THE EXCALIBUR DISASTER

ALSO BY JACK M. BICKHAM

Twister

The Winemakers

THE EXCALIBUR DISASTER

Jack M. Bickham

DOUBLEDAY & COMPANY, INC.
GARDEN CITY, NEW YORK
1978

All the characters in this book are fictitious, and any resemblance to actual persons, living or dead, is purely coincidental.

Library of Congress Cataloging in Publication Data

Bickham, Jack M
The Excalibur Disaster.

I. Title.
PZ4.B584Ex [PS3552.13]   813'.5'4
ISBN: 0-385-14169-6
Library of Congress Catalog Number 77-25577

First Edition

10.00/6.40 - 10/78

For my parents

PART ONE

The tragedy came without warning.

Weather was marginal over much of the Eastern Seaboard, with broad-spread rain and patchy ground fog and smoke. But that was not so unusual for an early summer evening. Thanks to a sharply controlled radar environment and sophisticated instrumentation, John F. Kennedy International Airport was landing the commercial jets only about forty minutes late.

At approximately 9:45 P.M., the Kennedy approach control facility routinely cleared the next of its jetliners waiting in an enormous holding pattern over Sandy Hook. Transwestern Flight 161, inbound from St. Louis, Missouri, was cleared to initiate its Instrument Landing System approach to Runway 4-Right.

Swinging the massive, wide-body jet out of the holding pattern and onto its new radar vector for approach, Pilot Jerry Emerson announced to his nearly two hundred passengers that they would be landing soon. He knew that some of them had been grousing about the delay and were impatient.

Emerson himself felt no such emotion. In more than nine thousand hours of jet flying, he had encountered many similar delays, and much worse ones, and an element of his professional attitude was that feelings got in the way of good procedure—and procedure was what kept you alive. He prided himself on his reputation as a pilot who flew not only by the book but with extraordinary firmness yet sensitivity to the aircraft.

None of them on the quiet flight deck had the slightest inkling. The Excalibur's trio of turbofan engines, situated far to the rear of the 175-ton aircraft, whispered gently at reduced power. Visibility forward, over the down-canted nose section, showed pitch blackness. But all was normal in the glowing buttons—red, yellow, and green—on the panels that extended across the front, over the low ceiling, and down the center console between Emerson and his second in command, Bill Terwiliger. The primary flight gauges—pale lemon and green—also indicated routine, and flight engineer Rudy Steiner, seated behind the pilots at a sidesaddle instrument panel, had called out nothing unusual from his array of more than seventy dials and hundreds of flasher-type lights and switches.

Flight 161 had now broken out of the rigidly controlled holding pattern and was being vectored by radar to the point where it would turn inbound on the Instrument Landing System and make its solitary approach to its designated runway at Kennedy. The Excalibur was idling in at an indicated airspeed of 150 knots and three degrees of flaps. Jerry Emerson's altimeter mode selector was off, the plane's estimated weight checked, reference speed and go-around EPR were set, shoulder harnesses on, emergency-exit lights armed, flight-control-hydraulic-power and yaw-damper switches on (annunciator lights out), SEAT BELT and NO SMOKING signs on, anti-ice being fed to engines and wings, altimeters and airspeed indicators set and cross-checked, continuous ignition switches on, fuel heat off, cabin pressurization set. *Check.*

The Excalibur's strobe lights, flashing inside cloud, made it appear that they were encased in a great, gauzy egg. They were ten minutes from touchdown.

Near the center of the airplane, in the 130-foot passenger cabin, stewardess Ginger Johnson made a last sashay up the center aisle, making sure seat belts were fastened and seats in the upright and locked position. Her fellow attendants, Martha Billingsley, Cheryl Hunt, and Tom Morrisey, were stowing gear in the forward galley, opening luggage-compartment doors, and collecting the last few cocktail glasses in First Class.

A middle-aged businessman caught Ginger's eye as she passed him. "Are we about to land?" he asked.

"In just a few minutes," she told him with a smile.

"Good. I'm bushed."

Ginger moved on, pausing to make sure a sleeping woman's belt was secure. She nodded to a young soldier, wide awake and looking lonely in the only occupied seat in his row of four. "Almost there," she told him.

"Do you fly on somewhere else tonight?" he asked her.

"No. Last stop for today, thank goodness."

The young man's eyes became eager, shy. "Staying in New York tonight, then?"

Ginger smiled but wished he wouldn't go on with it. Now thirty-three, she had the kind of face and figure that the airlines had once seemed to recruit in astonishing numbers. In this age of unisex, she almost always stood out in a crew because of exceptional beauty. The passes were always flattering but always a small problem, too.

"I stay with old friends in New York," she told the boy and started to move on.

He didn't take the hint. "Maybe you'd have dinner with me?"

"Gosh, that sounds like fun. But the amount of trouble I'd get into with Transwestern would be exceeded only by the trouble I'd have from my husband."

Leaving the soldier smiling with rueful disappointment, she went on to the front of the coach cabin, turned, and took a final look down its great length. The glance impressed her, as it always did, even though she had been flying the Excalibur five months now, ever since its introduction into the Transwestern fleet.

Excalibur, billed as the commercial jet for the 1980s, was the most flexible of all the new wide-body jets. It seated ten abreast in Coach, with a total capacity more than double that of the old 707, and yet it could operate economically on fairly short hauls. The public was accepting Excalibur, and so was Ginger . . . mentally. But she still sometimes had the feeling she was trying to serve meals in a bowling alley. The logistics on short flights was incredible.

Stepping into the galley area, Ginger nodded to her fellow attendants, then moved forward into First Class for a final glance there. It was not entirely necessary, but she took her responsibilities as senior very seriously.

Everything looked fine. There were only seven persons in First this evening. Two of them, however, were of more than passing interest —strange bedfellows thrown together by accident of flight selection.

The first was a man named Jason Baines. The slender, gray-haired man was president and chairman of the board of Hempstead Aviation, the California-based firm that built this new aircraft. Baines had been pleasant on the trip from San Francisco, and during the stopover in St. Louis he had showed quiet but intense pleasure when Ginger told him how much the crews appreciated the quiet and comfort of his aircraft.

The second passenger of interest was quite a different sort. Seated on the right, close beside a federal agent guarding him, he was a bulky, swarthy man of indeterminate age named Anthony Pronzani.

Pronzani, linked to organized gambling and syndicate crime, was hardly on a pleasure excursion. A grand jury in New Jersey was looking into allegations of tie-ins between certain oil companies and the Mafia. It was said that Pronzani would testify against his former friends in order to save himself in another case, on the West Coast. He could hardly be happy about the situation; his brother had also been scheduled to testify, a week ago, but had been killed in a rather gory bomb explosion in Houston, Texas, as he and another federal agent, like this one, started his car to drive to the airport.

Pronzani, Ginger realized, was watching her now. She mustered a smile. "Everything all right, gentlemen?"

The agent's eyes were like dull glass. "Fine."

"About to land?" Pronzani asked in a high-pitched voice.

"Yes," Ginger said. She was amazed: he was nervous about the landing. "We should be on the ground in about five minutes."

Pronzani raised a hand to adjust his tie, and a diamond of huge dimensions glittered bluely. "They're going to meet us?" he asked the agent.

"They'll be there," the agent said.

Ginger nodded to Jason Baines as she went back toward the galley. "Five minutes," she told him.

Baines smiled, the friendly lines crinkling around his keen eyes. "Tell him to land it gently, Ginger."

"Oh, he will, Mr. Baines. He knows he has the builder back here, taking notes!"

Baines's smile became a grin. "No, no notes. But I'm coming in to talk to some new potential buyers. It wouldn't be very good PR if we blew a tire or something, would it?"

"The pilots say it's a very nice airplane to land, and I love it, the way the dimple wing lets us come in so slowly. I wouldn't worry if I were you."

"Young lady, if I were the worrying type, I wouldn't have been building airplanes the last forty years."

"Well, you've built a nice one this time."

Jason Baines gently rubbed the fabric of his chair with his fingertips. It was a curiously loving gesture. "Yes," he said quietly. "We've built a very nice one this time."

Ginger went back to the crew seats near the galley and strapped herself in. Judging by the sound of the engines and the pitch attitude of the fuselage, they were on the ILS course now, and quite near touchdown. She felt a slight wobble as the plane moved through some turbulence, and then it was smooth and routine again. She closed her eyes momentarily. As soon as she got the passengers off, she thought, she would clean her contact lenses.

In the forward flight-deck compartment, Pilot Jerry Emerson had the aircraft dead on the flight path and localizer beam. Dense cloud and fog continued to obscure the windscreen in front of his eyes. Emerson watched the instruments, playing the controls with the tender touch of a musician. It was a beautiful plane to fly.

"Gear down," he ordered.

Terwiliger's hand moved to the console. There was a distant whine, then a slight jolt, and Emerson changed the trim to compensate for the drag of the big gear assemblies.

"Gear down," Terwiliger said. "Three green lights."

Behind them Rudy Steiner called, "Nose anti-skid release, brake pressure normal."

Emerson moved the speed-brake handle slightly and touched up the wing-slat control lever. No other aircraft in the world, he thought, had this latter control device, and it made all the difference. Across the surfaces of the wings, lost in the dark and fog outside, slats were moving farther open, exposing dimples in the wing's skin; the passing air was being forced to burble slightly, with the effect that the wing was capable of much greater lift at low speed. Emerson had never flown a large aircraft so gentle and responsive.

They were perhaps five feet above their glide path, but settling nicely. They were less than two minutes from touchdown. An electronic cone extended out toward them from the end of the target runway, and they were flying precisely into its point. A good approach made for a good landing, and this one was right on the money.

Flight 161 settled in routinely through the fog, rain, and smoke.

Eighty seconds later, dozens of drivers on the west side of Kennedy International Airport heard a great roar directly overhead and terrifyingly close. One of them claimed to have seen a flash of lightning. No one could verify this.

Many of them, however, did see an enormous silver airplane burst from below the clouds, its underside glinting in the visual approach lights off the end of the runway.

The aircraft was Transwestern Flight 161, an Excalibur, and its left wing was canted frighteningly low. Its nose, some witnesses said, was pitched over toward the ground. The engines blasted with full power as the plane bolted from the low obscuration.

A split-second later, the aircraft went into the watery landfill short of the runway. There was a thunderclap explosion and a blinding fireball.

Dense smoke rose instantly, obscuring the scene. There were more than a dozen wrecks on the adjacent interstate highway as drivers lost contol in shock or in trying to gape. Police cars raced toward the scene. Ambulances wailed. From the airport streamed emergency vehicles of all kinds. It was impossible at first to determine what had happened at the crash scene itself; small fires blazed in the wet, tufted marsh grass, giving the area an appearance of hell.

Forty minutes later, in a passenger ticketing area jammed with police, airport guards, stunned passengers, and dozens of hysterical men and women who had come to greet family or friends, a shaky ticket agent punched a change into the computer for Flight 161, and one woman somewhere in the lounge wailed with grief as the words displayed on TV sets on the walls:

Flight	From	Arriving
161	SAN FRANCISCO	CANCELED
	ST. LOUIS	

2

It was not yet 8 P.M. in California and full daylight remained beyond the curtains of Janis Malone's bedroom, when the telephone rang.

Janis's thoughts were far removed from her job as director of public relations for Hempstead Aviation. She had been standing in front of the full-length mirror applying a final touch-up to her short auburn hair, when the telephone sounded. A final glance in the glass told her that the new white pantsuit flattered her lithe figure, and she walked toward the other room with the thought that if the caller was Hank, he had better have a very good excuse for being late. *"I've been dieting for a month to be able to get into this outfit,"* she would tell him, *"and I'm taking it to dinner right this minute."*

As usual, Hank Selvy would not be able to tell with certainty whether she was teasing him. That would be fun. And it was far better to make a joke of their increasingly serious conflict if it was still possible.

"Hello?" she said, expecting Hank's deep voice.

"Janis? This is Ken Lis."

Janis stiffened slightly. A call from the general manager of Hempstead's Airplane Division at this hour was unusual. "What is it?" she asked.

"Have you heard what's happened?" Lis's voice was taut.

Janis braced. "Is it about Hank?"

"Hank?" Lis hesitated. "Oh. I see. No. Janis, an Excalibur went down at Kennedy."

Janis took a sharp breath. She had known this day had to come, the moment when the first of their new superjets crashed. But emotionally she was not ready. "How bad is it?"

"Very bad, I'm afraid. It looks like everyone is dead. Probably over two hundred."

"Oh, my God."

"Jason was . . . on board," Lis added, his voice choked with emotion.

"Jason *Baines?*"

"Yes. You remember he was going to New York . . . to talk to the Monravian ambassador."

"No," Janis said, closing her eyes. Then she opened them again, focusing on the rough texture of the painted wall directly in front of her as she leaned her forehead weakly against it. "Oh, Ken."

Ken Lis was a strong and capable man, one she had always admired. His voice now betrayed that he might have been on the verge of tears. "I have to call people in, Janis. We'll need you . . . some of your people. We already have a lot of reporters calling the plant—"

"I'll be there in twenty minutes," Janis cut in.

"I'll . . . appreciate that," Lis said as if dazed.

"Has Mrs. Baines been notified yet?"

"Yes. Transwestern called her. Then she called me. I just finished talking with her."

Janis could not resist asking: "How did she take it?"

Lis's voice became flat, bitter with control. "She gave me a number of specific instructions. She's . . . very much in control."

For a moment, Janis did not speak. Yes, she thought, Lydia Baines would be very much "in control." It would be easy to be in control, since there had been no love between her and her older husband. And no one had ever accused Lydia Baines of wasting emotion on any person who could not obviously help her toward whatever ruthless goal she might have in mind at the moment.

Former beauty queen, former movie star, much younger than her husband, and now the heir apparent to the Hempstead empire, Lydia Baines had always been the opposite of Jason Baines: hard where he was kind, unyielding where he favored compromise, cynical where he was idealistic and visionary. Lydia, Janis thought now, would waste no time mourning the dead; she would move to take the reins.

A father-son relationship had existed between Jason Baines and

Ken Lis. It was no secret that Lydia had been jealous. What would happen now, with Lydia in control?

But that was in the future. Janis realized that the crash took priority, and with an effort she got her mind back under control. "Ken, I'm leaving now. Just one quick question first: how did the crash take place? Do we know the cause?"

"It was a Transwestern flight, the one that originates in San Francisco with one intermediate stop in St. Louis. It dived into the ground a few hundred yards short of the runway in marginal weather. That's all we know now. We have people on the scene."

Behind Janis, the doorbell sounded. "I'm on the way," she said, and hung up the phone.

It was Hank Selvy in the doorway, his freckled face twisted in a grin. "Fabulous!" he told her, eying the outfit. "Sorry I'm five minutes late, but—"

"Hank," Janis cut in, "there's been an Excalibur crash."

Selvy didn't blink. "Where? How bad?"

"Kennedy. Everyone dead, and we don't know the cause yet."

"I'll drive you to the plant."

The drive across the outskirts of San Jose, with Hempstead Aviation's chief test pilot at the wheel and letting it all out, would have been frightening under any other circumstances. After briefly explaining the little she knew of the crash, however, Janis lapsed into silence and wished he would drive even faster. For his part, Selvy kept his hands locked on the wheel of the Toronado, his facial expression granitic as he concentrated solely on the twisting road ahead.

Despite their recent tensions, Janis felt a sharp pang of gratitude to him for understanding at least this once. A former Air Force bomber pilot and United Airlines captain for seven years, he had been Hempstead's chief test pilot throughout the Excalibur development program. For once, at least he could forget his jealousy of her job, or at least put it out of the forefront of his mind.

Looking ahead, Janis maintained her silence as grim thoughts raced through her mind. A major crash involving Excalibur was bound to create at least some problems for the new and revolutionary airliner. The death of Jason Baines might signal even worse crisis. For Jason Baines had *been* Hempstead Aviation, and Excalibur had been the company's greatest gamble, undertaken by him and the man who had just called Janis, Ken Lis.

Hempstead had been a giant during World War II, when its highly advanced twin-boom fighters first carried the war into Nazi Germany from long range. After that war, with the dawning of the space age, the future had looked bright. Hempstead, however, had chosen to gamble its future on a very strong, very safe, very conventional piston-driven airliner at a time when Lockheed was far advanced on the Electra and Boeing had the pure-jet 707 on its drawing boards. Hempstead's bulky passenger transport, the Zeus, came off the assembly line an instant antique.

Deeply in debt to build an airliner no one wanted to buy, the firm saved itself with several key contracts for the earliest space ventures. This stopgap income was only temporary, however, and did nothing to heal the deep financial wounds left by the failure of the Zeus. Hempstead shrank to a small percentage of its former size, sold off several subsidiaries, dabbled in submarine and tank technology for a time, and maintained its existence primarily through continued sales of a small light plane designed for private aviation, the 100-horsepower Wren.

It was out of the Wren Division that the idea for Excalibur came, in 1975. Ken Lis, the protégé of Jason Baines, made the proposal after lengthy personal studies. His suggestion: a new and radically different wide-body commercial jet that would serve the needs of the Environmental Age, the 1980s.

The aircraft proposed by Lis was to be called Excalibur. It was to be of wide-body design, but somewhat smaller than costly, long-haul jumbos. It was to have new-technology engines designed to operate more quietly and economically than any previously known. In order to be able to operate into many short-field airports with maximum flexibility, it was to be fitted with a new wing design that existed at the time only in the head of Lis's designer, Barton MacIvor.

It was to be a slat wing, a sort of dimple design that would increase the effective curvature of the wing at low speed, thus reducing stall speed and allowing maneuvering at much lower true airspeeds.

At the time Ken Lis made his initial presentation to Jason Baines and the board of directors, the slat wing worked only in theory. It had not gone beyond wind-tunnel testing as yet.

Jason Baines took the chance, mustering all of Hempstead's resources into what would be in effect a final, convulsive attempt to get back on top of the market. Lis was taken out of the Wren Division and placed in charge of a reorganized Airplane Division. Production of the Wren was halted. Excalibur became Hempstead's top priority—its ticket to survival.

Even during 1978, when Excalibur was being tested for certification by the government, and in 1979, when the first production models rolled off the line, some in the company doubted the concept. Partially to meet the simmering objections and partially to satisfy his wife, Jason Baines approved a second major endeavor toward the end of the decade, this one of quite a different nature.

Widely assumed to be Lydia Baines's idea for Hempstead's future, this project was the Eagle, a new, medium-sized air-to-ground ballistic missile with MIRV capability. Eagle was through research and development now; models had even been tested for the military. It was in the limbo of congressional study, with little indication that expenditure would be approved for its purchase any time soon.

Now, however, the status of Eagle was another matter that Jason Baines's death might change, Janis Malone thought. If the Excalibur crash signaled any serious trouble ahead for the airplane, Lydia Baines might press harder for Eagle than her husband had been willing to do.

Serious change was possible . . . serious conflict.

Hank Selvy drove off the highway and onto the access road leading to the Hempstead complex, a clutter of blocky white buildings against a murky pink horizon of California hills. Clearing the main gate in the high cyclone fencing that surrounded the grounds, he drove fast along the narrow entry road, rocking to a halt near the front doors of the sprawling main building. An attendant was just taking down the flag.

"I'll park and come on in," Selvy told Janis.

"It might be awfully late, Hank," she said.

"I'll try not to get in your way," he snapped.

"That wasn't what I—oh, forget it." Janis hopped from the car and ran for the entry of the building, angrily refusing to look back.

Once inside the building, she promptly forgot the seemingly endless feud with Hank Selvy over her independence. Her own office area was still dark, but she went through quickly and switched lights on, leaving a handful of notes for whichever of her assistants might arrive first. There was to be no information given out without her approval; all incoming calls were to be logged and returned later; the

R&D files on Excalibur were to be pulled, and work was to be begun on a complete and factual account of the testing that had gone into the plane prior to production.

That done, Janis headed downstairs to the office of Ken Lis.

In the outer office she met Kelley Hemingway, Lis's administrative assistant. Although she was almost Lis's own age, Kelley looked considerably younger. She was dark-haired and almost startlingly beautiful, and she, like Janis, evidently had been summoned from a social occasion; her pastel frock was quite unlike the severely tailored suits she usually wore to work.

There was no nonsense, however, in Kelley Hemingway's crisp greeting. "Janis, do we need to see you!" Turning from the secretary's desk where she had evidently been giving a younger woman some instructions, she strode to another desk, her own, and picked up a handful of telephone memoranda. "They're already swarming. Jones at the AP. A Miss Turner at UPI. Kincaid at the L. A. *Times*. Jarvis, New York *Times*. CBS News."

Janis took the slips of paper. "I'll get back to them, Kelley. Thanks. But first I'd better find out where we are on all this."

Kelley Hemingway nodded and Janis saw that she was pale. "There's no immediate indication of cause. It looks like some kind of systems failure or pilot error."

"And Jason Baines had to be on board."

A shadow passed behind Kelley Hemingway's large, expressive eyes. "Yes." She glanced briefly toward the open door into the next office. "It's been . . . a great shock."

"Is someone in there with him?"

"Mr. Coughlin."

"Do you think I should go on in?"

"Yes."

Janis started for the door.

"Janis?" Kelley Hemingway called after her.

Janis turned.

Kelley Hemingway's eyes were difficult to read. "We've already heard from Lydia Baines a second time. I'm notifying all division chiefs. In addition, Mrs. Baines wants us to set up a meeting of the board as soon as possible, to discuss future plans as well as the crash itself. . . . I wanted you to know that in case someone asks. But absolutely nothing is to be released."

"She isn't wasting any time, is she?" Janis asked angrily.

Kelley Hemingway parted her lips as if to speak, then turned away without a word. Janis understood: Kelley had too strong a sense of loyalty to say anything directly critical of Lydia Baines, but her essential loyalty was to Ken Lis, her direct supervisor, and it was no secret that Lydia Baines might not be as friendly to Lis as her husband had been. Under these circumstances, there was nothing Kelley might say without being disloyal to someone.

Janis walked into Ken Lis's office.

A division manager could have just about any kind of office he wanted, and Lis's reflected his no-nonsense approach to his job. It had steel walls and metal racks bulging with aviation magazines and technical reports. The desk was massive and of handsome wood, but very old. A large picture window, the draperies pulled back, looked out over the graveled corner of a roof to the oil-stained tarmac of the landing-field ramp area. In the distance, two Excaliburs stood surrounded by metal scaffolding beside the low-roofed Final Trim building. A tarnished sunset painted them a gleaming crimson.

Ken Lis, seated behind his desk, had a telephone in hand. Harvey Coughlin, chief of the Aerospace Division, stood near the windows, glowering into the distance. Lis, at forty-two, looked perhaps slightly younger. He was whip-thin, graying, a vigorous man wearing gray coveralls that made him look more like a pilot—which he also was—than a corporate executive. Coughlin was almost as tall, heavier, with a barrel chest and short-cropped hair that once had been red. His silvery suit was obviously expensive, and there was nothing out of place about him that might have spoiled his traditional newspaper tag as "the hero of Inchon."

Lis spoke into the telephone, his lips scarcely moving. "I understand. Call back as soon as you have further word."

He hung up and looked at Janis. There was pain around his eyes. "It's confirmed: no survivors. There was a fuel explosion and a . . . considerable fire."

"And Jason Baines is definitely . . . ?" Janis could not voice it.

Lis nodded, the lines in his face deepening. "Identification is going to be . . . very difficult. But he was on the passenger manifest. He's dead, Janis."

"God, I just can't believe it."

Harvey Coughlin straightened his shoulders. "It's a great shock.

15

But what all of us must do now is try to put our grief behind us and pull for the team. Jason would want us to go on—to be up and doing."

Janis stared at Coughlin, feeling a burst of irrational anger. Was he really this cold, or was he stupid? How could he mouth clichés at a time like this?

Trying to blunt her emotions, she turned to Lis. "Do we know more of the circumstances?"

Lis ran his hand through his hair in a characteristic gesture of stress. "Transwestern Flight 161, inbound to Kennedy on an ILS approach. As far as we know, it was a normal approach. Witnesses saw it come out of the cloud deck with the left wing low, the nose low also. There was engine roar as if a full-power recovery was attempted, but it went in nose first about three hundred yards off the threshold of the runway. It exploded—broke up—burst into flame."

Janis could not speak. She had never seen an actual crash, but she had seen photographs and read reports. The shocking force unleashed in an airplane crash was enough to turn the scene into one that must resemble hell: bodies were torn to bits—literally tiny *bits*—; the carnage was hideous. Now their proudest product, an Excalibur, was the mangled center of such a scene of horror, and Jason Baines had been among the innocent victims.

His expression studiously solemn, Harvey Coughlin spoke: "As I was mentioning to Ken, Janis, it should help us from a PR standpoint right now if I were to leak word to a few of my many friends in the press that there possibly was wind shear at Kennedy."

"Was that the cause?" Janis asked.

Coughlin frowned.

Ken Lis said, "There was no indication of wind shear. Other planes were landing normally."

"It doesn't have to be true," Coughlin said. "There will be no attribution, so no embarrassment. Merely the suggestion, however, should help us in the media during these first, critical hours."

"But how can we say that," Janis asked, astonished, "when it isn't even a theoretical possibility?"

Coughlin glowered. "*We* don't say it. The theory is *leaked* that Excalibur crashed because of wind-shear effect. It certainly won't hurt the reputation of Excalibur to suggest it as a possibility."

"The National Transportation Safety Board assigns probable cause," Lis said.

"I recognize that. I'm simply suggesting that planting the idea might help us. After all, we are in a time of tragedy here. That's why I'm here tonight. I came at once, to help. We all have to pull together now, for Hempstead."

Neither Lis nor Janis spoke. How quickly, she thought, Coughlin was ready to step forward to prove his dedication . . . now that the presidency itself was vacant.

Lis spoke. "We won't suggest wind shear, Harvey. We will not speculate at all. We'll wait until we have facts."

"That might take a long time," Coughlin argued.

"It might. But we're not going to panic."

"With Jason gone, don't you think it might be better if all of us worked together—pulled together on this thing? I'm here to help in any way I can. I urge you to consider a strategy—"

"I'm not thinking of strategy just yet," Lis cut in. "I intend to work with Kelley and Janis to handle the first press rush, and then I'll be getting on a plane to go to New York to see the crash site for myself. It will be time enough to talk about strategy after I get back."

"Is a trip to New York wise?" Coughlin asked. "Have you considered the PR impact?"

"I have to see for myself."

"But a trip by the general manager of a division will invest the crash with added importance in the eyes of the public, Ken!"

"That's hardly what I have to consider right now."

Coughlin drew himself up to his full height, his face setting in an expression that Janis Malone had seen often in newspaper photos of him. Middle age and a life without strenuous activity had softened him so much that the expression was now only a shadow of what it had once been, when he was a famous war hero, and later a force in state government. But Janis knew he was still a folk hero to countless Americans and still a force to be reckoned with both inside and outside Hempstead Aviation. However they might have first won their power of personal magnetism, the Harvey Coughlins of the world did not give it up gracefully; there was sheer pleasure in its use.

Coughlin said, "I'm offering friendly advice, Ken. I'm hardly a neophyte in dealing with the public. You'll remember that I was the one who put the Energy Compliance legislation through the state senate after I returned from Korea. That was sensitive . . . controversial. If it taught me nothing else, it taught me that every angle has to be figured before you make any public move during a time of potential controversy."

"I respect your opinion, Harvey," Lis replied. "But I have to make this trip."

"I can make some calls to Washington," Coughlin suggested. "With all my contacts, I can have us a direct pipeline of information right from the top of the National Transportation Safety Board. There's nothing you might learn that I can't get for us discreetly."

"I have to go." Lis's mouth set.

"I tell you, a trip there will just invest the crash with undue importance in the public eye! Don't make some theatrical move that will convince people the crash has all that much importance!"

Lis looked as if he could not quite believe it. "Harvey. Some two hundred people are *dead*. I think the crash is already important."

"Very well," Coughlin said, his face stiff.

Lis turned back to Janis. It was obvious that he was working under the burden of great emotion, but he was fully under control. "I want to explain to you precisely how we're going to handle all requests for information. Then I have an idea on an immediate news release. I also want a complete biography on Jason Baines pulled from the files and reorganized at once." His eyes shadowed. "Whatever else happens here, we aren't going to let them forget that Jason Baines was a great man."

It was hours later when Janis Malone had breathing time to look around her own hectic office and realize that she had not seen Hank Selvy since the parking lot. Was he angry again, jealous of her job? It was not a new quarrel, but his unwillingness to recognize the importance of this assignment tonight was a deeper hint of their ongoing conflict.

She felt angry and a little depressed. Looking down at herself, she saw that her lovely new pantsuit was peppered with typewriter smudges, freckles from spilled coffee, and eraser crumbs. Hank, she thought, would not approve.

He wanted a wife, and said a job had no place in his scheme of things. But if Janis had ever felt any inclination to give in on the point, she certainly felt none tonight. She was needed here more than she had ever been . . . and the days ahead, she sensed, were going to be more interesting than any she had ever known. She was going to stick it out.

3

It was after midnight when Ken Lis finally initialed the last interoffice memorandum pertaining to the New York crash. A flood of calls from the East Coast had added nothing of significance about probable cause, and there was nothing for him to do now but follow up on his original intention of flying personally to Kennedy at once. Already he was bone tired. *One step at a time*, he told himself. New York was next.

Walking into the adjacent office area, he was surprised to see Kelley Hemingway still at her desk. Head bent, she was writing swiftly in longhand on a legal-sized yellow tablet.

"What are you still doing here?" Lis asked quietly.

"I'm trying to organize all the information we have for a possible internal report. When the board meets, next week, we'll certainly need that."

Lis briefly studied her remarkable green eyes, seeing the fatigue in them. "You need your rest, Kelley. Tomorrow is soon enough."

She smiled. "I've got plenty of other work tomorrow."

"On Saturday?"

"We have the new budget projections; remember?"

"Christ." He had momentarily forgotten them entirely.

Kelley Hemingway tossed down the pencil and stood, smoothing her skirt over snug hips. "No problem. My working a few extra hours is the last thing we need to worry about right now, isn't it?"

Lis took a deep breath. "I guess it is, really. . . ."

"We'll all miss him," Kelley said. "I know you'll miss him the most. But a lot of us . . . cared very much for him."

"I know that," Lis said, and felt a stabbing impulse toward tears.

"What do you think is going to happen now?"

"I don't know. We'll have a full-fledged accident investigation, of course, and the way it looks at the moment we'll have a mystery on our hands for a while, anyway." Lis paused, thinking about the manifold problems that might arise. But then his fatigue and grief momentarily overwhelmed him. "Of all the God-damned planes," he burst out. "It could have been any other plane we have flying, any other time. Why did it have to be that plane? Why did Jason have to be on it?"

Kelley Hemingway watched him with cloudy eyes.

He added bitterly, "Just when we were finally starting to turn the corner, be ready to show a thin profit—just when his whole gamble on this thing was being vindicated! All the years he struggled, Kelley —all the bad times he put up with, and then he took this gamble with me, and production was just getting up to full capacity. And now, no matter what happens, he won't be here to see it. It's like he fought for all this, and just when he had the chance to start enjoying a little victory, he—ah, God, I'm not making very good sense right now!"

"You loved him."

"A lot of people wouldn't understand that. There's a school of thought that believes my relationship with Jason was entirely cold-blooded, a way to promote myself in the company."

"I don't know anyone besides Harvey Coughlin who might think that."

"Oh, there are others."

"I'd like to see some of them."

"With Jason gone, you may."

"Are you heading for New York right away?" she asked as they walked into the outside corridor.

"I'll go home long enough to grab a change of clothes and a toothbrush. The Learjet is waiting at the airport now."

"You ought to get a few hours' sleep first."

"There's no time. I can nap on the plane."

She did not argue the point, a fact he subtly appreciated. They walked down interior stairs and entered a lower hallway, dim and echoing with their footsteps. Her perfume was faint but pleasant, touching an unexpected chord within him.

They reached the yawning, glass-walled front foyer. Lis found that he did not want to separate from her. Was it that he could not face being alone in his grief? Or was it all grief? Was he also frightened, now that Jason was dead, about the uncertain future with Lydia Baines in control?

Or was he thinking of the stopover at home, and having to face Amy?

He did not know. But in this moment he was aware of Kelley as a woman far more concretely than ever before . . . aware of her shining hair, and the glisten of her pink lipstick, and the womanly firmness of her body. He felt a sharp, almost sickening jolt of electricity. He wanted to talk with her and hold her and make love to her.

"You're going home now?" he asked.

"After stopping for a hamburger or something."

"Maybe we could . . . do that together."

"That might be nice. I could call Jess and he could join us."

Jess Hemingway, her husband, was an attorney. He was bright, and a decent man. Lis liked him, but his mention at this moment was a harsh reminder.

"On second thought," he said, "there will probably be a sandwich machine at the airport. I'd better not waste the time. Good night, Kelley."

Her eyes narrowed. "Did I say something wrong?"

"No, of course not."

"One minute we were going to have a sandwich, and the next, you're in too big a hurry."

"I do have to hurry. Rain check, all right?"

There was a quick, half-hidden surprise in her eyes. "Good night."

He turned abruptly and opened a door leading into the production building and his usual short cut to the executive parking lot.

The building he entered, the three-story Main Assembly Building, was more than four football fields in length and half as wide. Brilliant lights shone down from a vast, girdered ceiling. Bare concrete reflected the slightest sound, magnifying it only to have it swallowed up in the vastness. Down the center of the long arena were a series of production-line Excaliburs, each in a different stage of assembly. At the far left, the airplane glowing dully from within its cocoon of workstands appeared almost finished, except for its tail assembly. At the opposite extreme end of the building, to Lis's right, the chuffing sounds of rivet guns and pinging of hammers surrounded a body section just beginning to take its initial form around a metalwork skeleton. Yellow factory carts and tool benches stood here and there in seemingly meaningless confusion. Only a single small crew was on the job at this hour, and the MA was gaunt, echoing, virtually deserted.

The MA was the oldest building in the present Hempstead complex, dating back to 1941. Thoroughly modernized now, it was the heart of the Excalibur operation. The four-story vertical tail fin could not be fitted here; the roof was not high enough. But almost everything else was accomplished here in a single line. Each $14-million airplane was subjected to more than three thousand team installation procedures after leaving the MA, but all that work would be on a recognizable airplane.

The Excalibur nearing MA completion at Lis's far left was No. 13 to be assembled. The first ten were in service, six with Transwestern and four with Eastern, and the other two were being outfitted at TW's maintenance facility in Oklahoma City prior to joining the company's fleet, within days. But the Excalibur crash in New York—of Excalibur No. 6—could change the timetable.

Lis knew better than most others the significance of that crash. Conceivably it could entirely rearrange all future scheduling and new sales of the aircraft.

Development and testing of Excalibur had taken upwards of five years and $150 million. More than twenty thousand hours of testing had gone into the prototype. Hempstead's investment was total, and only continued sales successes would make it pay off.

Sales orders were firm on the next sixteen Excaliburs due off the line. But another two hundred had to be ordered before the future was assured. Hempstead Aviation had to build Excaliburs, or close descendants, for ten years in order to reach a solid financial footing.

The New York crash cast a shadow of doubt on this future.

There was more in Lis's mind than the hard figures as he paused a moment under the broad wing of one of the assembly aircraft now, however. He looked up at the plane and felt a pulse of feeling that was close to genuine love. Excalibur loomed over him, its long snout more than thirty feet overhead, swept wings sagging with their flowing strength, gleaming metal skin an eerie green under a coating of protective plastic spray. The plane stood silent, mammoth, empty, a thousand overhead lights playing over the sleek curves of its body. It breathed beauty and speed and power.

We made you, Lis thought. *We dreamed you up and fought through all the design headaches and then we fought so you could be born. You belong to us and you're unique and lovely, and you're not just metal; you have our gut and sinew inside you somewhere. And Jason is dead, but you're his memorial, and you're going to be just as great as we dreamed. You owe us that, you big, lovely bitch. I'm going to hold you to it.*

He walked on across the MA, and reached the far outside door. He glanced back a final time and, despite himself, felt a doubt.

An Excalibur like this one was a mangled ruin short of a runway in New York. What kind of accident had it been? Could it possibly mean that this plane here, like the others so far produced, might carry within it some hidden flaw?

There was an answer to this question, and his job was to find it as quickly as possible. Despite his fatigue and burden of emotion, he squared his shoulders and moved briskly as he stepped out into the night.

4

Saturday's dawn had brought a steady, cool breeze in over the area surrounding JFK. The sky was blue porcelain. Perched in the right-hand seat of an airport jeep, Ken Lis was aware of a tightening in his midsection as Oxstetter, the public relations man at the wheel, pointed ahead.

"It's just up over that little grassy rise ahead. We're coming up on the runway extender."

Lis could see nothing over the gentle rise in the marshy land around them. To his right, across a drainage canal, was distant high fencing separating airport land from an interstate highway. To the left the land rose slightly, and he knew the airport was over there.

A roar began to swell overhead. He looked up and saw a TWA 727 swoop in from the right, gear down and flaps extended as if it were groping for the earth. Faint smoke issued from its idling engines, and the silver belly of the craft blotted the sky for an instant, and then it was past, settling into an all-engulfing roar of engine sound and wind, seeming to sink out of sight beyond the slight rise as heat waves mushroomed and the grass whipped. Lis heard the squeal of the tires at touchdown, then the more distant thrum of the engines as the pilot reversed thrust for braking.

It was the way, he thought, Transwestern Flight 161 had been planned to end. American commercial carriers made more than twenty thousand landings every day, and almost all were uneventful. Why had an Excalibur been an exception?

Oxstetter, a pale man with eyes that looked strained because his contact lenses didn't seem to fit properly, slowed the jeep and shifted to a lower gear as they went through a muddy depression in the dirt road. "Here we go, Mr. Lis. I guess you'd better sort of, uh, brace yourself. These things aren't very pretty."

"I know," Lis said.

They topped the rise.

There were trucks, jeeps, and fire wagons parked helter-skelter all over the ravaged grassy area. Close by, to the right, stood a clump of gnarled little trees. Beside them, a half-dozen policemen stood guard on a grisly mound of large black rubber bags. Ambulance attendants were loading some of the bags into their vehicles.

Ahead and to the left, the scene was like a battlefield. There had been scattered small trees or shrubs, but these had been uprooted or blasted into fragments. The tufted grass had been torn up, and areas here and there continued to smoke fitfully. Firemen walked around in heavy boots, spraying remaining smoking spots with hand-held extinguishers. Over the entire area were other men, some wearing business suits, others in firemen's regalia. They moved among bits of wreckage—sheets of bent aluminum, chunks of fire-blackened machinery, chunks of timber that had evidently once been cargo crating. Lis saw two mail trucks parked off to one side, and men loading things into mailbags.

Partway across the field, perhaps fifty yards distant, a giant section of Excalibur wing stood driven into the ground like a piece of abstract sculpture. Nearby, one of Excalibur's engines, ripped from all moorings, lay on its side in a smoking crater. And beyond this—beyond more chunks of airplane, and nearer the unseen runway threshold—the broken fuselage and remaining wing of the airplane lay crumpled, surfaces smudged by smoke and fire.

Oxstetter parked the jeep, and both men stepped down to the wet earth.

The air, despite a breeze, stank of kerosene and oil and something else, the sickening odor of burned flesh. All the grass had been scorched, and there were random holes and gouges everywhere as if pieces of the plane had hit, torn sod, and then bounced to rest somewhere else.

"This way," Oxstetter said, leading toward the area of worst devastation.

They moved among more scraps of metal and unrecognizable pieces of equipment. A large number of white-jacketed medical or hospital technicians were moving about, heads down as they minutely examined every inch of ground. They had black plastic bags. Lis saw one of the technicians bend over, examine something in the scorched soil, and then use a pair of bright metal tongs to pick it up and place it in his bag. Lis stifled a shudder.

As they approached the main fuselage section, the stench became heavier. Four men wearing business suits and carrying clipboards stood nearby, conferring. The evident leader was black, very slender, with thinning hair. His suit was rumpled and mud-stained and he appeared angry.

"Mattingly," Oxstetter said.

"National Transportation Safety Board?"

"Right. Chief field investigator." Oxstetter signaled to the black man, who nodded and continued talking to his subordinates.

After another few minutes, the black man finished with his companions and turned, scowling, to walk slowly and carefully through the burned, wet grass toward them, having trouble with his balance in the deep, uncertain soil. As he drew near, Lis saw that Mattingly was not as old as he had appeared at a distance, although his face was lined with fatigue and a suppressed rage of some kind. He was perhaps thirty-five, with furry black eyebrows, and he reminded Lis vaguely of a TV detective.

"Jace," Oxstetter said, "this is Ken Lis, division chief for Hempstead Aviation. Mr. Lis, Jace Mattingly of the NTSB."

Mattingly scoured his hand on his suit coat and extended it to Lis. "Sorry about the muck, Mr. Lis. Dirty job." Unsmiling, with only pain in his bright brown eyes, he studied Lis candidly. "No need for you to come out here."

"I wanted to see for myself," Lis said.

"Why?" The single syllable was almost an accusation.

"I'm not sure I know."

"Curiosity?"

"More than that, Mr. Mattingly. We built that airplane."

Mattingly glanced toward the wreckage. "Not much to be proud of at the moment, is it?"

"I think it's a pretty God-damned good airplane."

Jace Mattingly looked at him sharply. "Sorry. I tend to get upset."

"I do too," Lis told him.

Mattingly took a cigar from his inside pocket and patted himself in search of a match. "I don't imagine you're as upset as the people whose relatives died, though. For you it's just a business nuisance."

"The best friend I ever had was on that airplane."

Mattingly struck a wooden match and puffed dense clouds of smoke. "Again—sorry. I've had to deal with the FBI and everybody else already. I'm getting tired and the day doesn't even have a good start yet."

Lis turned to Oxstetter in surprise. "What's the FBI doing in on it?"

"They had an important witness on the flight," the PR man replied.

"My God, do they think it was sabotage?"

Mattingly exhaled a cloud of smoke. "Don't get your hopes up. There's no sign of a bomb or anything else that might hint of sabotage. The FBI will check it out for all it's worth, but in my opinion they're already running out of inspiration."

"If it wasn't sabotage, in your opinion, what was it?"

Jace Mattingly looked off into the distance, his tired eyes on a private horizon. This, Lis thought, is a formidable man. But Mattingly seemed more intent on his cigar than thought, until he finally spoke, now in a very quiet and controlled tone.

"Your airplane," he said, "is making a routine ILS approach well within normal limits on visibility and ceiling. The wind is light and steady. The pilot has been cleared to land, he's on the glide path, in the middle of the localizer. All radio conversation is routine. At just about the time he comes out of the clouds at an altitude of about four hundred feet, he is seen in a nose-down, left-wing-down configuration, with full power being applied. The pitch attitude continues forward, however, very rapidly, to a point somewhere past 20 degrees. The aircraft apparently begins to make a very slight recovery, but there is no time or altitude left."

Mattingly turned part way to his left and pointed. "First impact is over there, the left wingtip. The left wing is torn off and a piece of it punctures the left side of the fuselage about midway of the coach cabin, peeling metal like a can opener. The fuselage ruptures and cargo and passengers begin to be spewed out. The fuel ignites. The main section impacts over . . . there, and breaks in half. All sections are aflame within four seconds."

Lis was unable to speak for a moment. His imagination had leaped

27

to Jason Baines—to the roar, the vertigo, the split-second of fright, and then the incredible, tearing impact, pain, the gushing fire.

He swallowed hard to banish the vision. "Any preliminary guess as to the cause?"

"I haven't gotten that far yet," Mattingly said.

"When will you get that far?"

"We don't indulge in wild guesses."

"I know that," Lis snapped back. "You—"

"Gentlemen!" Oxstetter said, upset. "Let's—"

Lis ignored him, and continued his prodding of Mattingly. "I know how you operate. On-site inspection, interviews, tapes, photographs, reconstruction of the wreckage, public hearings, computer analysis—all of it. *I built this airplane.* When I leave here, I've got to go meet some people who might be thinking about buying it. If you have any preliminary ideas about probable cause, I'm asking you man to man, not on any official basis. *What caused this crash, if you know?*"

Mattingly glared at him in silence for a few seconds. "I don't know," he said finally.

"Wind shear," Lis prodded.

"No. Ruled out."

"Power failure."

"No."

"Autopilot malfunction."

Mattingly's eyes narrowed. "You know the autopilot is locked out on approach."

"Did you find the autopilot?"

"Yes."

"And?"

"It was locked in the OFF position."

"Ice?"

"Icing conditions were minimal. No other plane reported difficulty."

"The airplane had structural integrity when it hit the ground?"

"As far as we can determine now, yes."

"Pilot error?" Lis asked softly.

"It appears very unlikely at this time."

Lis did not reply at once. The most obvious likely causes were thus eliminated. The cause had to be deeper, then, and he felt a pulse of frustration and something almost like outrage.

A systems failure . . . somewhere.

This likely meant that finding the cause would not be easy. And it cast the shadow he had feared over Excalibur.

A few airplane accidents were easy to investigate. Lis remembered a notorious DC-8 crash in Denver when thrust reversers had functioned asymmetrically on landing, causing the jet to veer into a fuel truck, which exploded in flames. Or a freakish Pan AM 707 crash caused by lightning.

Most crashes, however, had a greater or lesser air of mystery about them. Even when there were survivors, they often could shed no light on what had happened. Some tragedies were solved only after tens of thousands of man-hours in the most meticulous investigation and analysis, and some were never solved at all.

Lis's impulse was to hope and believe that the cause of this crash would be found quickly and that it would prove to be some fluke. All new aircraft were subjected to prolonged testing, and Excalibur had been given the most brutal trials of any aircraft ever introduced into commercial aviation.

He also knew, however, that this aircraft now a mangled ruin had undoubtedly been subjected to more use and punishment in the few months since its manufacture than Hempstead had been able to give a prototype in two years of test work. Airline schedules were predicated on the idea of keeping aircraft in service; a piece of equipment earned no money while idle on the ground. This plane had not rolled out of the factory and crashed. It had crashed only after being used hard.

And it was a fact that some aircraft revealed a flaw only after such prolonged use. Lockheed's Electra had flown almost eighty thousand hours before first revealing a fatal structural weakness in its engine-pod mountings. The DC-8 flew for three years before its hydraulic systems began to fail with dismal regularity.

The thought uppermost in Lis's mind was related to these facts. He wanted to believe the crash was a fluke. But what if Excalibur was only now showing a flaw that it had carried from the drawing board?

"We'll co-operate in every way," he told Mattingly now. "That goes without saying."

"Fine," Mattingly said. "We have a lot of questions we'll want to be asking early on."

"We want to find out what happened as soon as possible," Lis pressed. "If there's anything wrong with Excalibur, we want to be ready for modifications quickly. And if nothing is wrong, we want to be cleared. We're not a Boeing, Mr. Mattingly. A prolonged investigation, if it were to erode public confidence, could hurt us badly."

Mattingly studied Lis's face, and there was a glint of anger in the investigator's eyes. "I'll give you one thought, Mr. Lis, on a basis of —how did you put it before?—man to man."

"What is it?" Lis asked.

"I'm not new at this. I've been around. I could be wrong, but I don't think so: My advice is not to pin too many hopes on a quick finding here. This one looks messy to me. Messy and nasty and probably complicated. I hate to say it for your sake, and I hate to say it for mine. But this has all the earmarks of one that is going to drag out."

5

Those who referred to Lydia Baines as "the queen of Hempstead Aviation" did not do so to her face, because their use of the title referred to her power and ruthlessness, and was by no means complimentary.

Driving up San Francisco's Russian Hill in the cool swirl of Saturday-morning fog, Harvey Coughlin was acutely aware of that incredible Baines power. Lydia Baines now held all of it, and he was about to face her.

The time was not long after dawn. Harvey Coughlin had left San Jose in the dead of night after a 3 A.M. telephone call. Mrs. Baines was at her town house in San Francisco, the male secretary said. Mrs. Baines wished to see Mr. Coughlin as soon as he could get there.

Harvey Coughlin had been driving since that time. He did not know why he had been summoned. But when Lydia Baines called, he obeyed. It was his mode of survival.

Lydia Baines, then known as Lydia Loring, had been one of the last great stars of Hollywood prior to the full onslaught of television. She emerged on the scene in 1949 as the sultry seductress in an adaptation from Tennessee Williams, and won an Oscar in this, her first, role. In the next four years she became Hollywood's hottest item.

An amazingly beautiful blonde, she starred in no fewer than fourteen major pictures, opposite the top male stars. No one claimed that she was a great acting talent, perhaps because she was too much a wish-fulfillment figure for American men. But she was able to project a sense of vulnerability—overlaid with hard cynicism—

that touched something deep in the fantasies of many men . . . and even many women.

Tall, with a tiny waist and lovely breasts and hips, Lydia Loring was said to have the greatest legs since Grable. Some said Grable simply was not competitive. But it was Lydia Loring's face, particularly her eyes and mouth, that made her a great star, though. Both were really too large for the oval of her face. Her eyes were dark, somehow mysterious, with a flinty quality that managed to convey a thrilling sense of danger. And her mouth had been called everything from sensuous to cruel to passionate, even vulgar. In a famous DiLorentioni closeup sequence in 1952, the camera had simply lingered on her mouth for more than three minutes as she silently watched her lover swim in a pool. That sequence was famous because it had never seen the light of day; censors of the time said it was so stirring that they must label it obscene.

It was a sensation, in 1953, when Lydia Loring married Jason Baines.

Baines, a widower at forty-one, was a storybook mate for her. He had been in the headlines since 1930, when he set new solo endurance records flying over the North Pole to Germany. He twice won the Bendix Cup, and in 1938 was among the first Americans to argue for a quick buildup of U.S. air power as a counter to the Axis. During World War II he commanded a legendary fighter team in the Pacific, and managed at the same time to continue management of Hempstead Aviation, a firm he had bought a few years earlier. He was accounted to be an aviation pioneer, an authentic war hero, an industrial genius.

Hollywood wags gave the marriage a month. "Lydia will get bored and go back to Hollywood," they said, "or Baines will drop dead from the excitement."

The wags, however, were wrong. Jason Baines built a large stone house for his bride in San Jose, and there was a legendary fight about it soon after their honeymoon. Lydia was soon discovered living a life of her own in San Francisco, and openly told reporters that she would never live "in that mausoleum" except for occasional visits. But the marriage did not founder, and Lydia Baines was soon clearly involved in her husband's operation of Hempstead Aviation.

She soon began appearing in various offices with good questions—

and demanding good answers. Within two years she had an office next to her husband's, and while Baines was clearly in control, his beautiful young wife also began having an obvious input into some decision-making. She was very, very smart. Old-timers whispered that Jason Baines was all that stood between them and Lydia's ruthlessness.

At roughly the same time Jason Baines gave the Excalibur development program top priority within the company, he gave his wife, almost as a seeming afterthought, complete control of the tiny and faltering Aerospace Division. A confidential memorandum said Lydia would be "project officer for reorganization and establishment of new aerospace priorities within general guidelines previously set by management."

It turned out not to be a simple reorganization. It was more a *Blitzkrieg*. The division manager who had held the division together with early space contracts now balked at certain of Lydia's proposals. He was fired. In what *The Wall Street Journal* called "the blood bath at San Jose," nine other executives were transferred, demoted, or kicked out. In came a new management team for Aerospace: brighter, younger men with fine backgrounds, the kind of aggressiveness Lydia Baines liked, and a clear understanding of who was the boss.

Since that time, Aerospace had done well. Not the cornerstone of the company, it had nevertheless turned a small profit each year. It was said that Lydia Baines would make Aerospace much bigger if she had her way.

Harvey Coughlin devoutly hoped the rumors were correct, now that Mrs. Baines did have her way. He had not made himself division manager easily, and his ambitions were far from satisfied.

He had managed to escape the famous blood bath, emerging third in line in his department. Later he had won a promotion from Lydia Baines by slipping her some confidential memoranda that might be interpreted as indicating potential disloyalty in his immediate supervisor, a kindly man who had gone out of his way to teach Harvey the business. A year later, during a congressional investigation of alleged collusion on certain subcontracts, Harvey had been the one designated by Lydia Baines to take certain files into the desert and burn them. For this he had gotten five thousand dollars in cash and another promotion just as soon as his new superior was made the fall guy in the government's prosecution. From that point, the step to division manager had been easy enough; the man in charge entrusted Harvey to handle some ticklish negotiations on prices, Harvey did a splendid job, and he let Lydia Baines know that his boss had had nothing to do with the success. The boss was fired. Harvey became the boss.

He did not know whether he was one of Lydia Baines's favorites, as some said, or not. He was much too frightened of the woman to consider himself secure. The long development of Excalibur, with Ken Lis obviously in the driver's seat, had been torture. But now Jason Baines was dead, and Lydia Baines had summoned Harvey in the dead of night. He was nervous but hopeful as he got out of his car and walked to the metal gates of the building.

He pressed the door-chime button under Lydia Baines's name and waited, burnishing one shoe, and then the other, against the backs of his pantlegs.

A soft female voice—not Lydia's—spoke from the tiny loud-speaker over the button he had pressed. "Yes?"

"Harvey Coughlin to see Mrs. Baines. I'm expected—"

"Yes, Mr. Coughlin. Please come up." The door lock buzzed and he reached quickly for it, entering.

The walk across the stone-floored lower courtyard was quick, and the ride upward in the private elevator even quicker. The doors swung open on another interior hallway, this one carpeted, with potted plants. An interior door leading to the Baines apartment was directly ahead. Harvey went to the door, pressed the button, and was ushered inside by a pretty young oriental girl.

"Mrs. Baines will be with you in a few moments, sir," the girl said, leaving him in the living room.

Harvey waited, resting his weight first on one foot, then on the other. The room was gigantic, with a high, timbered ceiling and rough stucco walls, painted stark white. The furniture was spare and contemporary. A rear wall was entirely of glass, giving a stunning view out over a balcony toward the bay, a huge bowl of creamy gray marshmallow.

Lydia Baines came into the room from a side doorway. "Harvey. How good of you to come." She was tall, very beautiful, wearing a floor-length gown of bright geometric designs. She showed no sign of grief over her husband's death but smiled thinly as she walked to him and extended both hands. "Thank you."

Her hands were cool. Harvey felt a deep chill, but managed to smile. "At your service, Mrs. Baines."

"Lydia," she corrected him.

He swallowed. "Lydia."

"Come, sit with me here on the sofa, Harvey." She drew him toward the long leather couch near the windows, and sat at one end, facing him at the other. The glare from the windows made it virtually impossible to see her face, and Harvey began to feel even more nervous and vulnerable.

"You realize, of course," Lydia Baines told him softly, "that my husband's death signals a period of change in our company."

"Yes. May I say how sorry I am—we all are—about this terrible tragedy."

Lydia Baines gestured impatiently. "Jason was not a young man, Harvey. While no one wants to die, it was much better than some lingering illness. I suppose, if he had to die, it was the kind of death he would have preferred."

Harvey felt a new and deeper chill. *She didn't give a damn.* "Yes," he murmured.

"We, the living, must go on," Lydia Baines added.

"Yes," Harvey repeated.

"Our meeting Monday will look at where Hempstead stands now and how we must plan for the future. The crash could be a serious blow to our long-term plans for Excalibur. We have to talk about that. We have to reconsider certain other alternatives—diversifications—which might become more pressing if the investigation of the crash were to drag out, with resultant trouble in sales."

She paused, so Harvey said, "I see," although he didn't see at all.

"I will be headquartering here, Harvey. I think you know I always detested that old house Jason put together for me. It looked ancient the day the carpenters moved out. Dust and mildew and isolation. Not my style. I prefer to be at the center of things. I expect, actually, to sell that house as soon as I possibly can. There are always fools on the lookout for houses that appear old and Spanish."

"Yes," Harvey said, mystified. "Of course, it's a big house—"

"My intent to live here, however, does not mean that I shall be remote from Hempstead operations. Quite to the contrary. I intend to take a much more active role. I will probably be at the plant at least two days each week, possibly more. And I certainly intend to maintain the closest possible liaison with key personnel whom I feel I can trust. I have always felt, Harvey, that I could trust you."

"Mrs. Baines," Harvey said, "I mean Lydia—you can be *sure* you can trust me! I am proud of my record of loyalty. I place Hempstead Aviation above every other interest in my life. Whatever you tell me to do, I will do, believe me!"

Lydia Baines crossed silken legs. "I am going to want two things from you, Harvey: information, and your total commitment to whatever priorities I may select."

"You have my promise."

"Information first. What have you heard about the crash?"

"The crash?" Harvey felt almost dizzy. He was being drawn toward the heart of power, and it made him giddy. He was desperate to say all the right things.

"Is there any internal talk," Lydia said, "about what might have caused the crash at Kennedy?"

"No—not that I've heard. I heard someone suggest sabotage—"

"Because there was a gangland thug on board? No. My sources tell me that has already been pretty well ruled out."

"Yes," Harvey said, sweating. "Well, that's the only theory I really heard."

"You are aware that the DFDR was severely damaged?"

Harvey tried to hide his shock. The Digital Flight Data Recorder, crash-protected and tail-mounted, was supposed to survive practically anything. If its tapes had been damaged, the best hope for finding cause had been eliminated. "I wasn't aware of that."

"It's true. So there's every chance we might face a long investigation. And that could damage our chances of placing new sales for the airplane in the foreseeable future."

"It might not be that bad," Harvey suggested. "We can hope—"

"Idiots hope," Lydia told him. "Intelligent persons plan alternatives. I expect you to furnish me with a continuous flow of the best intelligence you can gather inside the company about the crash, its likely causes, sales, and everything else that may be going on inside Ken Lis's division. That's number one. My husband and Lis got along very well. I expect to get along with Ken Lis too. But the relationship will not be the same, obviously. You can help me overcome any possible antagonism that might arise."

The prospect of antagonism involving Ken Lis was lovely to Harvey Coughlin, but he pretended otherwise. "Oh, I'm sure Ken will work with you, Lydia, in this time of—"

"Of course he will," Lydia snapped. "But we all protect our own backsides. If he or anyone else tries to hide anything from me, it's your responsibility to let me know about it."

"I'll do my best."

"It won't trouble you—make you feel that you're spying on a friend?"

"My loyalty," Harvey assured her eagerly, "is to Hempstead—and to *you*. I simply have to put that before any other—"

"Fine," Lydia cut him off. "Now, as to point two. With at least some possibility of trouble ahead for Excalibur, I believe it behooves us to move quickly and aggressively to try to broaden our sales base. This effort will affect you directly, because I am speaking about Eagle."

Harvey's chest fluttered with excitement. "You know Eagle is at the heart of my division and closest to my own heart. I wish there were something we could do to move it along, but as you know, it's tied up in congressional committee somewhere, and the anti-military lobby has kept it from even being put on a hearings docket—"

"I intend," Lydia cut in, "to announce at the meeting Monday a major new effort to diversify by pressing for approval of Eagle in Congress. The Pentagon wants the weapon."

"But Ken Lis is against Eagle. Your husband agreed with him that Hempstead is not big enough to give top priority to two such major systems as Excalibur and Eagle—"

"My husband is dead. I am in charge now. If both Excalibur and Eagle do well, we press both full speed. We expand. If Excalibur falters, I intend to make sure that Eagle production can take up the slack, if at all possible."

Mentally Harvey reeled. It was beyond his wildest hopes. His division could become tops in the company. No longer would he play second fiddle. But he could not allow himself to get too excited. "With Congress dragging its feet, I don't see how—"

"That's one reason I wanted to give you as much lead time as possible," Lydia told him, interrupting again. "Congress is no longer

37

going to drag its feet, as you put it. On Monday or Tuesday of next week, Senator Sweet's committee will receive motions for rehearings on several defense matters. Eagle will be on the list."

"None of my contacts in the Pentagon entertained much hope that this could happen. How did you ever get them to reconsider—"

"That doesn't matter, Harvey. The point is that it's been done; Eagle will have another chance. At the moment, it remains a slim one. But you can change all that."

"My friends and associates in the Pentagon are solidly in favor of Eagle. I can assure you of that."

"It's going to be up to you to see that our support is broader this time," Lydia Baines said. "You'll begin preparing yourself at once. You'll be our man in Washington, and I'll be depending on you to see to it that Eagle is approved by the committee, and then has clear sailing in Congress itself."

"Well, now, see here," Harvey said nervously. "I've been away from politics for a long time, Lydia. Of course, I still have my friends . . . and a wide support among the people of the country, I daresay. —*They* don't forget their heroes of battle as quickly as some of our nation's leaders evidently do! But—I know *very* few present congressmen and senators. Since joining Hempstead, I have eschewed politics; it was your husband's wish."

"You'll get back into the swing," Lydia told him, "and fast. You underestimate yourself, Harvey. Your name still has magic. You still command respect. Now is the time for you to use it."

Staring into Lydia Baines's beautiful, cold eyes, Harvey felt a mixture of eager longing for power and a contrary tug of fear. He had decided many years before that he would never again become actively involved in politics . . . after that very bad day when not even the endorsement of both Richard M. Nixon and Barry Goldwater had been able to win him the vacant senate seat from California. He did not now want to face the political arena again, even in the role of a behind-the-scenes influence operative. He had been glad to put that all behind him and throw all his energies into the private sector, Hempstead Aviation.

But it had always rankled, that defeat. He had been much younger then, and perhaps one of the dozen best-known men in America, fresh from Korea and wide acclaim as an authentic hero in a war short on heroes or material for pride. He had been asked to spearhead the California Energy Compliance Law, and its narrow passage had been attributed to his personal appeal. In those days anything had seemed possible, and he had not even been very surprised when his party then asked him to run for the Senate. At a time when the Republicans owned the White House, with Dwight Eisenhower and Richard Nixon, there had been precious few heroes in the ranks at the state level.

Harvey had run hard and well, but the close defeat embittered and sickened him, leading to the vow never to try politics again. Since that time, he had remained a very private citizen, except for a few speeches at American Legion conventions and once a seconding speech at the GOP nominating convention in Miami Beach.

Still, he knew he had potential power. Many Americans revered his name. He had never failed to receive a warm welcome at the Pentagon, where heroism was appreciated. He knew that he could at least get in to see many members of Congress on the strength of his name alone, if he so wished.

Jason Baines had told him never to use his military reputation for company advantage. But clearly Lydia Baines felt no such compunction.

And so he was challenged . . . and tantalized. He knew how he could use his personal power. He knew he could score points with certain members of Congress. He would enjoy the wielding of power, the enhancement of his name again.

In addition, he could see how much Lydia Baines was placing on him in responsibility. If he did this well, the rewards might be unimaginably great.

But there was also the chance of failure—the kind he had experienced in that Senate campaign.

Was it worth the risk?

Lydia Baines was watching him, and now snapped her fingers as if dismissing his uncertainties. "Harvey, you can do it. I'm counting on you. There will be no ifs, ands, or buts."

"It will be . . . very difficult," Harvey said.

"You can learn. I expect you to start at once. And you won't be alone. We have one valuable ally: Matthew Johns, the junior senator from Colorado. He is very much in favor of Eagle, and he will work as closely with you as appearances will allow."

"I only worry . . . about letting you down."

"You won't let me down. I know it. I believe you're the kind of man I will increasingly depend upon in this company in the years ahead."

It was the stuff of dreams. Aerospace could become the top division within the company. Harvey could vault right over Ken Lis and have everything he had always wanted.

Life as a corporate executive had disappointed him; there were always difficult decisions, nagging uncertainties, fear that he might make a blunder. But if he were in charge, at the very top, what more could he *possibly* fear?

He set his jaw. "Lydia, I won't fail you."

Lydia Baines abruptly rose to her feet. "Good. I'll see you Monday morning. In the meantime, any information you may collect will be helpful. Use as much of your own staff resources as necessary to prepare for the new hearings. I expect to be in contact with Senator Johns over the weekend, and I'll tell him that you are to be our man in Washington."

"Yes. I'll—get busy at once."

After Harvey Coughlin had been shown out of the apartment, Lydia remained standing where she had been, by the couch, for some minutes. The oriental maid came back, padding silently.

"He has driven away, madam."

"Thank you. That will be all."

The maid vanished. Lydia walked to a wall panel and pressed a button. Doors slid out of hidden niches, effectively sealing the living room off from the remainder of the apartment. Then, satisfied as to total privacy, Lydia turned toward the far end of the room, where a screen masked a small area.

"Matthew?"

A tall, youthful-appearing, and very handsome black man stepped from behind the screen, a cup of coffee in his hand. Senator Matthew Johns would have been recognized by millions of Americans.

"What do you think?" Lydia asked him.

"He *sounded* sure enough of himself."

"He can handle it," Lydia said.

"You have more confidence in him than I do."

"He never failed Jason; he won't fail me. Why do you think he would fail me?"

Johns frowned. "Harvey Coughlin was a great war hero. He's done fine things for Hempstead in terms of public relations—his very presence in the firm has benefits. But I wonder how competent he really is, beneath that façade."

"He's competent enough," Lydia bit off. "He has to get this done for me in order to survive. He's smart enough to recognize that."

"Would you really sacrifice him if he failed you?"

Lydia looked at him, surprised. "Of course. I'll sacrifice anyone. This is my big *chance*. No one is going to ruin it for me."

"I'll do everything I can to help him."

Lydia smiled. "Of course. And once Eagle is established, your own business associates in Colorado will be happier—and you may be one step closer to the White House."

"We'll call it the Black House when I get in there, Lydia."

"As long as our goals are parallel, you can call it anything you want. I want Eagle. You want more clout. We're going a long way together."

It was Johns's turn to smile. He raised his coffee cup in a small, mocking toast. "To our mutual interests, then."

"We mustn't fail, Matt. This crash makes it even more imperative. We don't have to work behind the scenes any more. We're in the open—it's my company now, and I don't intend to let anything damage it. You do understand how serious I am about that, don't you?"

Johns lowered his cup. "Oh, yes, Lydia," he said quietly. "I understand how serious you are." He was a powerful man, but there was a trace of something bordering on awe in his voice.

6

It was Saturday afternoon, less than twenty-four hours after the crash, when Janis Malone learned that her job, and perhaps everything about Hempstead Aviation, would never be quite the same again.

She was in the public-relations office, reading copy, while across the room one of her young aides was pecking away at a warmed-over "gee whiz" story detailing all the testing that had gone into Excalibur prior to its approval by the government for commercial use. She looked up at the sound of someone entering and saw Harvey Coughlin making directly for her desk, a legal tablet in hand.

As usual, Harvey's suit was expensive and immaculate. He gave Janis a crisp smile as he bent over the desk. "A pretty busy day, eh?"

"It certainly is." Janis smiled in return.

He tossed the tablet in front of her. "I hate to do this to you, but I have an added project."

She glanced at the first sheet, making out such topic headings, in Harvey Coughlin's blocky handwriting, as *Eagle Develop. History* and *Systems descrip. in common lang.* "Eagle?" she said, surprised.

"A complete update on all our information files for Eagle," Harvey told her. This is top priority, Janis."

Everything seemed to be top priority. "We'll certainly get busy right away, Mr. Coughlin."

"Glad to hear it! Excellent! Put your best people on it, and if you need extra help, I'm hereby authorizing whatever expense may be necessary. You can also have two technical writers out of my engineering department if you need them: Coldirons and Duffy. Hang the expense. This is vital."

When executives talked about hanging the expense, they usually were thinking about completing a project yesterday. "What's the deadline?" Janis asked.

"I'll have to have it all in absolutely top-drawer shape by Tuesday afternoon," Harvey Coughlin told her.

"*Next* Tuesday?"

"Yes. I expect to be heading for Washington not long after the old man's funeral. This material must be prepared, checked, and ready for the printer by midweek. We'll start with one hundred copies. Alert the printer for a rush job. And binding—we'll want them bound and with a color cover."

"That's expensive—"

"Any expense is approved!"

Janis, to hide her dismay, bent over the tablet, checking headings. Gathering the material was going to be another major job. Then, hearing new footsteps, she looked up to see Kelley Hemingway entering the office to walk over and join Harvey Coughlin.

"I don't think I ever saw so many people working over the weekend," Kelley said with a thin smile. "Not that it's a pleasant experience, under the circumstances."

"No, it's a tragic time for all of us," Harvey said. "But we have to go on. As I was telling Janis, our next major thrust is going to be on Eagle."

Kelley Hemingway's slightly raised eyebrows betrayed her surprise. "I thought Eagle was on the shelf."

"Well, it's off the shelf as of now. Aerospace has been given orders directly from Lydia Baines to press forward. I intend to leave for Washington next week."

"Does Mr. Lis know about this?"

Harvey Coughlin stiffened slightly. "I doubt it. Why should he know about it? This is Aerospace business. The Airplane Division isn't involved."

"Of course," Kelley said quietly.

But the mention of Lis had angered Harvey Coughlin, and he pressed it, his mouth a thin line. "Things are changing in our company. No division has favored status any more. My orders have come directly from the top." He turned to Janis again. "So, as I was saying before we were interrupted, this project gets all priority."

"Yes, sir," Janis said. "I have to tell you, though, that even with hiring of extra people, this is a big project for us. The printing will take a lot of time."

Harvey gestured impatiently. "Just get it done."

"We'll certainly try, sir."

"No 'try' about it! I want to make it clear, young lady: if anyone drags feet on this project, or tries in any way to thwart me—"

"It isn't a matter of trying to thwart you!" Janis replied. "It's a question of whether it's possible for us to do it!"

"Young lady, I'm giving you an *order* to do it."

Kelley Hemingway asked, "Do you really think this should take priority over the Excalibur right now, Mr. Coughlin?"

"I don't have to discuss it with you," he snapped. "The day when my division had to bow and scrape to some other division is gone. I want this work done and it *will* be done. I have my authority direct from Mrs. Baines. Is that understood?"

"I think we understand," Kelley replied, her eyes icy.

"If you have questions, Janis, contact me. I will be checking back on your progress." He turned and strode out of the room, his shoes making loud tapping noises on the hard tile.

"Ken doesn't know about this," Kelley Hemingway said grimly. "I'm sorry to be the one to have to drop more bad news on him."

"Is he back?" Janis asked.

"He walked in a little while ago, looking like death warmed over." Kelley paused and frowned. "*Damn*, I hate to tell him this!"

"Mr. Coughlin said he's going back to Washington. That means the entire Eagle project is heating up again. I thought that was just about doomed."

"Someone doesn't think so."

"He *said* Mrs. Baines told him to do this."

"She's not even waiting until her husband is in the ground."

Janis looked down at the legal tablet left by Harvey Coughlin. "I had better call my staff back in. We'll have to go right through the rest of the weekend. Mr. Coughlin said I could use Duffy and Coldirons, from Engineering. Even with them I don't see how we can make it. I'll have to call downtown. Maybe there are a few writers who could use some quick extra money, doing the more routine, straight writing."

"I'm sorry, Janis," Kelley said.

Janis shrugged. "We'll get it done . . . somehow."

"I'm not just sorry about that. I came down here at Mr. Lis's request to drop *another* project on you."

Janis stared at the older woman in dismay.

Kelley put the file folders on the desk. "Mr. Lis paid a call on the Monravian delegation presently visiting in New York. You remember doing the news release on their visit, and how Mr. Baines was going to New York to talk with them. Well, Mr. Lis made that call for him, and it now looks like Prince David Peltier of Monravia himself, and his whole entourage, will want to visit here during their two weeks in the United States."

"Visit *here?*" Janis groaned. "To Hempstead?"

"You're aware of the sales affort we've made on Monravia. If they go ahead with expansion of their small national fleet, to go after the tourist dollar in air fares as well as at their beaches and casinos, they're going to be buying a dozen or more new intermediate-range jets. We want that sale, because it would be a wedge into the entire European market."

"I know all that," Janis said. "But they're coming *here?*"

"Apparently Mr. Baines had already suggested it. The prince, it seems, is a pilot and aviation buff himself. He's evidently very impressed with Excalibur, although he has never seen it. Apparently there's a division of opinion in the royal cabinet about which airplane Monravia should buy, if indeed they go into international air competition at all. They're going to visit Boeing, Lockheed, and probably McDonnell Douglas. The prince wants to come here. Mr. Baines evidently thought it might be vital to the sales effort. Mr. Lis had no choice but to encourage the idea. Right now we're going to be scratching for new sales more than ever, and a Monravian sale would be great publicity to take the edge off news of the crash."

"That's all I need," Janis said. "Making arrangements to baby-sit a prince!"

Kelley's eyes crinkled in a smile. "That's not quite the right word. He's in his twenties, and from what I hear, quite dashing."

"I wish he would dash somewhere else right now!"

"You'll have to work it in, Janis. We don't know their precise schedule yet, but it won't be long. You'll have to contact our State Department about protocol matters, and local and state officials will have to be warned that it's coming up. Next Wednesday, you're to call the Monravian Prime Minister. His name is Lucian Derquet, and he's with the official party at the Americana, in New York. Mr. Derquet will probably have their itinerary by then."

"You have his name and number in your notes?" Janis asked.

"Yes, and a lot more. I'll try to help you with some of it, Janis. I know it's a dreadful load to drop on you, especially after Harvey Coughlin."

"We'll manage." Janis rubbed her eyes. "The prince of Monravia and his party! Good lord, ordinarily that might be a fun change of pace!"

Kelley nodded. "I'll get back to you on details. Right now I'd better get upstairs and tell Mr. Lis about this Eagle thing. I wish I didn't have to!"

Already preoccupied with thoughts of all the items that had to be accomplished, Janis did not reply, and when she looked up from the files on her desk, Kelley Hemingway had gone. Janis wondered, with worry, what kind of a portent Harvey Coughlin's new priority project might be within the company's operations. But she did not have the time for the luxury of wondering about this very long.

"Jimmy?" she called to the young man across the room who had been tapping away at the typewriter throughout.

Stein grinned ruefully and headed for the files. Janis turned to her room.

"Jimmy, get the locater list out of the top file drawer and start calling our people. If there is any way they can come back in, tell them I authorized double-time pay. We've got a couple of new projects. Tell them to plan to work *late*."

"I've got a date tonight, Janis," Stein pointed out.

"Cancel it," Janis said. "You try to leave here and I'll break your leg for you."

Stein grinned ruefully and headed for the files. Janis turned to her desk telephone, reached for it, and paused. There were two women in the city who had done free-lance jobs in past months, and she intended to call both. But Jimmy Stein's comment about a date had reminded her—not that she needed reminding—that the new situation required her, too, to cancel something.

Hank Selvy had appeared in the office shortly after noon, acting as if nothing had happened between them the previous night. He had been concerned about the crash and concerned about how tired he said she looked, and she had made an instant decision that, oh, hell, she would just pretend again that she hadn't even noticed his surliness when her job took priority over an evening with him.

So he had mentioned tonight, and she had readily agreed. That, she had thought then, would make everything all right again.

But now it was out of the question.

She did not relish the prospect of telling him so.

It crossed her mind that she might get everyone working at top speed, then slip out for, say, two hours. She could meet Hank somewhere for dinner, then make an excuse and come right back.

There was only one basic flaw in that plan. When you had been sleeping with a man occasionally for more than six months, he tended to assume that a nice dinner would be followed by a return to the apartment, music, drinks, and bed. Turning him off after dinner would be tougher than simply canceling the engagement entirely.

He would make a scene either way, Janis thought. He was a top pilot, a man liked and respected by all his associates, and usually great fun to be with. Janis had thought about it for a long time before taking him as her lover, but it was not really a decision she regretted, except at times like this. Her sexual experience was limited. Hank Selvy was capable of moving her more often and more intensely than anyone else. There were even days when she was sure she loved him . . . wanted to marry him.

But Hank Selvy's blank spot about her job was a mile wide, and obstinately total. No wife of his would ever work, he liked to tell her, sounding dismayingly like a cliché character set up for destruction in some liberationist polemic. He was jealous, jealous of her time on the job, jealous of her devotion to her job, jealous of every extra moment she spent involved in this work that meant so much to her.

He could not—or would not—understand why the job was so important to her.

She had now been with Hempstead Aviation almost seven years, since shortly after finishing graduate work at UCLA. She had never really done any other kind of work. It fit her, complimented her view of herself, and her background.

The daughter of a pioneer aviation family, she had known since her sixth birthday that aviation would somehow always be a part of her life. On that day, her father, a high executive with Lockheed, had taken her on her first airplane ride.

While most children had their first air trip in a small Cessna or Piper Cherokee, Janis's had been in the engineer's chair of a Lockheed Constellation. Surrounded by the massive banks of gauges and controls, watching her father competently handle the big plane while the chief test pilot sat smiling and relaxed in the right-hand seat, she had fallen in love with every aspect of flying.

She had her private license at seventeen, her instrument rating a year later, and she was a certified flight-instructor at twenty. Meanwhile, her father's position allowed her summer employment ranging from office jobs to a rivet gun in Primary Assembly.

Nepotism rules, a shakeup that changed her father's status, and then a fatal heart attack altered all her plans of moving in at Lockheed under her father's wing. She continued college, and after an undergraduate degree in economics and an MA in journalism, she began looking for another company, where memories might not make every day too bittersweet.

Ken Lis had been the man who gave her a chance.

Onlookers liked to say that PR offices in most large companies had to be equipped with high-speed revolving doors to handle the arriving and departing employee traffic. After three years with the company, Janis had found herself second in command. After another year, during the most exciting and trying time of Excalibur development, her supervisor had departed for a lower-pressure post with American Airlines in Tulsa. While ads were run seeking an older male for the top job, Janis took over on an interim basis. After two months of that, Ken Lis called for her one Friday and said, "I don't know what the hell we're looking outside for. The job is yours if you want it."

She wanted it.

Now she had been in the post long enough to be considered something of a fixture. Still young, she was a seasoned pro. She enjoyed it, even the tough times, like now. She had paid a price; she had never surfed, had never really had a vacation, had never read a poem at leisure or enjoyed a week hidden away with a lover. But the price was worth it, to her.

If only Hank Selvy could understand.

But Janis did not delude herself that he would. She dialed his apartment number with a sense of mentally gritting her teeth.

Hank Selvy answered promptly. She told him she was still at the office.

"Then, you better get your rear out of there," Selvy told her amiably. "Dinner theater starts in three hours, you know."

"Hank, that's why I called. I'm really sorry. I'm going to have to work."

There was a pause. "Why not leave the work for the peons?"

"I can't, Hank. I've got these two new incredible projects dumped in my lap. I might be here all night, for all I know."

"It strikes me as damned strange, dumpling, that other offices out there don't have to work seven days a week."

"You know we're a small staff, and emergencies like this just don't come up every day."

Hank Selvy said nothing. The line hissed.

Janis said, "Try to understand, Hank. Okay?"

"What I *don't* understand, chicken, is how I always manage to end up at the bottom of whatever priority list you happen to draw up."

"Hank, that's not true and you know it."

"Yeah." There was another pause. "Well. Okay. See you Monday, maybe."

"Well, I—" The line went dead in her ear.

She held the telephone a moment, listening to the dial tone. Her eyes stung. Because she had opened herself to this man, he had an uncommon ability to hurt her. She felt miserable and guilty and abandoned. Didn't he *see* that this was an emergency? Couldn't he understand *this once?*

Angrily, struggling against irrational tears, she slammed the phone on the cradle and bent to look up the numbers for volunteer help.

"Got a second, Janis?"

She looked up at Stein, who had walked over with his sheaf of typed pages in hand.

He told her, "I got everybody but Rick, and his line is busy. I thought while I was waiting to try him again, maybe you would want to look over this test-program copy."

Mentally Janis shook herself. She gave Stein a bright smile. "Let's have a look, Jimmy." And she reached for her copy pencil.

49

7

B arton MacIvor was seventy-one years old.
  He did not look it.

That was because old age was just one of a number of unpleasant aspects of normalcy that MacIvor simply refused to grant any official notice.

Sitting hunched over now in front of Ken Lis's desk, MacIvor tugged at a heavy pipe, making clouds of dense Latakia smoke. It had been a warm spring, but he had paid no attention to that, either. He wore thick wool trousers, very baggy, a red lumberjack shirt, and a corduroy sportcoat that might have been through the Battle of the Bulge. His brawny forearms, sticking far out of his sleeves, were deeply tanned. His stubbled face showed the ravages of the outdoors. Hair that was still partly the color of carrots hung over his ears and onto his collar in a wildly unkempt condition. He cocked his head to watch Lis with his good right eye, his left one off line toward the outside.

"It's not a good development, lad," he rumbled in a deep voice that carried more than a hint of his Scotch heritage. "Right on toppa th' crash, tha' wooman starts this business wi' Coughlin about Eagle again. An' poor old Jason not even in th' ground yit!"

"Pappy," Ken Lis reminded him carefully, "that's not your worry. What we have to talk about is Excalibur, and whether this crash means we should initiate some new testing."

MacIvor removed his pipe from his teeth and pointed at Lis with it. "The aeroplane is sound. The design is sound, the frame is sound, the wing is sound."

"Then, why did it crash?"

"It crashed because accidents happen! Why does lightning strike a tree? It's fate, is all! Somethin' broke. A rod, or a cable. But Excalibur is sound, I tell ye!"

"We're going to have to review all production records on that airplane," Lis told him. "Transwestern will scan all their maintenance documents."

"Shooer," MacIvor grumbled. "I know all that. But just because she crashed on approach, don't be tellin' me we gotta start a lotta new tests on the wing, or anythin' like that, because Excalibur is *sound*."

Lis watched his old friend, aware that there was no man closer to him, now that Jason Baines was gone. "Pappy, what about some new computer analysis? Heavier stress factors, more variables?"

MacIvor stood and banged his pipe on the heel of his hand in the general vicinity of Lis's desk ashtray. Fiery sparks showered in all directions. "Let me review a few facts for you."

"Pappy—" Lis began to protest. But MacIvor was bulling ahead.

"Six year ago," he rumbled, "I was not exactly a poor man. I was nice 'n' retired from Hempstead Aviation, had a nice cabin in the mountains, was doin' my fishin' 'n' my huntin' 'n' my nose-pickin' like a respectable retired gentleman oughtta do.

"I'm thinkin' I earned retirement. —Naw, naw, lemme talk! I'm thinkin' I *earned* retirement. Who'd designed the Scorpion fighter, thet carried it to auld Hitler, an' then the Japs? Who'd drawed the basic plan fer our little two-seater, a plane this company had for its bread 'n' butter for more'n ten years?"

"You did," Lis told him evenly. "I know all that."

"An' who," MacIvor went on, fixing Lis now with his slightly cocked left eye, "was havin' hisself a little fun, dreamin' up a nice new little plane—one you an' me talked about some, that we were thinkin' we might call Songbird?"

The memory touched a chord. "Songbird was a dream, Pappy. A kid's dream. The big money is in big airplanes. Hempstead had to have a revolutionary design. When I came to you, and we talked about it, I didn't have to twist your arm off to get you back here, out of retirement."

"Yer right about that, lad. I come back willin' enough. I took my wing design 'n' I planned it all oot, and run the tests, an' you said I

51

was daft, but I finally even convinced *you*. —An' fer these last years, when I coulda been workin' on Songbird, I worked instead with you on Excalibur."

MacIvor paused and his big chest heaved. "She might be my last aeroplane. I put everything into her. She's *sound*. Don't try to tell me she isn't."

"I'm not saying she isn't. I'm saying we ought to dream up new tests."

The old man struck a wood match on the underside of the desk and applied the flame to his pipe, showering new sparks all over his own lap. "Jason is gone," he said, puffing, "an' the wooman is a loon. She'll be givin' you hell. She'll be wantin' to make them skyrocket things in place of honest aeroplanes. Insteada talkin' aboot new tests of Excalibur, ye oughtta be thinkin' aboot how ye can git outta this place before bad things happen to ye."

"Pappy," Lis said with more sternness and certainty than he felt, "nobody is running out. We're going to see it through. You and me. And that means dreaming up some new tests, among other things."

MacIvor heaved himself back to his feet again. He started like a tidal wave toward the door. "All right! All right! I'll dream up some things!" He turned and looked back, his eyes sad. "But he's *dead*, lad. Things'll never be like they was . . . an' ye know it."

Lis sat back in his chair. It was late now and he was filled with regrets. Even the simmering anger about new emphasis on the Eagle project—news he had had to get secondhand from Kelley Hemingway—was not very significant at the moment. He was simply very, very tired.

Barton MacIvor's reference to Songbird had not helped—had brought back a related flood of old memories, buried dreams. Songbird had existed in vague sketches and rough plans done on butcher paper, before Excalibur had been dreamed of. Songbird remained so: a vague possibility thought of sometimes late at night, in the loneliness, and yearned for with a sense of regret . . . a four-place airplane for private aviation, with the quickness of response built into great fighter planes . . . high speed, great range, yet a wing design giving it the forgiving qualities of the gentlest, dullest little plane on approach and landing.

Lis knew in his mind how Songbird would look, and how it would fly. It was a dream he had shared with Barton MacIvor, and with

Jason Baines. One day, they had said, *one day* . . . after Excalibur had made Hempstead solvent again, they would pull out the plans. They would commit to the dream.

But now Songbird probably could never be. And everything that had happened argued against its possibility.

And Lis had to put it out of his mind and work with the given.

He got up from his desk. He could not continue tonight. He walked, aching, into the adjacent office. The drapes of his own office had long since been closed to the night, but behind Kelley Hemingway they remained open, and he was reminded of the hour: almost ten.

Kelley was speaking into a dictating machine, consulting notes. When Lis walked over, she cut the machine off. She smiled, but she looked tired too.

"You'd better get out of here," Lis told her.

"In a minute," she said.

"What are you doing?"

"The notice and agenda for the board meeting Lydia Baines wants Monday morning. We've notified everyone by phone, but I want this in everyone's box tomorrow afternoon."

"Kelley, tomorrow is Sunday. I don't want you in here again."

Kelley leaned back in her chair and said something that surprised him: "Do you think the board will elect you president on Monday?"

"I don't know," he said quite honestly.

"You're the manager of the biggest division. It's logical."

"I thought about it a little on the plane. It's possible."

"But what does this business about Eagle mean?"

"It means my chances are less than they appeared before that happened."

"My God, she wouldn't try to have Harvey Coughlin named president!"

"I hope not."

"What will happen if she *does* try?"

"Then, it will happen. It's her company."

"Damn!"

Seeing the flush of frustrated anger in her face, Lis was struck anew by the vibrant *aliveness* of her. Her anger was motivated by loyalty to him, and it pleased him inordinately that she felt so strongly where he was concerned. Youthful, pink with her rage, brimming with good health and a lively intelligence, she was an amazing woman, a thoroughly beautiful and delightful one, and he felt a strong, mindless pulse of desire. He wanted to grab her, pull her close, feel her against him. In his imagination, he stroked the velvet texture of her skin. *Jesus Christ! You have to stop this.*

She was a happily married woman, wasn't she? He had his own marriage to maintain, right? And had office hanky-panky *ever* worked?

He changed the subject, asking her about a report she had due on new sources for certain materials, especially plastic. She told him the status of the report and they talked about it briefly. It helped. The business talk eased the old barriers back between them. He thought perhaps she seemed more relaxed too.

After a while, he left the building to head home.

Reverting to Kelley Hemingway's anger about the possibility that Harvey Coughlin might become president, Lis considered things he might be doing to try to strengthen his own position. He could politick for it, he thought, with the other board members. But he was not going to do so. It was not in his nature. The idea was repugnant to him. Practically, for all he could know, there would be *no* new president as such; Lydia Baines might run the company on her own authority, without portfolio. Politicking simply would not do any good . . . which, he thought wryly, made it very easy to be moralistic about it.

As he drove, however, he found himself speculating about what the Monday meeting would bring. He did not look forward to it. He had a sense of dread. It seemed indecent to be meeting before Jason Baines had even been interred. But he could not let his emotions get the better of him, he reminded himself. He had to be calm . . . rational. He had to stay in control, for the sake of the company . . . for Excalibur.

As he drove along the empty highway, however, he saw lights of the city ahead, against a milky sky dominated by a half moon. There were lights all around him in the distance of the night, and beyond the lights, the blackness of unseen mountains, and beyond them, the ocean.

He was struck by a sense of disassociation. *Why are you here? What are you doing with your life?*

He did not really know, driving along now toward a home that had no joy in it, and a wife he hardly knew. All he knew was that somehow his entire life had pointed him toward this moment, and he had come.

He had been born and raised in Pennsylvania. With a degree in engineering from Penn State, he had gone into the Air Force.

After the service, he had flown for Eastern Air Lines, but his first love had always been engineering and administration, and he had moved to Hempstead Aviation in its darkest period, after the failure of Zeus.

He had been married by that time, and his marriage was already disintegrating.

Amy had been vivacious, a real go-getter, even as a sophomore in college, when Lis had met her: a student senator, an officer in the pep club, secretary of the Young Republicans, leader in her sorority class, member of a baffling number of clubs and volunteer organizations ranging from the Spanish Club to the school's poetry-magazine staff. He had been both flattered and puzzled when she dropped from school immediately to marry him, throwing all her energies for a time into being "the perfect wife for you, darling, that's all I want."

As the years passed, and especially when Lis's job with Hempstead Aviation consumed nearly all his waking hours, Amy Lis had drifted at first and then rushed headlong back into one volunteer activity after another. Outside her home she was known as the one woman who would always help with a worthy cause, as an organizer and a doer. Her picture appeared in the local newspaper regularly as spokesperson for some group or organizer of some event. She was almost universally admired by people who did not know that she kept herself going with amphetamines and sometimes alcohol.

Once, a few years earlier, she had had a serious crack-up after following liquor too closely with a particularly potent pep pill. She had been frightened enough to consult a psychiatrist for a few weeks. Then she came home one evening to tell Lis that she would go to the physician no more.

"He doesn't know anything," she snapped in her characteristically brisk, almost angry way.

"Have you given him long enough?" Lis asked.

"I don't have a lifetime to give the man, and he's a fool!"

"What did he say to make you so angry?"

She turned her back to him, looking out a living-room window. "He didn't say anything. He's a fool, I told you."

"Amy, what did he say?"

She turned and her eyes were bright with angry tears. "He said I'm not worth a damn and I'm wasting my time."

The psychiatrist, a youthful and athletic man who defied all the stereotypes of his profession, shook his head with a sad smile when Lis asked him about it two days later. "No, Mr. Lis. That's Amy's own personal beast talking for her. I didn't say that."

"Her beast?" Lis echoed.

"Most of us have one. Something we carry inside, a self-concept that isn't accurate but really bugs us. Usually it's a view of ourselves in one component of our personality that has some slight basis in reality but is mostly our own insecurity, our own magnified problem."

"And what's Amy's beast?"

The doctor leaned back, tenting his fingertips. "Amy went after every prize, every volunteer activity, every possible accomplishment goal, all her life, until she married you. You were a trophy, in a way. Please don't get me wrong. She loved you. She still loves you. But she can't be satisfied being a housewife, or even holding a single outside job. At some deep level, Amy is convinced she is worthless. She has to enter these activities, has to appear to be in charge of things and a leader, to give herself some antidote to the basic feeling of being worth little or nothing."

"I don't see why she has to be quite so extreme."

"Mr. Lis," said the doctor smiling, "there is nothing more extreme than the human personality."

Lis remembered that conversation, and the blur of years of anguish that had followed, as he now drove near his home. He was tremendously tired. He thought again of Kelley Hemingway but banished the thought as soon as it arose.

His home was in a residential area featuring very large lots and arrangements of trees that gave each home the feeling inside of being isolated in the country, because no other structure could easily be seen. Two stories, more than a dozen rooms, Lis's house was much too large for a childless couple. But Amy had wanted something that looked impressive.

Lis pulled into the carport at the rear and entered the house through the kitchen. The sound of the stereo system, from the living room, smote him in the face. The volume was sky-high, making articles in the large kitchen vibrate on shelves. Puddles of water in dishes piled in the sink and on the drainboard jiggled with the sound waves.

He walked through the connecting hall and into the living room, which was large, airy, with a wall of natural rock. Amy, wearing a slightly rumpled but very elegant linen suit, sat on the couch, her eyes closed. There were a vodka bottle and an empty glass on the coffee table.

Lis went to the stereo and switched it off.

"I was listening to that," Amy said, her eyes angry as he turned. She was blond, slightly overweight, her eyes puffy.

"How much have you had to drink?" Lis demanded.

"Not very much. Not enough. I had a late meeting and I had to unwind. What do *you* care?"

"You know I care."

"Do you?" she shot back. "You come in late from work, on the way to some other business session or some airplane, or bed, and ask me how much I've had to drink; is that *caring*, in your lexicon?"

"There's no use in my staying when you're like this. All you want to do is fight."

"How often over the years have you stayed long enough to find out if I want to talk about—or do—anything else?"

Knowledge that she might be near a truth—and a stab of guilt—stopped him. "It's my fault, is it?" he asked softly.

"A little of it might be! You may not be perfect."

He sat down on an ottoman, fatigue draining him. "They'll bury Jason Tuesday."

"I'm sorry about Jason."

The resentment boiled up. "You hated his guts, Amy."

"I didn't!"

"You blamed him for all the time I spent on the job. How many times did you make that clear to both of us, and to anyone else within screaming distance?"

Her face waxen with rage, Amy reached for the bottle.

"You've had enough!" Lis snapped.

"I haven't had nearly enough! Get out of this room! Take your nasty remarks and your perfect conduct somewhere else, and leave me alone!"

He stood and walked out of the room as the bottle clinked against the glass, pouring. It was not until he was upstairs, in his own bedroom, that he began to control the shaking anger.

It had been his fault, he thought. How often had this cruel streak surfaced in him, and the resentment come out? He had *wanted* to wound her. She had tried, for a moment there, and he had been the one who broke the spell. Why? How much of her problem *was* this coldness within *him*?

He thought briefly of going back downstairs. But then he heard the stereo start again, louder than before. New rage filled him. He slammed his bedroom door, unable to forgive and hating himself for his own weakness—and the way it made hers so much worse.

8

R eaction to the Excalibur crash went far beyond the confines of Hempstead Aviation.

In Oklahoma City, headquarters of Transwestern Airlines, meetings were held throughout the weekend. On Sunday, executives had completed a preliminary study of maintenance records of the ill-fated airplane and were setting up plans for extraordinary measures to check their remaining Excaliburs for any signs of hairline cracks in metal, flaws, or unusual wear in cables that might be revealed only by X-ray and scrutiny of maintenance books on all planes.

Two other airlines contemplating Excalibur purchases made informal but firm decisions to hold off, pending results of the crash probe. And a number of newspapers ran lengthy stories about the Friday-night crash and stories about air tragedies of the past. Travel agencies and airline ticket offices suffered a noticeable slump in orders, as is usual in such cases.

In Washington, Jace Mattingly returned to his apartment Sunday afternoon and found from his telephone tape recorder that he had had several calls from his supervisor at the National Transportation Safety Board office, George Pierce. Mattingly cursed ritualistically, made a cup of instant coffee, washed his face, and called Pierce back at home, per the latest recorded instructions.

"We want to have a meeting at nine-thirty in the morning," Pierce told him without preamble. "Can you make it?"

"I can make it if you tell me to make it."

"Make it."

"Okay. Anything else?"

"Any new developments or ideas?"

"The wreckage isn't cool yet. If you want miracles—"

"All right, Jace. All right. I was just asking."

"Well, I don't have anything. Neither does anyone else."

"Have you talked to the pilot's widow yet?"

"I just got back from New York five minutes ago!"

"All right, all right. But I want you to put that near the top of your list, Jace. Ordinarily someone else would do it, I know, but we have that damned train wreck in Georgia, with all those caustic chemicals."

"I'll feel like a ghoul, but I'll talk to the widow."

"We've already had a couple of congressional inquiries."

"Great," Mattingly said bitterly.

"Senator Logan, of course. If a Frisbee crashes, he wants more dope on it so he can issue his usual statement about how incompetent we are. The other one was from Senator Johns."

"The black from Colorado? What's his interest?"

"I don't know. The question came from his staff. Seemed friendly enough. But of course the guys on up the hall are paranoid already. This ties in with the FAA and a lot of other agencies, you know, Jace. The FAA certificated that crazy new wing on this airplane. Now if they start crashing all over the place—"

"One has crashed," Mattingly cut in. "It's not an epidemic. Jesus!"

"Well, I know that, Jace. But I'm just trying to let you know that there's a lot more than the normal heat on this one."

"I know, I know. You've told me."

"You'll be at the meeting?"

"Yes."

"And you'll interrogate the pilot's widow. You have the address we got for you? She lives right here, near the District."

"Yes," Mattingly said dully. "Very convenient. I'll contact her. Is there anything else?"

There wasn't, and the call was terminated.

Sipping his now-cold coffee, Jace Mattingly turned the known factors of the Excalibur crash over in his mind. He was puzzled and worried. It was not going to be an easy one. He was going to require all the patience he could muster.

Patience, however, was not an item Jace Mattingly had ever had in large quantities. He was the kind of man who sometimes found himself yelling at rude headwaiters. He had no patience with cruelty in any form, nor with stupidity. Even obstacles that could not be fit into these categories tended to make him furiously impatient.

He had needed considerable drive to get out of the ethnic ghetto of Chicago where he had been born. A baseball scholarship had gotten him a college degree at Michigan State, and the Air Force had taught him how to apply much of his knowledge to accident investigation. He had had to scramble a bit to get on with the NTSB staff, but made it. He later managed to add a second degree—this one in law—via the night-school process. This enhanced his position as an investigator, but even more important, gave him the sense that he better understood his job.

Early promotions had come partly, perhaps, because of his race. He was realistic enough to recognize that being a black man in a government agency low on its unwritten ethnic quotas was enough to give him an actual advantage. At times he had felt uneasy about this, even angry. But to hell with it . . . to bloody hell with worrying about it; he would take any advantage he could get, and he would be so good in whatever job they gave him that no one *else* could ever think the same thoughts that sometimes nagged and depressed him in the night.

Mattingly had needed the job even more in recent years, and for emotional reasons. After the breakup of his marriage, the job had become his life.

His ex-wife was remarried now, evidently very happy, living in Oregon. He had a picture of her somewhere, a handsome woman who looked younger and less harried than when she had been married to him; the picture showed her standing beside her new man, a younger man, with two small children. They had a third now. She was smiling in the picture, and the smile sometimes haunted him.

Jace Mattingly put his coffee cup in the sink with some other dirty dishes that had been collecting for over a week. He went to the dinette table, opened his briefcase, and took out some of his notes. He intended to review some things, but one of the first sheets that fell out was his recent notation of Nell Emerson's telephone number in nearby Hyattsville. He looked at the number, knowing he should go ahead and call her now.

He did not want to do so. He did not like intruding into someone's grief. The act made him feel cruel and somehow dirty, like a grave robber. He always ended up sitting there stiffly, pretending not to notice the tears, feeling like a complete shit.

In this case, also, he even less liked the prospect. Because there was a possibility about the Excalibur crash that had been teasing his mind, and he did not want to have to face it directly.

Nothing that had been uncovered so far showed a physical cause for the crash. The plane had banked and dived into the ground. Something could have malfunctioned, of course. But it was also barely conceivable that one of the pilots had simply made a very, very bad mistake.

Mattingly did not like the concept of pilot error as a solution to an investigation. He believed, like some airline pilots he knew, that attribution of pilot error had more than once been a way out of an otherwise insoluble puzzle for accident investigators. When all else failed, say the pilot must have goofed; it provided *some* idea to list on that bottom line of the form, at least.

So Mattingly did not want to consider the theory. And he certainly did not want to approach Jerry Emerson's widow with all the inevitable questions about fatigue, illness, medicines, marital problems—the crap you had to ask to try to find possible reasons for a fatal error of technique or judgment on the flight deck.

But he was going to have to consider it. The prospect was not pleasant, especially since Jerry Emerson had been TW's only black captain.

To delay that unpleasantness, or begin down the road toward it? Mattingly considered, walked to the telephone, and dialed. He would make a start toward getting it over with.

In Hyattsville, Maryland, about ten miles away, the telephone's jangle sounded loud, echoing through a house that seemed preternaturally silent without the customary racket of two small children. Nell Emerson walked from the kitchen into the entry hall and picked up the instrument. She expected it to be another friend or neighbor with the awful, nervous, strained comments of condolence. She braced herself for this.

"Hello?"

"Mrs. Emerson, please." It was a male voice, tense but polite.

"This is Mrs. Emerson."

"Mrs. Emerson, my name is Jace Mattingly, and I represent the National Transportation Safety Board office looking into the crash in

New York. I'm sorry to have to disturb you at this time, but as I'm sure you realize, the board investigation does include contact with the crew's next of kin in certain instances."

Nell leaned against the wall, closing her eyes against the ache. "I understand, Mr. Mattingly. You want to interview me. Is that it?"

"Yes. May I ask if I could possibly visit with you in the next day or two?"

The persistence of the question flared resentment within her. "I can't see you today," she said brittlely. "I just returned from the funeral home. Preparation of my husband's body was delayed, you know, by an autopsy ordered by your agency."

The voice did not speak for a moment, and when it did, it sounded tinged with chagrin. "We appreciate your co-operation on that, Mrs. Emerson. I'm sorry it was a necessary—"

"It was not necessary. I used to be a stewardess. I understand the rules and why they exist. I also understand that you would have gotten a court order for the autopsy if I hadn't consented. But I resent it. There's no way you people are going to claim Jerry was sick, or disturbed, or on drugs. That crash was not pilot error."

"Mrs. Emerson, would sometime tomorrow be convenient for me to come see you?"

"No, not tomorrow. I have a funeral to attend tomorrow."

There was another silence, then: "May I see you Tuesday morning?"

Nell breathed deep. There was no escape . . . no way to avoid an interview she knew was going to lacerate. "Yes, Mr. Mattingly. "Tuesday."

"Thank you. I'll call you before I come out Tuesday morning. I'm sorry to have bothered you today. You have my . . . sincerest sympathy."

"Good-by, Mr. Mattingly." Nell hung up.

Turning, she went back into the small kitchen. Her sister Robin and a man who had been one of Jerry's fellow pilots, Leonard Burns, looked up from their coffee cups at the table as she entered.

"It was the NTSB," Nell told them. "They want to ask me questions."

"That's routine, Nell," Burns said quickly. He was a tall man, white, with graying hair and a jutting jaw, and his expression showed his concern. "It won't be any big deal, really."

"It was not pilot error," Nell said. "It was *not* pilot error."

"They haven't made that suggestion," Burns replied. "And if they do, they'll have the pilots' association to fight. We've already decided that."

"I'll fight them too. They won't pin that on Jerry's reputation. I'll fight them all my life if need be."

"Nell," Robin said softly. "You've got to think of the kids, too. And the future. Try not to get hung up on this. It's like Lenny just said: no one has even suggested pilot error yet."

Leonard Burns rose from his chair, went to Nell Emerson, and awkwardly patted her arm. "Look, Nell, I have to get going. I'll see you in the morning. Jack Barstow and I will be by at nine-thirty. All right?"

"Yes," Nell murmured, staring into space. "The funeral is tomorrow." She appeared dazed, withdrawn.

Burns looked at her for an instant, torn. It had been a painful visit. Nell Emerson had been in the business and she had always known, as all the wives knew, that there was that slim chance of a Bad One. But it was proven that more pilots died in automobile accidents on the way to flights than they did in their aircraft. The chance of tragedy was always remote . . . until it happened.

Now Burns did not know what to make of her dazed anger, her insistence about defending Jerry's reputation. Burns did not take it for a good sign. It was the start of what could become a morbid preoccupation. He would have preferred tears, hysteria. Nell had to break, and descend into her grief, before she could begin to try to heal in order to move again among the living.

Knowing he could say none of this, Burns nodded to Nell's sister, "Take care," he said thickly, and walked out of the room.

Once inside his Volvo, Burns heaved a sigh of relief, and then felt guilty. He had sighed because he was intensely relieved to be away from Nell, and away from the unbearable quiet, tension, and grief of her home. He was escaping it now, going back to the everyday routine. But he realized that for Nell Emerson the ordeal was inescapable; and it was just beginning.

And in St. Louis, Missouri, there was also a sense of ordeal.

A brief spring squall had brought heavy rain pounding the dingy windows of the apartment. Thunder rolled, rattling the tiny glass boats and figurines on the shelves of one wall.

Standing in the middle of the cluttered little room, Harold Zelmer was only faintly aware of the storm.

He stood very still, bony hands jammed deep into the pockets of his jeans. He was twenty-four, tall, lank, with a shock of white-blond hair and vivid blue eyes. Some of the women who pursued him at the club where he played folk guitar each night said he looked like a famous Scandinavian tennis player. Since Harold Zelmer paid no attention to any sport and cared nothing about women, these comments had no effect on him.

Although his mother had left the apartment only Friday afternoon, almost exactly forty-eight hours ago now, Harold had already turned it into a mess. Always cluttered with mother's knickknacks and crochet work and fussy little plants, it was now strewn with magazines, last night's TV-dinner tray, empty glasses, soiled clothing, sections of the current *Rolling Stone*, empty Falstaff cans, Twinkies wrappers, crumpled cigarette packages. In one corner, several magazines devoted to male weight lifting and body building were strewn around on the old upright piano, the one with the ivory broken off brown keys. The piano was in flawless tune; Harold kept it that way personally. But like everything else of his mother's in the apartment, it irritated Harold, was a relic of an earlier time. His mother had already been a widow, and past forty, when he was born. She had already been living in the past when his life began.

Through the years of his growing up, Harold had never had to face any significant change in this place, which had always been home. The faded, pinkish picture of Jesus, wearing a crown of thorns and with a sword-pierced heart exposed in his chest, hung slightly askew over the greenish velveteen couch, as it always had. The cardboard painting on the east wall, of a shack in the mountains with deer looking out at it from a wood, had been the stuff of Harold's earliest fantasies. The radio console in another corner was a fine old Stromberg-Carlson, and the black-and-white television set an original Dumont, with a ten-inch screen.

Past the end of the couch two and one half steps was the little hallway with its gilt mirror and umbrella stand made of wicker. Turn to the right and you entered Harold's room, with the trundle bed he had occupied since his youth, the faded yellow newspaper clippings of big-game hunters on the walls, the cobwebby string of old flying-model airplanes, the olive-drab footlocker, always locked, packed

65

with more magazines like those on the piano, used in his sex fantasies.

At the opposite end of the little hall was his mother's room, with the brass bed, the religious pictures, the walls and ceiling stained by brown rain leaks when the roof failed, in 1954, the canary in its cage, the pervasive odor of decay and stale sachet.

The apartment had always been home and haven, unchanging. Harold Zelmer had always known that he had this place, with his mother in it.

But Harold's mother had left to visit a sick sister in New York on Friday. She had boarded Transwestern Flight 161.

Harold had shed no tears. That was not manly. The telephone call notifying him had been like a spear point inserted into his brain, and his sense of loss was so severe as to be disorienting. But he had not cried. He had never cried in his life.

He knew, intellectually, that he probably should feel like crying. Last night, after several beers, he had actually tried to cry, to seek relief. He could not. The only emotion he had ever known was far from tears. It was rage.

It was rage he felt now.

He had hated his mother in a way, but he had needed her. They had taken her away—had killed her. So now he did not have to hate her any more. He could hate them instead for killing her.

Harold did not know what he was going to do. His mother's body was being shipped back home. He had talked to the funeral home and everything was all set. He had thought about slipping into the funeral home, after Mother was in the coffin and everything, and climbing in with her so he could be buried too. He had thought about this, even calculating how long he might likely live after being buried. He thought the air would give out within two hours, which was good. It was not a very pleasant prospect, thinking of lying there in the dark beside his dead mother, day after day, being hungry and smelling her sachet and the embalming fluid. Worms might even get in. He hated to think about that.

He had decided that he could not hope really to get into the coffin. It would not be large enough. Or the bearers would notice the extra weight and would open the lid and see him and make him get out, which would be embarrassing. All his life, Harold had had ideas like this, but the doctor had helped him many times to see that the ideas were not really very rational and would only lead to embarrassment. So he had learned to hide most of his ideas, and how he felt; ordinary acquaintances considered him quiet and perhaps eccentric, but reasonably normal.

So he could not go into the ground. He had to stay alive. But to do what?

Pounding his fist softly against his forehead, he fought to be rational, the way the doctor always said. He tried to make a list:

1. Go to work as usual.
2. Arrange to meet Mother's body at the airport.
3. See to the services and funeral.
4. —

He could not *think* of 4! But he had to make plans. He was alone now. He had to ignore the sense of loss, and build his own life. But how? *How?*

He thought of the doctor. The doctor could help; he had helped so often before.

Hands shaking, Harold dialed the familiar number.

"Doctor Lindsey's office," the secretary answered cheerfully.

Harold struggled to make his voice calm and rational. "This is Harold Zelmer and I want an appointment as soon as possible."

"Mr. Zelmer, hello. Well, the doctor isn't in on the weekend, of course, and I'm in here only because we have this new filing system to set up. I shouldn't even have answered the phone, but it startled me. I don't know if I should make any appointments without asking the doctor—"

"*Please!*" Harold said.

She paused. "Well. Just a minute."

He waited, his chest in tumult. He could hear her rummaging around. He imagined the messy office, usually so cool and neat.

"Mr. Zelmer?"

"Tuesday afternoon at four?"

"Yes! Yes! You don't have anything sooner?"

"I'm sorry."

Harold drew in a ragged breath, trying to calm himself. "All right. Yes. Fine. Tuesday. At four."

He wondered how he could endure until then.

9

As administrative assistant to Ken Lis, Kelley Hemingway had been named secretary to the company board, without voting privileges, as one of her earliest assignments. Although she had assumed many more-important, decision-making duties as time passed, the keeping of board minutes remained as part of her job. It was one she enjoyed, because it placed her close to major policy discussions.

Heading to the ground-floor board room Monday morning, notebook and pencils in hand, Kelley had seldom experienced such a feeling of nervous anticipation before a meeting. But it was a feeling mixed with dread.

As she neared the board-room area, she met one of the members, Dean Busch, approaching from another hallway. The youngest member of the board, at thirty-seven, Busch was chief of Hempstead's smallest division, Consumer Products. The title of the division was actually a misnomer based more on old hopes than on reality; Hempstead's sales to the general consumer market were nil, a plan to branch out into housewares having been shelved a year previously, and Busch presided over a division that made control rods and altimeter housings for two small-aircraft firms, Cessna and Piper. Characteristically, Busch managed his job with casual good humor and some *élan*.

Meeting Kelly now, Busch gave her his usual wide grin, although his freckles seemed to stand out a little more than normal in his pallor. He held two large and heavy loose-leaf books toward her. "Just the lady I hoped to see. Will you carry these for an old man?"

"If I see an old man, I may offer," Kelley told him. "But you do look a little pale."

Busch straightened his rather loud plaid jacket and gave her a grimace. "Uncertainty makes me queasy."

Kelley fell into stride with him. She asked the question uppermost in her mind: "Do you think there will be talk of naming a new president today?"

"No," Busch said firmly. "Even Lydia wouldn't move that fast."

"I think she might, just because no one seems to expect it."

"Well, there could be some argument in favor of it. This whole place is going to be uneasy until the question is settled. But I just don't see her asking us to do that today. A temporary, acting president, maybe. *Maybe*."

"Will it be Ken Lis?" Kelley asked directly.

Busch looked thoughtful. "Sure."

"You feel that certain?"

"No," he admitted. "Hell. With the old man gone, who can predict anything?"

"Is that why you brought your homework?"

"Damn betcha. If the lady starts tossing around hard questions, I got my cheat notes here so I can have hard answers."

They were nearing the double doors that led to the board room, and ahead of them Kelley saw Richard Cazzell, the balding vice-president for finance, shuffling into the room. She told Busch, "You *are* a little nervous."

Busch scowled. "You better believe it."

They entered the room together.

It was a long and narrow room, deep in the building and with no windows, but brightly lighted by banks of fluorescent tubes inset in the acoustic-tile ceiling. The long and slender mahogany conference table dominated, with a single chair at the far end, the head, and four on either side. Two board members were already seated: the rotund Bert Jerno, chief of the Administrative Division, and Seymour Trepps, chief, Ocean Research.

Richard Cazzell, the lank, elderly man who had just preceded Kelley and Dean Busch into the room, had walked to a small side table containing a coffee urn, cups, and other paraphernalia. He was greeting Ken Lis, who had just filled a coffee cup. Kelley thought Lis appeared tense and fatigued.

69

It was less than three minutes before nine, so Kelley went directly to her accustomed place near the foot of the table. Nodding to the others, she sat down and prepared her notebook. As she did so, the last two members walked into the room together: Lydia Baines and Harvey Coughlin.

Whatever else he might be, Harvey Coughlin had never been entirely trusted by some of the others in that room. He was admired for his dogged determination, but Kelley knew that some of them saw him as a schemer. Jason Baines had used Coughlin but kept him in line.

For him to be entering with Lydia Baines, whom probably everyone felt at least wary of, did not seem a good portent.

Lydia Baines moved directly to the head of the table, as if she had always taken that place. She wore black, but the dress was stylishly cut, with a slit at the left side that revealed a long, tanned leg as she moved. She looked regal and totally in command. Kelley felt a slight chill, wondering what it must be like for a man to be confronted sexually by this woman. Lydia Baines would enjoy emasculating a man, and the stronger the man, the more challenged she would be to render him helpless, impotent. Was it a feeling like this that made her eyes flash so brightly as she took her chair at the head of the table and tapped a long, crimson fingernail for order?

Ken Lis and Harvey Coughlin were the last to take their chairs, facing each other across the width of the table at the places closest to Lydia Baines. Dean Busch and Seymour Trepps were on Lis's side, between him and Kelley, and with Coughlin were Cazzell and Jerno. The selection of chairs was very nearly symbolic of how a vote might split in any serious confrontation, the older men with Coughlin, the younger and more innovative with Lis. But Lydia Baines was the swing vote now, and Kelley felt a premonition of disaster.

"Thank you all for coming today," Lydia Baines said quietly. "The minutes, Miss Secretary, will show that the meeting began on time with all present. Please note the following. Quote. The members of the board extended sympathy to Mrs. Baines on the loss of her husband, and unanimously adopted a resolution praising the late Jason Baines as an aviation pioneer who would never be forgotten. Unquote. I have the exact working of the resolution here." Lydia Baines took a typed sheet of paper from a slender folder in front of her. She handed it to Lis. "Will you pass this down to the secretary, please?"

"Item two, if you please, Miss Secretary," Lydia went on. "The board approved naming of a new chairperson for the group, Mrs. Lydia Baines." She glanced around. "Any objections?"

"I so move," Harvey Coughlin said.

"Second," Cazzell said.

"Thank you," Lydia said with a frosty smile. "Adopted without dissent."

Dean Busch leaned forward, a tight smile on his lips. "Madam Chairman?"

"Dean?"

"I applaud the actions noted, but I must note also that I begin to get the impression that some of us could have stayed at the job. In the past, motions have come from the floor."

"Dean, you all know that my late husband discussed every aspect of the business with me. I've attended many of these meetings. I don't want to antagonize anyone, but we have a crisis here and we must move swiftly. Do you understand?"

Busch's face reddened. He seemed about to speak again, but withered before Lydia Baines's glacial stare. He sat back, silent.

Kelley saw that Lydia Baines's dangerous gambit had worked. She had dared immediate open conflict while they were all off balance, and had established her command.

"You know the time and place of the funeral," Lydia said. "I will appreciate your loyal attendance. Please do not bring friends or others outside of your immediate family. The services are closed to the public and will be very brief and simple, as I believe Jason would have approved.

"I will at this time call on Ken Lis to report to the board on any new developments in the investigation of the crash. Ken?"

Lis leaned forward, his face sober and strained as he examined the notes in front of him. "My report dated yesterday, which all of you have, includes all known information up to that time. There have been no significant new developments since then."

"Then, the cause of the crash is something of a mystery."

"That is correct."

"Then, production will go ahead normally and we really don't need to do anything in particular as a result of the accident."

Lis looked up at Lydia sharply, astonishment written on his features. "It isn't quite that simple. *Something* caused the crash. Hempstead has an obligation to look over all possible causes—re-examine all prior test data, for example. The crash appears to have been caused by a systems failure resulting in loss of control functions, or a slow-speed stall. It would be criminal if we ignored these possibilities and didn't do everything in our power to check possible causes."

Harvey Coughlin leaned forward. "Ken, I don't think I understand what you're saying. If they can't say it was a failure of the plane, why do we have to do anything except go full speed ahead with our production? Why *ask* for trouble with new tests or anything like that?"

"The NTSB will investigate, after all," Richard Cazzell added.

Lis frowned at his papers. "Under the circumstances, I believe continued production is feasible. We have orders, and our financial structure is such that a production delay at this time would not be justified. But I believe we have to institute renewed internal testing and evaluation, both on our own and in co-operation with Transwestern, and I have already taken steps to begin that process."

Lydia Baines said coolly, "If word gets out that we're retesting Excalibur, it will shatter public confidence."

"It will wreck the chance of new sales!" Coughlin added.

Lis's face darkened. "I could remind the board of a famous airplane still flying many of the air lanes today. It had a defective cargo door. The company that built that plane knew the door design was something out of Rube Goldberg; the company ignored the bad design and went ahead. Then there was a test failure. The company kept building. Then a plane in actual operation had an explosive decompression as a result of failure of that door, and the plane just managed to land, badly damaged. The company *still* did nothing. —Finally, you'll recall, there was a crash. Leaving abstract morality out of it entirely, what would you prefer—a shadow on our plane's reputation now, or the PR disaster that would come if we did nothing and the plane was later proven by the NTSB to have a defect that we overlooked?"

There was silence for a moment, Kelley heard her own pulse in her ears. She, like the others, watched Lydia Baines.

Lydia finished jotting a note on her tablet, then raised her eyes to Lis. "It sounds like you're ready to condemn the very airplane you, more than anyone else, brought into existence."

Lis shook his head. "No. I firmly believe Excalibur is sound. But we have an obligation to test."

"But the public is bound to misinterpret that."

"Transwestern doesn't think so. Their board has already approved a joint test program if this board approves. They'll take one of their remaining Excaliburs out of service and fly it here with a complete technical team. That plane, one with a maintenance and use record very near that of the one that crashed, will be test-flown by our people along with the prototype. We'll look for any signs of change in characteristics that might point to something developing after extended daily use in passenger service."

Lydia Baines shook her head. "I, for one, am very much against any joint test program. The public will take it as proof that something basic is wrong with the aircraft. We can't afford that kind of impression. I don't think I need remind anyone that this company is committed to years of production of Excalibur. Our target right now is a minimum of sixty new orders by the end of the year. If we don't have them—if something erodes confidence, and we don't have new orders flowing in. . . ."

She did not need to finish this statement. Kelley Hemingway, like everyone else in the room, knew that Hempstead would be out of work in MA without new orders before the end of the year. As few as a dozen new orders would allow continued full production well into the following year. But for maximum efficiency and economy in ordering materials and prefabricated subsystems, five times that number of orders should be in the files.

And given the tremendous investment on Excalibur, continued full-scale production was mandatory if the company was ever to pull out of debt and make the great gamble begin to pay off. A fall-off in orders now would be very nearly catastrophic; there was no other project to take up the slack.

Lis, however, did not flinch. "We can't take any chances on the airplane's safety."

"The airplane is safe," Lydia snapped. "Every aircraft is a compromise."

This was true, and unanswerable. Engineers could make an airplane so strong it might withstand almost any impact. But it would have to weigh so much that it would never get off the ground. On the other hand, Kelley recognized that Lydia Baines and Ken Lis

73

were speaking at cross purposes now, and there was more involved than the question of the wisdom of joint testing with Transwestern.

It was Lydia who spoke again, bringing this fact into the open. "I also must say, Ken, that I believe you overexceeded your authority, making tentative arrangements with Transwestern on your own. That sort of decision is for the board."

Lis looked sharply at her. "I've always made that kind of decision on my own."

"You will stop doing so."

The silence was embarrassed. It was Bert Jerno who broke it.

"I sort of hate to bring this up," he said, "but Sales tells me that we already have definite signs of a problem because of New York. It's sort of a factor here."

Lydia turned cool eyes toward the rotund administrator. "Explain."

"We've had telephone contact with both United and TWA this weekend, since the crash," Jerno said slowly. "You know that both of them have been considering placement of orders within the next quarter. Now they're both backing off a little—talking about possibly waiting until sometime next year."

"That settles it," Lydia Baines said. "We can't go into any joint test program with TW that might further erode confidence by suggesting we believe something is basically wrong with Excalibur. We have to exude confidence. We *need* those orders."

"Plans for the joint testing are already far advanced," Lis said.

"Cancel the plans."

Kelley Hemingway fought the impulse to speak out. The room was deathly silent. Jason Baines had never, to her knowledge, so directly affronted any division manager. By contradicting Ken Lis so frontally, Lydia Baines was doing more than changing the test situation; she was putting Lis in his place . . . a place of lesser stature than he had held under her husband's leadership.

Lis knew this. Every person in the room knew it.

His face drawn, Lis said slowly, "I believe, Mrs. Baines, that an action countermanding a division chief must be by vote of the board."

"You want a vote?" Lydia replied quickly.

"Ken," Bert Jerno said. "Don't push it . . . okay?" It was truly a plea.

Dean Busch held up his hand, his usually sunny expression solemn. "I'm with Bert on this, Ken. Look—hell! Can't we accomplish essentially the same testing with our own prototype, and maybe one plane off the line? We do continuing testing anyway. That won't call attention to anything we're doing. Let TW do their own testing, and we'll do ours." Busch turned toward Lydia Baines. "*That's* sensible and agreeable, isn't it?"

There was just the slightest crack of desperation—and of challenge —in the younger man's tone. He was saying to Lis, *You needn't surrender unconditionally.* And to Lydia he was saying, *I'll support you only so far; don't force it beyond limits of safety.*

Lydia Baines hesitated only fractionally. She read the signs. She even glanced at Kelley, and Kelley understood perfectly in this instant that the older woman was weighing the odds of a vote on Busch's suggested compromise . . . was perhaps even weighing whether insistence on total victory might eventually cost her because it could create sympathy for Ken Lis.

Lydia said quietly, "I see no reason why Dean's suggestion wouldn't work. Would that be acceptable to you, Ken?"

Lis's chest heaved. "Yes."

The sense of relief in the room could almost be touched.

Lydia rearranged some papers in front of her. "All right, then. I believe we can all see, especially in view of Bert's information about United and TWA, that any other sales we can make at this time are vital to show continued confidence in Excalibur. We have a visit upcoming from the Monravian delegation. Ordinarily we might have viewed this as a significant but not mandatory order. Now our situation is changed. We *need* that Monravian order. I suggest that we have another meeting of affected divisions the day after tomorrow, to make sure we have a full and complete program laid out to welcome the Monravian delegation and give them a maximum information and sales effort. Will ten o'clock, here, be agreeable?"

No one argued.

"Done, then," Lydia said, jotting a note. "Richard, after the meeting today, I want to confer with you awhile on an idea I have for a cash rebate plan that might be attractive to Monravia and other potential small buyers."

Cazzell raised furry eyebrows in surprise. "Mrs. Baines, the company has never gone in for anything of that nature."

"Times change," Lydia snapped. "May we move on, please?"

Again, no one missed the significance of this. An outsider might not have understood that the exchange was, in its way, nakedly brutal. Nothing was the same in this room now, nor would it ever be the same again.

Lydia Baines pretended not to notice. "The difficulty we now face as the result of a single Excalibur accident proves again something I often said to my late husband. This company needs to diversify its base. I believe there is no time like the present. We have another product which might provide great diversification, and potential large income. Of course I refer to the Eagle project."

There were varied expressions of new surprise. Seymour Trepps spoke for the first time: "Isn't Eagle hopelessly locked up in a Senate committee, Mrs. Baines?"

"Eagle has been hung up in committee partly because this company has not been willing to press vigorously for its adoption as a part of the nation's defense arsenal. I am pleased to report that I have already taken certain preliminary steps to push harder on the matter, and as a result, I have confidence that new hearings will commence shortly on Eagle. Harvey, here is already preparing new materials, and I have instructed him to be ready to go to Washington for some advance work later this week. I trust that this initiative on my part meets with your approval."

No one spoke. Lydia Baines, Kelley thought, seemed to have an infinite capacity for new surprises. Most of the men in the room evidently knew nothing of Coughlin's plans. If Lydia's idea was to seize control partially by achieving surprise, she was doing very well.

"Harvey," Lydia said with her first genuine smile, "tell us about the situation and your plans."

Harvey Coughlin, his jaw set, pulled his chair closer to the table and looked down at notes. "Well, the Eagle project is of tremendous significance, obviously. And may I state personally, Lydia, that I applaud your initiative in this area. I intend to take maximum advantage of your wonderful efforts."

Lydia's eyebrows knit. "Tell us your plans, Harvey. Please."

"Yes. Of course." Coughlin scowled at his notes again. "Naturally, everyone knows that Eagle is an advanced air-to-ground missile, a more compact and sophisticated system than any we now have in our arsenal. While size restricts its range to six hundred miles, it can be carried by several aircraft now flying in our Air Force, and it has two unique advantages over other existing missiles: a completely new guidance system designed to help it maneuver away from attacking missiles, and a full multiple-warhead capability.

"Eagle," Coughlin went on, warming to his topic, "can be slung under a bomber or even a heavy fighter. It can be released at either low or high altitude. It can elude anti-missile missiles. And it can be programmed to release as many as five independently targeted warheads as far as two hundred miles from impact area. The Air Force, as you know, has already tested our prototypes, and had formally asked Congress for authorization to buy this missile from us and add it to the nuclear arsenal."

Coughlin paused and reached for a water glass.

Ken Lis—as Kelley had known he must—spoke. "One of the reasons we haven't pushed Eagle is that at least some experts believe it might cause a complete breakdown of the latest round of SALT talks. The last administration in Washington was officially against the weapon's introduction."

Lydia Baines said, "That was the last administration. The new one hasn't taken a stand."

"A number of years ago," Lis added, "this company adopted a policy to avoid basing its financial well-being on defense contracts of any kind. That was why we took the gamble on Excalibur. Eagle was already in Research and Development, and we continued it. But it has never had a high priority, because company policy was against it."

"A great many firms much larger than we," Lydia Baines said, "base a considerable portion of their economics on defense work."

"And a lot of them are in trouble. Defense work comes and defense work goes. All morality aside, it's feast and famine when you're trying to deal with the Pentagon, and everyone knows that."

Lydia Baines's eyes snapped. But when she spoke, her voice was cool. "Eagle would be a feast for us, Ken. —Continue please, Harvey."

Harvey Coughlin cleared his throat. "Assuming new hearings are held in the immediate future, I believe we will have a strong case for Eagle and a more assertive strategy for influencing voters who may be wavering. . . ."

As he droned on, Kelley found her attention wandering. She had a great sense of watching a charade. The *form* of the meeting was as it had always been. The effect was entirely different. This was not a free and open debate, the kind of near free-for-all that Jason Baines had encouraged and enormously enjoyed. This issue was decided. Eagle was being given new and higher priority.

Glancing covertly around the table, Kelley knew that a vote, if forced, would also be a mockery. Harvey Coughlin, so self-importantly reading his notes, would obviously vote for Eagle pressure because it was in his self-interest. Richard Cazzell was old . . . nearing retirement; he would vote to preserve his security, i.e., with Lydia Baines. Bert Jerno was a nice man and Kelley basically liked him. But he was not a strong personality. He would twist in the wind—and vote out of cowardice. Lydia Baines could force him to knuckle under on any issue she chose.

This group—Lydia Baines, Harvey Coughlin, Richard Cazzell, and Bert Jerno—could provide a rubber-stamp majority on anything Lydia wanted.

Of the others, Ken Lis was the only man whom Kelley was sure of. He would vote his conscience. She thought Dean Busch, stubborn as he was and with the resiliency of comparative youth, would do likewise. But she was not even sure of Seymour Trepps. His was the weakest division, his future the least secure. Trepps now looked miserably unhappy. The last thing he wanted was a confrontation. He had no heart for it, no power base, and no possible hope that he could gain.

It was a situation made to order for an autocrat and Lydia Baines fit the prescription. It was clear that she was already wholly in charge now. It was her company. The victory was hers.

As Coughlin spoke on, a new and chilling thought occurred to Kelley. Because she was so firmly in control, would Lydia Baines push even further? Would there after all, be a new president named today? Was there any limit to Lydia Baines's audacity and lust for power?

It was far from a happy line of conjecture. Kelley waited, even more ill at ease.

10

At 10:50 A.M., the members of the Hempstead Aviation board filed out of the room. Lydia Baines headed for a second session with Bert Jerno and Richard Cazzell, while the others scattered. More upset than he wanted to show, Ken Lis walked directly to his own office.

Seating himself behind the desk, he closed his eyes for a moment. Green stars danced on the screen of his eyelids, then exploded and vanished. He had a headache. Slipping his loafers off under the desk, he wriggled his toes, seeking relief from the tension.

Dean Busch poked his head in the doorway. "You want to talk about it later?"

"Late today, maybe," Lis said.

"That bitch wants us all to be her puppets!"

Lis was aware of a need to hold things together . . . why, he did not know. "It's not that bad, Dean. It's just a period of readjustment."

"I don't know what the fuck we're going to do!"

"Let's huddle around five, all right?"

Busch nodded unhappily and went away.

Lis's intercom telephone button flashed at him and he picked up the receiver. "Yes, Barbara?"

"We had two calls from a Mr. Lucian Derquet, of Monravia, while you were meeting," the secretary told him. "He left a message the second time."

"What did Mr. Derquet have to say for himself, Barbara?"

"He said the Monravian delegation will not be visiting Hempstead for at least two weeks."

Lis straightened up in unpleasant surprise. "Will *not?*"

"Not for at least two weeks," the secretary corrected him. "He said the delegation has visiting plans for Boeing later this week, and then they'll probably be visiting two other companies the following week. He said he wanted you to know at once about the delay. He said he or a member of his staff will be back in touch with you in a few days to set up a new definite time."

"Thank you, Barbara." Lis hung up calmly, then examined the meaning of the delay. Monravia was giving priority to larger airliner-manufacturing companies, and this could not be a good sign.

He did not need another unfavorable development right now. He felt a stab of depression, which he threw off with some effort.

As he did so, Kelley Hemingway, her face pink with anger, strode into his office. "Got a minute?" she asked.

"Of course. Sit down, Kelley."

Instead, she stood over him, seething. "How can you be so calm?"

He made it a point to grin at her. "It isn't easy."

"She didn't even mention electing a new president!"

"She's a very clever woman."

"You're not upset? You're not angry?"

"Yes, I am," Lis admitted. "But I can see what a clever tactic it was on her part. As long as the naming of a new president is hanging over our heads, there appears to be at least a *chance* that she won't want that title for herself—that she may be content with the title of board chairman. And *that* puts the presidency up for grabs. Who is going to fight her on that board as long as they think they might have a chance for the top job?"

"She's going to ruin the company."

"Not if she can avoid it. Ruining Hempstead is hardly in her own interest."

"But what about the testing with Transwestern?"

"That's out," Lis said as calmly as he could. "I want you to call them and tell them that we've changed our plans."

"Are we going to test on our own?"

"Oh, yes. I'm going down to talk to Pappy in just a few minutes. We have to lay on an even better test program internally now. And I'd like you to draft a letter to the NTSB, too, Kelley. Ask them to let us have access to all voice tapes, and any recorder data, that they may salvage from the wreckage. Stress that it will help us to have access as soon as possible, since we're doing some testing of our own."

"I'll do it," Kelley said. "But I'm getting the feeling that I must be crazy!"

"Why?"

"That woman has just changed every method of operating that the board ever had! She insulted you, practically threatened two or three others, and gave Coughlin virtually a green light to push a project that the board repeatedly voted, in years past, to keep on the back burner. And here we stand, talking as if nothing had happened."

"We can't go around wringing our hands, Kelley. We've got a business to run."

"Aren't you upset? Don't you care?"

That stung, and Lis momentarily lost part of his control. "You're damned right I care! But I'm not going to let everything go down the tubes because I feel bad! It's up to us to keep this company going!"

Kelley bit her lip. "Of course. You're right. Sorry."

Lis was aware of an impulse to go around the desk and take her in his arms. He did not move. "I didn't mean to bark."

"What upsets me more than anything else is that she's so obviously setting you and Coughlin up for a head-to-head competition. You have to save Excalibur. She's dangling the carrot in front of him on Eagle, a project you personally despise. Winner take the presidency!"

"And in the meantime," Lis said, "each of us—in her view—will work harder to beat the other. Which she must assume will help the company."

"It's a damned sorry way to get performance."

"It's hardly unusual in business, Kelley."

"I wish I had your philosophical attitude."

He chose not to contradict her on this. If she thought he was calm, it showed that his control was better than it felt at the moment. He was both hurt and angry. His impulse was to clean out his desk. But his investment was too great for that. He reached for the telephone. "I'd better see if Pappy can see me now."

Kelley Hemingway threw up her hands and strode out of the office.

Lis dialed the number of the engineering-and-design lab, and a young technician switched him through to Barton MacIvor.

"Pappy, can we visit?" Lis asked him.

"Top o' the mornin'!" MacIvor boomed back. "Yer meetin' over?"

"Yes. I'd like to huddle with you about testing."

"You be wantin' me to come oop, or will you be comin' doon fer a spot of tea?"

"I'll come down."

Barton MacIvor's office, off in one corner of the sprawling engineering lab, was walled off by glass. The glass partition was covered with pasted-up blueprints, pencil sketches, sheets of specifications, and cartoons torn from MacIvor's favorite magazine, *Flying*. A decrepit wooden desk, a trio of old wooden straight chairs, a pair of filing cabinets, and a draftsman's table constituted the furniture, and everything was buried under blueprints and designs, manuals and reference books. More books and blueprints were perched on pulled-out desk drawers. Several old cups of tea or coffee, half consumed, stood around on precarious balancing points, and one had spilled a week (two weeks?) earlier on an out-folded blue-on-white engine design sheet on one corner of the desk. The stain, greenish black, was dried now, a trash man's Rorschach.

It was hard to believe, Lis thought, entering the mess, that out of this chaos could come sketches and designs of such unequaled simplicity, grace, and engineering elegance—that in this rubble could prosper a mind with the keenest edge he had ever encountered.

Barton MacIvor was at the drafting table, pouring water from a tin can into a plastic heater. "Wipe yer feet," he suggested.

"You cleaned the place up," Lis observed.

"Shooer." MacIvor shoved a mountain of drawings off a chair onto the floor to clear a chair. "A man has to have cleanliness for work. Now, will you be havin' yer tea?"

"There was too much coffee in the meeting, Pappy. I'll pass on tea, thanks."

"I heard there was more'n coffee in th' meetin'," MacIvor said.

"The grapevine works fast."

"Aye. The whoor was nasty, the way I hear."

"It wasn't so bad. Pappy, the reason I came down here was to talk about those tests we have to set up."

MacIvor raised the lid of a small blue teapot and sniffed the fumes. Nodding with satisfaction, he hunted around in the litter, evidently for a cup. He spied a paper container with something turgid half-congealed in the bottom. He poured this into the wastebasket and went to the teapot. "I been thinkin' ye ought to be tellin' young Scanlon aboot the tests," he said, pouring.

"Why?" Lis demanded.

"Wal, I been thinkin' it's time fer me to move on."

"No."

"Aye. With Jason gone, and that woman already putting the cat amongst the pigeons, it'd be better fer me to move on before I get myself in trouble with her."

"Pappy, we need you here. You can't walk out with Excalibur in trouble!"

MacIvor glared at Lis with his good eye. "The boys can handle the tests, an' if I should stay, the day would come when that whoor'd walk in here an' say, 'Oh, hallo, you'll be havin' your office cleaned oot for the new man by noon, won't you?'—I want to avoid that."

The thought of MacIvor's departure was depressing in the extreme. Lis knew he needed the old man for more than his technical genius. "Pappy, you can't leave now. Your guts are in Excalibur. See it through with me on this. Then—later—there will be time to get back to Songbird. I promise you."

"Ah," MacIvor sighed huskily, giving Lis a look of reproof, "you'll do anything to keep me, won't you."

"I need you, Pappy. Not just for the plane. I need you here because you're my *friend*."

"'S a new ball game now, lad. That whoor will ruin you. You should be thinking of getting oot yourself."

"And run from her? Give her exactly what she wants?"

MacIvor sipped his tea in silence, watching Lis over the rim of the paper cup.

"We've got to do what Jason dreamed," Lis told him. "We've got to make Excalibur the greatest, most historical airplane since the DC-3. We've got to vindicate the dimple-wing design. We owe it to him, Pappy!"

MacIvor put down the cup. "Ah," he sighed, making the sound infinitely regretful.

"Stick with me a while longer," Lis urged, shamelessly pressing the advantage. "I need you. You know that."

"You're a devil," the old man said. "You'd be arguing that it wasn't all that bad, and that we oughtta form a committee, if we were'n hell."

"Just stick it out with me."

"You are not like the others," MacIvor told him. "You're some kind of throwback. You belong back with Sopwith Camels 'n' Spads, 'n' fly her by the seat of your pants. You had a place with Jason, but this whoor will never give you freedom, and if you don't kiss her rear fer her, she'll throw you oot when you least expect it. Don't you *see* that, lad?"

"I'm going to try to hang in. Hang in with me, Pappy. Please. I'm asking you personally."

"Ah," MacIvor said. "Maybe I could hang around a little while." He walked around the desk and glowered down at Lis. "But don't ever say I didn't warn you!"

Lis stood. He started to offer the old man his hand, but MacIvor was occupied with his paper cup of tea. Impulsively, out of his relief and loneliness and love for the man, Lis threw an arm around his wide shoulders and hugged him.

"I'm still gonna build Songbird," MacIvor said, snuffing as if he had a runny nose.

"And I'm going to help you."

For a moment it was as if the dream were still very golden, very much alive.

It was MacIvor who broke the spell. "We git along, you fool, because we're one as daft as the other. You're committin' suicide and taking me along for a companion."

Lis grinned at him, weak in his sense of relief. "That's bullshit, Pappy, and you know it. Now let's talk about the test program."

11

George Pierce, the immediate supervisor of Jace Mattingly within the structure of the National Transportation Safety Board, was a very tall, very slender man with bright green eyes and a skull without a trace of hair. Pierce was already at a table inside the pancake house, morosely stirring his coffee, when Jace Mattingly walked in, Tuesday morning.

"You're late," Pierce said, faintly smiling.

"Naturally," Mattingly said.

"I assume you've been conducting vital interviews, and reviewing preliminary reports."

"Negative. I've been sleeping."

"You look like you needed it."

"Thanks."

Pierce signaled a waitress, who came over and took Mattingly's order, for coffee.

"You ought to eat," Pierce lectured him. "How can you walk into a place like this and smell the pancakes and coffee and syrup and bacon and not be ravenous? I've got a number seven ordered: a little bit of everything on the menu."

"My stomach wakes up about noon," Mattingly said.

"What's on your personal agenda today?"

Mattingly glanced at his watch. "I meet the pilot's widow in an hour."

"That's fast."

"You said to be quick about it. Personally, I would have waited a few days, out of decency for the widow, and then let one of the staff handle the interview."

"I want you to do it personally."

"Why?" Mattingly asked bluntly. "Because I'm the right color?"

Pierce looked genuinely pained. "Jace, God damn it, you know better than that."

"Why, then?"

"You know why. It's awfully damned early in the investigation, but it's going to be a tough one. We certainly can't rule out pilot error on the basis of the preliminary evidence."

"And we can't suggest it, either," Mattingly countered. "About all we really know is that the plane hit the ground at approximately 228 miles per hour and there were no survivors."

"What about the black box? Anything more on that?"

The "black box," actually a bright-orange metal container about the size of a breadbox, contained two vital instruments: the Digital Flight Data Recorder and the Cockpit Voice Recorder. Although it had been mounted in the tail for maximum safety, the box had been fished smoking from wreckage in the Kennedy crash, severely damaged.

"The word this morning," Mattingly told his superior, "is that the voice tapes are probably beyond repair. The metal foil was superheated, and the lab boys say it will be a miracle if they get anything off them, either."

Pierce accepted the bad news with only a deepening scowl. "The interviews?"

"Ahead of schedule. And the wreck site has been scoured, and we're building the frame to start reconstructing the plane from its fragments. Metallurgy will start testing structural components for stress fatigue or breakage within forty-eight hours. The engine test team is being brought together, and they'll start taking the engines apart for examination, including X-ray, by Friday. It's a hell of a lot too early to be saying we have to grope around for something like pilot error as a cause!"

Pierce eyed Mattingly somberly. "Does it bother you more in this case than it would normally?"

"Why should it?" Mattingly demanded. Then he understood. "That's a crummy thing to say! Listen, I don't care if the pilot is black, white, or speckled like an Easter egg! I just say, don't start talking pilot error out of desperation when the investigation is hardly started!"

"Okay." Pierce looked embarrassed. "Sorry. I'm feeling pressure, friend. Excalibur is not your ordinary airplane. This is not your ordinary wreck."

"There aren't any ordinary wrecks."

"Lecture me about it, Jace. You know perfectly well what I mean. I mean that new wing design. Everybody is manufacturing rumors, because the Excalibur design is so unique."

The waitress interrupted them, bringing pancakes for Pierce, coffee for Mattingly. They waited until she left.

"That wing was tested more severely than any in history," Mattingly said then. "There's no suggestion so far that it failed."

Pierce began slicing his pancakes with a knife. "The pressure comes for a variety of other reasons. For one thing, Hempstead is not one of your corporate giants. If we were to ground Excalibur, it could ruin them."

"Has someone already suggested grounding Excalibur, for Christ's sake?"

Pierce's eyes hardened. "It's an implied possibility, Jace. Don't play games with me. The director is already feeling some heat from certain senators who think they can reap a little publicity from yelling about unsafe air-transport practices. The New York *Times* is interested."

"And the director is feeling the heat."

"The director can take the heat. That's his job. But there's also pressure from the White House."

Mattingly put down his cup. "The White House!"

Pierce chewed thoughtfully before he spoke. "Several European nations have expressed some interest in Excalibur. It's considered ideal for shorter hops on the Continent, especially with the low noise levels. Monravia has a big delegation in the country right now to look at several aircraft for its expanded commercial fleet, and the word is that the prince himself is hot for Excalibur. If our investigation drags out—that's the term used by the White House, I'm told—then Monravia might go elsewhere."

"As long as they go to another United States company, why should the White House care?"

"They might not, but there's strong competition from Great Britain in this class of airplane. There's official concern that if Excalibur is in trouble, a lot of orders might go to the British. That could screw up the balance of payments for two or three years. And the official view is that we can't afford that setback right now, with the recovery in trouble anyway."

"What are we supposed to do?" Mattingly asked. "Give the plane a clean bill of health when we're not sure why it crashed?"

"No, Jace," Pierce said patiently. "I'm just trying to explain to you why we're all going to continue feeling pressure—why we need to have some sort of internal list of possibilities ready, not for publication."

"Are we going to put sabotage on the list?" Mattingly asked.

"You're playing games with me again. You saw that FBI letter. No sign of possible sabotage."

"That doesn't entirely rule it out."

"No," Pierce said. "So if you want to keep it on your mental list, fine. That makes the list include the following: sabotage; wind shear; approach-to-landing stall due to pilot error; control-system malfunction; asymmetric power surge; major-component structural failure; pilot disorientation in transitioning from cloud to visual. Have I left anything out?"

"Yes," Mattingly said. "Other."

"We're going to have continuing pressure," Pierce said ignoring the sour joke. "From the White House. From Congress. From Hempstead, from Transwestern and other airlines, from GE and all the other major-component-systems suppliers, from consumer-safety groups, advocacy groups—the works. Part of that is normal, part is extraordinary. We're going to follow our usual procedures. The director says we are not going to be stampeded. He means that. But in view of all the circumstances, he has approved one unusual measure, hoping it will provide us with a single source of the latest information at any moment's notice."

Mattingly studied his superior's face, trying to guess what the procedure might be. He could not, and remained silent, waiting.

"You're to be freed from all the usual procedural channels," Pierce told him. "You're our designated hitter. Move through the investigation as you see fit. Keep on top of whatever aspect looks promising. Do anything you can to expedite matters. —And be prepared to report to the director whenever he has to have the latest information."

"Oh, no!" Mattingly said, dismayed. "Not me!"

"You."

"I don't want any part of it. You're setting me up! If the probe goes sour, I'm the guy out front, taking the heat from all sides!"

"Make sure it doesn't go sour, then."

"Look, I believe in normal procedures. I *live* by normal procedures. Now you're short-circuiting everything—and making me the one who scurries around, gumming up the works for everyone."

"The director picked you personally, Jace. He knows you and he knows your reputation. You can be his personal trouble shooter in this one. If anyone can cut through red tape and channels and stay on top of this thing moment by moment, you can. —Who knows? You might even be pioneering a new system. If we can break this one in record time, we might see more investigations with a sort of free-lance trouble shooter in the act."

"You're asking *me* to come up with cause!"

"Well," Pierce said, "I wouldn't put it that way."

"We're not a one-man operation. We never have been. Now the director is trying to set me up as the one who might have to make a decision for him at any moment."

"It's a golden opportunity, Jace. Handle this well, and it's a big promotion."

"Get in trouble," Mattingly said bitterly, "and I go down the tubes."

"You won't go down the tubes."

"I could!"

"You won't, Jace. This is a chance in a lifetime for you. You have only one instruction: find the cause of that crash. No one is going to ask you how, or why, you proceed. Just get moving. No one can afford a year's investigation on this one—not the companies involved, not the Board, and not the country."

Mattingly sat back, staring at his coffee, numbed. "I can't believe this," he said. "I don't *want* this. It's too much!"

"Of course, you can write a letter to the director, refusing," Pierce said. "No one would hold it against you . . . he said."

"Yeah," Mattingly said. "Right." He knew better. And he also knew that he could no more turn his back on this challenge than he could look for another kind of work. Even as the challenge scared him, he felt his nervous system gearing up for it. He downed his coffee and dug into his pocket for change.

"In a hurry?" Pierce asked.

"I've got an interview with Mrs. Jerry Emerson, remember?"

"You're a big shot now. You could duck it—assign someone."

Mattingly stood. "Pilot error is the first possibility I want to ex off my list, friend. I'll see the lady personally."

Pierce went back to the remnants of his breakfast.

It was warm and hazy outside, and the coffee burned in Mattingly's stomach as he got into his car and began driving. It was not far to Hyattsville and the address written in his notebook, but he drove slowly to give himself additional time to readjust to his new situation.

He was still numb. After years of bitching about red tape and the bureaucracy, he was essentially freed of it. He had an enormous puzzle and could attack it any way he wished. His mind was racing ahead of him as he considered possibilities. It had to be orderly . . . careful. But he was at least free to range over any set of theories he wished to attack. After talking about freedom for so long, he suddenly had it, and he found that its first impact on him was frightening.

The designated address in Hyattsville was a modest frame house on Forty-first Avenue. There was a blue Datsun in the driveway, and Mattingly parked behind it. He gathered up his briefcase and tape recorder and walked to the front porch, where he rang the doorbell.

The white man who opened the door was a pilot. He wore no insignia on his rumpled red shirt and gray slacks, but Mattingly recognized him as a type immediately: rather short, dumpy, sandy hair going to gray, wide ears, freckles, smoke-colored glasses. Trouble, Mattingly thought.

"I'm Frank Bronk," the man said shaking hands. "I'm a senior pilot for TW. One of my friends and I thought we ought to be here when you talked with Nell."

"Friends of the family?" Mattingly asked.

"You might say that." Bronk escorted Mattingly through the living room to the kitchen, where two other people were at the kitchen table. One was clearly another pilot—the same age and characteristics—and the other was a beautiful young black woman whom Bronk introduced as Mrs. Jerry Emerson.

Mattingly put his briefcase and recorder on the table. "I'm sorry to put you through this, Mrs. Emerson. Regulations."

"That's quite all right," she said softly. She had risen as he entered the room. She wore a plain black jersey pantsuit, the sleeves of the blouse long, and absolutely no jewelry. She wore her hair short and natural, and this added to her effect of being totally clean and uncluttered. She needed no ornament, Mattingly thought. She was the most attractive woman he had seen in a long time.

"I'll record your comments if I may," he said.

"Fine," she said.

The other pilot, who had introduced himself as Leonard Burns, glared as Mattingly ran his power cord to the wall receptacle. "Is that really necessary?"

"Yes," Mattingly said. "We have to have a record."

"It looks like intimidation to me," Burns said.

Mattingly straightened up. "Look, friend. I have a job to do here."

Burn's eyes were hot with suppressed anger. "Coming in here the day after a woman's husband has been buried—what kind of a job is that?"

"Lenny," Nell Emerson said quietly. "He's doing his job. Now, you behave yourself."

Mattingly met her remarkable eyes and felt a kind of electric shock. She was incredible. "Thanks," he said. "I wouldn't be here if it weren't necessary."

"I know. Please sit down. I'd like to get this over."

Bronk, the quieter of the two pilots, leaned against the cabinets. "Do you have any objection if we stay, Mr. Mattingly?"

Mattingly saw that Bronk was trying to get along. "If Mrs. Emerson wants you to stay, then I think you should stay. The interview is with her, though, so I would appreciate it if you would keep out of it."

"We'll keep out of it," Burns said, "unless you start talking pilot error. We're not going to stand for that."

Mattingly ignored him. "May we begin, Mrs. Emerson?"

She nodded and he turned on the recorder.

"Now, will you please state your full name?"

"Nell Goodwin Emerson."

"Your husband was Jerry Emerson, the pilot of Transwestern Flight 161?"

"Yes." She studied her clasped hands.

"How long were you married to Captain Emerson?"

"Seven years."

"Children?"

"Yes. Two."

"Your husband was a senior pilot for Transwestern. Correct?"

"Yes."

"How long had he been flying the Excalibur?"

"Since it was introduced."

"Six or seven months, then?"

"Yes."

"Had he ever spoken of any difficulty with the airplane?"

Nell Emerson's expressive face showed surprise. "No. He always said it was the nicest airplane he had ever flown."

"The nicest? Could you explain that?"

"The most stable. The most forgiving."

"The most forgiving?"

Her eyes betrayed irritation. "You don't fly, Mr. Mattingly?"

"As a matter of fact, I have a private license," Mattingly said. "But I can't put my interpretation into this report. If you want to elaborate on your remarks, I will try to help you do so."

She nodded ever so slightly. "I'm sorry. I'm nervous."

"Take your time. Now. When your husband said the plane was forgiving—"

"He meant it was very easy to handle, with no hidden tricks. He said it approached so slowly to landing, with the dimple-wing design, that it reminded him of flying a Cherokee. He loved all the extra power, like the old Electra. A go-around was possible from practically any position, he said. He said he actually sometimes worried that some—" Nell Emerson looked stricken, and stopped.

"He said he worried what?" Mattingly asked quickly.

Nell Emerson showed that she thought she had made a mistake. "He said he worried that some pilots would practically go to sleep flying it."

"What do you suppose he meant by that?"

Burns leaned forward, face red. "He meant it was so easy to fly, a man might get lazy up there. But that doesn't mean—"

"Can I please interview the lady?" Mattingly cut in.

"We're here because we know how you guys always look for pilot error, and you're not getting by with it this time!"

Mattingly reached over and switched off the recorder. "Look, friend. We're not getting anywhere. I have a lot of questions to ask, and a lot of them touch on possible pilot error. A lot go to the airplane. I'm sorry, but that's the way it is. Now, are you going to keep quiet and let us do this, or must we ask Mrs. Emerson to drive all the way downtown to our office, where we can do this in peace?"

"He's right, Lenny," Nell said. "Please stay out of it."

"I'm trying to protect your interests, Nell!"

Bronk, the other pilot, slowly shook his head. "Come on, Lenny, shut up."

Fuming, Burns subsided.

Mattingly started the recorder again. "When your husband worried aloud about some pilot failing to remain alert enough on the flight deck, did he ever say that there was anything specific that worried him? Did he ever mention any anomaly about the aircraft that might make it bite if it were pushed too far?"

Nell shook her head. "No. He loved the plane. He thought it was perfect. It's the only plane he ever flew that he didn't find anything to criticize about."

Mattingly hesitated, reluctant to start moving toward more sensitive areas but compelled to do so. Nell Emerson had already touched some distantly responsive chord within him. At any time, he would have disliked probing into more personal areas; with her, he felt obscene.

He tried to begin gently. "Was your husband suffering from any minor illness prior to his last flight? A head cold? Upset stomach?"

"No. Nothing."

"His health was good?"

"He had just had his regular physical. He was fine."

"Had he been sleeping well?"

"Yes."

Burns was looking restive again but Mattingly went ahead. "Was he upset about anything?"

"No. My husband was fine. He had just gone back from his days off and we had had a lovely time. He was not upset or angry or anything else—not about *anything*. There was no reason why he should have been less than 100 per cent on that flight, and I'll fight anyone who tries to suggest otherwise."

For an instant, Jace Mattingly stared at her in mute admiration. She was more beautiful when aroused like this. *How lucky he was to have a woman like you, a woman willing to fight for him!*

Then he caught himself staring and spoke quickly: "I'm sure you understand we have to ask these questions."

Her eyes fired. "Yes, and I'm sure *you* understand that Jerry was a good pilot. He was the *best*. He did not make mistakes. This crash was not a mistake. If you or anyone else tries to blame it on pilot error, I'll fight you. . . . In court, if I have to."

Burns stuck his chin forward. "And the Pilots Association will be right there beside her."

"Could we get on with this?" Mattingly asked.

But he could never quite get the interview back on the tracks again.

After a little while, he switched the machine off again. "We may be back in touch. I want to thank you. You've been very helpful."

She watched him close the briefcase. "When will there be a decision?"

"Not for quite a while, I'm afraid."

"I want a cause found as soon as possible."

"We all do." Mattingly was fed up with the two pilots, watching every move as if waiting to pounce. He was fed up with questions that went nowhere. He was fed up, too, with feeling this intense attraction for a woman he hardly knew and with whom there obviously could never be a relationship. He was fed up with himself. "You can be sure we're working hard on it," he added, and picked up his gear.

"People call," Nell told him, also standing. "They say hateful things, like, 'Is this the wife of that man who killed all those people?' They say he was drunk, or drugged. Even the children have already heard things like that right here on the street, from other children." Her eyes began to brim. "I want the cause *found*."

"We're doing everything we can," Mattingly said. He was suddenly alarmed. "We want the public hearing as soon as possible—"

"He has to be cleared. I can't live with this over our heads!" And then her composure broke, and she began sobbing.

Mattingly stood there, stunned, as her shoulders quaked and the tears came. Leonard Burns moved to her side and put a protective arm around her. She shrugged him off, shaking her head violently. "I'm *all right!*" She wiped her eyes on her sleeve and angrily fought for renewed control.

There was nothing for Mattingly to do. He started backing for the door to the living room. "I'm sorry," he said. "Thank you again." He turned and fled.

As he drove away from the house, he spotted one of the pilots at the front windows, peering after him. It gave Mattingly a burst of hot resentment. It would have gone better, he thought, if he had been alone with Nell Emerson. For both of them. When he saw her the next time, he would make sure they were alone.

Then Mattingly took a quick breath, astonished at himself.

There was no need to see her again . . . was there? How could he have this certainty, then, that he would? And wasn't that crazy, on the basis of a single business call, to feel so strongly that he *had to* arrange it so they could meet again?

He was shaken. He had been dreading each day of this investigation, and remained convinced that it was going to be long . . . difficult. But suddenly his outlook, while more complicated, was less glum. There was a wild, totally irrational longing inside him now, and he knew: he *would* see her again.

Somehow.

12

Tuesday afternoon, promptly at four o'clock, Harold Zelmer walked into the office of Dr. Howard Lindsey. He had been in a coffee shop on the first floor of the thirty-story medical office building since before two, waiting.

"Gosh," he grinned at the receptionist. "I hope I'm not late. I almost forgot the appointment."

She was a brunette, and pretty. "The doctor will see you in a few minutes, Mr. Zelmer."

Harold waited and thumbed through a copy of *Time*. His hands shook, but he rested them on his thighs so the receptionist would not notice.

At five after four Dr. Lindsey opened the door to his inner office. A tall man with long dark hair and a full-fledged handlebar mustache, he was lean and young and Harold liked him most of the time. As usual, Lindsey had let his previous patient out through another door so there would be no meetings in the waiting room. As usual also, Lindsey looked fresh, rested, and unperturbed.

"Harold," he said soberly once they were inside and the door closed. "I heard the news about your mother and I want to say how sorry I am."

"I went to the airport," Harold burst out. "They brought her back. They made me wait until they had the box in the cargo area off to one side and then they let me in and I went over and the box was *small*. It was—only about four feet long and two feet wide, and I said, 'This can't be my mother, this can't be Mrs. Zelmer, she was a tall woman and she weighed almost as much as I do.' And they looked at the papers and said it was Mother, and they went away and then they came back with a man from the airline, and he was embarrassed and he said he should have met me, and when I asked him about it, he said it *was* my mother. But he said she was . . . she had been . . . he said, his words were, 'Sometimes in crashes, bodies are not recovered intact.' And what he meant was that she had been torn to pieces! I said, 'Is that what you mean, this box contains *pieces* of my mother?' And he got red in the face and said he was sorry. Then I said I wanted to see her, and they wouldn't open the box, so I went to the funeral home and talked to the director there, Mr. Jones, and *he* wouldn't open the box, either. I said, 'How can I know it's even my mother?' And he said, 'We've examined the contents, Harold, and we can vouch that this is your mother.' And I said I wanted to see for myself, and he wouldn't. They *wouldn't.* Today we had the service and everybody came, but I never saw her, she was in a regular, full-sized casket today, but the lid was closed. And it wasn't even her, Dr. Lindsey, it was just pieces of her, they tore her to bits and just put them in this little box like garbage and sent them back. She trusted them, she got on that airplane, and they tore her to bits!"

"And you're terribly upset, thinking of how she died," Dr. Lindsey said.

"Of course I'm upset! Jesus Christ yes, I'm upset! Do you think I'm crazy?"

Dr. Lindsey leaned back in his swivel chair and made a tent with his fingers. "Harold, the death of a parent is a terrible trauma under the best of circumstances. You've handled yourself like a mature person through this. I have some idea how difficult it is for you."

"She wasn't even a body any more," Harold said. "She wasn't even a person. They called her *contents.*"

"At least it was quick, Harold. At least she had that mercy. If you can try, as best you can, to look at it from that standpoint—"

"All I know is that she trusted them and they killed her and now I'm alone!"

The doctor studied Harold for a long minute, making Harold feel like he was being undressed. Then the doctor began to talk. It was unusual for him to say much; his usual role was of questioner, always asking those maddening questions, playing his Freud games, which Harold usually saw through as fast as they began but played with

97

him because maybe it would help even though he saw their transparency and stupidity.

But, this time, Dr. Lindsey talked for a considerable time, discussing grief. He reviewed Harold's years of visits to his office, and many of the things they had discussed. He pointed out all the progress Harold had made.

Listening, Harold knew this was all to bolster him. But he could also see that there was some truth to what the doctor was saying. It was true he seldom heard the voices any more. It had been years since they had frightened him even when they did occasionally try to come, whispering hotly, urgently, in his right ear. And it was true he had learned to control his tantrums. And it was true he had learned to get along in ordinary society. He had finished high school, and his job playing in the club paid a decent wage and gave him his days free to read or walk or watch daytime TV.

What Dr. Lindsey was suggesting, Harold saw, was that all his progress had prepared him for a tragedy such as this. Harold, the doctor was saying, was now capable of dealing with it emotionally. The very fact that he felt his sorrow so keenly, and recognized his rage for what it was, showed how far he had progressed.

"I know all that," Harold broke in finally in exasperation. "But what can I *do*?"

"Do?" Lindsey repeated.

"Do about Mother!"

"Harold, there's nothing anyone can do. Not now."

"I've done nothing but think about this," Harold said. "Even at the club, playing, what my mind has really been doing is thinking about this. I've gotten books from the library. There are always crashes. Sometimes the airlines are responsible. Sometimes the builders are responsible. All airplanes aren't safe, not at first. The Electra wasn't safe at first. The LC-1011 had a defect that killed people before they fixed it—"

"But your mother's death was sheer accident."

"But she was in one of those Excaliburs! That's a new airplane! I've read some things in back issues of *Time* and *Newsweek* about it. It has a new kind of wing! What if it wasn't safe? What if it was the airplane's fault? Isn't that just like murder? Didn't the company that built that airplane, and the airline that used it—and put people like Mother on board—just as much as *murder* them?"

The doctor's smile was more a grimace of reaction, the way it sometimes was when Harold had succeeded in shocking him and he wanted to hide it. "Let's have a reality check here, Harold. You're saying those companies are guilty of murder because a new-model plane happened to crash?"

"If they were negligent, yes! If they flew an unsafe airplane, yes! And they should be punished! But *will* they be punished? No! If *I* kill someone, they'll electrocute me, or shoot me, like Gary Gilmore. They liked that, shooting Gary. But if *business* commits a crime—if it pollutes a world or kills an ocean or directly *kills*, the way companies like Dow Chemical did in Vietnam, then it's all right; no one minds; big business can do no wrong in this country, because, who said it best? . . . The business of America is business!"

"Harold," Dr. Lindsey said, "I think we have to examine the string of logic here."

They did so, Lindsey carefully raveling out Harold's statements, Harold becoming more and more upset. Harold was furious and frustrated. He had come for *help*, not to play these Freud games. So he fought back.

Finally, however, he saw the doctor glancing at his watch on the desk, which always indicated time was almost up, and he was thinking how to wind up the session on a positive note, some bullshit to keep the patient going another day or week or month. And this reminded Harold that he had been dangerously frank during part of this hour. He had to mend his fences.

"Maybe you're right," Harold told him, holding up his hands in playful surrender. "I'll think about it. I don't *like* believing they killed innocent people!"

"They're just as upset as you are," Dr. Lindsey said. "I think I can assure you of that."

Harold stood. "Anyway, Mother is buried. I have to go to work soon, but first I'm going to clean the apartment."

"You plan to remain living there?"

"Oh, yes. If I moved, who would care for Mother's things?"

The doctor appeared about to say something, then thought better of it. He opened the private exit door and patted Harold on the back. "I want you to feel free to call me, Harold. I want to help you if I can."

"I feel better already," Harold said, and smiled as he walked out, confident that he had fooled him.

Once Harold was gone, however, a frowning Dr. Lindsey opened a desk drawer and took out a microphone to a Dictaphone machine. He pressed the button and dictated the file number, Harold's full name, and the date, and then details of the encounter in brief.

"Pursue the matter of caring for his mother's things," Lindsey concluded. "Further discussion of the alleged criminality of airlines and/or manufacturers should be avoided unless patient insists upon it. This area shows severe loss of realistic thinking and inability to cope. The patient has shown a marked deterioration as the result of this accident, and may be near a complete psychotic break."

13

The first week following the crash of Transwestern Flight 161 did not look well for Harvey Coughlin.

Boarding an airplane to return to California for the weekend, Harvey was filled with plans for telling Lydia Baines of all the progress he had made. In truth, his first days in Washington had been dismaying.

Among politicians, who often dealt in myths and patriotic symbols, Harvey's name was still magic, if by now a little faded by time. He had made his rounds of Senate and House offices and had managed to see a number of members of Congress. The greetings had been cordial and even warm, at least until he revealed that he was working to gain support for Eagle.

The Administration was maintaining a studiously neutral attitude on the matter. Having been drawn into a political blood bath over the new escort fighter a year before, the President and his aides would not get stung again. There was a very large figure in the budget for "new arms allocations," with no other specification for its use. The White House would let Congress decide which new weapons systems would get money from this general fund, and thus let the good senators and congressmen take whatever heat and controversy might be generated by their choices.

The trouble was that the congressmen were almost as leery of furor over new weapons as was the President. Eagle had been shelved once. There was general talk about reconsideration in committee, to be sure; but no one was eager to put himself in the cross fire between hawks and doves by openly supporting the missile's manufacture and procurement.

So Harvey had been welcomed in a friendly manner and then held at careful arm's length. He plodded his rounds, getting the same reception again and again. He had the feeling that he had accomplished absolutely nothing.

He was not a politician, and his days in Washington vividly reminded him of this. He still had clout, but it was potential, not focused on generating action. Washington was too complex; there were too many inside lines running in every direction, crossing one another. He was going to need more direct help from Matthew Johns, who had been able to give him very little this time due to problems at home, in Colorado. He had to let Lydia know this but in a way that would not betray any sense of his worry. It was going to be difficult.

The cabin attendant who brought him his drink once the plane was airborne leaned over with a bright smile. "Mr. Coughlin? Aren't you the Harvey Coughlin they made a movie about?"

Harvey grinned, jutting his chin at her. "I'm the one, but I think they miscast that old film." Then, as she appeared puzzled, he winked. "I'm a lot handsomer than James Garner, don't you agree?"

The girl laughed delightedly. Harvey leaned back, feeling marginally better. That line always worked. It was nice to have things you could count on.

In California, Friday evening signaled the end of the first phase of renewed Excalibur testing. The prototype had been stripped of seats, packed with instruments, and loaded to capacity with lead weights in the cargo compartments. Chief test pilot Hank Selvy and his crew then took the plane to twenty-six thousand feet and repeatedly flew the laden ship, gear down, to the brink of approach-to-landing stalls.

Nothing whatsoever happened. Excalibur dutifully sounded its warning, the stick-buffeting mechanisms worked, and the wing kept right on flying, providing total aileron control near the wing root while the tip was already stalled. Sensors recorded seventy-two different lines of data. Nothing appeared abnormal.

"Well, naturally nothing went wrong," Hank Selvy said in Ken Lis's office during the debriefing afterward. "We ran the same goddam test a hundred times before certification."

"We weren't loaded quite that heavily," Lis pointed out, "and we didn't push it quite that far. I thought once there you were going to get the full stall break."

"I did too."

"We'll get the full break next time."

The week had taken a toll on both men. After the meeting, Lis drove directly home. He found his wife waiting for him in the living room. She wore a dazzling new beige dress, and by the look in her eye, she was speeding. Lis tried to ignore it. He went to her and kissed her gently. As she raised her slightly puffy face to him, he smelled the whiskey heavy on her breath as well.

"We have to be at the country club in twenty minutes," she told him.

"What for?"

"The new officers are being initiated tonight. I'm the new secretary, remember?"

Lis took a deep breath. "I'll just change clothes."

"You don't have to act like a martyr about it," she called after him. "This is very important to me!"

Lis did not reply. His legs shot pains of fatigue into his torso as he climbed the stairs. The prospect of going to that club, smiling ritualistically, going through hours of meaningless conversation about nothing, filled him with despair. He needed quiet tonight . . . to relax, to try to rest and stop thinking for a blessed little while. He tried to hold the bitterness in check as he hurried through a change of clothes.

"Oh, Ken, you're not going to wear *that* suit!" Amy Lis groaned as he went back downstairs. "It makes you look like an old man!"

A hot reply leaped to Lis's lips, but he choked it back and gave her a slow smile. "Some days I feel sort of old, Amy. Do you?"

"I've never felt better," she said, her drugged eyes dancing. "Come on. Hurry. If we're late it will be just terrible!"

Across the city, at almost the same time, Hank Selvy had just arrived at Janis Malone's apartment. Wearing her floppy slippers and nylon robe, Janis opened the door to his crooked grin with a sense of dismay.

"Hi, chicken," Selvy said, coming in.

"Hank?" she faltered. "We didn't have a date!"

"I just got out of that hellhole they call Hempstead Aviation," he said, going to the couch and dropping onto it, "and I thought I couldn't stay away from you another minute. So what do you think of that?"

Janis smiled, torn between pleasure and irritation. "I'm holed up with my notes and portable typewriter. I've got a ton of work to do this weekend!"

Selvy put his feet on the coffee table and held his arms out. "C'mere."

Janis reluctantly sat beside him. "You goof. You have to get back out of here. If I don't work tonight, we can't go to the beach tomorrow afternoon!"

Selvy put an arm heavily around her while his other hand snaked inside her robe and lifted the weight of her breast. His fingers pinched her nipple too hard. "To hell with tomorrow. Work always did make me horny. How about a hamburger and a nice roll in the hay, dumpling?"

Janis pulled away, going cold. "Hank, you know I don't like it when you come on that way."

Selvy tried to pull her back, although his grin was fading. "C'mon back here."

"Hank—no!"

He let his hands drop. "I was thinking about all our little spats lately, you know? I was thinking we could put all that behind us— really have a night tonight. What do you say?"

"Hank, it sounds lovely, but I have to get this work out. You know that. I told you about it this morning!"

"Screw the work. Get dressed. We'll go eat and then come back here and get it on. How's that sound?"

"It sounds like what you want to do. But it isn't what I want to do."

"Why not?"

"Hank, because it just isn't, that's all! How can I explain it to you? I have to . . . sort of plan things ahead. And tonight I've planned to work until about ten, then shampoo my hair and watch the late show on TV, and then get up again at six to finish before we go to the beach. Now, you just be a nice boy and do it like we said we'd do it."

Her attempt at humor was feeble, and fell flat. Selvy's eyes were showing signs of the old anger now, and she quailed within. She patted his knee, trying to make it better. "All right?" she asked.

"You know," Selvy said, "I've had a hell of a hard day. Did it ever occur to you that I might need you tonight?"

"I know you might, Hank," Janis said regretfully, "But I've got this work—"

"Damn the work! It's not that important!"

"But it is, Hank."

"More important than us?"

"Oh, Hank, do we have to have this same argument every time we see each other? For God's sake, can't we just have a little *fun*?"

Hank Selvy's expression changed . . . became suddenly dead and calm. He pushed himself up from the couch and got to his feet. "I shouldn't have come. I'm bothering you—keeping you from your work."

"Oh, hell," Janis said. "Stay awhile, Hank. Sit down. Stop standing there like a big goof. We'll talk." She tried to make a joke of it. "All we have to do is not talk about my job, and we'll get along perfectly, right?"

"No," Selvy said, and his eyes suddenly were bright, as if he might be ready to burst into angry tears. "I know this is my problem, honey. I know I'm immature and all that shit. I'm sorry to give you such a bad time. I'm just going to have to try to figure myself out, right?"

"Sit down," Janis said, faking a big grin, "and we'll start right now."

"No," Selvy repeated like a man in a dream. He shook his head and started for the door. "I'll get out. I'll see you later."

"Noon tomorrow?" Janis said following him.

He opened the door and stared at her. "No. Not tomorrow. I'm going to cancel that, Janis."

"Oh, Hank. Don't do that."

A smile twitched at his lips, then vanished. "Sorry. I'm kind of tired. And I'm sick of being the heavy . . . you know?"

"Hank, you're not the heavy. Come back in here!"

"I just can't hack it this way, babe. I'm sorry."

"Hank—?"

He grinned crookedly although his eyes were devastated. "See ya."

"When?"

He had already turned to walk away.

Janis closed the door softly. She stood very still and listened, and heard his car start and drive away.

An outsider, she thought, would not have understood what had just happened. It was only as the culmination of their tensions that it made sense even to her. A relationship did not stand still. It became better or it became worse. Hers with Hank Selvy had been deteriorating for months, but she had refused to face it, because she could not bear to look at the consequences.

A broken date, a series of arguments, a real fight, a weekend of silence, renewed tension for a little while, and now this. It was not a little thing. In context, it was possibly the end for them.

Numbed, Janis went back to the dinette table and sat down again at her typewriter. She could not concentrate. She got up again and went to the bathroom for a glass of water. As she sipped it, she looked at herself in the brilliance of the full-length mirror.

On impulse, she opened the front of her robe and looked at her body. She examined the swell of her breasts, the flare of hip, the lines of her legs. She had learned to be proud of this body through Hank. She had learned to love it through him. She remembered a night not so long before when he had come up to her in the bathroom here, had slipped his hands under her arms, stroked her. . . .

And now was that all over? For nothing—because of so little? It was unbelievable and absurd.

She would not, she decided, let it bother her. Tying her robe firmly around her waist, she padded back to the typewriter, sat down, typed two lines.

Then she stared at the copy awhile, emotion flooding through her. It couldn't be over—not really. Affairs did not end so casually or quietly. Something big and dramatic had to happen.

With a renewal of concentration, she managed to type another sentence. Then she stopped and thought about it again, and her self-control began slipping fast. She left the typewriter. Work was impossible. Only a stubborn pride held the tears back.

14

During the second week of June—the second week after the Excalibur crash—a lull befell testing at the Hempstead plant as the first round of renewed flights exhausted obvious possibilities. Monravian representatives made definite plans for a two-day visit to San Jose during the third week. And at Ken Lis's request, NTSB trouble shooter Jace Mattingly agreed to bring audio tapes from the crash to the Hempstead offices for playback.

The meeting to play the tapes began promptly at 10 A.M. in Lis's office. There besides Lis were Barton MacIvor, a young engineer named Majors, and Kelley Hemingway.

Seated behind his desk, Lis appeared slightly more rested than he had on several previous days. Wearing blue coveralls, he had spent two hours earlier with mechanics tearing up the floor of the prototype Excalibur, looking for cable wear. But Kelley was encouraged by his appearance; some of the deeper lines were slipping from his face. She thought perhaps the worst of his grief over the death of Jason Baines had begun to pass.

Barton MacIvor, seated in front of the desk beside his young engineer, looked as sloppy and eccentric as the younger man looked efficient and neat. While Majors wore a pin-neat dark suit and striped tie, with black loafers, MacIvor's corduroy jumpsuit looked slept in, which it might well have been. One foot, hiked to the edge of Lis's desk, was encased in a garish yellow cowboy boot. Smoke from his big, curved-stem pipe already wafted like gray curtains through the still air of the office.

Jace Mattingly, Kelley thought, looked by far the most nervous of the group. He also looked tired. His suit was baggy, with lapels too narrow for the current style. His narrow tie was out of the fifties, and his tan brogans were down at the heels. The flesh drooped under his eyes. He was, Kelley realized, a comparatively young man. But his fingers were in constant motion as he lit one cigarette from the other, and he would not live to be old, Kelley thought.

"I have a tape for you to hear," he said placing a small Sony on the desk. "Maybe one of you can come up with an interpretation we missed."

"Exactly what's on this tape?" Lis asked.

"Crew voices just before the crash. Most of it came from the tower tapes, but a little comes from the Cockpit Voice Recorder."

"As long as we have a mystery on our hands," Lis said, "I'm willing to try anything."

Mattingly scowled. "I'm not sure it's a genuine mystery. It's more a complex technical problem that we haven't ironed out yet."

"Meanin'," Barton MacIvor interpreted, "ye haven't figgered oot what caused the wreck, but yer workin' on it."

"That's about the size of it," Mattingly admitted.

MacIvor puffed prodigiously on his pipe. "I'd be callin' that more'n a technical problem."

Mattingly took a notebook from his briefcase and flipped pages. "Let me briefly fill you in on where we stand. First, there's nothing to support a theory of sabotage. The FBI will continue checking the backgrounds of all passengers and crew, but neither their lab boys nor ours have found any hint whatsoever of explosive materials or any other known method of wrecking an airplane."

"I don't think any of us ever gave sabotage much serious thought," Lis said.

"Neither did we, frankly, but it's the kind of thing the FBI has to check out most carefully."

"You've had no more luck with the flight recorders?"

"We're still trying to reconstruct some of the digital data with computer massaging techniques. Maybe we'll come up with something, maybe we won't."

MacIvor stirred. "Are there any possibilities you can rule out?"

"We know there was no explosion, no decompression, and no fire prior to impact."

"How aboot engine or control failure?"

"Portions of the flight engineer's console were found virtually intact in the wreckage. Several gauges were frozen. The engines were at max climb. Normal primary-mode electrical systems were on and functioning. Gear were down and locked, all control surfaces, including the dimple-wing slats, were in normal position, and the airspeed —we have managed to massage that out of the recorder—right on the book figure. We have no indication that the airplane was off its glide path or course. Wind shear or other external factors have been ruled out."

Kelley Hemingway felt uneasy. "In other words," she said, "there was no weather problem of significance, no power failure, no control-system failure, no electrical problem, and no gross structural breakup."

"We have no evidence of any of those."

"And yet," Majors said, "the damned plane went in."

Mattingly looked at him for a moment. "Obviously."

"Maybe," Lis said, "we'd better listen to the voice tapes."

"It's confidential," Mattingly said, standing to operate the machine controls. "We have tower talk spliced in for time and space references." He pushed a button and the tiny reels began to turn. A hiss came from the loudspeaker. Then a deep voice, somewhat muffled, came through the bubbly sound of some kind of audio distortion:

"Well, he was a little long, wasn't he?"

Another voice, slightly higher-pitched: *"Yep."*

Mattingly raised his voice. "First was Jerry Emerson, the captain. "Second was Terwiliger, the copilot. They're on final, seventy seconds from touchdown, talking about Eastern Flight 41, that just landed ahead of them."

Kelley's arms chilled. They were hearing the voices of the men on the doomed Excalibur flight, the private conversation of men who could not know they were about to die. The expressions of Ken Lis and Barton MacIvor showed that they, too, were feeling a similar chill.

The tape hissed, silent. Then a new voice boomed through, much clearer and louder:

"Eastern 41, turn left next intersection, contact ground."

"The tower, of course," Mattingly said.

No one else spoke. Kelley understood: The Eastern flight, completing its roll, had been ordered to turn off the active runway to make way for Transwestern 161, one minute behind.

As if to verify this interpretation, the tape spoke again:

"Transwestern one-six-one, cleared to land, sky obscured, visibility one, fog and smoke, wind northeast at five."

The voice of Terwiliger replied scratchily, *"Roger."*

"Fifty seconds," Mattingly said, his jaw set with tension as he stared at the machine.

Kelley listened to the hiss of the tape, unwilling now to look at anyone else. She felt transported out of this comfortable office and onto the dark flight deck over New York that night: surrounded by the glow of red, yellow, and green lights, the whisper of engines far to the rear, the glide of steel through cloud. Had they had any sense of foreboding? Of course not. If they had, they would have acted—would not now be dead.

The recorder stirred, making a series of noises that were recognizable as voices only by stretch of the imagination:

"Jujubunchee."

"Nawbathow."

"We think," Mattingly said, "that Emerson said there, 'Just a little bumpy,' and Terwiliger said, 'Not bad, though.'"

"I don't know how you figured that out," Kelley said.

No one else commented. The recorder hissed, then went through a series of noises that might vaguely resemble humanoid mutterings. Then it was quiet again.

"We don't have any idea what they said there," Mattingly commented.

The tape spoke again, Terwiliger's voice: *"Ten feet low."*

"Right. Coming up, though. Plenty of power. Plenty of power. Just a little elevator climb, see? What a nice airplane!"

The tape hissed in silence again.

Terwiliger's voice: *"Kind of pretty, coming in this way. Too bad we can't see it. We're high now."*

Emerson: *"We're coming out in a second."*

A third voice: *"That's the view I always get. Like the inside of a hat."*

An appreciative chuckle came through clearly.

Mattingly said, "That was the flight engineer last."

"*American Flight four-eight, continue, contact departure control, one-twenty point four.*"

"The tower, talking to a parallel-runway takeoff," Mattingly explained. He glanced at his notes. "Twenty seconds."

Kelley closed her eyes. She imagined the rain-gleaming Excalibur, strobe lights flashing, its powerful landing lights reaching out into the cotton interior of the cloud, gliding in ever lower, gear and flaps down, feeling for the welcoming earth so close below.

"*Well, here we go now. We ought to be—*"

The voice was interrupted by a hoarse shout, so loud that Kelley jumped.

The voice screamed something wholly unintelligible. Then, "*How about it! How about—*"

"*Power!*"

"*Christ, look!*"

There was a shout: "*ANTELCOUGH!*"

Another shout answered, and there was a burst of garbled sound. Then: "*Can't get—Christ!*"

"*More!*" The sound broke, came back: "*—on that side!*"

The loud noise vanished magically from the tape. Kelley stared at the machine, her pulse thumping sickly in her ears.

"Impact," Mattingly said.

The tape spoke again, carrying the voice of a man whose tone shook under tremendous effort at control: "*TWA Flight four-zero-one, execute a three-sixty-degree turn now. Eastern Flight seven-eight, discontinue approach, execute missed approach, contact approach control now. Delta eight-one, hold. All aircraft in the Kennedy area, attention. Hold your present position. Emergency in progress. Emergency in progress.*"

The tape fell silent once more. Mattingly reached forward and punched a stud. The reels stopped turning. No one spoke or moved. Mattingly flicked his cigarette lighter. The sound was loud in the room.

Exhaling smoke, he coughed and cleared his throat. "That's it. The unintelligible shouting could be tremendously significant, but we simply don't have enough tape left to rebuild it. Could any of you make anything of it?"

"It happened very fast," Lis said.

Mattingly nodded. "At one point, someone yells, 'Look there!' or something like that, indicating they saw a malfunction light or *something* that told them what was happening."

"They could have been dropping out of the cloud and seeing the ground," Majors suggested.

"It's possible," Mattingly conceded in a tone that hinted he did not believe that interpretation. "If we could just unscramble the rest of it right along there, maybe we would know what went wrong."

"Play it again," Lis suggested.

Mattingly stood and rewound the cassette. He punched the forward button and again the sounds and voices boomed from the small speaker:

"*Power!*"

"*Christ, look!*"

Kelley strained, awaiting the unintelligible shouts.

They came:

"*Theantelcough—*"

"*Shovelack!*"

"*Itrialastalt—*"

"*Can't get—Christ!*"

Mattingly stilled the machine once more. "It's obviously an exchange. Voice-pattern analysis indicates Terwiliger yelled first, then Emerson replied, then Terwiliger again, and it's Emerson's voice we hear saying, 'Can't get,' there at the end."

Ken Lis shook his head. "I can't make anything of it. How about you, Pappy?"

"It's a mishmash, shooer."

"Kelley?"

"No."

"Don?"

"I don't have the first idea," Majors admitted. He appeared shaken.

Mattingly bit his lip. "I was afraid of that, but it was worth a shot. If you think of anything—"

"Could we get a copy of that tape?" Lis asked.

"It's confidential. You'll keep it that way?"

"Of course." Lis stared at the machine. "I was thinking, if I played it over and over—"

"I'll get you a copy. But I won't have a lot of hope, Mr. Lis. I've played the thing a hundred times, and it just gets worse."

"It might contain exactly the information we need to understand what happens," Lis said. "That puts us so close to a solution to this mess—and yet so far."

"We're going to find what happened," Mattingly said setting his jaw.

"If this is a copy of the original tape," Lis said, "maybe you could leave it with us, rather than mailing a duplicate."

"That's all right. I'll do that."

The conversation went on, ranging over a variety of topics relating to the crash, but it was anticlimactic after the tape. When the meeting broke up, at lunchtime, it was with mutual assurances that any new evidence found on either side would be made available immediately. But Kelley could read expressions, and she knew the facts. They were no nearer a solution than they had been two weeks earlier —were actually in worse condition, because so many theories had already been tried and found unhelpful.

She went to lunch alone in the company cafeteria. When she returned to the office, trying to turn her mind to plans for the Monravian visit next week, she heard faint sounds issuing from behind Ken Lis's closed office door. They sounded strange, and then she recognized them. She stood listening.

It was the tape. He was playing it over and over.

15

Unable to make anything out of the garbled portions of the crash tape, Ken Lis was forced to turn to other pressing matters during the remainder of the day. There were civic arrangements to make for the Monravian visit, and many internal decisions to make concerning it. In addition, there was a particularly harassing problem with a parts supplier that was having a lengthy strike, and a conference with key members of the Administrative Division about a broader employee insurance program he wished to begin before the summer was out. As a result, it was past five o'clock when he checked incoming telephone memos and found that Lydia Baines had called earlier, requesting only that he return the call before leaving that evening.

It was past five-thirty when Lis dialed the familiar number of the hillside estate. An unknown voice answered and had him hold for about two minutes before Lydia Baines's voice came on the line.

"Ken," she said in the cool, cultured tone he knew well. "Thank you for returning my call at last. I have a matter to discuss with you. Would it be possible for you to stop by the house here on your way home?"

Lis almost smiled. "On the way home" took him nowhere near the Baines estate, and she knew that. But he said, "I'd be glad to stop, Lydia. I'm about to leave now. Say in twenty minutes?"

"That would be grand. I promise not to keep you long, but it is something I believe we should discuss in person."

"I'll see you then."

Leaving his office after a brief colloquy with Kelley Hemingway,

Lis went to his car, in the executive lot, and pulled away. The drive across the corner of the parking apron beside the MA Building took him within the shadow of the prototype Excalibur, deserted for the moment and silent.

Lis felt a stab of actual resentment as he drove past the plane, and although he knew how irrational the feeling was, he recognized its basis. Earlier tests of Excalibur, during the development phase, had been a source of elation when it performed flawlessly. Now, with a shadow of doubt about some hidden flaw within it, every smooth flight was only a source of new frustration. At the same time, he could not yet quite believe that the aircraft was at fault; he found himself almost *wanting* it to show some anomaly so that the crash cause might be known . . . modifications might be studied.

There had been a few cases in aviation history when an airplane entered service with a fault that better testing or more careful examination of data by a greedy management might have corrected, and thus prevented tragedy later. But in most instances the flaws had been found only as a result of prolonged wear. However they were found, they were often very costly.

In 1960, when Lockheed had found the cause of some Electra crashes to be unstable whirl mode, the firm had been forced to spend more than $25 million in a massive structural modification program. Then more than three thousand violent turn-and-takeoff procedures had been tried before engineers were fully satisfied that the "fix" was permanent, that the engine pods would no longer tear loose from the wing because of certrifugal force.

If Excalibur held such a flaw, and the cost to repair it was comparable, the repair itself could plunge the company into deepening fiscal crisis. But the repairs would have to be made if necessary; the alternative was an unsafe aircraft that no one would buy, and obvious financial ruin.

Driving toward the hills and the Baines mansion, Lis mentally reviewed some of the testing that the Excalibur had gone through before ever being offered to the government for certification. The memories were disconcerting, because it was hard to imagine that a fault could have gone undetected. The fuselage and wings had been submerged in giant water tanks and subjected to pressures fifty times any that might be encountered in flight. Surfaces had been bombarded with three-inch artificial hailstones, the engines flooded with tens of thousands of gallons of water and sludge ice under extreme pressure. Critical wing and engine mountings had been cut halfway through and then subjected to drop and twist forces four times those likely to be found in flight. The landing gear had been forced to bear impacts seven times greater than the weight the airplane could get off the ground. In the wind tunnel, models had withstood violent maneuvers subjecting the frame to five times the force that might be met even in a flight emergency. A special "destruction machine"—an old commercial crane—had repeatedly picked up a finished Excalibur and dropped it from a height of ten feet, and then a wrecking ball had been attached and the crane began systematically beating the airplane to pieces to see what parts would give first. It took five hours to make the right wing come off, and by that time little about the airplane was recognizable even though basic structural integrity had been maintained.

For all these reasons, Lis's gut feeling was that the plane had nothing wrong with it. But the fact was that more than one hundred persons were dead. An Excalibur *had* crashed. Now, if the shadow was to be removed soon, he had to hope paradoxically to find evidence of a flaw he could not really believe in.

The great old Baines house was on a hillside, nestled among trees. As Lis neared it, he first noticed a number of cars and panel trucks parked in front. By the time he reached the parking area and stopped his own vehicle, he was alarmed to see that something definitely was going on.

The front doors of the house had been thrown open. Across the front porch were arranged many chairs, sofas, tables, and other items of inside furniture. Other items stood around on the sloping lawn: more furniture, cardboard boxes, rolled rugs, table and floor lamps. It looked as though the inside of the house was being cleaned out.

As Lis got from the car, he saw two college-age men come out of the house, struggling together under the weight of an old china cabinet. He hurried to intercept them at the foot of the steps.

"What's going on?" he asked.

The boy on the front end of the cabinet grinned under his load. "You're a day early, friend."

"A day early for what?"

"The auction. It starts tomorrow."

"What auction? This is Jason Baines's house!"

"You better talk to the lady inside, friend. I just do what I'm told."

Lis hurried into the house. The central hallway had been stripped, the floor covering gone, the gilt mirror vanished from the wall, the chairs taken away. His footsteps echoed, as did the voices of other movers, upstairs somewhere. He saw another youth, coming down with a chair in his arms.

"You looking for Mrs. Baines?" the youth asked.

"Yes," Lis said. "Where is she? Do you know?"

"I think she's back in the kitchen."

Lis went back past the empty living room, down a corridor past the game room, where the billiard table stood like a lean-to against a wall, its legs already removed. He found Lydia Baines in the huge kitchen, watching two black women wrap dishes and pack them in large cardboard barrels.

"Ken," Lydia said, turning to greet him. "You've found us in something of a mess." She wore hip-hugger slacks of pale ivory, which accentuated the golden tan of her bare belly. Her blouse, semitransparent, revealed the outlines of dark, hard nipples freed of the restrictions of a bra. She looked very beautiful, and about twenty-five.

"Lydia," Lis said, "what the hell *is* this?"

"Well," she said, glancing at the dish packers, "there's no sense getting rid of everything. I always rather liked some of the things in the kitchen."

"Where's everything going? What are you doing?"

"Oh. I didn't tell you, I see. I'm selling the house. It will be easier to sell without the furnishings, since Jason's tastes were so baroque. So the public auction is tomorrow, and then we put the house on the market this weekend."

"You're selling Jason's house?"

"Possibly I should be more sentimental, but let's face it. I always detested the place. I'll never use it. So I'm converting the white elephant to cash, which I *can* use."

"You're selling it *all?*—all Jason's things?"

"Yes. But if there was some item you had a particular sentimental attachment to, Ken, just say so. I'm sure we can work something out." She put her index finger to her lips as she pondered it. "Let's see. The billard table? You and Jason used to play billiards, I recall.

That will be hard to sell anyway, since it can't be taken down to small parts."

"No," Lis said huskily. "I don't want it. It's like—"

"One of his shotguns? You used to shoot, I remember. I have a collector coming for those early tomorrow, but you can have your choice."

"Lydia, Jason loved this place. Everything in it—he collected everything in it, and put it there."

"Ken, you always were the great sentimentalist."

Lis avoided her gaze. He was having difficulty maintaining a semblance of calm. Shock mixed with a consuming rage. He patted his pockets for cigarettes, which he never allowed himself to carry any more.

"Here," Lydia said, extending a pack of Kents.

Lis took a cigarette and lighted it with her small gold Zippo. He inhaled raggedly, deep.

"I asked you to come by," Lydia told him, "because that snag in Washington is about to be worked out and it looks like Harvey Coughlin will be going back East within a week at the outside. In the meantime, he's very busy preparing. I have a related project that I want to assign to you, because you're always so good at expediting matters."

Still dazed by the surprise of the stripping of the house, Lis braced for this new angle of attack. "You mean something to do with Eagle?"

"Yes. It's not in your division, but it's an area you're expert in: manpower management."

Lis waited, inhaling again.

"I want a study made on full production capability for the Eagle," Lydia Baines told him. "You know we originally spoke of using the old maintenance building, and we still have the plans for modification of the structure. I'd like those plans updated and new cost estimates made. I also want figures on manpower availability, likely wage scales, how many skilled personnel could be diverted from the Excalibur line to help with on-line training for Eagle, and so forth. I know it's a tall order, but I'm sure you have the people to get it done for me."

"You're definitely going ahead, then, if possible?"

"Of course. I thought that was understood."

"Any new production line is going to strain our budget severely."

"The risk is worth it."

"Finding skilled people will be virtually impossible. The on-line training will be tremendously costly."

"I just told you that we'll divert a certain number of skilled people from Excalibur. The people on the Excalibur line know what they're doing. We can divert a few dozen without hurting quality, and they can be the nucleus for the Eagle team."

"Lydia, you know how opposed I am to this."

"May I have a progress report in ten days?" Lydia asked.

"Yes," Lis said, accepting it with great difficulty.

"Good."

"Was there anything else?"

"No, that will be all, Ken; thank you."

Lis looked around the kitchen, overcome by a sense of loss.

"This really does upset you, doesn't it?" Lydia said.

"I just hate to see it go."

"You could always buy the place, you know," she told him.

"Could I?" he asked, turning to face her again.

"You're not serious."

"How much are you asking?"

Her eyes sparked as she met him directly, relishing her words and showing it. "Two hundred and fifty thousand dollars."

He tried not to flinch. "I see."

"Good heavens, Ken. Take a gun, or the billiard table or something. Don't be a fool."

"I'm not a poor man. I could probably swing it."

"I'm very well aware of what you make. Jason was very generous with you."

"I earned my money."

"I didn't mean to imply that you hadn't, Ken," she said in an insulting tone that treated him as a child to be humored.

He took a deep breath and ground the Kent out under his heel. The irrational thought came that if it was going to be his house, he could do anything he wished to the floor. "I'll be in touch, Lydia."

"Of course. Thank you for coming."

He hurried out, hating to see more bare walls, more furniture being carried out. Once in his car, he started the engine quickly and backed around to depart.

As he did so, he looked up briefly at the great, shambling structure, seeing it in a way he had never done before. It was not in good repair. Certain basic maintenance jobs—painting, guttering—had been neglected, as Jason Baines had been preoccupied with other matters. It would take work to make it livable in Amy's terms.

He wondered if he was really going to do it. If Amy wanted it, he thought, he would do it. The purchase would be more than a wildly sentimental gesture. It could become the kind of showplace home Amy had always wanted—even needed, for her sense of prestige. It could become the first step in mending their marriage.

With that thought, he pressed hard on the accelerator, eager now to get home.

16

K en Lis found an empty house when he reached home, and
   Amy's car was not in the garage. Dishes in the kitchen sink
and untouched mail showed that she had not been there since morning. There was no note.

It was an irritation, but not unusual. Lis paced the living room,
thinking of arguments in favor of buying the Baines mansion. He
imagined a scene with Amy in which she would be enthusiastic,
touched, happy. He ranged over financial arrangements that would
have to be made, and then just as quickly found himself thinking
how silly the idea was, how he should drop it immediately.

Walking to the kitchen patio doors, he peered into the fenced
backyard. It had been badly neglected, none of the spring work
done. Last fall's leaves still filled the small goldfish pond and choked
the flower beds. The roses had never been pruned and were vining
on the ground. The grass was long and shaggy, already browning
here and there because he had done nothing toward fertilization or
early watering.

Stepping out onto the patio, Lis was struck by a sense of regret
that they might leave this place where once they had known considerable happiness. All the times had not been bad here. He could
remember the high excitement of the early Excalibur planning, the
fine days he and his wife had had planning and planting most of this
yard. They had been trying very hard then. It had been in the days
before she went to the first diet doctor, and started on the pills, and
the drinking worsened.

But if the house had seen them happy, Lis told himself, it had also seen their marriage become the mockery it was today. A new start might be what they needed. He had read that everyone's life went through roughly five-year cycles of renewal, willed or not. Moving to the Baines mansion, seen in that light, was not merely a sentimental gesture. It was a genuine attempt to begin again.

The idea of buying the Baines mansion would also be a commitment, Lis saw, to remaining. His roots here were deeper than any other he had ever known, and he yearned to drive them deeper, more permanently, into the California soil. Buying the house would tell Lydia Baines—and anyone else who noticed—that he intended to endure.

He heard a car in the driveway, and then Amy came into the kitchen, carrying two thick sheafs of correspondence of some kind, which she placed carelessly on the countertop. She wore a white summer dress with a scooped neckline trimmed in tan, and it emphasized her full breasts. She did not look so overweight in the outfit, which was new, and large, dark sunglasses hid her eyes.

"Hello!" Lis called to her through the open patio door.

She smiled and came over, swinging her small white purse. It was his first hint that she had been drinking again.

"Planning some work out here?" she asked, smiling behind the glasses.

Lis's pulse thumped. "Amy, I have some big news, I think."

She seemed not to hear. "What we need is a part-time gardener. You never have time any more, and I'm much too busy. With all my new duties, I'll simply never have time again to get out here and clean it up and stay after everything. It depresses me. Why haven't you looked for someone part-time to work out here?"

"I might consider that, Amy. But listen to what I want to tell you."

She removed her sunglasses, revealing sun-dazed, tipsy eyes that did not focus on anything specific as she looked around the messy yard. "Gwen and Carole and I went to the hospital auxiliary meeting. Do you want to hear about the election? I was elected secretary."

"That's great," Lis said, feigning enthusiasm.

"Heavens knows it will be extra work, but that means I'll be president in two years. That's a feather in my cap!"

"That's wonderful, Amy. Congratulations."

"After the meeting we had to go by the Republican Women's Club a while, and we've decided to have a fund raiser toward the end of August. Jill Jimmerson and I are in charge of arrangements. The paper came and took a picture."

"Amy, there's something I'd like to discuss with you."

"After that we went to the club and had a few drinkies, and Gwen and I beat Carole and Pauline Clemons something like seven thousand points." She shook her head and made a face. "I'm thirsty. Fix me a nice martini on the rocks, darling."

"I think you've had enough for right now."

Her puffy face stiffened. "Then, I'll fix it myself."

He followed her into the house and watched her put ice cubes into a water tumbler. She poured perhaps four ounces of Tanqueray in on the cubes and expertly added a few drops of vermouth before dropping in a twist. He saw the film of sweat on her forehead and knew he was going to say something about the drinking even though it was not tactically wise; he felt driven.

"That's a stiff one, isn't it?" he asked.

"Yes," she said with relish, going to the couch and dropping down.

He followed her again and sat opposite her. He was aware that her legs were carelessly revealed and that she still had sexy legs.

"I think I'll just skip supper, darling," she told him, sipping. "You wouldn't mind a TV dinner, would you? I have that fund raiser at eight o'clock and they'll probably have some snacks, and I'm really trying again on getting my weight down a little. I haven't had anything at all today except some crackers and a few drinks to help keep me going."

"Amy, are you sure you're not drinking a little heavily?"

Her eyes warned him he was on dangerous ground. "If I am, it's my business. I can control myself."

"You're drinking," he told her, goaded, "and taking that speed you get from that diet doctor. That could be a lethal combination. It's *damned* dangerous."

"I never take any of the pills with a drink. I keep them separate. I know what I'm doing and I don't need any lectures from you. Besides, the pills seem to have very little effect on me any more. The body gets used to them, you know."

"I know," he said. "And you take more and more of them."

"I'm not a fool, Ken. I don't know why you try to treat me like one. Other people respect me. They see my good qualities. Then I come home and get lectures."

"Amy, I see your good qualities. I just don't want you to hurt yourself. I keep thinking about that other time when you kept going faster and faster, and drinking more and more to knock yourself out at the end of the day—"

"That was the flu," she snapped. "I came right back from it."

He wanted to shake her until her teeth rattled. "Just take it easy," he said. "All right?"

"I never felt better, Ken. I don't know what you're talking about. I only take a few little things now and then to keep me going. I'm so busy these days!"

"I just don't want you to overdo it."

Amy put down her half-empty glass with a clatter. "And I just don't want to hear any God-damned more about it, Ken!"

"All right," he said, throwing up his hands.

"Since when did *you* care, anyway? You don't give a damn. How long has it been since you've touched me? I run my own life, and that's the way you want it, anyway."

"All *right*, Amy! Let's just forget it, okay? There's something else I wanted to talk with you about anyway—"

"You haven't cared for me," she shot at him, "since you had your obscene little affair with that girl."

It was a body blow. Lis inhaled slowly, watching her. "We agreed that that was past."

"But you've never stopped thinking about her—wanting her."

"It was ten years ago. Aren't you *ever* going to let me live it down?"

"Do you still fantasize fucking her when you occasionally conde-scend to make love to me?" she asked with fierce rage. "Is that why you say I look bad, because you're comparing me with her?"

"Amy, it was *ten years ago!*"

"I know when it was. I know how long it went on while you were fooling me, laughing at me behind my back. I know you still think about her."

"It happened," Lis said. "I wish it hadn't. I ended it. I'll carry my regret to the grave. I was an idiot. But she lives at the other end of the country. I haven't seen her again, and I never will. I've been faithful ever since. I will be faithful. I've tried everything I know. I know my job keeps me away from you too much. I know your problems. But we have to try. We have to get ourselves straightened out, Amy! This evening—today—I came home with tremendous news to talk over with you. I was hoping it would make you happy, and we could look back on today sometime in the future as our new start."

He had finally gotten through to her. She narrowed her eyes. "What news?"

"Lydia Baines is selling the mansion. I know you've always wanted a bigger house. We could buy it, Amy—redecorate it. Would that please you?"

Her face twisted in disbelief. "Jason Baines's house?"

"Yes. When you had your parties and meetings, can't you imagine using that big front living room? We would have to have some domestic help, of course, but we could swing that—"

"You actually think," she asked, "that I would live in Jason Baines's house?"

Lis stared at her, the last vestiges of his hope beginning to drain.

She told him, "I'm too busy for a house like that. And I would never live in Jason Baines's house. *God*, Ken! Won't you even let him go when he's *dead*?"

"You always said you loved that house."

"That house stands for everything that's made our lives miserable: your lap-dog dedication to Jason Baines, the endless nights you spent there or somewhere else with him, working on plans, rather than with me—"

"All right, forget it. Just forget it! I thought I was doing something for you—"

"You haven't done anything for me in years! Face yourself just a little, will you? If you want Jason's house, it's because owning it would be a big ego trip for you. —For *you*, not me!"

"You're wrong. You're crazy!"

"Am I?" She walked out.

17

F or Harold Zelmer, the weeks following his mother's death had become an increasingly confused shuttle between mindless elation and frenzied outrage. He had made no essential changes in the apartment, although it was quite filthy by now. He thought about hiring someone to clean it up but knew he could not let anyone in among his valuable mementos. He went to church every day and prayed very, very hard for his mother's soul, and for guidance. He had an increasing feeling that there was something that had to be done to set things right . . . something *he* was destined to do. But he did not know what it was.

On many afternoons, he went to the large public library and pored over old magazines and technical journals. He became obsessed with Excalibur, and with the workings of Transwestern Airlines. He began filling notebooks with names and data—company officers, technical information on the airplane, its cost, deliveries, testing, everything he could get his hands on. He did not know why this was important, but he knew it was.

He went to the club each night like a sleepwalker, and really had little awareness of his surroundings. Thus it came as a considerable new shock when the manager called him into his office that Friday night.

The manager was an enormously fat man named Gilbert. Harold did not know if that was his first name or last. It was all anyone had ever called him. Gilbert sweated heavily, and always. His cubicle office stank of his sweat and his cigars.

"Harold," Gilbert said, scowling over piled magazines and newspapers on his old wooden desk, "I guess you've noticed how our crowds have been falling off lately."

Harold had not. Now, thinking about it, he realized that there had been many vacant tables during what should be the busiest part of the evening. "I guess it's the season, Gilbert," he said.

Gilbert used sausage fingers to flick an ash from his cigar, missing the ashtray. "It may be and it may not, Harold. But you know, I'm in business here, and when a businessman sees business slumping, he has to do something, you know what I mean?"

Mystified, Harold nodded.

"I hate it like sin, Harold," Gilbert told him, "but I got to change our image a little bit. Maybe folk music like you perform is in a slump right now, who knows? I've talked to other owners and they're having similar experiences, crowds dropping, so it's no reflection on you. But what I have to do," Gilbert sighed heavily, "is try to change the image to start getting our crowds back, see?"

"You want a different kind of music?" Harold asked.

"Harold, with your mother's death and all, I really hate this. I mean that sincerely. As I said, it's no reflection on you. But what I'm going to have to do is, I'm going to have to let you go."

Harold stared. His pulse thudded. He could not believe this.

"I'm going to try some up-tempo stuff, a little Dixieland combo," Gilbert told him. "And then, on Tuesday night, I got this magician coming in. He's really terrific. Well, Harold, you know you wouldn't fit in with that kind of entertainment. You would be miserable. So, Harold, I have to let you go. I'm real sorry. But I know you won't have any trouble finding a new gig."

"I've worked here for four *years*," Harold said unbelievingly.

Gilbert handed an envelope across the desk. "I'll tell you what, you don't even have to play the last show tonight. Hell. There's nobody out there anyway. And here is three weeks' severance pay, Harold. I don't have to give you that by law, but you deserve it. You've been loyal. This will be a nice bonus for you, assuming you find a new gig right away, as I'm sure you will."

Gilbert stood and held out a hand, his jowls drooping in a grin. "No hard feelings, right, pardner?"

Harold cleaned out his locker and went home, arriving much earlier than usual, before midnight. He switched on the T.V. set and found a late-night talk show that he had often heard discussed. He opened a beer and drained it. The apartment was dark, with just the penumbra of bright light from the television set, and he felt jerkily nervous. He did not know how to handle this new shock. He knew he would never find another job. He had money saved, but the job had given some structure to his life, some marginal meaning. *Without it he was nothing.*

He was shaking. He went to the medicine cabinet for one of his pills. As he was about to open the little metal door, he looked at his own reflection in the dimness. There were rings under his eyes. Sweat glistened on his forehead. His eyes looked crazy.

The pills were doing this, he thought. Dr. Lindsey had strengthened them last week, and these made him sleepy and dopey-feeling through part of the following day.

With an angry gesture, he slammed the metal door. He would take no more pills.

Trembling, he walked back into the living room. The picture of Jesus looked down at him in the dim, reflected light from the TV. *Jesus, what is it you want me to do?*

He opened another beer, then another. He began to feel better, but even more jumpy. The voices were not there, but they were almost there. *What am I going to do about a new job? What am I going to do about Mother? I can't just sit here.*

He could not hear the TV. The other sound in the room was that of his own guttural sobs of anger and pain and confusion.

18

O n the day following Ken Lis's meeting with NTSB trouble
shooter Jace Mattingly, a confidential memorandum concerning the session went from Lis's office to the San Francisco town
house of Lydia Baines, carried by a messenger. The memorandum
remained unopened until midafternoon, when it found its way, with
other correspondence, to Lydia's hand while she luxuriated in her
tub.

Lydia Baines often opened mail and studied business matters
while in her tub, a tiled enclosure roughly eight feet wide and
slightly longer and sunk in the floor of the large bathroom like a
small pool. There was a plastic-topped desk, which swung out over
the tub from the wall, complete with a dictating machine, writing
materials, and a telephone. The desk was the only businesslike item
in a room that otherwise reflected Lydia's taste for the bizarre and
sybaritic. Large tropical plants created a lush jungle across one wall;
color television could be projected onto a four-foot screen by remote
control, or the room could be filled with stereophonic music. Golden
heating panels flooded the area with a lovely and warming light, and
a small fountain bubbled over rocks in a far corner. There was room
enough for a couch and a chair, and a small but well-stocked bar.
The room could be entered only through an elegant dressing room
connecting to Lydia's bedroom. It was a place where Lydia enjoyed
relaxing, luxuriantly conducting her correspondence, and sometimes
entertaining a lover.

She was immersed to the neck in hot, foamy water, with the built-
in whirlpool device in operation when she idly opened Lis's mem-

orandum and read it through. As she did so, her relaxation vanished and was replaced by a mounting rage. She pulled her telephone from its desk compartment and angrily punched buttons, direct-dialing her number in Washington.

"Senator Matthew Johns's office," a secretary answered.

"Let me speak to Senator Johns, please," Lydia snapped.

"I'm sorry, ma'am, Senator Johns is in conference."

"This is Lydia Baines calling. Put me through."

The girl's slight gasp showed she knew Lydia's importance in the office. "One moment please, Mrs. Baines."

Lydia waited impatiently and then heard a different line being picked up.

"Lydia," Matthew Johns's voice said warmly. "What a surprise!"

"Are you alone, Matt?"

"As a matter of fact, no."

"Can you get rid of them for a minute?"

"That, ah, might be rather difficult."

"Matt, this is God-damned important."

There was only the slightest pause while Johns evidently considered whatever politics might be involved with his visitor. Lydia allowed him this. If it was impossible, it was impossible. He would call her back soon in any event. Whatever their personal relationship, she did not make demands such as the one she was now making unless it was vital, and he knew this.

He said, "Will you hold, please?" The line clicked and sounded dead as she was placed on "hold" for about thirty seconds.

When Johns came back on the line, his tone was attentive and businesslike. "All right."

"I hope it wasn't anyone too important, Matt."

"As a matter of fact, it was Clifford Sweet and we were talking all around the edges of Eagle."

Sweet, as chairman of the committee that had to bring Eagle up again on its agenda for the project to get rolling, *was* vital. Despite her own concern, Lydia sharpened with interest.

"Is he going to get Eagle back on the committee agenda?" she asked. "Or are we facing more delays?"

"Cliff is still very much against Eagle, I'm afraid. But it looks better all the time. I'm not pushing him too fast, but there are two factors helping us. There's an electronics firm in his own state that evidently has hopes of manufacturing a key electronic component for you if Eagle goes into production, and it's the kind of plum that no politician likes to be accused of ruining for the local voters. Second, Cliff needs some help from me on the new urban housing bill. Some black support might just push it through. We're fencing at this point, but I feel surer than ever that it's coming."

"When?" Lydia demanded impatiently.

"I was overoptimistic before. I don't want to make that mistake again. I can't pick a date, but I think it will be soon."

"If it would help for us to encourage that firm in Sweet's home state, let me know. We can do that, I think."

"I've thought of that, Lydia. The information is secondhand and I don't even know the firm's name yet. But I'm having it checked out and I'll get back to you on it."

"Good. The reason I called, Matt, is that Ken Lis had a session yesterday with a man from the NTSB, Jace Mattingly."

"Yes," Johns said. "I've met him. Good man. They've given him a very unusual assignment on the Excalibur matter to try to expedite it."

"Lis's memo," Lydia bit off, "makes it sound like they have *no* idea of what caused the crash yet. Lis raises the specter of an investigation dragging on into early next year!"

"My God, we can't have that. Excalibur has to be selling, and selling well, to fund all the plant expansion for early Eagle production, doesn't it?"

Lydia paused an instant, thinking of the financial wreckage she had found in the company's records. She chose not to confide that at this time. "It would be damned helpful to have the Excalibur payments coming in regularly, Matt."

"I'm glad you let me know about this at once. I'll call a few people and have them make some calls. Those bureaucrats over there at the Board are just going to have to realize that a lot of important people have a stake in a quick finding on this one. I was hoping they already realized that, but it looks like someone is going to have to jack on some more pressure."

"Can you talk to the President?"

"Christ, I don't know. He wants Eagle. He hopes to make defense a big issue in the next campaign, and Eagle is the kind of thing he wants to point out as an accomplishment. But you know he has this thing against apparent interference with normal agency procedures."

"Try it," Lydia urged, "if you think there is any way at all that you might speak to him without it backfiring, or revealing our own interests. Damn it, we have to get that investigation wound up and Excalibur sales moving again! And we have to get those hearings going on Eagle!"

"I'll do what I can, Lydia, and I'll be back to you as soon as possible."

"Would it help in any way to send Harvey Coughlin back there at this time?"

"No," Johns said after a slight pause. "As soon as hearings are set, I want him here and I plan to use him. He's just the kind of simple-minded, goodhearted fool we need to make friends with some of these people. But I don't want him running around until the situation is such that I can direct his efforts in a subtle way . . . make maximum use of him."

"Whatever you say on that, Matt," Lydia said. "I'll be waiting to hear from you."

"All right, Lydia."

Lydia hung up the telephone, swung her desk back out of the way, and readjusted the whirlpool to maximize its swirling pressures.

The simple fact was that Excalibur had to be vindicated, and soon, if the future of Hempstead Aviation was to be secure. It was not only a matter of having income with which to fund Eagle. It was simply a matter of survival.

After her husband's death, she had scanned financial records with a greater concern and detail than had ever been possible during his life, and had been shocked by what she saw. She had known the general situation, and worried about it. But Jason had kept fine details to himself.

The gamble on Excalibur had been total. All reserves of cash had been thrown into the effort, and Jason had secretly borrowed very heavily not only against all company holdings but personally. In the present year the gamble had begun to appear to pay off. Originally planned to sell somewhere in the $10-million to $12-million class, Excalibur already had been pushed upward to $14 million per airplane. This remained competitive with lesser craft still on the drawing boards and allowed a healthy profit margin per plane.

Hempstead Aviation still required the constant inflow of new cash from new purchases, however, to keep going. Jason had committed everything to the project, and certain of his long-term notes were due prior to the end of the year. All the obligations could be met nicely with forty to sixty new orders and the required minimum down payment on contract. Without them—

Lydia did not like to think about that possibility. It was devastating.

The Excalibur probe had to be concluded, and successfully. New sales were mandatory.

And beyond that, Lydia Baines was very well aware how certain people within and outside the industry had always considered her a kind of charming accessory to Jason Baines, a pretty watch fob for a great business and engineering genius. The image rankled, and she was determined to prove to them all that she was fully capable of not only sustaining Jason's company but making it an empire.

Eagle was only the first step in her ambitious dream. Certain of the company's submarine-research material had never been published or shown to anyone. With Excalibur providing a basic, long-term cash flow, Hempstead Aviation could go ahead with Eagle and make a tremendous—and rather quick—profit. That profit could be plowed back into a submarine project built around the concept of using underwater vessels to poison huge areas of ocean to deprive an enemy of all commercial fishing and other ocean-related sources of food. Beyond that project, Lydia believed the United States would be back in space exploration on a manned basis within another decade. Her dream was for Hempstead to be the builder of the manned exploration of Mars.

It was not an idle dream. It was a burning need within her that would be met or she would destroy herself and everyone else in the seeking. No one ever again would look at her as a sex symbol . . . she would never again have to grovel before any man. Hers would be the ultimate power, that of great wealth.

Thinking of this possible future, Lydia remembered something that had happened to her when she was fifteen years old. She had been a very precocious fifteen, fully developed physically in terms of beauty and attraction for men.

Her mother had taken her to a studio, trying to get her a part in an upcoming movie. Her mother had once played bit parts for the producer to whom she took Lydia, and they knew each other well. He was a fat man, bald, smiling. He chucked Lydia under the chin and said she was a darling child and asked her how much she wanted to be a movie star.

After a while, Lydia's mother had left her there alone. The producer talked to Lydia a while longer, casually went to his door and flicked a security lock, came back to where Lydia was seated, and standing over her, worked the zipper of his trousers. . . .

Lydia remembered. She remembered the shock and horror and fear, and the terrible eagerness to please, closing off her own mind and becoming an automaton for the part in the movie. . . .

The part that went to someone else.

It was a thing she would never forget. She had vowed that no man would ever have such control over her again, and she had finally made herself a star, and had seen powerful men grovel, begging her to do parts. That had been heady stuff, sheer pleasure.

Making Hempstead Aviation into a true giant would be even greater.

Nothing was going to stop her from making it come true.

19

The warehouse, specially procured for the purpose only a short drive from New York's Kennedy Airport, had been transformed in the weeks since the Excalibur crash, and wreckage of the airliner now filled the central cavity of the building, looking like an engineer's nightmare.

Under jury-rigged floodlights, a massive supporting platform of lumber, mostly two-by-fours, had been constructed. With the exception of certain instruments and servomechanisms to be tested in labs near Washington, every piece of the wreck had been trucked in. Diagrams and photographs recorded in minute detail where every scrap had been found after the crash, and in what condition. But here the parts were being reassembled, as perfectly as possible, in the original Excalibur configuration.

Wire and cables spider-webbed the support platform, with steel posts and cross girders here and there as needed for extra strength. From the wires were hung every part of the plane. Here was a large, torn section of the fuselage, and close beside it, in proper placement, a bent and scorched bit of wing root only ten inches long; here was a massive wing section, bent and blackened but placed exactly in the place it must have been in the intact aircraft, and beside it, suspended on wire, was a wingtip light.

The major pieces were all in place. Now, in bins and boxes along a seventy-foot work trestle, technicians were sifting much smaller bits, identifying them, fitting them into the gigantic puzzle.

Watching, Jace Mattingly knew that the work would continue for weeks.

"Sometimes," he confided to the technician standing beside him in the warehouse, "I wonder why we go through this."

The technician's name was Teed. A middle-aged white man with parchment skin and rather heavy spectacles, he had never betrayed the slightest hint of a sense of humor in Mattingly's presence. He did not spoil his track record now. "It's only when we identify every fragment, and juxtapose them in the mockup, that we can be sure we have every item. There have been cases when we discovered a failure in structural integrity through this procedure when any other—"

"Right," Mattingly said wearily. "But you haven't found anything so far?"

"You've seen the preliminary, partial reports. Given the force of impact and fire effects, major components appear within normal parameters."

"Meaning you haven't found anything."

"Well, yes. Of course we've *eliminated* many possibilities."

"That seems to be what we're doing all over the place."

"I heard," Teed said, "that the strip-down on the engines showed no mechanical failures or deviations prior to the crash."

"The bird had its power."

Teed stared at the wrecked airplane being reconstructed before them. Its sheet metal reflected in his glasses, making silvery patterns. "The work gets slow now, and tedious."

"I'll check back later in the week."

"You can be sure we'll notify you at once if we make any major finding."

Mattingly watched a technician carry a piece of landing-gear strut underneath the platform and start wiring it. "All you guys need," he said, "is a haystack to look in."

"What?" Teed blinked myopically.

"Nothing. Thanks for the report. See you in a few days."

Teed had already turned back to his clipboard by the time Mattingly waved and walked away.

It would have been easy enough to fly to Washington, but Jace Mattingly's agency was feeling a budget crunch, and driving gave him time to think, anyway. Heading south on the highway, he chain-smoked and mentally reviewed what he saw as a worsening situation.

Worsening not because anything new had happened to complicate matters but worsening because absolutely no evidence had been found, despite extensive effort, that might begin to solve the mystery of why TW Flight 161 went down in the first place.

The engines, as he had confirmed for Teed, had been torn down and examined in fine detail. They had been functioning perfectly at the time of the crash. Metallurgical tests on engine bracing, wing-root members, vital fuselage bracing, and the remaining major segments of the empennage had shown no breaks that could be proven to exist prior to impact, no sign of stress or wear on moving parts, no evidence of fatigue.

Flight-deck controls and instruments had been checked and reassembled elsewhere, by specialists. There was nothing to hint that any instrument or cluster of gauges had malfunctioned. The major controls, including wing slats, trim, flaps, and power, had—as far as could be determined—been in normal modes and working.

There had been a brief flurry of theorizing that a freak wind shear might have occurred. Consequently, flight crews working in and out of the airport over several hours had been contacted and laboriously interviewed from a preset group of questions carefully designed to neither hint at nor deny the possibility of turbulence at the threshold. When these efforts all were negative in eliciting a hint of wind shear, the questioning extended to three small private airfields in the area, with similar results. Then a special meteorological profile was ordered from weather experts, who used all available data in order to draw up an independent portrait of weather conditions as they existed when TW Flight 161 descended, that fatal evening.

The chance of wind shear or severe turbulence, this profile indicated, was on the order of one in five hundred thousand.

Mattingly had been on some tough ones before but never one in which there seemed to be no hint whatsoever of what had caused the destruction and death. Every new interview, every new test, only did as Teed had dryly suggested—eliminated some other possibility.

Mattingly, however, was not interested in eliminating possibilities. He wanted a probable cause. Pressure was mounting in the office as questions persisted from the press, the public, and Congress. There had been some nasty lawsuits involving Transwestern. The agency simply could not avoid a public hearing more than another few weeks . . . not in this case, and while there did not have to be a verdict any time soon after the hearing, it was going to be pretty bad politically if the hearing took no form whatsoever and the press could conclude that the NTSB had no damned idea whatsoever what had caused the crash.

Given that situation, Mattingly knew, the theory of pilot error was bound to surface. When every other probable cause has been ruled out, or has failed of proof, then revert to human fallibility. Sometimes it was the cause. Sometimes it was simply the best way to hide the fact that the cause had never really been found.

Mattingly had pored over Jerry Emerson's history. He simply did not believe that Emerson could have made such a fatal error, especially not on short final approach, a time when even low-time pilots know they have to give maximum attention to their task or pay the consequences.

No, Mattingly thought, driving. It was the airplane. Something in the airplane had broken, gone sour. But, lacking proof of this gut conviction, he was going to be under pressure in that public hearing to hint at pilot error. And what the hell was he going to do about that?

By the time he reached Washington, he had no more answer than before. He found a message that "P" wished to see him at his earliest convenience, and went immediately to the office of his superior.

Faded sunlight entering from a window at the back of the small room glinted off George Pierce's bald head as he looked up when Mattingly entered.

"Glad you're back," he said. "Nothing new at the warehouse, I assume?"

"You assume right," Mattingly said.

Pierce leaned back with an unreadable expression. "We are going to start making arrangements for the public hearing."

"*When?*"

"As soon as possible. As soon as the depositions have been properly prepared and the lab findings can be typed, and schedules arranged."

"It's too early," Mattingly said. "Someone is pushing too hard. We won't be ready."

"Jace, we're going to *have* to be ready."

"All right, who's pushing so hard?'

"Several senators. Several representatives. Transwestern. Somebody high up in the White House, because of the balance-of-trade thing. The press." Pierce took a deep breath. "Everybody."

"How long can we hold off the public hearing?"

"A month or two."

"All right." Mattingly did not try to hide his deep disgust. "We'll be as ready as possible."

"We'll be ready," Pierce corrected him.

"I keep telling you, this is not even your normal tough one. This gets worse every time we run a new test. We have no *sign* of why that plane crashed!"

Pierce seemed not to hear. "I've authorized in-depth psychological profiles on the crew."

Mattingly tingled. "*What* crew?"

"The crew of Flight 161, of course."

"We *have* that information!"

"We have the usual psychological data from the airline physicals. What I'm talking about is an in-depth personality profile on the pilot, copilot, and flight engineer, done by a panel of independent psychologists working from file data, interviews, biographical studies —anything they think they can dig up to give a complete picture of the state of mind and emotion of each of those three men the day they flew toward Kennedy in Flight 161."

"Pilot error," Mattingly snapped.

"I'm not saying that."

"You *are* saying that! Why else would you have the studies made?"

"Maybe the profiles will give all three men a perfectly clean bill of health."

"That's crap and you know it. Nobody has a perfect life, a completely placid outlook. Those shrinks will dig, and find some worms, and be ready to make it look like Jerry Emerson was ripe for pilot error!"

Pierce's eyes had grown unaccountably cold. "I'm covering bases, Jace."

"You're fixing to protect your own backside by having evidence to support a theory of pilot error if we're not clever enough to find what really happened!"

Pierce's hands twitched on the desk top. "I won't debate it with you. Pilot error has to be considered until you or your people come up with a better probable cause. If you don't like the pilot-error theory, then find something better."

Mattingly stormed out of the office and returned to his own glassed cubicle in a much larger, open work area. Staring at reports on his desk, he felt thoroughly stymied and angry. He was making a great deal of commotion, with no progress. The idea of a public hearing that might openly suggest pilot error—even though a final finding might take many more months after the hearing—shocked and dismayed him.

He tried to probe his feelings. How much of his feeling that Jerry Emerson was blameless, he asked himself, was based on fact? How much was based even on normal intuition? He had to be honest with himself here. How much of his instinctive support for Emerson's reputation stemmed from the fact that he had been a black man?

And how much from the fact that his wife had been Nell Emerson?

Mattingly continued to think about it. He considered the possibility of calling Nell now, and trying to arrange a meeting with her. There was justification. He could update her on the investigation, perhaps give her warning of the new pressures that might jeopardize her dead husband's reputation.

He recognized, however, that these were only rationalizations. The truth was that he had been thinking about her almost constantly. He wanted to see her on any basis; it was as simple as that.

And for this reason, he told himself, he could not grasp at excuses. He had an official status here. He would not trade on it. He would see her soon enough—he told himself—in the normal course of events.

So he did not reach for the telephone, but in the following hours his eyes kept returning to it as the hunger to see her again continued to plague him.

20

Almost precisely on the appointed hour of 10 A.M., Thursday, June 18, the Trident passenger jet, wearing the cream-and-blue colors of the Kingdom of Monravia, touched down on Hempstead Aviation's airstrip. Tensely checking on last-minute arrangements, Janis Malone made sure that the small group of dignitaries near the welcoming ramp were properly aligned for the ceremonies. A crisp California wind crackled the flags held at attention by a local Boy Scout troop, and behind the distant cyclone fencing a crowd of perhaps two hundred cheered raggedly. Janis signaled the extra security guards to maintain their positions against anyone trying to break through for an autograph, again promised the local television people that they would have plenty of time for their shots, and gave a hand wave to the leader of the small military band grouped off to the right. As the gleaming jet hissed and thundered up to the parking location, guided by a mechanic with signal paddles, the band raggedly struck up the Monravian national march.

Shielding her ears from the jet blast, Janis again looked around for possible glitches in the protocol, but saw none. Standing at the red-carpeted platform where Prince David Peltier would be led for introductions were Ken Lis, a beautiful Lydia Baines in an off-white dress and hat, the mayor and manager of the local chamber of commerce, Harvey Coughlin, Barton MacIvor, and a protocol man from the U. S. State Department named Hawkins. Everyone—and everything —looked fine. *If anything goes wrong,* Janis thought, *I'll kill myself.*

Planning for the visit had been good medicine for her after the breakup with Hank Selvy. She was tired but perhaps not as strung out as she might have been if she had had time to brood. Hempstead had never experienced anything quite like this before, and Janis had been at the center of all the planning. Under any other circumstances she might have actually enjoyed it.

The Trident turned massively on signal from the mechanic with the paddles, and Janis, standing out in front of the reception area with a security man, caught a glimpse of the pilot peering down through his side cabin window. His face partially obscured by aviator's sunglasses, he was handsome, dark-haired, and surprisingly young. Janis turned away as he went out of view, the plane continuing to pivot, to make sure the crew rolled the platform up beside the plane to accept the stairs when they folded down, and then the engines were cut, and as they unwound, the silence was vast, punctuated by the wind and the sound of the flags over the playing of the band.

There was a predictable delay as chocks were placed under the massive wheels of the plane. Monravia, richest of the tiny countries that cling to existence in the shadows of France and Italy along the shores of the Mediterranean, had created a stir like this at each of its stops in the United States. Janis had seen newspaper coverage from each visit, and was anxious that this one be the smoothest of all. She also was honest enough with herself to admit a considerable curiosity about Prince David Peltier, only son of Queen Sophia and head of this delegation. His pictures had made him look youthful and handsome.

The door of the plane was swung open, and portable stairs were extended. Once the stairs had been locked, there was another momentary delay while two elderly men in considerable military gold braid conferred at the door above. Then one of them came down, to be met by Ken Lis, who had walked forward. Janis stayed in the background now, watching, as another man came down from the plane. He was short, round, with well-oiled black hair and a little mustache. Janis recognized Lucian Derquet, the Prime Minister, from other photographs. The two men put their heads together in quick conversation.

The security guard standing beside Janis nudged her. "Miss Malone, I think they're waving at you."

"Me? Who?" Janis looked around and saw him pointing up toward the door of the plane. Another military man was standing out of the doorway and out of view of the people in front. He was signaling frantically to Janis.

"Me?" she said, pointing to herself.

The general, or whatever he was, motioned more vociferously, signaling that she should come up to the plane.

Janis hesitated fractionally, looking toward Lis for instructions. He was, however, in conversation with Derquet. The band was still playing and everyone was waiting. Janis had to make an instantaneous decision, and made it. She quickly went up the shaky metal stair to the door of the plane, and stepped inside.

It was cool and dark in the corridor of the Trident. A half dozen military and civilian officials were standing around. One of them was the young pilot.

"What is the schedule?" the pilot asked her tensely. He had removed his sunglasses, and his eyes looked dazzled by the sunlight flooding into the doorway. "Is there supposed to be a speech here? No one mentioned a speech!"

Janis was irritated. "I made the arrangements with Prime Minister Derquet, and I'm sure he and Prince David understand the plans even if you don't. —And the plans certainly didn't call for me to be summoned up here to be interrogated by a member of the crew."

The pilot's face went blank. "I beg your pardon?"

"I said—" Janis began.

"*Madam!*" one of the aides said, his voice hoarse with shock. "You are *addressing* Prince David!"

Janis stared. She had been thrown off by seeing him first at the controls of the plane and then by the odd light here in the doorway. But it was unmistakable: the dark hair, the bright blue eyes, the jutting jaw. It *was* Prince David Peltier, his coat removed, his collar open and tie pulled down.

"Oh, good God," she said. "I'm sorry, Your, uh, Excellency, I—"

"It doesn't matter," Prince David said quickly. "But do tell me. Are you the Miss Malone we have had contact with? Miss Malone. Am I supposed to make a speech here at the airplane? What is the plan?" The prince grimaced. "I don't want to commit some kind of official indignity!"

Janis relaxed a little; he was more nervous than she was! "Just a few informal words will be fine, Prince David. Then we'll go inside,

143

you will have a few minutes with the press in our conference room, and then the official part of it will be over."

"Fantastic," Prince David said, suddenly beaming at her. "Thank you, Miss Malone. I did not want to make some mistake. When we visited Seattle, I thought the mayor was a Secret Service man. When we were at Lockheed, I got in the wrong bus and the people in charge almost had a stroke!"

Janis smiled at him. "We're keeping it simple here."

"Thank you! Fantastic! All right!" He looked around. "Has anyone seen my coat?"

Two flunkies struggled with one another for the honor of holding the jacket. As the prince shrugged into it, Janis turned, still smiling, to go back down the stairs. She felt considerably better. Then she was almost knocked backward by Derquet rushing up the stairs and into the plane again.

"What are you doing in here?" Derquet flung at her. "The arrangements were explicit! We do not need sensation seekers!"

"I asked her to come up to tell me the protocol, Lucian," the prince said. "Since you had neglected to inform me."

Derquet's angry expression instantly vanished and he became oily and conciliatory. "A thousand pardons, Miss." He turned to the prince. "All is in readiness, Your Excellency. A few remarks from the platform, and then—"

"Miss Malone has informed me, Lucian," the prince said, a light of combativeness in his remarkable eyes. "Since you neglected to take care of all the details, it was necessary for me to turn elsewhere. Now may I suggest that we deplane without further conversation?"

Derquet, his face splotched with rage, bowed from the waist. "Of course it will be as you say, Your Excellency."

Prince David stepped forward, the same reckless, happy light in his eyes. He put his arm through Janis's, locking it. "Will you accompany me, Miss Malone? These things frighten me to death!"

Astounded, Janis found herself being propelled out onto the stairs on the arm of the prince. The band was playing and the crowd cheered. He paused, hanging onto her for dear life with one arm while he waved the other and grinned broadly.

"I'll never get used to crowds," he said under his breath. "What if I were to trip in going down the stairs, like one of your presidents did once? My country would be forever in disgrace. My mother would probably have me beheaded! —Is that Mrs. Lydia Baines there in the white? Of course. I have seen all her motion pictures. What a formidable woman! She frightens me more than anything else! Stay close, Miss Malone, I beg you!"

So it was that Janis Malone found herself going down the stairs to meet the official welcome that she herself had devised. She didn't know what to do—was caught by the prince's impetuosity. She didn't even know whether to smile. It was a funny mixup—she hoped. But Lydia Baines was glaring daggers.

21

After the first confusion, the visit by the Monravian party began going well and smoothly. Ken Lis, at least, was able to view it with a sense of good humor.

"I'm mortified," Janis Malone told him in the hallway while the prince was meeting the press. "I didn't know what to *do*."

"You handled it perfectly," Lis said. "And you got to meet the prince right away, and he obviously likes you."

"Lydia Baines doesn't," Janis said.

"Even Lydia can't fight success," Lis said. "Relax."

"I thought he was the *pilot*."

"Well, he did fly it down from San Francisco, so it was a natural mistake."

"Mr. Derquet didn't like my presence one little bit!"

Lis nodded, remembering his meeting with Derquet in New York. "He has a very high position in Monravia, and he's supposed to be the prince's top adviser. But I get the impression there's always tension between them."

"I can see why," Janis said. "The prince is so informal—so dynamic. And Derquet is such a—such a toad!"

Lis chuckled. "He does take himself awfully seriously."

Janis glanced at her watch. "Is it time for us to go in and save him from the press?"

They did so. After a few more questions, many aimed at general interest in a wave of minor earthquakes that had rattled Monravia several days running, Lis and Janis escorted the prince out a side door into a private hallway.

The prince mopped his forehead. "Those lights are too hot! Thank you for rescuing me!"

"We have to get up to my office now," Lis told him. "We have five minutes to relax, and then, if we follow the schedule, we'll start the first session introducing Excalibur design factors to your party."

Prince David nodded. "Good. Excellent. You know how much I admire Excalibur, Mr. Lis. Nothing in our visits to other builders has changed my interest. May I ask if you have recent word on investigation of the crash in New York?"

"I'm afraid the investigation is still under way," Lis told him.

"I feared as much. Some of my group, I must tell you, have spoken against Excalibur as a result of that crash. Lucian is one of them, and he has great influence in the cabinet that advises my mother, the Queen. But I intend to continue pushing for acceptance of your aircraft because of its advanced design. Will I be allowed to fly it? I would like that very much."

"I see no reason why you can't handle the controls in flight," Lis told him.

"And pizza," the prince said.

Lis was thrown for a loss. "What?"

"Pizza! American pizza! I have been in New York and all over your country, and every place we have stopped, it has been some kind of steak or chicken! American pizza is the greatest food in the world! The Italians have no idea how to make pizza as Americans do! Tell me: do you have a Pizza Hut in this part of the country?"

Lis laughed at Janis Malone's expression of total wonderment. "We have one not ten miles from here."

The prince rolled his eyes. "If there is any way you can get me to that pizza, I will be forever in your debt!"

Lis glanced at his watch. "I'm afraid we're using up our entire five minutes of spare time. We're going to have to go direct to the conference hall for the presentation."

Prince David threw up his hands. "If my official duties prevent me from having even one visit to a Pizza Hut, the trip will be a complete disaster!" Then he grinned and made a mock salute. "It is as you say, Mr. Lis. Duty first. Lead on."

The session in the conference arena was the first strictly between Monravian officials and members of the Hempstead team. Fewer than two dozen persons were in attendance. In the front of the pit-

147

shaped room, office-type armchairs were grouped in a large semicircle facing a platform equipped with a blackboard, display easels, a large cutaway model of Excalibur, and push-button devices to operate slide and motion-picture equipment.

Lydia Baines, regal and cool and showing no signs of any irritation she might be feeling toward Janis Malone or anyone else, opened the meeting with a few words of additional welcome. She was obviously aware of how striking she appeared, and was enjoying this fact despite her stern effort to be businesslike. Her eyes repeatedly stole toward the handsome prince seated in the first row.

"Now that we are out of the glare of publicity," she said, "please allow me to welcome you to the business portion of your visit to Hempstead Aviation. You have your schedules, worked out in advance. I'll be very brief in reviewing them. This is a general session designed to introduce all of you to a few of the basic concepts and facts about Excalibur, which we consider the jet airplane for the Environmental Age. After this meeting, we will have an informal lunch in the executive cafeteria, in this building. At 1:30 P.M., engineering talks will begin between your experts and Mr. MacIvor and his staff. At the same time, the first Excalibur demonstration flight will begin. After that flight, at approximately three o'clock, we will break up for individual conferences. At about 4:30, transportation will be standing by to take you to the two motels reserved for you. The reception and dinner for city and state officials will begin at the country club at seven. Our meetings resume here tomorrow morning at ten, and your departure, as you requested, is scheduled directly after lunch."

Lydia paused and looked around briefly. "Whatever we can do to make your visit both informative and pleasant, please be assured that we want to do so. Now let me turn the platform over to Ken Lis, chief of our Airplane Division."

Lis moved to the platform. "My remarks will be generalized and brief. I have a few slides I want to show you. —Janis?"

Janis Malone was already at the side control panel, and even as he called her name she had touched the button that lowered an electrically controlled screen behind him. At the same time, a slot opened in the back wall of the room and Lis saw the brilliant bolt of light that signaled readiness of the slide projector, with its long-throw, 300-mm. lens.

"The HE-14 Excalibur is the jet commercial transport for the Environmental Age," Lis began, and as he did so, the lights dimmed and a huge color picture of an Excalibur in flight was thrown onto the screen behind him. "It is not the largest jet, not the fastest, not even the most luxurious. Planes like the 747, LC 1011 and Concorde can claim all the world records in those departments.

"Excalibur, however, is the most practical and safe jetliner offered today."

The slide changed, showing a chart. It would change on Janis's command through Lis's brief presentation.

"In the 1960s the aviation industry saw an unlimited future, and the problem seemed to be how to carry all the passengers that the projections showed clogging the airports of the future. In that pre-environmental time, the answer from the industry was the wide-body jet, capable of carrying a lot more passengers per flight, and/or planes like the Concorde SST, which could carry considerably faster on the long hauls. It was in this period that we saw introduction of the 747, at $25 million per airplane, and the LC 1011 and DC-10, at about $15 million. Despite cries from environmentalists, the Concorde began service.

"In the middle to late seventies, however, a number of things went wrong. The Arab nations drastically boosted the price of fuel. Environmental groups began filing—and winning—more lawsuits aimed at air pollution and noise around airports. Late in 1976, the government ordered a definite abatement of jet-engine noise in the decade of the eighties.

"At that time, the backbone of domestic fleets was formed by the 707, the 727, and the Lockheed Tristar, essentially, along of course with others, like the DC-10. Even before changing conditions made it obvious that radical change had to come sometime in the eighties, the 707 was already being phased out. It was a fine airplane, but even at that time it was more than twenty years old. And the 727, a newer plane, was reaching the logical end of its development pattern with the stretch model.

"While other aircraft companies decided to modify existing designs to meet the new, emerging picture of jet air travel, Hempstead Aviation elected to begin development of a radically new airliner.

"With passenger totals slumping, wide-body designs were no longer as attractive as they had been in, say, 1972. From 1973 through 1976, not a single U.S. carrier ordered a wide-body jet, and some had their recent deliveries mothballed rather than endure the high price of flying them half empty. The price of fuel simply made the situation impossible; a 747, as you probably know, carries fifty thousand gallons of fuel . . . some of the wide-body trijets as much as thirty-six thousand.

"Excalibur's design philosophy, then, was for a large airplane. A normal capacity of about 170 passengers was selected, with option for narrower seating and a reduced galley area that might raise capacity to near 230 if desired.

"In terms of environmental concerns, Excalibur engineers worked with both General Electric and Pratt-Whitney in developing a new, cleaner-burning, quieter fan-jet power plant. Due to its unique wing design, Excalibur can operate at considerably lower levels of power than other jets of comparable size, which in itself tends to reduce both noise and smoke. In addition, the Excalibur engines recycle smoke and noise back through the combustion area, in effect giving the engine a self-canceling effect. The result is the cleanest, quietest jet aircraft on the market.

"Economy is also a concern, of course, and from the start we were determined that Excalibur would be the cheapest plane in the air on a ratio of fuel per passenger. That goal was met. Our tests show that the Excalibur averages about 14.5 per cent less fuel per gross weight than its competitors. Reports from Transwestern Airlines in the first months of operation were even better—savings of 16 per cent over the 727, for example, on identical routes.

"Finally, I want to point out to you that the airplane of the future will have to deal with more-varying circumstances than those of the recent past. The day of flying jumbo jets into widely scattered airports, loading them to the gunwales and barging off three thousand miles—that day is passing. Today, airlines have to have the long-distance capacity; they need fairly big planes. But they also *must* go into smaller cities for their fares as well, and they can't do that with airplanes that are too costly for shorter hauls or simply can't operate into fields with runways less than two or three miles long.

"Excalibur handles this problem also. Probably its greatest single advantage lies in its historic wing-design breakthrough, sometimes called the slat or dimple wing. Put in its simplest terms, the Excalibur wing flies at lower airspeeds than other wings, and lifts greater weights, because the effective curvature of the upper wing surface is increased by making the air burble over controlled dimple patterns.

"A wing flies, of course, because the air traveling over the upper portion has to reach the rear of the wing at the same time the air traveling under the lower surface reaches the same point. If the upper surface is curved, that air has to travel faster to get to the back at the same time the air underneath does traveling a shorter distance. The result of the air traveling faster over the upper, curved surface is that a partial vacuum is formed and the wing is sucked upward into that partial vacuum—and flies.

"In the early days of aviation, for this reason we had some very thick, 'fat' wings to get maximum lift. But there are two factors that limit the effective curvature. One is simply that a wing can get so fat that the air breaks up rather than flowing over the top. The other is that a wing must be made increasingly thinner, to slice the air cleanly as speeds are increased.

"Conventional jet aircraft solve this problem in part by having basic wings that are very thin, for speed. But designers then add extensions, flap-like devices that can be mechanically extended from the front and rear portions of the wing to give the wing's effective surface more length and curvature at lower speeds. Excalibur uses these aids but also adds its dimple system—thirty-eight indentions per wing—which can be exposed by sliding slats in the wing surface. The air burbles slightly over these dimples on the upper wing, greatly increasing the effective curvature.

"The result," Lis went on as a slide illustrating the dimple-wing design was thrown onto the screen, "is an aircraft that is amazingly docile and forgiving at low speeds. While other aircraft of its size land at about 150 miles per hour, for example, Excalibur lands at a book speed of 111.

"Our studies show that this reduced landing speed, together with a correspondingly improved short-field takeoff capability, opens up to Excalibur more than eight thousand smaller municipal airports for possible service well within the safety designs. We have, in short, a plane that is quieter, cleaner, more economical, safer, and capable of operating into many more fields than any other.

"All the details are in your information packets, and some of you have conferred with our European sales representatives on other occasions. While at least two other manufacturers have planes somewhat like Excalibur on the drawing boards, ours is the only one in production now, and flying."

Lis paused and the lights in the room were raised again to normal levels. "I now want to turn the session over to Miss Janis Malone, of our public-relations office, who will tell you about company and customer reactions to Excalibur."

Lis left the platform and Janis Malone walked to the lectern, carrying a small folder of notes. As he sat down, Lis could not help but be struck by the contrast between Janis and the hard-edged, classic beauty displayed by Lydia Baines only moments earlier. It was a refreshing contrast. In her simple summer frock and medium white heels, Janis appeared slightly wind-blown, pink with controlled excitement, and enormously young and appealing. Her eyes, as she surveyed the group briefly, brimmed with life and enthusiasm. There was nothing artificial about her, and Lis wondered how anyone here could possibly fail to believe anything she told him.

A little while later, during the coffee break, Prince David remarked about this as he stood with him momentarily alone in a corner of the room.

"A remarkable woman," the prince said, his eyes on Janis across the room.

"We're lucky to have her," Lis agreed.

"The way she gave out facts without ever looking at her notes! A fantastic mind! And when she walked onto the airplane, I thought she must be some local Miss America girl you had brought in to be part of the welcome. Most women are either beautiful or intelligent, and if they try to be both, they are hard, like your Mrs. Baines."

Lis was interested both in that he had made the observation so soon, and was willing to express the view so openly. "Mrs. Baines has been under pressure of many kinds since her husband's death," he said carefully.

"Yes," Prince David said, his eyes sober as he turned slightly to view Lydia at the table a dozen paces away. "But she is tough, that one. I think she and Lucian are a good match."

"They seem to be getting along."

"I wish," the prince said suddenly, "she had not planned that reception and dinner tonight. If I investigated, I think I would find a letter somewhere from Lucian, suggesting it. Everywhere we go, there is a reception and dinner—horrible little drinks and hideous lit-the soggy sandwiches, and then more of your roast beef, and I smile and bow and act my part, and inside I am dying for pizza!"

Lis grinned at him. "I begin to think you're serious about pizza."

The prince rolled his eyes. "Mr. Lis, I am a . . . wait, I want to say it the right way . . . I am a freak! I am a freak for your pizza! Now I face return to my own country within forty-eight hours, and there will be no pizza. I am distraught."

"We might try to get some frozen pizzas," Lis suggested. "You could take them back with you."

The prince made a face. "That was Lucian's suggestion. I have tried frozen pizzas. They are as bad as pizzas in Italy! I have two great chefs on the staff at the palace, and I have given them at least a dozen recipes for pizza. But those are not right either. There is nothing like a pizza from an oven in one of your Pizza Huts—nothing! Everything else is pale imitation, a sham and a fraud, and an abomination in the eyes of mankind!"

"Prince David," Lis said, "we are going to have to figure out a way to get you some pizza."

Across the room, Lydia Baines and Lucian Derquet had turned from a brief private conversation and were now walking toward Lis and the prince.

"Not a word of this to Lucian or that woman!" the prince said. "Lucian would fill the airplane with hideous imitations, and *she* would probably serve me with a pizza at the dinner tonight—some great, swollen, obscene thing with artichokes and papayas on it! Ah, God! I am trapped and cheated."

"I never knew the life of royalty was so hard."

"Mr. Lis," the prince said sadly, "you have no idea." At this point, Derquet and Lydia Baines had reached hearing distance, and the change in the prince's expression was magical. "My good friend and my *new* good friend!" he exclaimed, beaming.

"You are ready to resume, Excellency?" the saturnine Derquet asked.

"If you will just be so kind as to allow me to finish my coffee, Lucian," Prince David said. There was a subtle bite in his tone, but Lis did not think anyone else caught it.

"We hope you're finding the visit informative so far, Prince David," Lydia said. "We want to do anything we possibly can to make your stay pleasant!" She linked her arm through his, continuing to give him her most brilliant smile.

"My dear lady," the prince said, "you could not possibly have planned any aspect of the visit to please me more. And you are a most charming companion."

Lydia began maneuvering him away from Lis and Derquet. "I see why so many Americans love to visit your country, Prince David, if your charm is any indication of the welcome they receive. My only regret is that you were unable to visit me in my home in San Francisco during your brief stopover there. I have some things there I would have so much enjoyed showing you."

The two of them moved away, toward another group of people.

"I wish to apologize," Derquet said softly, "for any embarrassment that might have been caused by the prince's rash actions during the arrival."

"I thought everything went very well," Lis said.

Derquet's waxed mustache twitched. "The prince is very young, Mr. Lis. Although in his middle twenties, he has lived a life that has been relatively sheltered. Queen Sophia is a very strong person, as perhaps you are aware. The prince is not always as sensitive to protocol as perhaps we might wish. His impetuous actions in the door of the airplane—if they caused you embarrassment, please accept my apology."

Subtly, Lis saw, Derquet's words were more than a formal apology. They tended to set Derquet up as the center of authority and wisdom, and simultaneously denigrate Prince David in a way that no one could ever call intentional. It was a tactic that Lis did not like.

All he said, however, was, "Think nothing of it."

"The prince always allows his enthusiasms to run away," Derquet said. "The incident at the airplane, for example. And now, in addition, I feel that I must warn you that the prince is very enthusiastic about your Excalibur."

"Why should I be *warned* about that?"

Derquet frowned as if troubled by weighty matters of state. "It may be, Mr. Lis, that the cabinet of Monravia will eventually advise the Queen to purchase the Excalibur. But as the chairman of the cabinet, I have seen it sometimes go against the wishes of very high personages. It works slowly, and with great care, for the good of our beloved nation. I myself, for example, am not convinced that any aircraft is superior to the others. It would be a great shame if you were to misinterpret the prince's enthusiasm and so count on a sale you may not have."

Lis was listening carefully and liking it less all the time. "I hope we can convince you, Mr. Derquet, because if I interpret you correctly, it's vital that we impress you."

"I would not try to persuade you, Mr. Lis, that I am an important figure in Monravia." The little man sighed. "Fate has given me a critical position of great responsibility. I try to discharge my responsibilities as well as my limited capacities allow. But if I am, as some newsmen have suggested, the second-most-powerful person in Monravia, it is only because I love my country and my queen, and work hard to serve. I personally am nothing . . . seek nothing for myself."

"Still, Mr. Derquet," Lis said making a show of sincerity, "I see that you're crucial to any negotiations. I certainly want to work closely with you."

Derquet gave him a slight nod. "It will be my pleasure, Mr. Lis. But please remember that any power I may have is from the Queen, and it is power that must be exercised behind the scenes. Nothing could more distress me than to have any outward manifestation of the fact that I bear the greatest responsibility of all those on this trade mission."

"You're very loyal," Lis said.

"I thank you. —And now I see that Prince David has finished his coffee. Perhaps we should resume?"

Lis moved dutifully to follow orders. As he got the session going again, however, he was troubled. There was more than he had discovered in Derquet's reaching for power here. Why did the minister feel it necessary to undercut the prince? What were the political realities in Monravia? And what did Derquet think he might gain through the Excalibur negotiations?

The water had just gotten deeper. Lis now had additional reasons for watching his step.

22

During the luncheon in the executive cafeteria, Prince David Peltier twice complained of a headache. His personal physician, a kindly elderly man who wore wire-rimmed spectacles, prescribed Empirin, and the prince smilingly assured everyone he felt fit enough for the afternoon demonstration ride in a production Excalibur that had been prepared for that purpose. Accordingly Lis ducked out of the luncheon a few minutes early to go on the ramp where the new airplane stood gleaming under the bright afternoon sun.

Hank Selvy, his copilot, and his engineer were already on board, conducting preignition checks, while several mechanics swarmed around the outside of the plane, double-checking small details. Lis climbed aboard, stepping into the flight-deck area. Selvy was in the left-hand seat. Lights glowed on the panels, and switches were being thrown. The sun had made the cabin warm, and it smelled of new upholstery, sweat, and warm electronic components. Selvy and his aides were stripped to tee shirts.

"Ready to light up," Selvy told Lis.

"Good. What's the flight plan?"

"Just what we asked for. Depart to the west, swing out about twenty-five miles over the ocean, then turn northbound to flight level three-five and our demonstration maneuvers. Then east and south, coming back over the Bay area, south of Lodi, Stockton, and home."

Leaving the flight deck, Lis went back into the first-class cabin area, where a secretary assigned by Kelley Hemingway was stowing soft drinks in the galley compartments. He went on to the rear of the airplane, into the coach section. Of course this had all been checked earlier, but Lis did it partly to make doubly sure everything was right and partly because he enjoyed it. He loved this airplane.

The rear cabin was dim and quiet and warm, with the odor of plastics. The curving murals, beige carpeting, and red seats were perfect. Lis found nothing out of order.

Going back to the door and descent staircase at the head of First Class, he saw that Prince David, Lydia Baines, and about another dozen persons were waiting on the tarmac below. The prince had changed to a pale green jumpsuit and looked more like a race-car driver than a member of royalty.

Lis went down to meet them. "We're all set. You can board."

Lucian Derquet turned to the prince with obvious concern. "You are sure you wish to make the flight, Excellency?"

Prince David frowned and rubbed his forehead. "I think I am feeling better, Lucian."

Lydia explained to Lis, "The headache seems to be back, and getting worse."

"We can postpone the flight," Lis said.

"No, no," Prince David said quickly. He smiled. "I'll be fine."

They climbed the stairs and began arranging themselves in the cabins. The prince asked Lis if he could have a peek into the flight deck, and Lis obliged him. They stood behind the pilots, and the prince asked a number of sharp questions about control and instrument functions, showing no sign of the distress he had been demonstrating only moments earlier.

"Shall we fire it up?" Selvy asked.

"Yes," the prince said eagerly. "Can we stand here until we are ready to taxi, Mr. Lis?"

"I see no reason why not."

"Fantastic!"

Out over the canted nose of the Excalibur, a ground man waited, his ears encased in big red headphones. Hank Selvy signaled him that the brakes were set at PARK. The ground man acknowledged and twirled his hand, signaling to start the top engine.

"Ready to start number one," Selvy told the crew.

"Ready," the copilot said.

"Start switch on."

A faint whine came to them from the back of the aircraft, and a few needles stirred in gauges.

"Start valve is open."

"Pressure is fifteen. Pressure is twenty. Start lever."

Lights momentarily dimmed. The flight engineer reached overhead and flicked a toggle. Excalibur throbbed from end to end as the number-one engine caught hold and began to spin under its own power.

"Okay; generator-drive light is out."

"Roger; fuel flow good. Oil-pressure light is out."

"Forty per cent."

"Start switch off."

"Duct pressure normal."

"Okay, going to idle."

"Everything looks okay."

"Prepare to start number two."

Prince David's eyes shone. "The procedure is very much like Boeing airplanes. I could start this airplane!"

Lis put a hand on his shoulder. "We'd better get back and take our seats for takeoff."

"Yes, of course. How I would like to watch it all from up here!"

"Are you still going to want a try at the controls once we're at cruising level?"

"Yes! Of course!"

"I thought your headache might be too bad," Lis said, puzzled.

The prince frowned. "Oh. Yes. My headache. —Mr. Lis, when we get back on the ground, I want a few minutes alone with you if you can manage it."

"Certainly," Lis assured him, pressing him back out of the front area and into the galley in front of the first-class cabin.

Once in the passenger cabin with the others, the prince was much more subdued, again frowning and rubbing his head. This puzzled Lis, because there had been no symptoms on the flight deck. Was he so eager to pilot the plane that he was hiding genuine pain up there? It worried Lis a little.

Lydia Baines had arranged it so that she and the prince shared a front row of seats, with Lucian Derquet relegated to the row behind them. Lydia was charming and informative during the remainder of the engine runup procedures, and the prince smiled and replied for all the world like a man thoroughly fascinated but in some discomfort.

The exit door had been swung closed earlier, and with full engine operation, now the air conditioning was bringing the temperature down rapidly. A signal bonged overhead and the SEAT BELT and NO SMOKING signs flashed on. Lis took his seat across the aisle from Lydia and the prince. The engines advanced slightly, there was a gentle little jolt as the brakes were unlocked, and they were on the taxi. Heat waves shimmered off dun-colored grass choking cracks in the pavement as they moved along ponderously toward the far end of the landing strip. Lis caught snatches of conversation:

—From Lydia: "Of course, this is the standard interior, and custom work is quite possible. . . ."

—And from Derquet, to Janis Malone: ". . . have been said to exert as much influence in my country as your own Henry Kissinger so recently exerted here. However, my own view of myself is a humble one. . . ."

Then the conversations were drowned out by the groaning of brakes as the plane slowed and wheeled onto the end of the strip. The brakes locked after the turn was completed, and the engines smoothly advanced. After a brief, slightly vibrating test, the brakes slipped off and Excalibur began to roll.

The flight could not have gone better, from Lis's standpoint. Ten minutes out, they were over the ocean at an altitude of thirty thousand feet. Lis took Prince David forward, and a place was made for him in the copilot's chair. With Hank Selvy closely watching, the prince took the controls. The left wingtip dipped momentarily, a sure and traditional sign of tense nerves in the pilot, drawing the yoke down on that side, but then the prince grinned, heaved a deep breath, and flew well. Selvy guided him through a series of increasingly complex maneuvers.

"Fantastic!" he kept muttering like a child with a new toy. "So much power! Such quick aileron response!"

He kept the controls through the far turn in their course, and had to be coaxed to relinquish them as they neared the San Francisco Bay area. As he climbed out of the chair, he met Lis's eyes. "It is a docile and beautiful airplane, Mr. Lis."

"The more you fly it the better you like it," Lis said.

Prince David maneuvered into the tight aisle behind the flight engineer's position, and leaned his head closer to Lis so he could speak so low that he was hard to hear. "We must have more talks, my friend. I must be sure you understand the political situation in my country."

"Maybe when your headache is better," Lis said.

"The headache never existed. I only played that I had a headache, in case I need a good excuse to slip away from some of the terrible state formality of the dinner and reception tonight."

"If that's the case, why don't you just tell Lydia and Derquet that you don't want any part of it?"

The prince surprised him by being serious. "That is part of the politics you must come to understand. Lucian is a very powerful man. My mother, the Queen, has absolute power. But she listens to the cabinet, and there Lucian has great influence. . . . I am careful not to offend dear Lucian, my friend, and you should be also!"

"It sounds like selling Excalibur to Monravia may be more complex than we imagined."

"*That*, my friend, shows understanding! I myself prefer your airplane. I already know this. But we are going to have many difficult moments together, you and I, if we are to make a sale a reality!"

"You make it sound as if buying Excalibur is very important to you, and not just for its own sake," Lis probed.

The prince studied his face for an instant before replying, and then seemed to select his words carefully. "Until I become King, Lucian Derquet has great power and influence, as I have explained. The things I want . . . now, until I become King . . . must in effect be approved by dear Lucian."

"I see," Lis said.

It *was* more complex than it appeared on the surface, then. Derquet's influence depended upon the Queen. Perhaps a part of his game was to undermine the prince's ideas and projects subtly, trying to delay the day when the Queen would be ready to step aside and let the prince assume the crown. Perhaps, too, Derquet saw what Lis understood in a flash of intuition: when Prince David became King, Lucian Derquet's days in office would be numbered.

Excalibur, then, was more than an airplane in these negotiations. It was a symbol of power in a Monravian game within a game. And it seemed Monravia would order Excaliburs only if checkmate was called by Prince David.

23

Meanwhile, in New York City it was late afternoon, and Harold Zelmer stood in front of a camera shop across the street from the Transwestern Building. Traffic clogged the street, the fumes making Harold slightly nauseated. Sweat-soaked and hungry, his head aching dully from the constant din of the voices trying to speak to him from within, he nevertheless maintained a calm exterior so no one would take notice of him. This was vital to his operation.

For this was what it had now become, an operation of revenge and an example to the world that even giant corporations could not kill without paying for it.

The idea had grown slowly; it was now fully formed.

Harold had a hotel room, rented by the day, and had been moving forward slowly on his plan, changing and improving upon it as he progressed. Since the night when he first heard the voices clearly, a week or more ago, he had acted with the sole intent of learning all he could about Transwestern Airlines, the better to single out the person or persons on whom he would visit his vengeance.

Research had led him to Nolan Trenor, the vice-president who had been responsible (according to both *Newsweek* and *Fortune*) for TW's final decision to purchase Excalibur. Trenor, according to *Time*, was also considered the heir apparent to the TW presidency. So by getting Trenor, Harold would have not only revenge for the evil decision that had led to his mother's death; he would also deal Transwestern a mortal blow in terms of its executive plans for the future. Trenor was the ideal choice.

Since making this decision, and finding the new photograph that would aid identification this evening, Harold had been ferociously busy. He knew Nolan Trenor would leave the TW building, walk to nearby Grand Central, and get a commuter train. *Fortune.* He knew the city to the north where Trenor lived. *Newsweek.* He had even visited that city earlier today, leaving a rental car at the train station to facilitate following Trenor all the way to his home tonight. It had been a very difficult and busy day, but Harold was right on schedule with his plan.

Harold consulted his watch. It showed four fifty-nine. Nolan Trenor never left before 5 P.M. *Business Week.*

At four minutes after five, a tall, rather slender man carrying an attaché case hurried from the double glass doors of the Transwestern Building. Harold jerked to attention inside, because recognition was immediate, thanks to the new photograph. Even with dark glasses masking his eyes, Nolan Trenor was unmistakable.

As Harold had imagined he would, Trenor turned right and proceeded south on Madison. Harold left the storefront and walked south on his side of the street, paralleling Trenor. They crossed the next two intersections, and then Trenor crossed Madison at 43rd and walked past the façade of the Biltmore, toward the station. Harold followed, and within moments he was trailing his prey past gleaming silver commuter-train cars.

It was hot and stale. People jostled Harold, causing him to lose sight of Trenor for a few seconds. Cursing, Harold ran to catch up. He did so, and slowed down again, gasping for air through his teeth.

Mother had always said it was bad to breathe through your mouth. She said the nostrils filtered out germs but the person who breathed through his mouth gulped them all down. Well, no matter. Harold seriously doubted that he had time for any germs to take effect before he had his revenge.

After what seemed an interminable walk past one gritty silvery car after another, Nolan Trenor swung up into one of the commuter cars. Harold waited a few seconds, then swung up after him. He would risk riding in the same car, to be sure of continued surveillance.

Most of the seats in the coach were already occupied, and the air was dense with cigarette smoke. Harold saw Trenor take a chair toward the front, so he took one toward the back. The view down the aisle was perfect.

After a while the train jolted and began to move. It glided past the sides of other trains, the platform filled with people, and a row of pillars, and through a brick tunnel that seemed endless.

Gathering speed, the train finally emerged into fading daylight. Accelerating, it began to rock gently on the rails. Harold watched the passing panorama of Manhattan, trying to breathe through his nose.

Within minutes, the train followed an elevated right-of-way past playgrounds, expressways, gigantic rows of apartments, and narrow streets, past older, dirtier buildings, and then past the endless blocks of gaunt, black-and-red slums that were the warrens and burrows of the poor. Fighting a sense of claustrophobia, Harold Zelmer thought about his plan.

Just as Nolan Trenor was an ideal target for revenge within Transwestern, so there was a perfect person inside Hempstead Aviation, in far-off California. Harold had already located this man, too, and was studying about him in his spare time. As soon as Trenor had been eliminated, Harold would be ready for the next phase of his operation.

It was impossible to make everyone pay. But these two would stand for all. One on the East Coast, one on the West. Harold's revenge would span the continent. He liked that.

After completing his revenge, he did not know what he might do. He did not think he would ever return to St. Louis. He thought he might go work on a farm somewhere, or he might return to a city like New York and marry a chorus girl and become the president of a bank. He knew he could accomplish anything he set out to do. He had always known this. It was merely a question of making decisions. He could decide after the two men on his list were dead.

The commuter train slid northward in the gathering heat-haze of the evening. The terrain began to change again, trees and hills showing now. The train came to a small town after a while and stopped briefly to disgorge a few passengers, then went on. Harold looked out the window fitfully, seeing a highway and more trees and, once, a river.

In the front of the car, Nolan Trenor had taken some papers from a briefcase and was reading. Occasionally he would jot a note in a margin of a page with a gold fountain pen. Somehow the jotting with the gold pen infuriated Harold. It was so ruthless, the way Trenor jotted notes, probably making decisions to put other mothers on other defective airliners.

Less than an hour after it had ground out of Grand Central Station, the train changed its rocking momentum again, signaling another small town ahead. Harold had studied the line map, and knew this was where Nolan Trenor would depart.

Up ahead, Trenor closed his briefcase, straightened his tie, and peered out through the dirty window with what appeared to be anticipation. A slight smile touched his lips. Harold saw this and was thrilled. *He likes it here,* he thought. *That makes it the right place for his killing.*

The train came to a halt. Many men on the car got to their feet and moved toward the exits. Harold waited until Trenor had gotten off before joining the crowd.

Stepping off the train, he was struck by a breath of cooler, fresher air, a slight breeze that smelled faintly of flowers and living green things. There were trees everywhere and a small stone depot in immaculate repair and a small park with curved driveways and flowers. Beyond the park were some small buildings, the downtown area of the town.

Nolan Trenor had walked to his left after leaving the train, toward a curb area where a number of cars waited with engines running. Harold saw him walk to a dark blue Plymouth station wagon, open the passenger-side door, and get in. There was a silhouette of a woman—Mrs. Trenor—behind the wheel.

The cars were all held up momentarily while commuters boarded, and this gave Harold his chance to run across the street and into the park, where a small lot was reserved for renters who wished to leave their cars by the day or week. He knew exactly where his rented Pinto was, and went to it unerringly. He got the little motor started quickly, backed out, and was waiting at the head of his lane to pull out into traffic when the blue station wagon glided past his position.

He pulled in directly behind it.

At the far corner, nearer the business district, the station wagon turned left into traffic. But the woman behind the wheel seemed in no hurry, and Harold was able to keep up, pushing the Pinto hard.

After another block there was a traffic signal, but he got through on the amber to maintain a one-car-length gap between himself and his quarry.

The station wagon headed out of the small downtown section on a curving country road now, where the houses were well back from traffic and guarded by huge old trees and great walls of shrubbery. The road became narrower after another little while, and for a mile or so a third car got in between Harold and the station wagon but presented no problem and soon turned off.

Five minutes later, the right-turn signal of the station wagon began blinking, Harold slowed and watched it turn off into a driveway flanked by a rock wall. There was a large two-story house back among the trees on a hillside.

Harold drove on past the driveway. There was another car close behind him, and it honked irritably when he pulled off onto the narrow gravel shoulder without a signal. Shooting the other driver the finger, Harold dug in the glove box and took out a pair of small, folding binoculars. Sliding across to the right-hand seat for a better view, he rolled the Pinto window down and trained the glasses on the distant house on the hill.

The house was larger than he had first estimated, with steeply slanted roofs, multiple wings, and a bricked front-driveway area leading to a large porch with round pillars. As Harold watched, the station wagon pulled up in front and Nolan Trenor got out. His wife, a handsome woman with graying hair, got out on the other side. Together the couple walked up the steps toward the front door. The door opened and a younger couple came out to greet them. There were also two small children, who ran to the Trenors. Nolan Trenor picked up the little girl and held her over his head. Harold could see his grin.

Grandchildren, Harold thought with a fierce burst of pleasure. Nolan Trenor's daughter or son. And grandchildren. A fine house, a handsome wife, a son or daughter, grandchildren.

This made Harold very happy. It would have been terrible to find his prey was a sour old man to whom death might be a blessing.

Harold continued watching until they had all gone into the house. Then he put his glasses away and slowly drove on up the road, checking out the neighborhood. There were other houses fairly nearby. All had large lawns, handsome gardens. One or the other would need temporary yard help, he thought, with summer coming on. He would enjoy working in the out of doors for a few days or even weeks while he watched the Trenor house and perfected the plan for Nolan Trenor.

PART TWO

1

BOARD SCHEDULES AUGUST HEARING
IN JETLINER CRASH

New York to Be the Site

NEW YORK—Public hearing into the May crash of a Transwestern Airlines "Excalibur" which carried 199 persons to their deaths will be held in New York City in August, the National Transportation Safety Board announced here today.

The public hearings, scheduled to run for two days, are designed to adduce evidence in the crash at Kennedy International Airport, it was stated by Gen. (Ret.) Burkham Collins, director of the NTSB.

Collins acknowledged in a press conference at the downtown Hilton Hotel, where he made the hearing announcement, that strong public pressure and persistent reports of mystery surrounding the Kennedy crash were among motivating factors for holding the hearings somewhat earlier than is the practice in most major disasters of this kind.

"It may be well into next year before a formal report is issued," Collins added, "but in view of intense interest in this crash, we want to have all the known facts presented in an orderly manner according to normal procedures.

One hundred and ninety-two passengers and a crew of seven died in the evening crash, which saw an Excalibur jetliner apparently lose control and dive into the ground just short of Kennedy's Runway 4-R.

It was the first mishap for the Excalibur, a radical innovation in commercial aircraft featuring a wing that has a surface whose texture can be changed to add extra flying ability at low speeds. Excalibur was introduced into commercial operation late last year after the longest and most comprehensive testing program ever undertaken by the FAA, which certificates all new aircraft.

During NTSB public hearings of the kind announced for next month, the Board calls all witnesses and brings out all testimony, including technological studies and reports, bearing on the accident involved. The hearing does not preclude later findings, and delay of the formal report is normal.

Reaction to the NTSB announcement was quick in Washington.

One of the Board's strongest critics in the Excalibur case, Senator Johnson Davis (D-Miss.), said he was pleased.

"If Excalibur is an unsafe aircraft," Senator Davis said, "the public has a right to know the facts at once. There should be no delays when safety is involved."

Senator James West (R-Calif.), the state where Excalibur manufacturer Hempstead Aviation Co. is headquartered, commented, "A prompt public hearing should clear the air and remove vicious rumors about the world's safest airliner."

Mrs. Lydia Baines, chairman of Hempstead, issued a statement saying the company has co-operated fully with the NTSB and expects Excalibur to be cleared.

Mrs. Baines's husband, Jason Baines, formerly president of Hempstead, was killed in the Kennedy crash.

Officials at Transwestern Airlines were not immediately available for comment.

"We're running out of time," Ken Lis told Barton MacIvor and Hank Selvy. "We've *got* to find something ourselves, or those public hearings will leave an air of mystery that can destroy all hopes for future sales."

"They can't hurt the aeroplane," Barton MacIvor said exhaling a cloud of smoke that curled over Lis's desk. "The aeroplane has no faults."

"We've simply got to intensify our testing. Otherwise the hearings could ruin us."

Hank Selvy looked skeptical. "We've got two flights laid on this week already."

"I want at least five flights."

"Impossible! We can't change test gear and plan the tests that fast!"

"Don't tell me what we can or can't do," Lis shot back. "In a matter of a few weeks, the NTSB is going to have those hearings. If we aren't a lot more ready than we appear now, we'll have *had* it."

"We might test forever and never get the right combination of circumstances that made that TW flight go in."

"God damn it, Hank, I don't want to hear any of that kind of talk! Lay on the extra flights. And I want you to start taking her right through the stall, and not only in level flight but in accelerated-maneuver stalls, too."

"That's a lot more risky—"

"I know that. We don't have a choice any more."

MacIvor relighted his pipe in a new cloud of dense smoke. "I been thinkin'."

Whenever he said something like that, Lis listened. "Yes, Pappy?"

"I think we ought to be gettin' the simulator boys to rig up some special effects, a special film. Everything they can come oop with to cause visual disorientation."

"Simulating what?" Lis asked.

"An approach to Kennedy's 4-Right."

"Pappy, we decided at the outset that talk of pilot error was bullshit. Something made that plane crash, and it wasn't the pilot."

"We're gettin' short of time, lad," MacIvor said. "You pointed that oot yerself. Aw right, then. If we can't find anything else, had we not better be ready to try to show it *could've* been pilot error?"

Lis hesitated. He did not like the suggestion, but there was so little time now . . . so little time. "All right," he said. "We'll add that program to the testing too. At this point we can't overlook anything."

In Washington, meanwhile, investigator Jace Mattingly had finally yielded to nagging desire and called Nell Emerson. Contacted at the lawyer's office where she worked, the widow first sounded reluctant to meet him but finally agreed when he insisted that it related directly to the crash probe.

The attorney's office was in a suburban shopping and business mall, and Mattingly met her near a cafeteria shortly after noon. His throat ached when he first spied her, lovely and trim, like chocolate ice cream in her white summer dress. He told himself this was business, and tried to be formal. She shook hands but was cool. They went through the cafeteria line, and she took only coffee, while he selected a chicken-salad sandwich and iced tea, and even at that she was quick to have her change in hand to deny him the pleasure of paying for what she had chosen.

They found a table off to one side and sat down facing one another. She was very much in control of herself and heartbreakingly beautiful.

"I thank you for seeing me," Mattingly said.

"I assume it relates to the story in the newspaper," she said putting cream in her coffee.

"The hearings will be difficult," Mattingly said. "You'll be asked to appear, and you ought to be warned how they may proceed."

"Warned?" Her eyes were suspicious.

"They're working up a deeper psychological profile on members of the crew. I can see by your face that you're already guessing what that means. You're right. I'm sorry. But they haven't found a thing —*we* haven't found a thing—that really explains the crash."

"So they're going back to the possibility of pilot error?"

"It was always a possibility."

"You told me you didn't believe it."

"I still don't."

"Then, why a new psychological profile? You lied to me!"

"I *didn't* lie to you. The fact is that I don't run the agency. There's pressure. Every aspect has to be considered. I don't like it, but I can't really say they're 100 per cent wrong in wanting every base touched."

"And this is why you had to see me, to tell me?"

"Yes."

She tilted her head to look at the way he was beginning to learn signaled new suspicion. "Why couldn't you say it on the phone?"

"I . . . didn't think that was proper."

Her eyes narrowed. "Perhaps I shouldn't say this, but I think there's something more involved. I think you grabbed any excuse. . . . Am I wrong?"

Mattingly met her eyes and knew he was defenseless. "Not entirely."

"Mr. Mattingly." She was irritated, very much under control. "It may be that in your line of work you find many women impressed by your high position, the glamour, and so on. My marriage was a very happy one. My . . . grief . . . is still very much with me. I resent subterfuge. I will not see you again, and if you try to bother me—"

"I won't," Mattingly cut in. "But you don't have to treat me like that, lady. I'm not a Lothario, going around and chasing women all the time. I wanted to tell you this in person, not over the phone. I wanted to *help*, if there's any way I could. Sure I wanted to see you again . . . for other reasons too. But I haven't said anything out of line. I haven't done anything to you to give you call to treat me like some slum nigger."

She studied him for a moment. "I'm sorry," she said. "It's just the . . . stress. You're right. I apologize."

Mattingly grinned at her through the anger. "And then you have only coffee, so I have to handle this crummy chicken-salad by myself."

"Your iced tea looks pretty bad, too. I'd say you really struck out on all counts this time, Mr. Mattingly."

"Yeah. You don't know the half of it. I came through the line without getting any mayonnaise, too. Without mayonnaise I don't know if I can get this thing down."

Nell glanced over the surface of the table, then reached for a small white bowl in the center, with the napkins and sugar and salt and pepper. She raised the lid of the container and then looked up at Mattingly.

He mumbled. "Good God! Do you suppose all those cafeterias where I've eaten all those dry chicken-salad sandwiches had mayonnaise in a container like that right in front of me?"

She smiled. "Probably."

"The mighty, trained investigator," he said glumly, shoveling mayonnaise onto half the sandwich. "I hate these things."

"Why do you eat them?"

He patted his stomach. "There are only so many types of food it will accept."

"You have an ulcer?"

"Well, not quite."

"You shouldn't smoke so much," she said, eying the smoking butt in the ashtray.

"Tell my nerves."

"If this job makes you that nervous, you should quit."

"And do what?"

The question surprised her. "I don't know—"

"No," he said. "This is my meal ticket. I'm *good* at this. I'm sticking."

"Even if it gives you ulcers."

He almost replied jokingly, in the same vein, but something about her eyes, and the wary look in them, broke through. He leaned toward her, all his intensity coming out. "Look. I just wanted you to know the score. I'll do everything I can to help you, but some of those psychologists are probably going to say bad things about all the crew. That's what they're paid for, to prove everybody is nuts. And when they question you, they'll poke around in your private life, try to get you to hint that your husband was . . . nervous . . . or unstable in some way. That's all I wanted to say. I *could* have said it on the phone. I'm sorry."

She nodded, a slight smile on her lips. "I think you're an extraordinary person, do you know that? And I'm sorry for what I said earlier. We managed to get off on the worst foot today, didn't we."

Mattingly bit into the sandwich. "Yeah. But the mayonnaise makes all the difference."

And a little later, in California, it became clear to Harvey Coughlin that the NTSB announcement had had its effect on Lydia Baines, too.

"Harvey," she told him on the telephone, her voice as brisk as metal against metal, "I want you back in Washington by this evening."

Harvey glanced at his Pulsar. It showed eight-forty, and he was just having his morning coffee at his desk. "Has something gone wrong, Lydia?"

"The opposite," she snapped. "*Nothing* has happened. And that's what's wrong."

"Well, Lydia, the last hearing postponed action for a while, and there was a chance they might have killed our line item entirely—"

"Now, however," she broke in crisply, "the setting of a date for the Excalibur hearing could have a detrimental effect on the company's entire image. Just having the hearing scheduled a month from now could dim our image with some of those jackasses on that committee. So we have to intensify our efforts to get Eagle out of that committee and headed for the floor."

"I don't know how we can accomplish that," Harvey admitted.

"I do. I've convinced Senator Johns to take a more active role. He's having a party at his home tonight. If you can get there in time, he can help you meet some influential people who have been avoiding you. Including Senator Boudoin."

Generally considered one of the three most powerful men in the Senate, D. L. Boudoin had twice been his party's candidate for President. Harvey had not gotten past his second administrative assistant. "That would be great, Lydia! I've always said, if I can talk to a man, with my arm over his shoulder—"

"Get on the next plane," Lydia said. "Contact Matt Johns the moment you land. It's time for you to *push*, Harvey. You understand me?"

"I understand," he said.

After the connection had been broken and he had his secretary making a call about the next flight east, Harvey had to admit to himself, however, that he understood the need to push but not the precise way he might do the pushing. What was he to do? Threaten? Cajole? Try to intimidate? Try to wheedle? Washington infighting continued to baffle him.

Whatever was necessary, he told himself, he would do.

With a sense of having entered a new phase, he looked up as his secretary walked into the office.

"Mr. Coughlin, there's a flight in about ninety minutes, but I don't think you can make it to the airport."

"Call Operations," he ordered. "I want the Learjet to be ready in fifteen minutes. My personal authorization."

The woman stared, wide-eyed. "I don't know if the crew can be ready to fly you to San Francisco that fast, sir—"

"They'll be ready," Harvey said, "because I'm ordering it. And they aren't flying me to San Francisco. We're going direct to Washington, so tell them to get cracking on a flight plan."

175

The secretary hurried out, wobbling on high heels. Harvey smiled to himself. The corporate jet had been used little of late, as economies were practiced. But there would be no compromises now. Not with this mission. He could not fail. Lydia's tone had made that clear.

2

Senator Matthew Johns's home was in a fashionable section of a Washington suburb, an old brick mansion behind heavy oak trees that virtually masked it from view from the street. A large number of cars were already in the long, curving driveway when Harvey Coughlin got out of his taxi at nine thirty-five that night, an hour he devoutly hoped was proper—neither too early nor too late.

Walking up onto the front porch, he heard the music of a small combo playing somewhere back in the house. There was a rumble of many voices and the inevitable tinkling of glasses and other party sounds. Harvey pressed the doorbell button and was escorted into a blazing foyer by a butler—a white man.

"Your name, sir?"

"Harvey Coughlin."

"Yes, sir. Will you wait a moment, please? The senator wished to be notified as soon as you arrived."

Harvey waited, able to see across the large empty foyer to double doorways leading into the first of probably several lighted rooms. This first one was crowded with people, many of them surprisingly young. He recognized the youthful lawyer types and the dazzlingly pretty career girls they tended to bring to parties such as this. Harvey felt very much alone, and even more worried about his mission.

He had arrived in Washington without a change of clothing, due to his hasty departure in California, and no idea of precisely what he was going to do to speed up the movement of Eagle out of committee. A trip to the hotel men's store had solved the first problem, but a call to Matthew Johns's office had not done anything about the second.

"Harvey," Johns had told him briefly, "I'm between roll-call votes and I only have a minute. You can be at my home tonight?"

"Yes."

"Excellent. I'll fill you in there. I've made some plans. Every move is crucial now, Harvey!" And with that, the connection had been broken.

Waiting now, Harvey could only hope that the plan was a good one, as promised, and that he could carry it out. The flight in, and rushing through this alien city, had gnawed at his synthetic confidence. *Could* he get Eagle out of committee? He did not know. He was worried.

The servant came back followed by Matthew Johns, a drink in his hand. The black senator wore tight dark trousers and a flaming silk shirt open halfway down his chest to reveal a luxuriant growth of curly black hair and a collection of heavy medallions on separate gold chains. He shook hands and grinned broadly as he drew Harvey off to one side. "Wonderful you could come, Harvey!" Then his grin died as they moved out of view of the guests in the adjoining room. "All right, my friend. Your timing is good."

"I didn't know how late I should be—" Harvey began.

"There are three people here who can help us, if you handle them right," Johns said. "One is Black Jack Mallory, another is Jake Steinell, and the third, of course, is Boudoin. Steinell is already here. The others will be here shortly. I want to introduce you to a lot of people, but you ought to zero in on those three."

"I've already talked with General Mallory a number of times," Harvey said, sweat trickling down under his collar. "He supports Eagle—"

"Yes, but some of those think-tank people over there have been pushing air-to-air as a priority and he's wavering. Do you think you can pump some confidence in Eagle back into him? We need all the backing we can muster across the river."

"I'll certainly try," Harvey said, relieved to hear a familiar task. "The general and I talk the same language; I can certainly talk with him man to man."

"Excellent. Now. Jake Steinell is a nationally syndicated columnist, and I'm sure you recognize the name."

"Of course," Harvey said. "But I fail to see how my talking with him could—"

Johns silenced him with an upheld index finger. "It's the way the game is played, Harvey. If you want something passed, sometimes the best way to convince those on the fence is to get word out that the thing is sure to pass with or without them. The bandwagon philosophy. So what I want you to do is butter up Steinell a little. Shouldn't be hard, he's an arrogant little bastard. Then let it slip that you think Eagle is in the bag and approval should be forthcoming."

"That's all?" Harvey asked. "It sounds too easy."

"Steinell is sharp. You have to handle it just right or he'll know he's being conned. But it's worth a try even if it *won't* be easy."

"All right," Harvey said. "But what about Boudoin? What can I possibly say to enlist his help? I *know* he's close to Senator Sweet, who runs the committee. But how can I possibly influence a man like Boudoin to put in a good word for us with a man like Sweet? This sort of thing—"

Johns silenced him with a hand on his shoulder this time. "I trust you to find some way, Harvey. I guarantee that I'll get you a few minutes with him. That's as much as I can do. Just don't blow it."

"I'll do my . . . best."

"All right. Now there's someone else I want you to meet. Her name is Dena Forbes, and I think you'll find her company most enjoyable. You don't have any objection to spending part of the evening with the sexiest blonde in the house, do you?" Johns grinned as he asked.

"What for?" Harvey blurted. "I mean—"

"Both Black Jack and Steinell are skirt chasers," Johns said. "Having Dena by your side is going to help you get their attention, believe me. She works in my office, and would like to meet you anyway. I think it's a case of hero worship. So she's your date for the evening, unless you object."

Harvey paused only an instant, aware of the quickening of his pulse. "I don't object. Far from it. I—"

"Come on, then," Johns said, taking his arm.

Feeling that he was being propelled into some adventure beyond his control, Harvey followed the senator into the first party room. Johns made a beeline directly across it and into the second, where an even larger crowd milled. Here was the combo, and a large bar in one corner, and patio doors open on a large, dimly lighted interior garden.

Following Johns across this room, Harvey saw ahead of them a group of young people, three of the energetic lawyer types and two girls, both very pretty. The blonde, he noticed, was probably the most attractive young woman he had yet encountered there, medium height, her black cocktail dress baring creamily sun-tanned shoulders. She turned at Johns's approach and smiled, a pink smile that lighted her wide-set eyes. Harvey held his breath. This was too good to be true!

It was true. Johns drew the girl away from the others, and Harvey found himself facing her with a sense of shocked pleasure.

"Dena," Johns said, "I want you to meet a very good friend of mine, Harvey Coughlin. Harvey, this is Dena."

She smiled broadly and extended a small, warm hand. Her touch sent a small, electric excitement through Harvey. At close range she was exquisite, with remarkable green eyes, lips that glistened under her pink lipstick, golden-tanned breasts partly revealed by the low neck of her dress. Her scent reached him, adding to his sense of being captivated.

"Hello, Mr. Coughlin," she said. She had a rather low, musical voice. "I've seen you on television, and this is a real pleasure."

He held her hand for an instant. "The name is Harvey, Dena, and the pleasure is all mine. I understand you work for the senator?"

"Yes." She smiled, making eyes at Johns. "And he's a slave driver." Then she put her hand to her mouth in genuine chagrin. "Oh, my God! I'm sorry! That was a stupid thing to say!"

Johns held his smile, seemingly unconcerned. "When you say something like that because you really forgot race, Dena, the *last* thing you want to be is sorry. So forget it." The senator looked over the crowd. "I see some other people I have to greet. If you two will stay put for a minute or two, I'll get right back and we'll see if we can't start some wheels moving."

Dena Forbes watched him walk into the milling group nearby. Her pretty forehead wrinkled. "That really was a dumb thing for me to say. I guess I'll never learn how to handle myself."

Harvey grinned down at her. Her head came to his chin, and in the back of his mind was a sexual fantasy that he knew was impossible. "Dena, I think the senator was sincere. It was an innocent remark."

She sighed. "He's an *awfully* nice guy, isn't he?"

Harvey wondered, and was jealous. "Yes, he certainly is."

"I hope I can help you tonight," she said, swinging those amazing eyes back to him. "I hope I don't goof."

"You won't goof, Dena. I just need to have some words with a few people who might be able to, ah, help me with a little project. Having you with me will make it seem less like I'm here only for the purpose of doing business, although—" Harvey hesitated, then plunged ahead with a feeling of being reckless—"although how anyone in his right mind could actually imagine that a beautiful young girl like you might actually be on a date with a staid old businessman like me—"

"Staid?" She smiled. "Old?" She looked him up and down. "We hardly look like May and November to me."

"Well," he said, flattered, "you know what I mean. Every man in here is covertly watching you."

"How very nice of you to say that!"

"It's true."

She tilted her head, studying him. "But you're the famous one. If anyone is out of their league here, it's me."

"Nonsense. I might have had some . . . notoriety once. But that's long ago, Dena."

"When the senator told me about your plans to be here tonight, I knew your name at once. Then I looked you up. Now I know *all* about you. All the medals and everything. You're still a *hero* in this country!"

Harvey could not restrain his grin of pleasure. "I think you're overstating by about a mile. But you're awfully good for an old fogey's morale."

"I hope we get a chance to talk later. I mean *really* talk. There are so many things I want to ask you."

Harvey hesitated, not knowing what to say in the face of this exciting stroke of good luck. Before he could formulate a reply, he saw Matthew Johns pressing back through the throng to join them.

"Okay," Johns said. "Those obligations are taken care of. The general is just arriving, and I understand D.L. is on the way. In the meantime, there are some other people I want to be sure you meet. Come on."

With Dena Forbes close by his side, Harvey was led across the room and into the next, where more partygoers were clustered. Johns introduced him and Dena to a pair of congressmen and a Pentagon aide whose name Harvey did not catch. They stood and talked for a few moments, and the men clearly were fascinated with Dena, whose dimples showed as she parried their wit. Harvey saw what an asset she could be to any man in a social situation such as this one, and his admiration for her increased in another quantum jump.

In another moment or two, Johns was leading them away again. "Patten, the fat one we just talked with, is on Ways and Means," he said softly. "You might remember him. A courtesy call could possibly do us some good."

"I'll remember," Harvey said. "And the other representative's name was Johnson?"

"He's nobody. Forget him."

"Where are we going now?"

"I'm looking for Steinell."

Harvey did not relish the prospect of meeting the syndicated columnist, but having Dena beside him bolstered his confidence. Johns had said that an item in the Steinell column about Eagle might be helpful. Harvey thought he could handle that sort of plant. And even if he hadn't been sure that it was a good ploy, he reminded himself, there had been no uncertainty in how Lydia had told him to put himself in Johns's hands.

In the next room, they found the newspaper columnist standing alone near a fireplace. He was a lanky man, not as old as Harvey had expected, and with a sparse black beard. His eyes seemed to X-ray Harvey as Johns made the introductions, and he had only a nod for Dena Forbes.

"Coughlin," Steinell said as they shook hands. "That would be Hempstead Aviation, correct?"

Before Harvey could react, Johns said, "Can I trust you alone a few minutes with the bionic brain, here? I have to see about recent guests."

"I'll take good care of him, Matt," Steinell grinned.

"Just don't tell the man anything," Johns told Harvey with mock nervousness. "He never takes a note but he has a tape recorder inside his skull. Dena, you protect Harvey, okay?"

"How," Steinell asked innocently, "could there be any news in Mr. Coughlin? Hempstead Aviation . . . Excalibur . . . Senator Peering is at this party and his committee oversees the NTSB, which is investigating the Excalibur crash in New York. . . . What could anyone make of that?"

Johns winced and tapped his forehead meaningfully. "You see what I meant, Harvey? Bionic." Shaking his head, he moved away through the crowd.

"Quite a man," Steinell said following Johns with his eyes.

"Are you good friends?" Harvey asked.

Steinell appeared sincerely surprised. "Are you kidding? He hates my ass. But he knows how I like to dig for information. If he didn't invite me to his parties, I'd get one of my associates to come anyway, under some cover. This way he can keep an eye on me and hope to neutralize my effectiveness."

Harvey chuckled dutifully. "Of course you're kidding me. There must be an adversary relationship, but I knew he spoke highly of you."

"He also knows," Steinell bit off, "that I'd gut him or anyone else if it meant a story." Seeing Harvey's surprised expression, he softened his tone. "You might as well know me for what I am, my friend, and be warned. But hell. I'm not on duty tonight, and we can be thankful the weather abated, anyway, can't we? Did you ever experience muggy heat like we had here yesterday?"

"I heard it was very bad," Harvey said.

"You weren't in town?"

"I arrived today."

"Oh, sure." Steinell craned his neck. "Here comes General Mallory. Is that his mistress with him?"

Harvey spotted his old friend and the striking young redhead at his side. "I wouldn't know," he replied tensely.

"I thought you two were old friends."

"Well, you might say we are. But I don't know anything about his personal life."

"Seen him on this visit yet?"

"No," Harvey said, resenting the prying.

Steinell sensed it. "Sorry. I seem to probe for information even when I don't have any intention of doing so. Old habit, I guess. Listen. Let me ask you another question, but no ulterior motive, I assure you!—Do you enjoy good music?"

"Yes," Harvey said. "Why do you ask that?"

"There's that big concert next Monday night. I have a couple of comps for it that I'm not going to be able to use. Would you like me to send them around to your hotel?" He turned to Dena Forbes. "What do you think, Dena?"

Harvey said quickly, "I doubt that I'll be in town that long. And Miss Forbes and I are . . . only casual acquaintances."

"Too bad," Steinell said, smiling at Dena. "On both counts. Well, I've got another offer, then. Thursday night. I've got some useless theater tickets. Do you like theater, Dena?"

"Oh, I love it," she said enthusiastically.

Harvey looked down at her as she turned, her eyes questioning. He saw what she was asking. *She would go with him if he asked*. This rocked him.

He told Steinell as calmly as possible, "Theater tickets might be very nice if they're really about to go to waste."

"Sure." The reporter took out a small notebook and pen. "I'll send them around to your hotel. Where are you staying?"

Harvey told him.

"Done," Steinell said. "And for God's sake don't think about it later and get all paranoid about how I'm trying to butter you up to get a story out of you. I know you're here to sell Eagle, above and beyond anything else, and I intend to cover that story anyway. Tell me this, though: do you really think you have a chance to break that log jam in the committee and get the Eagle appropriation out onto the floor where it might have a chance?"

"Oh, yes," Harvey said carefully. "I'm very encouraged about the prospects at the moment."

"The committee is split badly. You feel things are moving your way?"

"Yes, definitely. The latest developments on the international front—the stories about more powerful Soviet lasers, and so on, are bound to affect thinking here in Washington. And my reception everywhere has been very thoughtful and positive. I find that once I tell the real facts about the Eagle system, most opposition tends to vanish right away."

Steinell cocked his head. "What do you do about Cliff Sweet? He runs that committee with an iron hand. And a liberal like Sweet is not going to change his mind. With the chairman against you, how do you get the thing to a vote in committee?"

Harvey smiled at him, aware of sweat dripping from his nose. He had to say this right, and be very clever. "Senator Sweet is one of the finest men in Congress, in my opinion. I haven't yet visited with him personally, but I hope to do so. I believe that once I've had a chance to tell the Eagle story, things will go our way. This is bigger than a question of liberalism versus conservatism, or Democrat versus Republican. This is a simple question of keeping America strong and secure."

Steinell nodded. "Okay. Good luck to you." He jotted a line in his notebook and put it away. "Hey, there's the great congresswoman herself. Harriet. Have you met her yet, pal? Dena?"

"No," Harvey admitted, and Dena likewise shook her head.

"Come on, then."

Having done well, Harvey relaxed as he and Dena followed the columnist across the room to the point where a large and portly woman was regaling several other representatives with some long story. Everyone was grinning. Harriet Tinker was in good form.

As she saw Steinell approaching, however, she stopped and registered mock horror. "My gawd," she bawled. "Here comes the press. Hide the jewels and silverware, everyone!"

"Harriet, you sweet thing." Steinell kissed her on the cheek.

"Chauvinist," she growled.

"Harriet, let me present a new friend of mine, Harvey Coughlin."

The congresswoman extended her right hand and began mangling Harvey's fingers. "Coughlin . . . Coughlin. Oh, sure. The Eagle hearings. You testified for the manufacturer."

"Exactly how far I got," Steinell said. "Now, bore in, baby, and find out for me what he's doing in Washington this time."

Harriet Tinker ignored him. "The Eagle is a good system, Mr. Coughlin. I hope some of my rock-headed colleagues figure that out before adjournment."

"You know the Eagle system?"

"There isn't a hell of a lot that escapes me, friend. Tell me: what do you think of the prospects for getting it out of Sweet's committee and onto the floor? We've got the damned votes on the floor."

Harvey almost stammered, pleased and flustered to be asked an opinion by this famous woman. "I don't really know what the chances are," he said. "That's one of the reasons I'm here—to try to find out."

"I'll tell you one damned thing," Harriet Tinker added. "I'd a lot rather send a sophisticated missile out to fight my wars than send the poor blacks and chicanos and white trash. I'm in favor of push-button warfare and I don't care who knows it."

"Hear, hear," Steinell said and elaborately yawned.

"Prick," Harriet Tinker said, but she grinned.

Steinell patted Harvey's shoulder. "I need to circulate, since I'm obviously not going to get any news out of you people. See you later."

"Right," Harvey said and watched the reporter amble across the room. Then he turned back to Harriet Tinker's group.

"Watch that guy, Mr. Coughlin," one of the men said.

"He seems friendly enough," Harvey said.

"He's a gold-plated bastard," Harriet Tinker told him seriously. "I sort of like him, but I knew a hangman I liked once too. He's had recorders under half the illicit beds in Washington. He'd steal the gold outta your teeth. Hell, he'd steal porcelain."

"And," one of the men added grimly, "half the time, you don't know what he's really looking for. He's a master of indirection."

Harvey smiled more broadly, feeling better now. "Well, he certainly didn't get anything out of me."

"You *hope*," Harriet Tinker said. Then she brightened. "Which reminds me of a story I heard the other day, gents. There was a new committee being formed, see, and . . ."

Harvey, however, did not hear the anecdote. In the past few seconds he had had a lightning-bolt self-discovery. As he assured these people that Jake Steinell had gotten nothing from him, he had suddenly had a mental review flash through his mind, and he now realized with sickening clarity what had happened.

In a few seemingly casual moments, all Steinell had learned was

—that Harvey was to be in Washington less than a week,

—that he had just arrived today,

—that he was staying at the Sheraton,

—that he knew General Mallory,

—that he had not previously met Harriet Tinker, and

—that he was here to look into the vote situation on Eagle.

All he knew, in other words, was *virtually everything Harvey knew*.

Standing there, seeing this, Harvey felt mounting humiliation and worry. Had he let anything slip that could be damaging? Had he—instead of using Steinell—been used?

Dena was frowning at him in concern. She put her hand lightly on his arm. "What is it?" she asked softly.

Harvey moved away from the Harriet Tinker group, and to a deserted area near the wall. He looked down at Dena Forbes's obviously concerned expression and slowly took in a deep breath. "Nothing, I suppose," he said. And he hoped that was true.

For the next few minutes, they chatted alone. Dena prattled on about her year in Washington and how fortunate she was to have a job with someone as important as Matthew Johns. She pointed out a few newcomers to the party, which seemed to be growing all the time and changing personnel; clearly she was fascinated with Washington power and had done her homework. As they talked, Harvey relaxed again, feeling her spell. He wondered if there could be any way possible that he might get her out of there and somewhere alone. It seemed a forlorn dream, but it was constantly in his mind.

General Black Jack Mallory walked close by, spied Harvey, and came over. The woman with him was stunning, a statuesque brunette of perhaps twenty-five, and clearly, as Steinell had suggested, the general's mistress. Harvey wondered how a man of such fame could openly have a younger woman this way. He thought of his own dull wife. He was very thankful that Dena was beside him. Mallory, he realized, probably assumed that *they*—it was very nice indeed.

After speaking with Mallory for a few minutes and promising to visit his office the next day, Harvey guided Dena away and to another area where they could continue talking alone. He thought he had done well on his assignment tonight. Boudoin, he thought, was not going to appear.

It was just at that point, when he was relaxing and turning all his attention to Dena, that Matthew Johns sought him out again.

This time, Johns was not alone. Beside him was the tall, patrician man whose face would have been instantly recognized by most adult citizens of the nation.

"Harvey," Matthew Johns said, "I have a friend I want you to meet. This is Senator D. L. Boudoin."

3

D. L. Boudoin was not as tall as Harvey Coughlin had somehow imagined. Harvey realized that the years of public exposure had invested the man with an assumed stature that did not actually exist. And yet the senator was no less impressive for that; handsome, with the bearing of a man accustomed to getting his way, he fairly reeked of power.

Harvey introduced Dena. D. L. Boudoin eyed her appreciatively, then returned his eyes to Harvey. "It's a pleasure, Harvey. Of course I've known of you for many years. That was a great feat of courage at Inchon."

Harvey felt a moment's stab of irritation. He did not regret the few hours when something almost beyond himself had allowed him to lead an attack against impossible odds, and win. But would there never be a moment when he topped that day, so long ago? Would he always be recognized for what he had done, rather than for what he now was?

He said, "It was long ago, Senator. The pleasure is mine."

"I caught some of the Eagle hearings on the tube recently. You handled yourself well. Are you back now to try to build more support for that?"

The truth was the best policy. "Yes, I am. And very frankly, sir, I need to have a few words with you on the subject."

Boudoin nodded. "Fine. I'm very interested in hearing what you have to say. Of course, with my aviation background, I'm also interested in Excalibur. Tell me: do you have any inkling what really went wrong at Kennedy?"

Harvey hid his irritation. "No, sir, I don't. But we have confidence in our aircraft. I personally believe it was pilot error."

"I see." Boudoin glanced around, then at Matthew Johns. "I wonder where we might have a chat. I have to be brief, unfortunately—"

"How about the garden?" Johns asked, inclining his head toward the open glass doors. "It doesn't look like anyone is out there at the moment."

"Satisfactory?" Boudoin asked.

"Of course," Harvey said.

Boudoin smiled at Dena. "If the lady will excuse us?"

Harvey followed the senator across the room, agonizing when he paused a moment to speak to someone else. Then they went outside together, as if for a casual breath of air. The interior patio was densely foliaged, and lights from the house did not penetrate deeply. Boudoin followed a narrow brick walk; Harvey followed, hearing the faint tinkling of water. In a moment they were at a small pool with an artificial waterfall. It was quite dim there, and Boudoin was little more than a shadow. Harvey could see no one else.

"So?" Boudoin said, facing him.

Harvey decided to be bold. "Senator, the Eagle is a fine system, and many of us believe it's vital to America's defense through the eighties. We are working hard to get it out of committee, but a word from you in the right ears could have a profound effect in helping us."

"Well, that's direct. I like that."

"I believe in being direct." Harvey hoped his laugh did not sound hollow. "I'm just a country boy who doesn't know how to act devious."

"And you think that the right words from me might spring Eagle out of Cliff Sweet's committee with a do-pass recommendation?"

"At this point, Senator, we would settle for having it reported out in a neutral fashion and let it stand or fall in a general vote on its merits."

Boudoin was watching him closely in the gloom. "With Excalibur in some trouble, moving right along on Eagle becomes much more vital to a firm the size of yours, does it not?"

"I won't try to kid you, Senator. Yes."

The senator sighed. "So many people want so many things from me, Harvey."

"Eagle is vital to defense, sir."

"I think that's an exaggeration. I think we need Eagle about as badly as we need another Watergate, to be candid about it. What's your answer to that?"

Harvey swallowed. "I disagree, sir, and I have figures—"

"Anyone can make figures prove anything."

Boudoin's voice was hardening. Harvey knew he had to take more desperate measures. He groped mentally. "Even if you were correct, sir," he said, "which I cannot concede, let's be hardheaded realists here. There will be a new missile system within the next two or three years. We think—"

"Why do you feel so sure of that?" Boudoin cut in quietly.

"The military establishment has to introduce new systems— upgrade things on paper—to prove that it's making progress. It's time for a new missile system."

"And what if one is not needed?"

"There will be one anyway. And my point is, if you *were* right that one is not needed—which I can't agree with—but even if that were so, then my point is that it's certain we'll have one anyway. In such case, why not Eagle? It's the best!"

"Perhaps because it could start a new round of arms escalations on both sides."

"The Soviets are already beginning manufacture of their Strabda V, Senator."

"You know about that, do you?" Boudoin was interested.

"I do my homework," Harvey told him.

"Strabda V is highly classified."

Harvey said nothing, hoping he had not gone too far.

Boudoin sighed again. "If I were to help you in some small way, there would, in all candor, have to be some kind of *quid pro quo.*"

Harvey stared, trying to read his expression through the dark. "I'm sure we would do anything reasonable, Senator, but I can't imagine what a company such as Hempstead Aviation could possibly do for a man of your stature."

"Friends help friends."

Harvey did not reply. He did not understand, and was afraid he would botch whatever progress he might already have made. He would have to wait now, and let Boudoin be clearer in his own way.

Instead, the senator surprised him by extending his hand. "It's been a pleasure visiting with you, Harvey. I intend to think about this matter. I will make some independent decision within a very few days."

Harvey's heart sank. He had said something wrong. "If I can answer more questions—"

Boudoin turned and walked him back toward the lighted doors of the house. "I intend to do my own research. I appreciate your calling the matter to my attention." He paused a beat, then said, "By the way, are you interested in private investments?"

Puzzled, Harvey answered cautiously. "I have a small stock portfolio. . . ."

"My son-in-law, Joe Wind, has a small investments firm. Fascinating field. There's a young man who's really going places. I recommend him, if you ever are looking for new opportunities."

"I appreciate the tip very much," Harvey said as they went back into the house.

Boudoin was immediately intercepted by several others, and Harvey was left to his own devices. He drifted away, puzzled by much of what had just taken place, and in search of Dena. He first found Johns, and reported briefly.

"Excellent," Johns said.

"Do you understand what he meant about investments?"

Johns smiled thinly. "I'm not sure, but I have the feeling that it will come clear before many moons pass. Tell me: is there anyone else here you think you ought to meet?"

Harvey looked around slowly. "Not that I can see offhand. . . ."

"It's been a good evening's work," Johns told him. "Unless someone appears, let's say that the business is over and we can relax. I intend to get some feelers out tomorrow, and I may have suggestions for others you ought to contact in a more formal way."

"Excellent," Harvey said, relieved.

"Enjoy the party." Johns turned from him and walked toward another room.

Feeling very much alone, Harvey drifted in the other direction. For a number of minutes, he could not locate Dena Forbes. When he did so, it was with a sharp sense of regret: she was talking with Jake Steinell, the columnist, and evidently enjoying whatever tale he was telling.

As Harvey began edging back out of the crowded room they were in, however, she looked up and spied him. She smiled and waved, said a few words to Steinell, and detached herself from him at once to hurry toward the place Harvey was standing.

"There you are!" she said. "I was beginning to think you had forgotten about me!"

"I've been dismissed from more work," Harvey said. "So I suppose . . . your obligation to stay with me has been removed."

She linked her arm in his. "That's grand. Then you can get me a drink and we can start having that real talk I've been wanting."

"Do you mean it?"

"Of course I mean it! Why shouldn't I mean it?"

"I—I told you before: I'm a staid old businessman—I mean, I did one exciting thing in my life, long ago—"

"Harvey, if you knew how seldom a girl in this town gets to meet *anyone* who isn't totally filled up with himself and bragging about all his power plays—! I enjoy your company, all right? I want a drink, all right? You're *not* going to get rid of me without saying I bore you to tears, all right?"

Harvey grinned so widely that his face ached. He felt foolish and young and tremendous, all in a flash. "All right," he said. "But after we have a drink, I'm warning you: I intend to try to take you away from all this, so I can have you all for my very own."

It was Dena's turn to beam. "It doesn't sound like a warning, Harvey; it sounds like a very nice promise!"

He wondered if he could believe the evidence of his senses.

4

I
t was the same evening in California when Ken Lis heard his wife, Amy, fall.

He was at his desk in the bedroom upstairs, poring over the latest confidential reports on Excalibur sales efforts. Two crack members of the sales force had paid a return visit to United Airlines' headquarters. Their reception had been friendly, arousing some initial hope. United without question had to find a way of buying at least one hundred new jetliners in the next four years but had delayed making purchase orders because of the enormity of the required investment. The time was now drawing close when the company had to commit itself, and Hempstead Aviation had been practicing the soft sell for more than two years, confident that it would get at least a piece of the huge order when it finally came.

With uncertainty remaining over the NTSB investigation of the Excalibur crash, and other majors delaying placement of orders, Lis had instructed Sales to renew efforts at United in a more positive way. The telephone contacts had been promising, and after an exchange of correspondence the two Hempstead experts had made their personal visit.

Results, judging by the memoranda Lis was restudying at home, had been only faintly promising. In view of the general situation, they could easily be discouraging. United was interested. But gentle attempts to press for a firm commitment had been rebuffed. There were also hints of early negotiations between the carrier and Lockheed.

Sales had now recommended a tougher effort with both United and the recalcitrant TWA. The offer suggested was in effect a deferred payment plan, allowing the companies to make partial payments for delivered aircraft until 1985. The proposal, Lis thought, just might be so attractive that United or one of the other majors would accept it regardless of concern for the NTSB probe. For this reason it had to be considered carefully. On the other hand, payments, flowing into Hempstead between now and the middle of the decade would be so slight by comparison with needs that additional long-term borrowing would be required. It was a complex problem, one that Lis was thinking deeply about when he heard the awful noise downstairs.

He had come home earlier to find Amy missing, a brief note on the table saying she had gone to a reception somewhere. As he studied the sales memos, he had vaguely heard her car coming into the garage and had even glanced at his watch to see the time: almost ten o'clock. He had known when she entered the house, but she had remained downstairs. She had not called upstairs to him, nor had he gone down to greet her.

The first sound he heard was her aborted outcry, and then the loud thumping noise, which he translated instantly, throwing his chair back, as the sound of someone falling down stairs. Rushing into the hallway, he plunged down its length to the stairs.

Lying at the bottom, legs sprawled on the lower steps and head down, lay Amy. She had evidently been carrying her purse; its contents were strewn all around her. With jerky, unco-ordinated movements, she struggled to a sitting position as Lis reached her side and knelt anxiously beside her.

"Amy, good lord! Are you all right?"

She shook her head as if dazed. "Think so." She laughed breathlessly. "Oof. Foot slipped . . . something."

Her breath hit his face and he saw her eyes as she spoke, and instantly he saw how drunk—or drugged—she was. His temper hit the flash point. "God damn it, you could have killed yourself!"

Ignoring him, she turned over and tried to get to her feet. Her left ankle turned and she cried out in pain, clutching at him for support. "Twishted . . . my ankle."

"You're so drunk you can't stand up! You drove home that way? What the hell is wrong with you?"

She shook her head blearily. "Only had a few drinkies."

"How many? Six? Eight? Jesus!"

"Jush . . . a few. Tired. Need a little pill—"

"How many pills?" he shouted at her. "How many already today?"

"No' . . . many. . . ."

"*How* many?"

She shrugged. "Eight . . . nine. Dunno. . . "

"Amy, listen to me!" He held her by sheer force, forcing her to look him directly in the eyes. "You're in the same vicious cycle you got into once before. More and more pills, more and more liquor! Where is it going to end? You've got to go back to the doctor! You've got to get yourself back together! You could have crippled yourself with this fall!"

She tried to wrench free. "Lemme 'lone."

"Amy—!"

The telephone rang sharply in the nearby alcove.

"Ansher it," she mumbled. "Prob'ly somethin' 'portant—"

The telephone kept ringing insistently. Lis hung onto his wife, struggling with her. "You've got to see that doctor! You can't keep going this way! This is the worst you've ever been—"

"Ansher phone," she said thickly, pulling free and reeling back against the wall.

Lis hesitated, almost overwhelmed by the urge to hit her. The telephone kept ringing and he was so outraged and upset that he did not know what to do. He saw the touch of blood at the corner of her mouth where she had struck her head in the fall, and he knew that if he kept arguing with her, he *would* hit her.

Turning, he rushed in and grabbed up the persistent telephone. "Yes!"

"Mr. Ken Lis, please." The voice was that of a long-distance operator, and the woman had a thick accent.

"This is Lis."

"One moment, please. Monravia is calling."

Lis froze. This was totally unexpected and he had no idea what it meant. He turned and saw his wife moving unsteadily up the stairs, clinging to the banister.

"Wait and I'll help you," he called at her.

She turned partially and flipped him a finger.

"Then fall and—"

The telephone crackled in his ear: "Ken Lis?"

"Yes," Lis said, swallowing and turning his back on the sight on the steps.

The voice was unmistakable on a good connection. "This is David Peltier. How are you today? What time is it there?"

"It's past ten," Lis said, fighting to get himself together. "Where are you?"

"In my country. In the palace. I have been trying to call you from a secure telephone for several hours. It is four o'clock in the morning here. I finally went to bed with instructions to the palace operator to awaken me when the circuits were clear. I have news."

Lis leaned against the wall and rubbed aching eyes. He did not dare to hope. "What is it, Prince David?"

"Mr. Lis, we have had seven cabinet meetings on aircraft purchases since our return. The question of my country's entry into the tourist air market is now firm. Monravia will purchase eighteen medium-range jet transports and ten airplanes of the 747 class within the next two calendar years."

"And where does Excalibur fit in, Prince David?"

The sound of the sigh came clearly. "We had a crucial meeting yesterday, Mr. Lis. It lasted more than four hours. This is why I have called. We are now in general agreement on entry into the European market as soon as feasible, and into the trans-Atlantic competition within two years if possible. But the question of which airplane to buy for the medium-range hauls is still very much undecided."

It was a blow, but not unexpected. Lis turned and looked up the stairs. Amy had gotten up all right and could not be seen. He turned back the other way, concentrating on the telephone call. "Do you expect a decision soon?"

"Mr. Lis, the cabinet is almost equally divided. I have won over several of them to my point of view, which is favorable to Excalibur. But some of the others believe further investigation is necessary. Lucian Derquet leads the faction voting for more research into several aircraft."

"Doesn't your mother ultimately decide?"

"Yes, the Queen makes the decision, but her decision then is ratified by the National Assembly. Lucian has powerful friends. My mother would not likely make a controversial decision without support of a clear majority of her cabinet in any case, and in this one,

197

with Lucian clearly against any immediate decision for Excalibur. I fear she will not act."

"Then, we're simply hung up indefinitely?"

"Mr. Lis, I have spoken to my mother about this. She understands my eagerness to see a sale consummated . . . and yours. She has made a suggestion which I believe has merit."

"What is it?"

"Many in our cabinet have not seen the Excalibur. Neither has my mother. Fly an Excalibur to our country. Repeat the demonstrations you gave for us in California. Meet my mother personally, as well as all members of the cabinet. —I believe that this, Mr. Lis, could swing the pendulum in your favor."

"Mounting an expedition to Monravia isn't something we can just do tomorrow. We would have to get State Department approval, probably, and I don't know if there would be complications with the Common Market. It would take a full flight crew and backups, a mechanical and engineering team, and probably a cargo hold full of spare parts, just in case—"

"Mr. Lis, if you can make this trip, it can turn the tide for us."

Lis swallowed. "We could fly it through Greenland and Scotland. No problem there. . . ."

"Mr. Lis, allow me to begin preparations here. We continue to be bothered by recurrent but minor earthquakes, but these appear to be smoothing out. If this visit is to take place, it should be between now and late in the summer, when my mother and I traditionally go to the island of Lajos for a brief vacation. This is politically important to me: to win this battle. Allow me to make preparations at this end. You begin checking with your people . . . and with Mrs. Baines. If it can be worked out, the visit would be greatly beneficial."

Lis's mind raced as he considered complications. But the memoranda about United showed that Excalibur still badly needed a prestigious foreign sale, like one to Monravia. That sale might still prove to have impact far beyond the actual number of airplanes purchased at this time.

He said, "I'll begin checking it out right away, Prince David, and get back to you as quickly as I can. Probably in a day or two."

"Fantastic! I look forward to your call, my friend."

Lis hung up the telephone. His thoughts were filled with problems, plans, possibilities. But the ugly scene that the telephone call had interrupted would not stay out of his mind. He turned, setting his teeth, and went upstairs to look for his wife.

She was in the bedroom, the one he no longer shared. She had undressed and donned a gown and robe. After he knocked and she bade him enter, she faced him. She looked as though she might have been sick to her stomach. She was shockingly pale, standing near the bed, one hand on a post for support.

"Are you all right?" he asked. He had no heart for another fight tonight.

She nodded. "I'm sorry."

"I won't lecture you, Amy. You have your own life. But I wish I could make you see—"

"You have made me see," she interrupted with an eerie, controlled calm.

He studied her ravaged face.

She told him, "I don't want to see that doctor again. But I've been pushing myself too hard. You're right. I got myself almost over the edge tonight, and it scared me. I don't want to go over the edge, Ken. I'm going to try. I'm not going to drink any more, and I'm—" She stopped. A sob escaped her. She appeared suddenly unsteady, as if she might fall.

Lis rushed to her side, helping her remain on her feet, and she began to sob brokenly, her face against his chest.

He held her. He wondered why his feelings were so remote. Was it that he had lost the capacity to hope, or that he was simply the kind of cold, cruel, selfish bastard she had in the past accused him of being?

5

H arvey Coughlin's next day in Washington saw critical developments that were destined to have far-reaching consequences.

Harvey showered and dressed early, then lingered happily in the room for a little while, staring at the rumpled bed to reassure himself that last night had not been a wild dream. Dena Forbes had remained with him until almost dawn, and there had been no sleep. She had been passionate, eager and wise in ways he had never before imagined, and he had been delighted to learn that he was not so old after all, that he could respond to her, and please her repeatedly. When she finally departed, leaving him with a lingering, murmuring kiss at the door, he had never felt so much a man.

She was to be very busy during the day, and knew he had vital matters to take care of too. She made it clear, sitting up beautiful and naked on the rumpled bed, that she wanted to see him again, would not ask anything beyond the pleasure of his company, and would "never be a pest." Harvey assured her she could never be a pest, and they agreed that she would call him late in the evening to arrange a drink and another meeting.

"You're sure you want to see me again?" Harvey asked, still naggingly unwilling to believe his good luck.

"My God, yes," Dena told him. Then she stretched deliciously and gave a little moan of half pleasure, half pain, as she stole fingertips along her inner thigh. "I'll be sore for a week, but how could I say no to you now?"

Feeling unbelievably smug, Harvey breakfasted alone in the hotel coffee shop. Covertly eying other men and women in the room, he almost pitied them their humdrum lives. *I am no ordinary person!* he wanted to tell them triumphantly. *If you could only know what I did last night!*

So confident had the night with Dena Forbes made him that he began his calls on congressmen with a new sense of mission. His first visit, to Senator William Jacobs, was a pleasant one, because Jacobs had already been friendly during the recent hearings on Eagle, and the senator seemed even more sure of his pro-Eagle position now.

The second visit, to Senator Clifford Sweet's office, was not so good. Sweet was in committee, an aide said, and would not be available at any time this week. Sweet was crucial, and this development sobered Harvey a bit, but he made his next two calls with considerable enthusiasm remaining.

The first was to Senator Murphy, another friend. Although he could give Harvey only a minute or two, he assured him of continuing support. He urged Harvey to speak with Senator Jeremy Kusman, another of the opposition, and Harvey went immediately from Murphy's office to that of the other senator.

"I wish I saw it differently, Mr. Coughlin," the bluff Hoosier told Harvey. "I blow hot and cold on some of these defense projects. Dammit, there are so many of them, nobody can keep track of everything."

"In that case," Harvey said, "please study the information packet I've provided your staff."

"I will if I find time, sir, but Cliff Sweet is an expert in this field and he's my chairman. As long as he's against Eagle, I frankly don't see how I could possibly buck his opinion."

It was only one more indication of how crucial Clifford Sweet was in the ultimate committee decision. As long as the Southerner wanted to block Eagle in committee, it was likely to remain there, thwarted. Harvey left Kusman's office with a slight but growing sense of claustrophobia.

The afternoon was little better. Lunch with a lawyer from Matthew Johns's office revealed that a proposed afternoon meeting with officials at the Pentagon had been postponed indefinitely for unknown reasons. Instead, Johns suggested that Harvey visit other members of the committee. Harvey did so, finding only one more in his office and available, and that was one of those meetings he had begun to see as characteristic of Washington meetings: a long talk during which he was given no indication of how Senator Proxman felt on the basic issue.

When he returned to the hotel, a little after 4 P.M., Harvey was dragging from discouragement and the intense July humidity of downtown Washington. He found a call slip in his key box from Matthew Johns. Going to his room, he returned it immediately.

Johns was out, but his aide who took the call said that Johns wanted Harvey to know that two officers of Interspace Industries were in town and staying at a nearby hotel. He gave Harvey the number.

Harvey was well briefed on Interspace, the southern electronics giant headquartered in Clifford Sweet's home territory. It was hoped that Interspace, an early high estimator on a portion of the Eagle guidance system, might be drawn in to help apply subtle pressure on Sweet's office, on the basis of needing Eagle for its impact on the home industry. Two guardedly worded letters to Interspace in recent weeks had brought no reply, but word that officials were in Washington was a good sign. Things were moving. Interspace must be interested.

Harvey called the number given him but was told by the hotel operator that Mr. Gravvner and Mr. Clyne were out. Harvey left his name and number.

As he hung up the telephone, it rang. "Yes?"

"Mr. Coughlin? Harvey Coughlin?" The voice was high-pitched and reedy.

"Speaking," Harvey said.

"Good. How are you today, sir? This is Joe Wind."

Harvey remembered instantly: D. L. Boudoin's son-in-law. Wonderful! Although he did not know yet exactly what the call would mean, it signified that Boudoin had certainly not forgotten him. Now . . . what had Boudoin spoken of? . . . A *quid pro quo*? Harvey knew he had to be alert.

"It's a pleasure to hear from you, Mr. Wind. A mutual acquaintance mentioned you only last night."

"Yes," Wind said. "Right. Well, sir, I understand you have some interest in foreign investments of the type I handle."

"By all means, Mr. Wind. I believe we should talk."

Wind surprised him. "It would have to be fast, sir. I leave for

Paris and Vienna in the morning. Perhaps you would prefer to wait a week or two?"

"No," Harvey said instantly. Whatever advantage Wind might give him with Boudoin must be pressed. "I think we should talk at once. Is there any chance of that?"

"Well," Wind said, sounding reluctant, "I suppose I might come over right now."

"I wish you would do that."

"All right, sir; in that case I can be there in just a few minutes."

"Good. I look forward to meeting you."

Hanging up, Harvey smiled to himself. He had no real interest in whatever kind of foreign investments Joe Wind might offer, but if it took some investment with him to make D. L. Boudoin a better friend, then the investment would be made.

It was to be hoped that the investment could be reasonably small. If possible, he intended to handle this out of his own funds. No one needed to know about this at Hempstead. Let Lydia think he had worked a miracle, if all went well. Let Ken Lis be amazed and disheartened. Once Eagle was approved, there would be bonuses enough to recoup whatever had to be laid out to such a small operator as a Joe Wind.

Washing up, Harvey reflected on how complicated things were becoming. He had to make contact with Interspace Industries in the hope that home-town pressures might influence Clifford Sweet, who might in turn influence undecideds like Jeremy Kusman. He had to be nice to a man like Joe Wind in hopes that this would bring about some action by D. L Boudoin that could also help. He was working now three or four steps removed from the desired objective, and congratulated himself on his keen perception of how such things were done.

The telephone rang again. Harvey answered it.

"Mr. Coughlin? John Gravvner. Interspace Industries."

"Yes." Harvey felt a pleasurable added tension. "It occurs to me, Mr. Gravvner, that Interspace and Hempstead Aviation ought to have a chat."

"That sounds good to me, Mr. Coughlin. My associate and I could meet you in the bar of your hotel in an hour, if that would be convenient."

"That would be fine."

"Fine, sir. Then, we'll see you at that time."

Harvey hung up, again congratulating himself.

Eight minutes later, there was a tap on the door. Harvey opened it to meet Joe Wind, a short, intense man with curly black hair and a rather loud sport coat.

Sitting on the edge of the bed, Wind opened a slender attaché case and pulled out a number of duplicated sheets. "I'm in a rush, Mr. Coughlin, and I know you're busy too. I thought I might leave these with you, and you can contact me sometime in the future if you feel like it."

Harvey glanced at the papers Wind handed him. They appeared to be factual descriptions of certain municipal-type bonds offered in Europe. There was no indication that any was current, and a few appeared quite old. Harvey looked up at Wind, not attempting to keep the question from his eyes.

"Just examples," Wind said. "My advantage for a man such as yourself is that I travel the world, seeking out maximum-return investments for select clients. I investigate a local situation. I move fast. Here is how I work: The client gives me a basic investment amount. I place that in my investment pool. When I see a good thing, I am authorized to invest all or part of the funds on hand in whatever proportions among clients that is equitable.

"Let me give you an example. Suppose I go to Europe this time with an investment pool of one million dollars. Suppose I find a good thing for five hundred thousand. I take it. If you have, say, fifty thousand dollars in the pool, and another client has twice that, I take twice the amount from him that I take from you, buying him twice the investment. The more you place in the pool, the more action you get on a good deal."

"You don't ask the client's authorization?" Harvey asked, astounded.

"That's how I operate. I work too fast for telephone calls and telegrams. My client trusts me and I do the job for him. I have no formal contract with anyone. Keep it simple, keep it loose. That's my motto. It helps some of my clients with taxes, too."

Harvey was beginning to understand, and his amazement grew. Joe Wind was, at best, on the frontiers of the law. He was a fast-talking, faster-moving, one-man shell game, the kind who sometimes made fortunes overnight. This kind of deal usually sounded like nonsense, but people had gotten rich this way. There were also people in prisons because of operations not much different.

"So what's your initial reaction, sir?" Wind asked earnestly.

Remember Boudoin, Harvey told himself. "It looks very good, Joe! I believe this is just the kind of thing I've been looking for!"

"Well, sir, you think about it, and if you're still interested when I return from Europe, perhaps we can discuss it further."

What was this? Harvey felt a tinge of panic. He could not let Wind slip away. It was imperative to invest with him *now,* and cement the *quid pro quo* with Boudoin. He said, "I don't think I need to consider it further, Joe. I definitely want in. What would be a minimum investment?"

Wind studied him with cool, sagging eyes. "You could get into the pool for ten thousand, sir."

"Ten thousand!"

"If that's too much, perhaps sometime later—"

"It's . . . more than I had in mind," Harvey admitted lamely. Then, however, he did some feverish mental arithmetic. "But I believe I could swing it, assuming you wouldn't mind a personal check on a San Jose bank?"

"That would be fine, sir," Wind said. "But I want to repeat to you that I don't operate under written agreement, for tax reasons. I make no guarantees. There is risk. Your money may go into a foreign investment, or it could go to a certain real estate plan I have."

"Whatever you think," Harvey said, digging for his checkbook. "I trust you implicitly."

Still acting glum and reluctant, Wind took his check, handed him a few more meaningless mimeographed sheets, and departed. Harvey was left with a feeling of panic about how low he had reduced his personal checking account. But he told himself it had been mandatory, and would pay. Changing clothes for the meeting with John Gravvner, of Interspace, he found himself glancing at the telephone, hoping Dena would call. That would come later, he told himself. She would call. She would not be able to resist . . . was probably even now thinking of him yearningly.

On the way out of the room for the meeting, he looked at himself in the mirror and liked what he saw. He winked at his reflection. "You devil," he told himself, grinning.

John Gravvner and his younger associate, Clyne, were waiting in the bar when Harvey arrived. Gravvner was a portly man about Harvey's own age, and both the Interspace executives seemed like solid types with no nonsense about them.

After Harvey had taken his place in the booth with them, drinks were ordered: martinis for Gravvner and Clyne, a bloody mary for Harvey. Gravvner explained that he and Clyne were in Washington to discuss details of an Interspace contract for subsystems on the proposed Saturn probe. It was not until after the drinks were delivered that they got down to the business at hand.

"We were delighted to learn that Eagle is alive again, Harvey," Gravvner told him. "We hope you win final approval for it and that Interspace can play a part in the production."

Clyne added, "Interspace was impressed with the designs forwarded for bids two years ago. It would be a plus for us to be part of the program."

Harvey nodded, again aware that he was treading on eggs. "I'm sure that if the project is approved, we will move swiftly to review all the old bids."

"You need a southern subcontractor," Gravvner said. "It will provide a firm national basis for the production, diversifying the input beyond merely California and a few northern industrial states. Interspace has fewer labor problems, being in the South, also. And there are, of course, other . . . shall we say . . . political advantages."

Damn them! They were perfectly aware of the need to have them on board as a lever to use on Clifford Sweet. If Interspace were the likely contractor, local concerns other than that company would benefit. Sweet's entire state would be boosted economically, and he would be made vividly aware of this. It was the kind of home pressure that not even he would be able to ignore without peril.

There was a problem, however, and Harvey had to be out front with it. "When we took the preliminary estimates two years ago, there was a wide variety in the bids received. I should tell you that your estimates were not in line with certain others."

Gravvner and Clyne looked at one another as if that was news to them. The Interspace proposal had been fully 30 per cent higher than several others and almost 40 per cent above that of a California-based company that happened to be owned by an old friend of

Harvey's. Surely these men knew how high their company's figures had been!

Gravvner now asked an incredible question: "Would it be out of line, sir, to ask if our bid was out of line by being too high, or too low?"

"Too high!" Harvey said. "You were way high!"

Gravvner frowned at Clyne. He turned back to Harvey. "We appreciate knowing that."

"Of course," Clyne added, "when our estimates were prepared, a two-year price escalation for labor and materials was built in. That's standard operation for Interspace. We don't want anyone to be confronted by any nasty surprises in the way of cost overruns. There's enough of that in military spending, I'm sure you agree."

"Oh, yes, indeed," Harvey said. Here again, however, he was being polite in the face of nonsense. No normal inflationary escalation could account for the amount Interspace had been high. "I'm sure," he added, "refiguring of all estimates would bring them closer in line today."

"Mr. Coughlin," Gravvner said, folding thick hands on the table top, "allow me to be candid with you. Interspace wants the Eagle contract. I believe there are advantages to your company by having us designated as the supplier. I think it behooves both sides here to reach an informal agreement at once."

"I'm not in a position to commit Hempstead Aviation," Harvey said, startled.

"I recognize that, sir. But you are a vice-president in charge of the division responsible for Eagle. Correct?"

"Yes. . . ."

"This is what I propose: A confidential memorandum, signed by you, stating that Hempstead Aviation definitely plans to contract with Interspace for the missile-guidance package. This memorandum would not be *legally* binding, of course, and we both recognize that. But it would give our company something firm. We could begin planning more definitely."

"Also," Clyne added, "it would give us something to show others, don't you see. . . . That could possibly help win quick approval for Eagle."

Harvey saw, and was both astounded and frightened. Interspace wanted this job badly, and at the inflated price they asked, Harvey could easily see why: enormous profit was involved. And Interspace knew he needed its help with Sweet, and perhaps with other southern senators if and when the issue went to the floor of the Senate and House. The confidential memorandum would give Interspace its assurance and its proof for use as a lever politically.

Harvey could write such a memo. As they said, it would not stand up in court anyway and could be worded somewhat ambiguously. But such a matter ordinarily would be a matter for the board to decide, and there he knew Ken Lis and some of the others would balk. He could not even be sure of Lydia Baines on this issue. She was stubborn.

He wanted to accept the offer and write the memorandum at once. It might mean just the leverage he needed. But with other, lower bids in his files at home, he was taking an enormous personal gamble. He might be second-guessed on this . . . accused of bad judgment.

He was damned if he did and damned if he didn't. If he said yes, he risked discovery and the accusation of shady dealing as well as improper financial management. But if he said no, Interspace might never help with Senator Sweet, the entire project might be doomed, and *he* would be the man who faced Lydia Baines's wrath as a failure in negotiations vital to the future of the company.

All this passed through his mind in a moment. Gravvner and Clyne sipped their martinis and watched him.

"Well, Mr. Coughlin?" Gravvner said now. "What do you say?"

"I just don't know. It's a complex question . . . if I had some time to think about it—"

"I wish we could offer more time, sir. Unfortunately, we see several key people in the morning, and after lunch with Senator Sweet, we head back home. It's the kind of thing we really need to settle right away, don't you see."

Harvey did see. He had to be a man of action, had to take one step or the other. An Interspace agreement might cost Hempstead needless millions. But without it there might be no Eagle at all. He could not risk that. His future rode on it. He could cover up the other bids somehow, he thought frantically. He could—

"Well, Mr. Coughlin?"

"I believe," Harvey said huskily, "a memorandum would be helpful."

It went quickly, after that. Clyne left the bar and located a public stenographer. Fifteen minutes later, Harvey and the two men were in his hotel room, where the memorandum was dictated. He tried to make the wording very vague, they politely suggested alternative wording that was too strong. A compromise was worked out. They did not seem particularly happy about the final draft, and Harvey was terrified of it. But shortly after seven o'clock he signed it, kept two copies, and let them leave with the original and one, after handshakes all around.

Harvey paced the floor after they left, sweat streaming down his face in nervous worry. Now he had to begin subtly to lay the groundwork for an Interspace contract, once approval was won for the project in Congress. There were things in his files that he had to . . . deal with in some way. This had to be kept secret. He was already in an agony, worrying how it might look if it came out.

But they had every bit as much at stake in keeping it secret as he did, he told himself. It would be all right. It had to be.

He was still thinking about it when the telephone rang again. His mind leaped to Dena Forbes and he answered quickly.

"Harvey?" It could be no one else!

"Where are you?" he asked gladly. "Will I see you tonight?"

"You'll see me in thirty minutes if you want to."

"You know I want to!"

"Have you had a good day?"

"I've wanted to see you."

"You know what I mean, silly. Have you made lots of good contacts for Eagle?"

"I think it's been a splendid day in that regard," he said. "You seem to have changed my luck."

"It sounds exciting!"

"It has been, Dena. I'll tell you all about it when you get here."

"Then, that gives me at least two reasons for hurrying," she told him, and hung up.

Harvey whistled happily while changing clothes and thinking about the evening ahead.

6

At about the time Harvey Coughlin was taking Dena Forbes to dinner that same evening, Harold Zelmer finally took the first major step in his careful, frenzied plan of revenge for the death of his mother.

Dusk was giving way to full night. The Scott family, one of Harold's part-time yard-work employers, were away for the week. His car was parked in their driveway, out of sight. He was out of the car, moving toward the estate of the Scotts' neighbors, the Nolan Trenor family.

Harold had been exceedingly patient, covering all his bases. Twice he had sent short letters back to his doctor in St. Louis, using a remailing service in Detroit. The visit to his aunt and uncle in Michigan was going well, he had told the doctor, and he was thinking about entering college there. So much for the doctor.

During this time, however, most of Harold's time had been spent doing general yard work in the town and learning about the Trenor family and home. Twice, late at night, he had slipped up to their house when they were gone, and once he had gone inside, tingling with excitement as he learned the layout of rooms. He was now ready, and tonight was his chance.

Crouched in the thin woods separating the two estates, he had a heavy revolver in his right hand, still wrapped in a red industrial towel. He had been on the Scott property for some time, carefully watching the Trenor house, seeing Mrs. Trenor leave for her usual visit to the church, two miles away. Harold had timed her before, and he knew she would be gone another forty-five minutes at the minimum.

Plenty of time.

Two lights glowed inside the Trenor house. One was in the kitchen. This one burned all the time, evidently to discourage prowlers, and meant nothing. The other glowed upstairs, behind the draperies of Nolan Trenor's study, and meant Trenor was up there alone, working.

Harold regretted having to enter the house, although he was fully prepared to do so. It would have seemed neater and more just, somehow, if Trenor had come outside to him. But Harold could not wait for such a great stroke of luck; he had been uncannily lucky already, and Mrs. Trenor might come home earlier than expected. And Mother could not wait any longer to be avenged.

Climbing to his feet, Harold moved out of his brushy hiding place and walked directly toward the Trenor house. His pores shrank and he felt nakedly exposed, but he resisted the impulse to slink or hurry. This way, if by some fluke Nolan Trenor opened his drapes and saw him, Harold could pretend an innocent mission . . . his open approach would be his best defense against suspicion.

There was no challenge.

Harold reached the side of the house and walked around to the back porch. The ivy growing on the trellis tried to grasp him as he went up the steps to the back door. His pulse hammering so hard he was afraid he might be sick, he tested the handle of the back door. If it was locked, he intended to risk the faint tinkle of breaking glass in order to reach quickly inside.

The door handle turned easily in his gloved hand, and the door swung open. Harold stepped inside, into the kitchen.

A single light glowed over the stainless-steel sink. There were a dinette table and chairs, many cupboards, countertops, a refrigerator, an electric range. It was a large, country-type kitchen, and very grand in Harold's eyes. The money had come from risking innocent people's lives, he thought.

Moving through the kitchen, Harold unwrapped his revolver, shoving the rag into his hip pocket. The gun was heavy in his gloved hand. It was fully loaded with new bullets Harold had purchased, hollow-nose bullets such as were favored by police officers for maximum damage on impact.

211

Beyond the kitchen, Harold was in a hallway that smelled faintly of old wood and furniture polish. He moved through it into the dining room, quiet, with faint light glowing on mahogany and the glass of a tall china cabinet. The thick carpet masked all sound from Harold's cautious but quick footsteps, and he felt better now, less ill, more committed. He felt strong.

The staircase leading upward was at the corner of the dining room, and Harold started up, gun ready. As he reached the halfway landing, he paused, nerves singing, tight with alarm. *He heard a voice upstairs, talking.*

In an agony of disappointment, Harold froze against the wall, straining to hear more. If Nolan Trenor had a guest, the revenge was off for tonight. Harold would not take any additional risks. He was taking quite enough already.

Standing with one hand clutching the gun and the other to his ear to capture the faint sound of the voice, he realized that it was Nolan Trenor's voice he was hearing. It sounded monotonous, and when it paused, Harold could not hear a reply from the other person.

This was puzzling. Sweat stinging his eyes, Harold crept higher up the stairs and paused to listen again.

Trenor was talking, but the other person was not answering. Try as he might, Harold could not make out a second voice.

What to do? He bit his gloved fingers to keep from crying out in fright and frustration. Why was the second person here? Why wasn't he or she *saying* anything? Harold had to be sure before he ran away. What if Nolan Trenor—he thought suddenly—were talking to himself?

That was possible. People did that. Harold did that sometimes.

He had to find out. He moved on up the steps to their head, standing now in the upstairs hallway with its framed mountain painting on the wall. The door to Nolan Trenor's office was ajar, light streaming out, at the far end. The voice was continuing, and now for the first time Harold could make out part of what was being said.

". . . further," the voice droned. "I believe any scheduling in that area would be contrary to our interests in the southern route. Please make three copies of that, Cindy, for my signature."

Harold felt weak with relief. *He was dictating into a machine!* He was alone, after all!

It was even better, Harold realized. Trenor would be preoccupied, and his own voice would mask any creaking floor boards that might otherwise have given Harold away as he closed in. This last bit of good luck fired Harold's resolve to new heights.

"Memo to file," the voice began again. "On the Sanderson matter."

Clutching the gun more tightly, Harold moved down the hall toward the door. It was a nice hallway, a nice home, the kind Mother should have had instead of a coffin. Mother would never have a nice home now, because Nolan Trenor and other evil men had placed her in an airplane that was unsafe.

Harold reached the office door. Taking a deep breath, he swung the door open and stepped into the room.

It was a large room with bookshelves lining the walls. A desk was at the far end, near the window, and Nolan Trenor was there, his feet hiked on the edge, his swivel chair turned so that his back was toward Harold. Trenor was speaking into a small tape recorder's microphone. A snifter of brandy stood on the desk, and a cigar smoked faintly in a gold ashtray.

Harold took a step nearer him. Trenor, warned by some primitive sense, stiffened and dropped his feet to the floor, pivoting the chair sharply. His eyes shocked wide as he saw Harold.

"What do you want?" Trenor asked hoarsely.

The fear was already naked in his eyes, and it was a moment Harold might have liked to prolong, for the punishment value. But the tape recorder was still going and Harold was not stupid. He would not give them a voice to try to identify. And he would not waste time.

He aimed the gun, holding it in both fists as the book had shown.

"No!" Trenor screamed.

Harold squeezed the trigger. The gun erupted smoke and an incredible explosive noise as it rocked back against his hands. The bullet hit Trenor in the chest, high, hurling him sideways and out of his chair. He hit the far wall and sprawled on his back, then struggled, one arm flopping, to sit upright.

His emotions rioting, Harold moved closer.

Trenor managed to sit up. He coughed, and red flowed out of his mouth and down his chin. His eyes held the confusion and shock of a hurt child. "Help me," he said.

Harold aimed carefully and fired a second time. The bullet hit Trenor in the middle of his face and his head simply exploded in a mess that appalled even Harold.

Turning quickly, he ran from the room and outside. Partway across the lawn, which was now dark, he fell to his knees and vomited. But then he felt better and ran on to his car, wrapping the revolver in the towel and hiding it under the spare tire. He took care to drive slowly, once he left the Scott-house grounds.

There was no makeshift procedure in his plans. Four hours later, he was on a plane for Chicago. There he would rest a few days, and do nothing, before flying on to California.

7

The new office Lydia Baines had had prepared for her use was now a brilliant white, with thick-piled aqua carpeting and a desk of slabbed glass flanked by two large ferns in suspended urns. A number of other, larger tropical plants created a cool, jungle-like atmosphere in a far corner. Lydia Baines herself, wearing a white summer suit, was seated behind the immaculate desk when Lis was shown in by one of her secretaries.

"Ken," she said with her cool smile. "Thank you for coming promptly. I have only a few minutes. Please sit down."

Lis took a chair in front of the desk and waited with a sense of foreboding. Lydia arranged a single sheet of paper in front of her, and glanced at it before speaking.

"The new owners took possession of the house today," she told him. "I'm glad to be out from under that white elephant."

"I knew it was sold. They got a fine home."

"You were wise to reconsider your idea of buying it, Ken."

"I might have bought it. My wife persuaded me against it."

"I think Amy showed good judgment."

Lis refused to rise to this bait. He had not been called to talk about the sale of the house he had loved, and knew it. He was not going to engage in small talk about a subject that she must know still hurt.

He said, "I have a test crew waiting on the ramp, Lydia, so we need to make this short if we possibly can."

"I thought you had burned out the brakes on the test Excalibur."

"The fully instrumented ship, yes. I have people working on it

215

straight through, day and night, and it will be ready again tomorrow, or else. In the meantime, we can run the high-speed taxi and rotation tests with the older plane, No. 2."

"You're pushing people hard on these tests, Ken."

"If we don't get some results, I'll push them harder than that."

"I like that kind of talk."

"The pressure warrants it. We're down to weeks now—a handful of regular working days. Transwestern has practically stopped its own Excalibur tests and history examinations. Everything indicates that the NTSB is at a standstill. If we don't come up with something new and positive, we're going to be saddled with hearings that leave us in the kind of limbo that won't inspire confidence for *anyone* to buy our plane."

"At least they won't be able to prove product failure."

"That's not good enough! I want the plane cleared, or guilt established and a fix made. We've got to have one or the other, Lydia, or we're badly hurt."

"I know you're doing your utmost."

"I'm going to have an answer, a definitive one."

"Good." She leaned back. "Actually, however, I asked you to come by to talk about something else."

"All right. What is it?"

"You've heard about Harvey's promising trips to Washington."

"I've been preoccupied with Excalibur, but only an idiot wouldn't be keeping one eye on Harvey's project too."

She smiled coolly. "Everything gives us more hope in that regard. You know, the way a number of borderline defense proposals are being handled this year either gives us a golden opportunity or offers us a danger of a complete disaster. Eagle is a good example. It was in the Pentagon's requests for budgeting last year but was passed over. It came back to the House in the President's request for supplementary military spending, but the President is not about to get caught in the open on something possibly as controversial as a new missile system or that X-ray submarine project. You understand how he gave them to the House?"

"As I understand it, they're in a package of items that the House can add or subtract, virtually as it sees fit," Lis said.

"Yes. And Eagle is one of five such packages handed to the Sweet Committee. If the committee reports them to the floor, then we'll have a vote, and a fighting chance. But if the Sweet Committee sits on them—if it simply does nothing—the package will simply lie there until next year, again."

"As of the moment, however," Lis pointed out, "the committee has Eagle on the table."

"Yes, but I'm sure you've heard the rumors and analyses saying the committee may report several controversial defense spending projects to the full House."

"I've heard something of that nature."

"You've heard," Lydia Baines went on, glancing at her paper, "that the committee apparently is going to reconsider Eagle shortly."

"I know the rumors."

"They appear to be more than rumors. Harvey and I are confident that a new hearing on the matter will be called early in August, and perhaps before that. All our indicators are favorable."

"I see."

"We spoke before about studying the possibilities for diverting manpower to a new Eagle line, and your report on the subject is excellent. I know your trip to Monravia next week is top priority, but I want you to have Ms. Hemingway begin immediately to implement the first phase of the Eagle production capability plan as you outlined it."

"Building changes?" Lis asked.

"Yes. I also want plans moved forward for transfer of the first forty supervisory personnel, for training purposes, by September first."

"Isn't that a bit hasty?" Lis asked. "We're in vacation time on the line, and will be until October. It's going to slow us down to transfer that many people out. Retraining new line crews—"

"New personnel will not be authorized for the ones who transfer out," Lydia Baines cut in.

Lis stared at her, disbelieving.

She smiled thinly. "With the NTSB probe going on, it can't hurt if we slow production somewhat. Actually, it might be a good tactic. It will delay the time when we might have to have real layoffs due to lack of orders."

"It's much too early to think about slowing down," Lis said. "Any slowdown in the Excalibur line will take months to overcome. We haven't had any other difficulties with any of the planes now in service. The more we test the surer I become that we don't have any serious problem. That's why we're going to Monravia with a plane—to try to push through their order and get some of the others as a consequence. Slowing our production line now would be a very serious mistake."

"That's your view," Lydia told him. "I've studied the circumstances and decided otherwise."

"Then, it doesn't really matter what I think?"

"Things look good on Eagle now, Ken. We have to be realistic. The moment we have authorization, we want to be able to start tooling up for immediate production."

"I'm still against giving anything like Eagle a priority," Lis said. "The entire thrust of our plan for the eighties was away from defense-oriented production. We were going to establish Excalibur, and then we were going to turn our design people loose on Songbird."

"Songbird is a dead end. Forget it."

"We've been talking about that little plane for years!"

"By all means, continue to talk about it! If it helps you hold men like MacIvor, let some of them fiddle with plans a little if you like. But we have Excalibur, and your job is to sell it. We're going to have Eagle, and I expect everyone in the company to bend every effort to make it a complete success."

Lis took a deep breath. "You're not going to follow any of the plans he had made."

"Don't take it hard. You're a young man. You can still prove yourself adaptable." She leaned forward, her eyes narrowing. "Hempstead Aviation is going to grow in these next few years beyond anything Jason ever dreamed of. I know this; I plan to make it happen. Someone is going to be the president of that larger, growing company. There are very few men I would consider for that post. Who else inside the company can I consider? Richard Cazzell is too old. So is Jerno. Trepps is a non-entity. Dean Busch is too young and brash. Harvey Coughlin is a good man, but he lacks your depth and intelligence."

"All I have to do is play ball?" he said.

Lydia's eyes hardened. "You will obey orders."

"Is there anything else?"

"Yes. I have instructed Cazzell to provide you with an open account for the trip to Monravia. In addition, I have ordered him to provide you with a cash fund which you can carry with you on the airplane for whatever emergencies may arise. I want you to understand that the cash fund is entirely at your discretion; it is being disbursed outside normal channels and will not be accounted for in the usual way when you return. A personal report to me in spoken language will be sufficient."

Lis looked at her, and as he did so, understanding dawned. "I don't think that will be necessary, Lydia."

"I hope it won't be. But let's be realistic. Companies have been forced to grease the skids with cash more than once in the past. I don't want any of my people in a situation where a few dollars could pave the way for a deal and then have them be without quick cash."

"I don't think it will be necessary."

"I hope you're right. But Cazzell will give you the cash and I expect you to take it—and use it if it becomes necessary. You understand?"

The cash would come from some account in a way that only Cazzell would ever understand, Lis thought, and it would not be traceable. It would be money he could hand to an official without fear of ever being held accountable.

He realized that, in her warped way, Lydia Baines was probably trying to make him feel more assured in his mission—was giving him a unique trust. She could not understand, surely, how her method made his skin crawl. He knew many companies used bribery, that in some circumstances it was almost assumed as a fact of life. But he had never been involved in such a transaction, and—to his knowledge—neither had Hempstead Aviation.

And so another shadow zone had been entered, another set of moral values compromised, and as a loyal employee he was to acquiesce. He knew it was completely futile to try to argue. If he did not carry the cash fund to Monravia, someone else would be found . . . someone else corrupted in his place.

"I'll carry it along," he said now. "I don't plan to use it. I'll report about that when I get back."

"Fine." Lydia smiled. "I think we understand each other."

Lis stood. "Will that be all?"

"Yes. I'm leaving for Washington in the morning and may not be back before you leave. If I don't speak with you again before your departure, good luck!"

Lis shook her hand, and left.

Alone, Lydia Baines resumed her place at the desk and briefly reviewed the meeting. It had been short and sweet, just as she had wanted it. For perhaps the first time, she allowed herself some hope that Ken Lis could really be salvaged. He would be very useful if it worked out.

At first she had kept him on only because she knew what a crisis it would cause internally if she precipitously let him go. But with each passing week she had seen more and more of the leadership quality that her husband evidently had always been aware of in him. His report on personnel transfers and building changes for Eagle had been terse and really quite brilliantly done, even though she knew he hated doing it. He had handled the Monravian visit well, she thought, and was quite right in being anxious to meet Prince David's request for a visit to that country. He was respected by everyone in his division—was practically a cult figure with some of the younger people, and was admired by the old-timers.

He could make a fine president, she thought. The Monravian trip and the Excalibur hearings in New York might go far toward determining whether he was tough enough to fulfill his promise.

If not, she thought, there was Harvey Coughlin. He was doing well in his Washington work. It amused her to know from Matthew Johns that Harvey had a girl, a relatively new employee in Johns's own office. But that was all right; Lydia could overlook slight shortcomings in people close to her, and even encourage them, because they gave her an added potential for power over them in a crunch. If Ken Lis faltered, perhaps it would be Harvey Coughlin to whom she could hand the torch.

8

The heat on the ramp was almost unbearable, sunlight blasting off oil-stained pavement to bounce back with an intensity that shocked the eyeballs. The test Excalibur to be used in the taxi runs —not the one loaded with flight instrumentation but a second and older ship with airspeed collectors and other instruments fitted to nose and wing surfaces—glittered so brightly under the sunlight that it could not be looked at directly.

Despite the heat, fuel trucks were pulled up beneath the plane's broad, backswept wings, pumping jet fuel in to capacity. A half dozen technicians in white uniforms were atop the wings, checking attachments for wind-speed, flow, and stress instruments temporarily attached with metal straps. More workers were inside, adjusting equipment there, and one of the flight crew was on the flight deck, visible faintly through the side window, checking controls. Hank Selvy and a mechanic were near the left main gear, going over test details on a clipboard.

Lis went over to join them. "Are we on time?"

"As much as can be expected," Selvy said irritably.

"What's the problem?"

"I just completed the other flight thirty minutes ago—no results, as usual—and Bert Beggs was supposed to take this one. But he's got a virus. So I took the liberty of going to the toilet between tests, which will run us a *little* late but not much."

"If you're too tired, Hank, we'll cancel."

"I'm not that tired," Selvy snapped. "We can't take time to get tired, isn't that right? Do or die for good old Hempstead."

"If you're that edgy, cancellation is mandatory."

Selvy took a deep breath. "No. I'm okay, goddammit."

"Is the plane ready?"

"Just about. We can get aboard and start up some air conditioning, anyway."

They climbed the portable stairs and entered the stifling interior of the No. 2 Excalibur. This one had most of its regular inside trim, including a full complement of seats in First Class and Coach. The limited instrument allocation was bolted and hung in what normally would have been the forward galley. After speaking briefly with the technicians there, Lis joined Selvy up front, where preliminary checks were already well under way.

Within ten minutes they were ready. With the airplane interior rapidly cooling as the air conditioning took hold, Selvy taxied out clear of the MA Building and to the northeastern end of the landing strip. Lis ran through the last of the checklist items, and Selvy briefly reviewed the procedures they would follow, taxiing rapidly—almost at takeoff speed—almost the length of the runway, before braking, on each run. The nose wheel would be raised by rotating the aircraft just short of takeoff angle, and readings made of air flow over wing surfaces in the ground effect.

"Going to be dull," Selvy observed.

"Let's get going," Lis said impatiently.

They taxied into position at the end of the runway, facing into the slight breeze. Final instruments were checked once more, the engines were run up to 20 per cent power, and the brakes were released.

Excalibur began to roll, slowly at first, then faster and faster, rocking on its massive landing-gear system as the pavement became a blur beneath the wheels. The one-fourth marker flashed by on the edge of the runway, and Lis saw the air-speed indicator, corrected for temperature and density altitude, reach the rotation mark. "Vee one," he called.

"Rotate," Selvy said, drawing back on the yoke.

Excalibur's nose rose massively, gently, as the entire airplane settled backward onto its main gear, tail low, nose canted up toward the sky. Another few knots of speed, and the plane would fly off in this attitude, but the additional few knots were not supplied. Digital readouts flashed red. Vital power readings held to the mark. The plane flashed past the halfway mark on the runway. Selvy held the nose high. Excalibur swerved marginally this way and that on the grooved pavement as he kept making tiny corrections in the direction to stay in the center of the runway. On either side, stunted brown grass was whipped by the force of the roaring engines. They reached the three-fourths mark on the runway, Selvy's right hand moved the ganged throttles back, and the nose slowly settled forward as the nose wheel "landed" again.

With only one quarter of the runway left, Slevy jumped on the brakes. The braking force slammed them forward in their seats. But the brakes performed as designed and Excalibur came to a shuddering stop at the end of the runway.

"Taxi her back?" Selvy called over the noise. His face was covered with a heavy film of sweat.

Lis nodded and taxied the big plane back up the runway through the settling fumes and rising heat of the previous run. It would be forty-eight hours before all the data could be fed into the computers and analyzed. Any anomaly would take that long to show up. More tests would be run in the meantime. There was so little time now before the NTSB hearings. And so much would depend on them.

The second run went as the first one had, and the third was similar. By the time they began the fourth of the six runs, a routine had been established, and Lis, like the others, felt more comfortable with the speed and hairbreadth control required to maintain the center of the rather narrow runway during a high-speed run.

They were at the halfway marker when it happened.

There was a tremendous, distant explosive sound. Dirt flew up on the right side of the airplane, and instantly it swerved sickeningly to the same side. Hank Selvy yelled something and instantly cut back all power to the engines. Excalibur was already running as if insane, skewing off to the right at a 40-degree angle, massive wheels bouncing over the edge of the pavement and onto the sun-hardened dirt. The nose came down faster than Lis had ever seen it, and the nose wheel crashed solidly home, bouncing before biting in a shower of red dirt and flying torn grass. Emergency lights were going on all over the place and Lis had his hands full trying to help Selvy keep the plane going reasonably straight. It was fully off the runway now and plowing across the scorched grass, heading for a distant fence. There was a sound of metal being torn. He smelled burned rubber and hydraulic fluid, and Excalibur slowly rotated as it skidded, right wing going out in front, and then the wingtip dipped and hit the earth and dug in a bit, throwing a geyser of sand and sod.

Slowing, going on with inexorable mass, making more screaming noises, the plane turned on around and skidded backward a few yards, bumped one last time, and was suddenly at a halt with a cloud of dust coming up from behind to envelop it.

Going by memory and drill, Selvy barked orders as they started through the emergency shutdown procedure. The back doors were already open, and Lis thought the technicians were going down via the emergency slide but didn't have time to look. He heard a siren and saw one of the company emergency trucks shoot into view. The fire crew unloaded in a hurry, running with hoses and foam gear.

"Okay," Selvy ordered, throwing the last switches. "Let's get out and let her cool off."

They exited the flight deck one at a time, moving fast but without too much hurry. Excalibur was shut down thoroughly, and barring a burst fuel system somewhere, the danger of catastrophe was already past. First the engineer, then Lis, then Selvy went down the crew escape slide to the ground, where the emergency crew helped them.

Two tires on the main gear on the right side had blown almost simultaneously, the force of the one explosion blowing the other, and Excalibur had been dropped onto the main-gear assembly itself without the cushion of a rolling wheel. The result had thrown the big aircraft sideways, off the runway, and across about four hundred yards of sun-scorched grass to the east of the runway, ending in a slow, massive ground loop. Excalibur now faced the way she had come, down on the right side, the wingtip on that side crumpled, dirt and grass fragments all over the wings and body. Settling dust resembled smoke, but was not smoke.

They had been lucky. It was the first genuinely serious accident of the entire test program, and they had emerged unscathed. It had not even happened to the plane with the bulk of test equipment on board.

"Mighty lucky," Selvy said as they walked stiffly back toward the MA seemingly a mile distant.

"If we were so lucky," Lis asked, "why do my legs feel like Jell-O?"

9

It had been three days since Amy Lis's fall on the stairs. In those three days, as far as Lis could determine, she had been making a real and frighteningly difficult effort to turn her life around.

She had not—and he felt sure of this—had a drink in those three days. She had volunteered the information that she was tapering off the diet pills, reducing the dosage by 10 per cent each day. She was trying a regimen of exercise, and had opted out of three or four club meetings.

The first day had obviously been harrowing for her. She was in bed when he got home, and appeared seriously ill. He wanted to call a doctor, but she refused. She sat up far into the night, sipping endless cups of hot tea, which he took to her, and watching anything that happened to be on the bedroom TV set. He tried to engage her in conversation, but she burst into tears and begged him to leave her alone until she was a little better.

On the second day, she had gone to the grocery, and a luncheon. Lis took her to a small restaurant nearby for supper, but she could not eat. Still she seemed better to Lis's searching eye; although her hands shook as badly, her color appeared healthier, and once when he made a feeble joke she smiled in response.

This morning the improvement had been more dramatic. She was up before he left the house, and the sound of her exercise bicycle hummed through the upstairs hallway while he shaved. She was evidently in the shower when he departed, and he did not see her, but she called cheerfully in response to his call of good-by.

The truce between them, as he saw it, was an infinitely fragile thing. He was taking each step as it came and trying not to intrude upon her in any way. He knew the cost of effort she was paying, and he held his breath. He had not been making idle threats when he told her how close he thought she might be to total breakdown. He had seen all the symptoms once before.

Now, driving up the street to his home, he was aware of a gearing up to hide whatever worries he really felt, in order to spare her. He had not even told her yet of the scheduled trip to Monravia. He had wanted to give her a few days, if possible, before such a change in routine had to be presented to her. He certainly would not tell her about today's near disaster during testing.

Parking his car in the garage, he touched the hood of her Vega and found the metal cool. She had not been out recently. He considered this a hopeful sign, indication that some of the frenetic activity was winding down. Taking a deep breath, he entered the house by way of the kitchen door.

Amy was at the counter by the window. Beyond the patio doors, the long-unused charcoal cooker smoked through its lid vents. The table was set, with fresh flowers in the center. Amy was tossing a salad. She wore a pretty yellow sun dress and her hair was freshly brushed and she had makeup on. She looked better than she had looked in a long time.

She turned and smiled. "Hi."

Something about her vulnerability touched Lis deeply and he went to her and kissed her on the cheek. "You look great, Amy."

"You're a damned liar," she told him with good humor. "But I'm better."

He gestured at the neat table and salad. "What's all this?"

"I thought you might enjoy a home-cooked meal, if you didn't faint from the shock."

"Listen, I'll manage not to. It looks tremendous."

"Don't get used to it. As soon as I get back on my feet, I'll be busy again."

He wanted to argue—to point out that "being busy" had gotten her to the brink of breakdown. But he did not want to spoil things. "I wouldn't want you to be a spoiled *hausfrau*."

"Good. Now, what kind of dressing would you like on your salad?"

"Oil and vinegar?"

"Making it easy on me. Good."

226

"Can I help?"

"No, but you can go wash your hands. My timing isn't what it once was and I'm afraid you won't have time for a drink before those steaks are ready."

Lis patted her ample flank and obediently went to the downstairs bathroom, where he washed quickly. She was, he thought with pleasure and hope, an amazingly strong woman. Few could have bounced back this far so swiftly. It gave him real hope, and as the hope dawned, he was aware of quite a different sensation, the beginning of a mild sexual fantasy and a faint throbbing in his groin. He tried to think of the last time they had made love. It had been that ugly scene, more than six months before, when she flung herself drunkenly on the bed, spread her legs, and told him to hurry. Naturally he had gone instantly soft. In the time since then there had been the nagging aches of desire for Kelley Hemingway, the occasional moments when the flash of some other woman's eyes, showing mild interest, stirred him distantly. But except for the periodic awakenings in the night, with his painfully stiffened penis disgorging itself onto the sheets, there had been nothing. In recent weeks, at least, his preoccupation with work had been so great that he had not had time to brood about his celibacy. But now the stirrings of desire told him that he was still alive, that even the slightest hope could galvanize him.

Walking back toward the kitchen, he thought of the Monravian mission and wished it were not so soon . . . that he did not face the prospect of telling Amy about it. It was the kind of trip that had often depressed her, the kind she refused to take with him, preferring in some contrary way to remain behind and resent his going. He had never understood this, and now worried what the impact of his announcement might be. But he could not delay telling her sometime tonight . . . or in the morning.

The kitchen was neat and silent. Amy was not there. Lis felt an instant of panic, hurrying to the sink. Then he spied his wife out on the patio beyond the closed door, smoke billowing around her as she used long-handled tongs to remove the steaks from the grill and place them on a platter. Frowning, she looked nevertheless younger and better than she had in a long time. Her waist was not quite so thick, as if the exercise had already begun to peel away a few of the excess pounds. *It really is going to be all right,* he thought.

Following hard upon the heels of this thought was another, a tinge of regret. He wondered if he *wanted* it to be all right with his wife. He thought of Kelley. Guilt resulted. He clamped it off and slid the door back so Amy could get inside.

"Need help?" he asked.

"Just a hearty appetite."

"I can supply it."

"If you want wine, you'd better open some."

It was the first time in as long as he could remember that she had not had at least one bottle of partially consumed wine in the refrigerator. He did not comment on this obvious change. "I think I'll have coffee or tea."

She put the steaks on the table. "I'm having iced tea."

"I'll have the same, then."

She went to the refrigerator. As she removed the ice tray it was clear how badly her hands shook. She was making a superhuman effort.

It was a good beginning. As they ate their meal, Lis felt his spirits rising. He knew how to distinguish between her genuine sobriety and the many initiations she had almost perfected. She was staying away from the liquor, and evidently reducing the pills. Already there was more of a calm about her, she did not move so jerkily as she did when the speed was rushing through her blood stream.

The conversation was mostly light. She told him about a telephone call she had had earlier in the day which had struck her as amusing. A friend had called in amazement that she had missed a meeting, the first she had failed to attend in more than two years.

"If you need any help," Lis told her carefully, "I mean if it gets rough, and a doctor would help—"

"Doctors," she said firmly, "are the ones who got me started on the diet pills. And if you mean another psychiatrist, I think I've had as much of rummaging around in my childhood as I can bear for a while."

"Fine," he said. "I just mean . . . whatever you need. . . ."

"I know."

She asked him about his day at the plant, and he told her only those things that had happened that involved no pressure and no real problems. She nodded, and did not inquire about the ongoing NTSB probe or Eagle, although he knew she was fully aware of both in general outline. It was as if they had entered a silent pact to make this time idyllic.

She suggested they take their dessert, small glasses of sherbet, into the living room. He carried the two dishes in to the coffee table in front of the long couch, and she brought more tea. They sat side by side, casually touching at the knee, as they ate. But for Lis it was not entirely casual. There was a persistent sexual tension, and he wondered if she could possibly be entirely unaware of it.

"Do you have a cigarette?" she asked when they had finished.

"I probably have some hidden somewhere."

"I think I'd like one with you."

"You haven't smoked for more than two years."

"And you've been quitting for twice as long," she told him fondly. "Since I'm jettisoning all my old vices, I thought I would just resume a *really* old one."

Lis got up and went to the bookcase in the corner of the large room. There were several small drawers in it, and he found a half pack of Kents.

"These are probably a year old and dry as a bone," he told her.

She took one and turned slightly to face him more directly as he resumed his place beside her. "I'll risk it."

He lighted her cigarette, then his own. The smoke was dry and harsh, but welcome. It curled around them as they sat close, half facing. Her skirt was carelessly high on her thighs and their knees were pressed together. Her color was higher. Now, he thought, she was aware.

"That's lovely," she said huskily.

"It's been a long time since we smoked together."

"I'm going to be all right."

"Yes."

She squinched her shoulders. "I remember once you told me you thought it was very sexy when I smoked a cigarette."

"You used to be the sexiest cigarette smoker in this hemisphere."

"Used to be?"

The lines were still in her face, the puffiness in her body, the ravages of her recent life all there to see. But the tawny challenge in her tone broke his control. He put his arms around her and kissed her uncarefully, his desperation suddenly all on the surface, trying to pull her through his own flesh and inside his own body. She gasped, then clung, her fingertips at his throat as her mouth opened and he plunged his tongue inside.

As she disengaged her mouth from his and held him closer, her breath warm against the side of his face, he was in an agony of need. Since it was she, he told himself that it was love. But it might have been anyone in this instant of letting all self-control go.

Amy put her cigarette on the ashtray and stroked her long hand up the inside of his thigh, and to the bulge. She held him with her eyes as her hand worked his zipper. Then her hand was inside, on him, drawing him out.

He reached for her.

She pulled back slightly, stiffening. Something twisted momentarily in her face. "Ken—I'm sorry—I'm just not ready yet."

The disappointment was shattering and it must have shown clearly. She looked down at his straining penis. In the strangest, calmest little voice, she said, "More dessert." Bumping the coffee table heavily with her hip as she moved, she slid off the couch and went to her knees in front of him.

"Amy," he said. "Don't—"

"I want to," she whispered, and moved her mouth down, and over him.

Her quickness had frozen him for a few seconds, and as sensation rioted through his body, he looked down at her without the will to resist. She was being very fast and almost rough in her seeming eagerness, and already for him it was too late. He tried to push her away, to spare her the conclusion. She made a little whimpering sound and clung more tightly, and fire bolted down through him and lanced out.

As he fell back on the couch, enervated, she continued. He put his hand down weakly into her hair. She kissed, nibbled, looked up at him smiling, and climbed quickly back up to curl in the corner of his arm, her head on his chest.

"Amy—" he whispered.

"Hush," she said cuddling.

"But after all this time, I couldn't—"

"I know, I know. Just be quiet."

For a few moments he held her while his mind reeled in consternation. "You've been trying so hard," he said. "You're not well yet. That wasn't fair. I shouldn't have—"

She dug a stiffened finger into his chest. "That's one of my new resolutions too. Cigarettes and that. They'll make me well."

"What can I do for you now?"

"Nothing. Not . . . yet. In a few more days perhaps."

He closed his eyes and held her. The act was not new for them in terms of their total marriage. Once, they had had a joke, a large blue ribbon he had presented her, in a small gilt frame and without any hint of its significance. But she had known. The joke had been that if they only had a state-fair competition in *this* category. . . .

But it had been so long since any intimacy had been between them. It was as if she had wanted to re-establish the totality of their relationship in a single act. He did not know the ultimate significance of this, but he was dazed, happy, concerned. Had they gone too fast?

He went to the bathroom for a minute. His hands shook. He stared at himself in the mirror and decided he would wait until morning to mention Monravia. But when he went back in to the couch, he blurted it out immediately.

"Amy," he said, taking her hands. "I have to make a trip next week. I know ordinarily you haven't ever gone with me, but come with me this time. Please."

Her eyes changed. "Where do you have to go?"

"Monravia. You remember we're trying to sell them some airplanes. They want us to fly an Excalibur in and demonstrate it. You can go. I want you to. It will only be four or five days, total, and Monravia is one of the most beautiful countries in the world, everyone says that. We can play on the beach and get a tan, and try out their casinos. While I'm in meetings you can see their old churches and castles and museums—"

"How long have you known?"

"Just a little while—a couple of days."

"How long did you intend to keep it from me?"

Lis recognized the symptoms. He had made a mistake. Only moments ago it had been the old Amy, the woman he had married. But now he had ruined things and the other Amy was facing him, her eyes bright with angry accusation. Amy's bitch was out.

He said, "I wanted to tell you at the right time."

"So now you've gotten what you want out of me, that's the right time?"

"Oh, Amy. Jesus."

Her lips formed a hard line. "I hope you'll have a lovely visit."

"Will you come with me?"

"You know I'm not strong enough to make a long trip like that."

"There will be plenty of room on the plane. You'll be able to stretch out or anything you want. And we'll have a night over in Scotland. There won't be any pressure on you—"

"No pressure?" she shot back. "Walking around on tiptoes, afraid I might commit some *faus pas* that could damage you or almighty Hempstead Aviation?"

"My God, I don't know what you're talking about, you've never commited a *faus pas* in your life! —Look: think about it. I know we could have a great time."

Amy Lis's eyes were like ice now, and every line of her body was rigid, unbending. "I don't want to go. I don't want *you* to go."

"Amy—I've got to go!"

Her face began to crumble. "I'm making an effort. Don't you see what an effort I've been making?"

"Of course I do! That's why—"

"I need you here with me," she interrupted, beginning to cry. "I'm not one of your libbers. I'm not emancipated. I have my organizations, but I'm not strong. Not really. Not inside. I could have been a good mother, but I was barren. And then you took up with that girl—"

"You're getting hysterical." He tried to take her hand.

She pulled away. "Were you ever alone in this house? Did you ever listen to the silence in this house? If you listen very carefully, you can hear the laughter of the children I wasn't able to bear for you."

"Calm down, okay? Please!"

"And now I'm old," she said, the tears splashing onto her clenched, puffy hands in her lap.

"You're *not* old!"

"I am forty-one years old. I feel eighty. I'm fat and I'm addicted to diet pills, and all I know how to do is chair stupid meetings that don't mean anything and hope to get my picture in the paper again and hope they'll use the wrong picture—the one—the one that makes me look like I'm still an attractive woman!"

Lis tried a different tack. He forced his voice to be quiet and calm.

"But that's all changing. It's a new start. Come to Monravia with me and it will all be different."

"I *can't*—don't you see?"

He stared at her ravaged face, seeing the tears, the age lines, the sagging folds of flesh along the line of her jaw, the way her eyes dropped in little cups of loose flesh. *She was a stranger.*

She asked, "Do you have to go?"

He hesitated. He could not abandon her. "No," he decided. "I can figure a way to let the others handle it. I'll . . . stay here if that's what you want."

"No," she said. "They want you. I know they do. They always want you. You'll lose your deal and then it will be my fault."

"It wouldn't be your fault! Hell, I don't have to go if it's that important to you—"

"No, then you would hate me for keeping you here, and don't you see how much of a failure as a wife I am already? . . . You go to Monravia. I'll stay here."

The feeling was one of total frustration. He should never have mentioned it tonight—should have let *this* night, at least, be a sort of dream. Now they were at an impasse where he could do nothing that was right.

"I want you to be happy," he said. "You don't know how much I just want you to be happy."

Amy Lis fled from the room.

Lis rejected the impulse to hurry after her. More words right now would only make it worse. He forced himself to remain on the couch where she had left him.

If he had been wiser, he thought wearily, he would have handled it differently and it would have been all right.

But he knew instantly that that was not true. There was nothing he could have done with such infinite tact and wisdom that this break would not have come. Perhaps in an insanely logical way they had both been looking for it—seeking a way to go back to the game they had played for what seemed decades. There had been so much pain, so much failure. Each failure over the years had eroded the chances of repair, and now they were like two old fighters in the late rounds, circling, flailing away at one another, past the point when anyone could win, and new blows could only add to the exhaustion, hurt the other in some viciously additional way.

233

Some time passed, perhaps twenty or thirty minutes. Lis carried the dishes and cups to the kitchen and cleaned things up, and started the dishwasher. He went back into the living room and lit the lights and sat down again, sunk in depression. He could not believe the past two hours. He wondered if he was going mad.

Amy came back downstairs, wearing her blue robe and some fluffy mules. Without looking at him she walked to the big stereo console and opened the sliding lid and turned on the radio portion.

The station specialized in "golden oldies," but unlike some that thought music by Fats Domino fit into that category, this one often played tunes dating back to the forties and even earlier. The song that filled the room now, as Amy Lis rotated the volume control, was a very old one: "Deep Purple." A big band, reminiscent of the Glenn Miller era.

Amy stood at the console with her back turned to him, listening.

You could not live in the past. It was gone. Your only hope for survival was beyond simple acceptance of change; one had to embrace it.

This was what Ken Lis had always told himself intellectually.

But he was almost overwhelmed by his sense of things lost. He could not allow everything to be lost. He had to help his wife get through this and be whole again, no matter what the pain or how long it might take. He had to be her anchor. But he was torn by his other commitments as well, and equally. He owed his loyalty to the airplane he and Jason Baines and Barton MacIvor had built. He owed all the effort he could muster to the younger people, like Janis Malone and even Dean Busch, whom he had recruited and asked to cast their lot with him in the company. And he did not know how he could fulfill so many obligations, or any of them.

Amy turned to him, a slight smile on her face. She looked better. She was trying again.

"Like to dance?" she asked.

Lis rose and went to her. She held out her arms and he took her, and began to move. But as he did so, it was not with the feeling of hope that he had felt as he went toward her. It was with something else, a subtle horror.

He had caught the odor on her breath as he took her close, and knew where she had found the strength to come back and try again.

She was drinking again.

10

When Hempstead Aviation's group departed for Monravia in a new Excalibur, the wire services took note of it in a small item. With the public hearing on the crash so near now, there was considerable public interest. But some of those most directly affected needed no news account to tell them about it.

On the morning of his departure, Ken Lis stood in the hallway of his home, holding Amy close. He knew she was trying very hard again today.

"I can still cancel," he told her. "I can let someone else go."

"No." She smiled at him, although her eyes betrayed her tension. "I'll be fine."

"You're *sure* you don't want to call your sister? See if she can come and stay with you?"

"I'm a big girl, darling. Don't worry about me."

"I'll call while we're fueling in New York," Lis promised. "And the minute we're in Monravia."

She made a little face. "Not if it's three o'clock in the morning here!"

"I'll remember that." Lis held her closer. "Amy . . . I know you're trying. You can whip this thing. Both of us can. Please keep thinking that."

"I will," she assured him, hugging him for an instant and then stepping back. "Now you'd better hurry or you'll be late!"

He held her for another instant, pulling her into his arms again, and then went out too quickly. Amy Lis stood in the front door and waved, smiling until his car was out of sight at the corner. Then she went inside quickly, and the tears came.

He was leaving unaware of how shaky she really was. She had hidden the fact only by dint of enormous effort. Cutting down both the drinks and the pills are harder than anything she had ever tried to do.

This morning, surely, was a special occasion and she could pamper herself just a little. She could not get through this day without some help, and that was obvious.

Having mentally debated the issue, she went into the kitchen and poured three ounces of scotch over two ice cubes.

For Janis Malone it was also a rocky morning. Meeting the rest of the Hempstead team at the airplane, she was more than ever aware of how much she loved her job; how many women her age got a free trip to Europe?

She intended to have a blast, too. If the prince got close enough, she would flirt. And if *he* didn't, someone else surely would. She intended this to be a romantic fling if she could make it so. She had it coming.

Oh, hell, who was she trying to kid? The truth of the matter was that she had never been less sure of herself and her dedication to work and independence than she was that morning. It had been a long night with Hank Selvy, and ultimately a beautiful and troubling one. Now she didn't know *where* she stood.

They had almost gotten into one of their endless fights, but both had been intent on avoiding that at all costs. Instead of replying to one of his barbs early in the evening, she had gone from her living room into the kitchen and brought back a well-chilled bottle of champagne. Then, when it was *she* who said something snippy a little later, it was of course Hank who not only refilled the glasses but nuzzled her throat and teased her as he began fiddling atrociously with certain zippers and buttons.

She did not remember any night that had given half the pleasure of last night. Both of them had been under such a variety of pressures, strained by so many conflicting demands, that they had seen each other very little except for brief encounters in the coffee shop or some similar situation that only heightened their frustration and need. Once their old pattern of arguing was discarded for the evening, they fell upon each other with a naked desire that neither had allowed the other to see during all their previous affair.

Now physically sore from some of their incredible antics, Janis was shaken in other ways as well. She had not known she had such a capacity for the erotic. Hank Selvy had awakened her to things about herself that she had not known existed, and already she hungered for more. She was not as happy about leaving for Europe as she had thought she would be. She was not as happy about anything in her life. A tiny voice whispered the question, what was *wrong* with being a wife and mother if it meant she could have more and more of pleasure like last night's? Was she being a dried prune when she spoke of the joys of a career? Had she only been substituting?

What she had to do, she told herself, was have a wonderful time in Monravia. She had to forget as much about last night as she could in order to remain firm in her convictions about career versus marriage. And my God, this Monravian visit was going to be a real thrill . . . wasn't it? *Wasn't it?*

In Washington, Jace Mattingly was aware of the Excalibur departure for Europe, but it was a sidelight to his day. Foremost in his mind was the issuance of rough-draft reports on the Kennedy crash.

The mystery was as impenetrable as ever. Final engine reports showed no failure. In the warehouse near the crash site, technicians continued to sift thousands of tiny fragments of hull and wing, but all data so far indicated that Flight 161 had been intact—and functioning with maddening normalcy—when it hit the earth.

In other aspects of the investigation, the lab boys had given up further attempts to massage data from the Digital Flight Data Recorder and the Cockpit Voice Recorder. The fluke damage and fire results had made the tapes useless. The verdict on the basis of so little information: no verdict at all.

Metallurgy had also issued a negative report. Excalibur had not crashed because of metal fatigue or breakage. Engineering studies showed no signs of structural failures prior to impact. Checks of other Excaliburs had failed to detect *any* abnormalities, when in fact the same rigorous checking of almost any airplane in the world would have likely found a dozen to eighteen minor defects of the kind that could be corrected during the next regular maintenance overhaul.

Added to Mattingly's headache was the letter from Ken Lis that outlined tests conducted by Hempstead Aviation into possible pilot disorientation factors due to windscreen or cockpit design; the tests at Hempstead, too, had been negative.

It appeared a dead end, with the public hearings already being set up in terms of room arrangements, stenotype reporters, and credentials for the press. Mattingly was filled with angry frustration.

As he had said he would do, he called Nell Emerson late in the day to report the latest findings in brief. Her voice was calm and friendly, but evenly controlled as she took the bad news. They both knew quite well what it portended. Unless something was found quickly, Jerry Emerson and his crew were almost certain to be branded posthumously as incompetents—good pros who had made one unforgivable mistake.

Mattingly tried to cheer Nell, holding her on the phone longer than necessary. When she said good-by, she sounded somewhat better. Mattingly returned to his dogged study of reports, plagued by a new realization, one he had known all along but was just really beginning to face at the conscious level.

He was falling hopelessly in love with Jerry Emerson's widow.

Kelley Hemingway's day, meanwhile, had already begun to assume the more complex dimensions she had known it would take on once Ken Lis was on the way to Europe. Sitting at her desk, surrounded by paperwork to expedite and telephone memos to answer, she strained mentally to stay completely calm as her secretary dropped more work on her desk.

"The meeting with the union's grievance-committee chairman is at one," Kelley's secretary told her. "That means you'll have to get back from the Chamber of Commerce awards session and luncheon an hour before you would if you stayed for everything."

"Okay, Barbara," Kelley said jotting a note. "My speech is ready?"

"Jana is doing the final typing job with the big type now."

"Fine. Are the materials here somewhere on the agenda for the meeting with the grievance chairman?" Kelley lifted the corners of piles of paper in search.

"The yellow sheets," her secretary said.

Kelley found them, scanned them. "I don't have any information on how Mr. Lis wanted to handle the problem on the overtime."

"I'll check if he left a memo on the machine or anything."

"Good. Also, call Steiner at United and explain why we'll have to postpone a session between him and Mr. Lis for a few days."

"What if he insists on wanting to go ahead?"

"Then, I'll talk to him." Kelley shuffled papers. "On this problem with getting enough titanium rods, please set up a meeting with Roscoe in purchasing and Jimmy in design at, ah, let's make it three o'clock."

"You have the meeting with Mr. Cazzell at three, to go over the draft of the new employee booklet."

"Damn. All right, then, make it four."

"You had dictation scheduled to start at four."

"Move that back to four-thirty."

"Do you want to return that call to Burns, at United Petrochemical, now?"

"Let me go over his letter again first. And please pull the files on all our fuel-cell negotiations and transactions for the last six months."

Barbara pointed at the telephone. "Those are all for you."

Three lights were blinking on the base of the pale green telephone half hidden under Kelley Hemingway's latest batch of paperwork. "Damn," she murmured, picking up the instrument and punching line No. 1. "Hello?"

In the instant before her caller replied, Kelley felt a pulse of sheer pleasure. She loved this, all of it: the confusion, the overwork, the complexity of decision, the responsibility. And she was good at it too, and knew it. She intended to keep everything going absolutely smoothly while Ken Lis was out of the country if she could possibly do so, not only because he obviously needed no complications but for her own fun in meeting the challenge.

It had taken years to reach this level of competency and understanding of how Hempstead Aviation operated. Even as she realized how much she liked the job and enjoyed the challenge, it also crossed Kelley's mind that she might never again get such an opportunity with another firm, or learn the job as well. Her constant, interior tension about the Excalibur situation was more than businesslike. At nights, sometimes, in the quiet while her husband slept, she imagined the worst: the dissolution of Hempstead Aviation. Where then would she be?

Where then, in fact, would any of them be?

Each passing day increased that pressure, and it was not at all the kind she or anyone enjoyed.

The trip to Monravia simply had to go well.

She thought momentarily of Harvey Coughlin, whose return from Washington had coincided with the departure of the Lis team for Monravia. Things would be far different if Lis failed and it turned out to be Coughlin in the driver's seat in the future, she thought. She was glad to be where she was right now, and not up there on the next floor with Coughlin's minions. Was it only her imagination that made the people up there seem unhappy even by sight?

". . . so we can't get the job done without help," her caller said.

"I understand, Charles," Kelley said sympathetically. "Look, let's talk about it. Suppose we get together at, ah, how would five o'clock be for you?"

11

arvey Coughlin had returned to California from Washington, but his tensions had not eased. In his office, he impatiently jammed the office intercom button.

His secretary came on the line. "Yes, sir?"

"What about my call to Sunset?" Harvey asked angrily.

"Sir," the girl replied, her voice faltering nervously, "the lines are all still busy—"

"How long ago did you try?"

"About ten minutes ago—"

"Damn it! Try again right now! I'm sitting here waiting for that call to go through!"

"Yes, sir—"

Harvey slammed down the telephone, cutting off whatever additional feeble apology the girl might be wanting to offer.

His nerves were bad. He had spent a miserable weekend at home with his wife, his thoughts tortured by memories of Dena Forbes. He had even come to the office on Sunday afternoon, using the pretext of work, to try to call Dena's Washington apartment on his credit card. The telephone was not answered, and he went home again plagued by jealous thoughts of Dena with one of those young lawyers, taking a drive or visiting a gallery or having drinks or—Christ! —making love as she had with him. Jealousy was new to him, sexual jealousy. His nerves were in tatters even before this morning, and the departure of Ken Lis and the others for Monravia, and the telephone call.

When the long-distance operator asked for him by name and said she was calling from Washington, Harvey's first thought was of Dena. As he picked up the telephone, he knew this was absurd, and expected the voice of Matthew Johns or one of his aides. The surprise was unpleasant.

"Harvey? This is Joe Wind! How are you today?"

"I thought you were in Europe," Harvey said, fighting to keep a snarl of disappointment out of his voice.

"I just got back, Harvey, and I'm going again tomorrow. That's why I called you. I'm onto something truly fine this time, Harvey."

Harvey squirmed, wanting to hang up. The last thing he needed was the braying sound of Joe Wind's voice on the telephone. He thought he had done with the man by handing him, no strings attached, a check for ten thousand dollars while in Washington. Was he going to be a continual pest?

Aloud, however, remembering Wind's connections, he said calmly enough, "Will you be making my investment in this thing, Joe? Is that why you called?"

"Your other sum is already working, Harvey," Wind yelled back. "This is something even better. The base sum is a half million, and I can let you in on the ground floor for as little as seventy-five hundred!"

"*Another* seventy-five hundred?"

"Harvey, if you have more, I would encourage the investment. But seventy-five hundred is the minimum I can handle. Actually, I'm stretching it a point to let you in at this level, but I like you."

"I'm rather, ah, tight right now, actually, Joe."

"The last thing I would ever want to be accused of would be high-pressure tactics, friend. If you choose not to go on this one, fine and dandy, fine and dandy! But this is one of those truly rare gems. I really urge you to come in. I really do. I can take your check for the amount and hold it a few days if that would help."

Harvey wanted to say no. He ached to say it. But they were within a hairbreadth now, apparently, of having almost a formalistic new hearing and sending Eagle's appropriation to the Senate floor. Lydia Baines had called only yesterday to say that Matthew Johns believed it would come within the next week or ten days.

Clearly D. L. Boudoin had had some influence on Clifford Sweet. Harvey did not know what tactic had been used and did not want to know. But it was working.

Did he, under these circumstances, dare offend Boudoin's son-in-law?

"Harvey?" Wind said. "Are you there, buddy?"

"I'm . . . here," Harvey said.

"What do you say, pal? Can I look for your check in the next mail?"

Harvey thought of his savings situation. If this was going to go on, he would strip himself bare. But he could not tell Lydia about this. He was in it on his own; it had to remain secret. And if Eagle was approved, the rewards would far exceed this loss, even if Joe Wind never paid him back a cent.

"Harv?"

"I'll . . . put a check in the mail at once," Harvey said swallowing hard.

"That's a mighty wise decision, Harvey! You'll never regret it! Oh, and incidentally, my father-in-law asked me to send his regards the next time we talked."

"My regards to him, too."

Moments after the connection was broken, the intercom light pulsed.

"Yes?" Harvey snapped.

"Sir, the lines are still busy to—"

"Don't tell me your problems, God damn it! Just try again! Keep trying until you get through!"

"Yes, sir."

The new call from Joe Wind was very upsetting. Harvey now had the terrifying vision of more calls . . . endless calls . . . always wanting more and more investment cash. Right now, he had to keep Joe Wind happy. And perhaps . . . just perhaps . . . he was being alarmist. Perhaps these investment opportunities did not come up frequently. Perhaps Wind's promises would be verified in a high return per dollar.

And at any rate, once Eagle was approved, he would not have to gamble any more with Joe Wind or anyone else.

This was a more cheering thought. Harvey told himself he would cling to it. He turned his thoughts back to the call he was trying to put through to Sunset Electronic Systems.

Sunset was a struggling young giant founded almost a decade earlier by a close friend of Harvey's named John Klepner. Harvey and Klepner had gone to college together, and their wives had always been close. They exchanged telephone calls regularly and saw each other at least twice a year.

Thanks largely to this friendship, Sunset had been given advance notice when the original cost-estimate requests went out on Eagle. As a result, Klepner's firm had come in with one of the first estimates—and the lowest—for supplying systems modules for the Eagle guidance package. At the time, Harvey had been delighted because he had helped a friend and gotten Hempstead a good probable bid.

Now, however, thanks to the new letter of intent he had signed for Interspace Industries, the package of engineering drawings and estimates nestled in the central files and bearing the Sunset name plate was a dagger pointed at Harvey's heart. Even allowing for the fact that Interspace was necessary politically, he could never justify handing them the guidance-system contract as long as Sunset's much lower estimate remained on file. Harvey had to get Sunset's records out of the files as if they had never existed.

When the telephone call finally went through, a few minutes later, he smoothly put his plan into operation.

"Jack, how in the world are you!" he asked his friend Klepner.

"Busy times, Harvey." Klepner's voice sounded more tense than usual, with blurry edges of fatigue. "When are you going to get down for some serious drinking and maybe some sailing?"

"Soon, I hope," Harvey told him, leaning back and hiking his feet onto the edge of a desk drawer. "It's been too long."

"It sure has, buddy. We were talking about you just the other night."

"We're extremely busy here, Jack. I suppose you are too?"

Klepner paused, then spoke in a lower tone, one that did not hide a note of discouragement. "Harvey, to tell you the truth, we've been having a little slump here."

"No."

"Yes, I—well, hell, I can tell *you*. I had to lay off about eighty people a couple of weeks ago. We took a real flier on that ham radio gear, and then they changed all the frequency allocations and we're having to take back all the transceivers and rework them. We're out the other end on that transponder modification for the Air Force, and . . . well, things have just taken a downturn generally."

"I'm genuinely sorry to hear that, Jack." Hearing the worry in his friend's voice, Harvey thought briefly about canceling his plan. But he knew just as quickly that he could not do this. Business was business. It was too late to turn back. "I trust things will turn up for you shortly. They can't keep a good man down, you know."

"I was hoping," Klepner said, "that you might be calling about Eagle starts. I know we have that good bid there with you. The papers say things look good. Eagle would really bail us out, Harvey."

"Jack," Harvey said, "I *was* calling about Eagle, but I'm afraid the news isn't the kind you want to hear."

There was a pause. "I don't know if I can hack any more bad news right now, Harvey."

"I'm calling you to save you grief, actually."

"What do you mean?"

"You remember your estimates as you submitted them originally?"

"I should. We spent a thousand man-hours on that document. I was up with it myself for days running."

"You remember the double redundancy on crucial components?"

"Sure. We built that right into our base figures."

"That's the problem, Jack. It now looks like we won't be asking for double redundancy. The military is going to ask for a triple-backup system."

"Triple! That's going to raise the price per unit by 20 per cent!"

"I know that," Harvey said. "Now, of course, your estimates say they cover, as I recall the language, quote, normal redundancy as required by user, unquote, without specifying double or triple or anything else."

Klepner's voice now betrayed a new kind of alarm. "Harvey, it was just assumed that it was double redundancy! My God, if we were asked to put in *another* backup set of components, at the price we quoted, we couldn't come out ahead at all! We would lose money on the deal!"

"I know that," Harvey said. "That's why I'm calling. Now, Jack, you know those estimates were not legally binding, in the real sense—"

"I can't stand behind them for triple redundancy! We can't make them for that figure! We would be ruined!"

"—and of course most of us recognize that," Harvey went on calmly. "Now, admittedly, there probably are some legal bloodhounds on our staff who would want to try to hold you to the bid or at least pay the prescribed penalty for withdrawal—"

"Harvey, this could ruin us."

"But I don't want any of that to come about," Harvey added. He was sure he had the hook set now, so he began to reel in. "I feel I can handle this for you, Jack. Informally. That's really why I called. You feel you can't stand behind the estimates in file here?"

"There's no way, Harvey! My God!"

"All right, then. Listen. Suppose you write me a letter at once. In it you simply state that you wish to withdraw Sunset's estimates. You can cite the long delay and rising materials costs if you like. But keep it vague. That way, our lawyers can't try to hold your feet to the fire on a technicality. I'll personally pull your estimate files and return them to you."

"Can you do that?" Klepner asked hopefully. "Legally, I mean?"

"If you ask for the file back, it's your file," Harvey said. "And I can put your letter requesting withdrawal in the file as my justification."

"You won't get in trouble? I mean, I don't want you sticking your neck out just because we're old friends."

"I'll be glad to do it."

"All right," Klepner said, his voice somewhat easier with relief. "I'll dictate the letter immediately. You should get it tomorrow. And you can then pull our estimates and mail them back to me."

"I intend to pull them now," Harvey said. "No sense letting them catch any lawyer's eye in the interim."

"Harvey," Klepner said with obviously sincere emotion, "we needed Eagle. I'm going to get my people to work on a possible new bid if it's approved. And we'll build in triple redundancy this time."

The added cost, Harvey thought, would put the bid almost in the same price category with Interspace. It could then be rejected on the grounds of lateness. "That sounds perfect, Jack."

"We're on shaky ground. The original Eagle contract could have saved us. But your warning helps us stay afloat a little while longer, anyway. I really appreciate it." Klepner sounded as if, in his tension, he was actually on the verge of tears. "When things go wrong, they really go wrong. But you helped and I appreciate it."

"Jack," Harvey said, "what are friends for?"

After completing the call, he went immediately to Central Filing.

It was easy to find the Sunset file in the maze of brown envelopes. He pulled it, putting it under his arm, and substituted a printed card which read WITHDRAWN—REQUEST OF BIDDER. When Klepner's formal letter arrived, it would take the place of the temporary card.

Returning to his office, he locked the Sunset file in his desk. He felt considerably better. Let Ken Lis make a grandstand trip to Europe, he thought. While he was gone, Eagle could become a reality.

12

A small patch of heavy weather diverted the flight into Monravia, so that the approach was over the sea and the cliffs. A late-afternoon sun lighted the cliffs and their plumes of spray in a crimson light. These, Janis Malone recalled from the guidebook, were the famed Cliffs of Blood, where ancient Monravians had withstood the attacks of a dozen angry neighbors. Janis wondered how many of those old-time attackers had come with greater real desperation than this trade mission concealed. Hempstead Aviation simply had to have Monravia's order.

Beyond the cliffs, Janis saw high, flat plains dotted with cattle and sheep and, here and there, a meandering fence line of piled rock. She spied a tiny village with twisting streets, and then, as the plane continued turning, the towering bulk of the mountains rose up in her window, peaked with snow of the purest white. It was an incredibly beautiful view.

The plane came around toward the east, descending more rapidly. Ahead loomed resort hotels on the golden beaches that had made Monravia famous in the contemporary world, and then the plane's wheels came down and they were skimming quite low over the old interior city: church steeples, tortured little streets, gray buildings with red clay roofs, green parks, and colorful squares. Janis momentarily spied a jewel-like golf course with a clubhouse whose red roof had turrets on the corners. Then there were some small lakes, a tree-lined boulevard clogged with traffic, a serenely curving river spanned here and there by old bridges with Roman arches, and then a modern highway and some open grassland. The plane sank lower, its engine note changing, and there was a power line, and the large painted runway numbers on the end of the concrete slab, and the plane whooshed gently down.

At the administration building, an old structure with multiple roofs and gargoyles, and modern wings extending out in both directions along the ramp, there were a number of black Cadillacs pulled up and waiting, a small crowd, and a military band.

"Looks like we get welcomed." Ken Lis smiled, slipping his suit coat on.

"Aye," Barton MacIvor said. "I just hope their meetin's are as friendly as their greetin's."

The Hempstead team filed off the plane: Lis, MacIvor, Janis, four more executives from Sales, the seven representatives of the mechanical-and-engineering team, and then the others, including the protocol man assigned by the State Department. Janis had a sharp sense of fairyland as she went down to the ramp, the band playing. There was a fresh, warm breeze, carrying with it the scent of jasmine and sea spray.

She did not see Prince David in the group of welcomers.

Lucian Derquet, a carnation in his lapel, came forward to shake hands and make introductions. "The royal family awaits you at the palace," he told them. "It is our greatest pleasure to have you with us."

Close beside Janis, MacIvor whispered for her ears only, "Did ye ever wonder aboot the fire hazard with all that oil?"

Janis stifled a giggle as MacIvor left her and lumbered over to Lis's side, where he hovered like a big guardian bear.

There was brief pomp on the ramp, with the honor guard smartly presenting arms—ancient Garand rifles—as Lis and the two men from the U.S. embassy walked down their line with Derquet and another Monravian functionary. A handful of newsmen stood behind restraining ropes, and a few flashbulbs went off. Then Janis and the others were escorted toward the limousines, one of Derquet's assistants nervously directing them toward different cars by some prearranged plan.

Janis found herself shepherded to a limousine along with pilots Bert Beggs and Jeff Riordan, and the three of them lined up on the wide back seat, facing a strikingly beautiful young woman who introduced herself as Monravia's assistant minister of commerce, Dorothea Telreaux.

"We look forward to most fine presentation from Hempstead Aviation," the beautiful young woman told them as the cars smoothly departed the ramp. "It will be most pleasure to speak of America with such as yourself."

Bert Beggs was bulky, balding, phlegmatic, and he blinked at Dorothea Telreaux and said nothing. Copilot Jeff Riordan, however, was considerably younger, and good-looking in a lean and hawkish way. He grinned at Dorothea Telreaux and leaned slightly toward her. "You've got beautiful country. I hope we get to see some of it."

Dorothea gave him a cool smile. "Thank you. Yes."

She was the kind of woman, Janis thought uncomfortably, who could turn a man's head. Her accent, possibly French, was thick. But, combined with her husky voice, it was charming. Her navy dress was cut in the latest fashion, with a white kerchief at the depths of a rather low neckline. The length of the dress, and her position on the rather low jumpseat facing them, revealed great legs. Her long black hair, combed and tucked tightly in a bun, was not so severe that it detracted from the classic beauty of her face, lighted by large dark eyes. Janis did not fail to notice—as Jeff Riordan obviously had also noticed—that beneath the coolly elegant exterior was a body that would be stunning in a bikini. Dorothea's deep and lovely tan indicated that she indeed must find time enough for bikinis.

"Have you been to America often?" Janis asked as the motorcade moved onto the major highway and picked up speed.

"Nevair," Dorothea Telreaux said. "But on my most recent trip, to the Soviet Union, Prince David has promise me that I will go with him when he goes to America the following time."

Janis was aware of a stab of jealousy. "Do you travel often with Prince David?"

"Oh, but yes. I did not travel to America last time because my duties are of considerable busy then, but otherwise I would made trip then."

Jeff Riordan stirred. "You and the prince pretty close, are you?"

Dorothea showed him twin rows of small, perfectly formed teeth. "But yes. You see, I am of royal family also, much remove. Fourth cousin. So we are vairy close."

Janis stifled an impulse to say something obscene. She said nothing at all. The woman facing her was elegant and cool and perfect, while her own linen suit was rumpled from the flight from Scotland, her skin felt oily and soiled, and her hair hung limp in the humidity. She wished she hadn't come on this junket.

The high-speed drive continued. Fortunately for Janis, Jeff Riordan indicated a lively interest in the sights along the way, although every time Dorothea turned to explain something they were passing, he seemed really more interested in her legs.

They soon reached the palace, which was a small city in itself, behind tall yellow stone walls. As the car jolted through an iron gateway, its tires bumped over ancient cobblestones of a huge central courtyard. A number of impressive stone buildings looked down on this courtyard, but by far the largest and most impressive was the main building, the palace itself.

The car stopped in front of this structure. It shadowed the warm cobblestones. Janis, like everyone else, got out of the car. A small band off to one side began playing something that might have been recognizable as a medley from *Oklahoma*, if the tempo had been right.

The main palace building loomed up incredibly. Janis stared at its bulk, frankly amazed. Walls of huge granitic block towered up—how far? six stories?—and beyond were gables, turrets, acres of red tile roof. Rows of windows stared down. An enormous portico fronting the glittering bronze front doorway was draped with Monravian and American flags, and even the state flag of California. The band was now playing "California, Here I Come."

"Come, my dear," Dorothea Telreaux murmured, touching Janis's arm to guide her toward a spot where all the others seemed to be congregating.

Feeling a little like a head of cattle, Janis allowed herself to be nudged into her place in the line. She waited. Barton MacIvor shot her a wink. The little band stopped playing.

The honor-guard captain barked a muted command. Heels clicked and rifles came up to salute. It suddenly grew quiet in the compound. Janis became aware of an old man off to one side, standing beside his pushcart. He had removed his cap and was standing at attention, his rheumy eyes alert.

The front doors of the palace swung open. Another guard captain stepped out smartly, slamming his heels together at attention. The band began playing a martial song. Two elderly diplomats came through the doors, and then another captain in smart uniform, and then Prince David Peltier.

Grinning, he came down the steps quickly. In a nod toward formality he wore a gray leisure suit, but the shirt was open at the collar. His eyes swept the line as he approached, and for a split second they rested on Janis. Her heart leaped.

Just as quickly, however, he reached the place where Ken Lis was standing with the U.S. ambassador. There was handshaking and some smiling conversation. Then the group began to mill slightly as the prince moved from person to person in greeting.

Janis, well at the end of the line with Dorothea Telreaux, was aware that her heart was beating very fast. She had mentally rehearsed this moment many times. Now she was acutely aware of how dumpy she must look beside the statuesque Dorothea. What would he say to her? Would he even remember her that clearly? Of course he would. She knew that.

Prince David reached her in the line. He grinned widely at her, squeezing her hands. "So we meet again, Miss Malone. I want you to enjoy our country." He turned to Dorothea Telreaux. "I want you to take especially good care of this one, my dear."

"Yes, David," Dorothea said. "Of course."

The prince moved on down the line. Janis was left with a tingling sense of aftershock. She realized that she had been harboring some awfully crazy daydreams.

With a shuddering breath, she put them behind her. Now, at least, she could concentrate on the job, she told herself.

13

After being escorted to a large and richly decorated bedroom on the third floor of the palace, Ken Lis had only ten minutes alone before someone rapped on the door and he opened it to admit Prince David Peltier and a young woman of perhaps twenty-five. She was dark and pretty, and wore a dress with a slightly military cut, which Lis had noticed on several other women in the palace.

"A thousand pardons for interrupting you," Prince David said anxiously. "Is it all right for us to visit with you briefly?"

"Of course," Lis told him. "I'm sure we need to put our heads together."

"Mr. Lis, may I present Chris Ingels."

Lis shook hands with the girl. "You're American?"

"No," she smiled. "German. But I attended your Columbia University."

"Chris is a member of the palace staff," Prince David explained. "She's excellent at news releases, and helps entertain guests and plan our social functions. She is also a former Olympic swimmer, an incredible golf player, a fantastic tennis player, an expert in five languages, a chess genius—"

"Oh, wait, wait!" Chris Ingels laughed.

"I think I agree with you," Lis told her. "I'm getting intimidated."

Prince David grinned, then turned serious. "Chris is also a trusted and good friend, Mr. Lis. She understands the palace intrigue. If at all possible, I want you to have some time with her during your visit. Perhaps through her you can understand some of our plots and counterplots. You will need this information to see how perhaps to handle some of the members of our cabinet."

Lis sized Chris Ingels up, noting that in addition to being attractive she appeared exceptionally clear-eyed and quick. She had the body of a good athlete. "Maybe we can even get in a couple of sets of tennis," he suggested.

"Do you play well?" she asked with a slight smile.

"I'm afraid I've been playing mostly racquetball the last year. It plays faster—provides exercise in a shorter period of time."

"Possibly we can try a set or two," she said.

"May we sit down?" Prince David asked, indicating chairs near a window.

"Of course. Forgive me." They took chairs in a semicircle. "Your official welcome at the airport and here at the palace was really something."

Prince David grimaced. "If some elements had their way, our guard would still be wearing armor. It was all I could do to keep them from bringing out the cavalry and the large band. We are tradition-bound, Mr. Lis. It is a great cross to bear."

"Prime Minister Derquet told me on the way from the airport about some of your more colorful history."

Prince David leaned forward with keener interest. "Did he also speak of our meetings? What did he say?"

"He started to mention the agenda," Lis said. "But one of your other ministers—is it Katrokos?"

"Katrokos. Yes. Our Minister of Culture."

"Katrokos pointed out the old castle just as the subject of the agenda came up, and we never got back to it."

The prince smacked a fist into his palm. "Ah, that Katrokos! He is a good and loyal man, but he will be the death of me! He should have kept quiet!"

"Don't you know the agenda for our talks?" Lis asked, puzzled.

"Yes, of course. But I had hoped you might be able to get some hint from Derquet's conversation about the strategy he plans to employ, what points he plans to attack most heavily."

"He's openly opposed now to buying Excalibur?"

"He is a very devious man. He talks out of both sides of his mouth, and after spouting confusion that paralyzes the cabinet with indecision, he says he is only trying to view all possibilities. Ah! He will drive me insane, that one!"

"I was under the impression that it might be the Queen we really have to convince."

"Ultimately, yes. But she will not act without a consensus in her cabinet. Lucian and some of his henchmen have great influence."

Lis glanced at Chris Ingels.

"Do not wonder that I speak out in front of Chris, my friend," Prince David said. "If something is to be known in this palace, she already knows it. And she is, as I have said, a good and trusted friend." He frowned. "Of whom there are far too few these days."

"I don't pretend to understand the internal politics," Lis replied. "But we have a complete presentation ready, and we hope to take cabinet members for a demonstration flight if they wish. No one will be able to say there are unanswered questions by the time we get through here."

"What about the crash investigation?"

"It stands where it did."

"No conclusion?"

"None. But the fact that no cause has been found is significant to me. Especially after all the tests we and Transwestern have run on our own. For a time I was shaken—thought there might be a hidden flaw. But TW has flown hundreds of takeoffs and landings in regular service since New York, and there have been no incidents of any kind. Their crews are under orders to report the slightest oddity in flight, and the worst they've come up with are routine instrument malfunctions and problems with radios, matters of that sort."

"You believe, then—?"

"I believe Excalibur is sound. The crash was some sort of wild fluke that will never happen again. I would not have flown my people over here in a new production Excalibur if I weren't completely confident in its performance."

"Is this—please forgive me, my friend—but is this a true personal belief, or the voice of a businessman speaking?"

"It's the truth," Lis told him.

"Good! Excellent! I am relieved. If dear Lucian spouts worries about a crash, do you have figures on how many flights have been made since the accident?"

"Oh, yes." Lis paused, then decided to go ahead and say it. "I get

255

the impression that you think Derquet may be playing a power game of his own here, fighting Excalibur for reasons that may not be very sincere."

"Sincere?" Prince David snorted. "Lucian does not know the word! The deviousness of the man is fantastic!"

"Then, maybe we've wasted our time."

"I hope not, my friend!"

Chris Ingels said, "The Prime Minister is mercurial. He has been known to change his mind in a brief time span. You remember the case of the railroad, Prince David."

The prince nodded and looked brighter. "Competing companies visited us to discuss extensions of our rail system, with new links into the Eurorail system. Lucian was adamantly opposed to the company favored by a majority of the cabinet, and held enough votes to make my mother pause. Then, as if by magic, he studied the matter further and became a most enthusiastic supporter of the plan, which is now being carried toward fruition. So I believe, as Chris says, there is hope, Mr. Lis. Perhaps if you flatter him . . . cajole him. . . ."

"I'll do my best," Lis promised.

The prince scowled and held up one finger. "And Dorothea."

"Dorothea?"

"Dorothea Telreaux. She rode in the car with your pilots and Miss Malone."

"She's a member of the cabinet also?"

"Yes. And another thorn in my side, believe me!"

"She's a striking young woman."

"She is, sir, what could I say, it is like when a hen lays an egg." The prince frowned and then brightened as he found the word. "A cluck. Yes. Cluck, cluck! She is a cluck, that woman! My God, sir, I believe that woman was sent into my life for a purgatory. And my mother adores her. She is a cousin. A *distant* cousin. I only wish she would be much more distant."

"She's on Derquet's side?" Lis asked.

"She pretends to be on my side, but actually she sides with him most often. My mother says this proves her intellect. Intellect! She has the intellect of a dead cow and the fiendish guile of a deadly snake. My mother talks about how I could marry the cow and re-unite old bloodlines. I tell you, Mr. Lis, to marry that viper would be a crucifixion!"

Lis had to smile at the prince's passionate hyperbole. "Are we talking about the same woman? The one I met was a knockout."

"A knockout? Yes. Beautiful? Yes. A stinging scorpion has a kind of beauty. A coral snake is beautiful."

"But she has a place in the cabinet."

"Yes," Prince David sighed bitterly. "My mother believes the proximity will make me marry the tarantula! And Dorothea is clever in this regard. She sides with Lucian, tempting me to be nice to her to win her to my position. Twice she has spoken against your airplane, and she knows as much about airplanes as she knows about the planet Jupiter."

"Perhaps you ought to tell me about the other members of the cabinet."

The prince raised his arms and slapped them against his sides. "If you convince Lucian and Dorothea, you will have broken the back of the unholy alliance speaking against your airplane. But it will not be easy, this I warn you. Perhaps the black widow spider hopes to establish a dominance over me that will end in a marriage. Perhaps the camel plays some deeper game with Lucian. How does one read the mind of such a vile microbe? I have given up!"

Lis looked at Chris Ingels. She smiled grimly. "Dorothea has been pursuing very hard lately."

"She makes nausea rise in my throat!" Prince David grabbed at his neck and made a violent gagging noise. "I go horseback riding, and she is there in a dress that hikes high on her legs, as if she will seduce me! I go swimming, and she is there in her black bikini, as if the sight of her bare belly will overwhelm me with passion and I will throw her down and mount her on the spot! I go driving and she manages to find a way to come along, making her little *eeks* and *awks* as if she were frightened by speed! I tell you, sir, that shark knows no fear, and she is continually circling me! Only by inventing a crisis for her department was I able to keep her off our plane when we visited your country."

"And I'm supposed to handle this lady in some way?" Lis asked.

"Charm her. She is vain, like all peafowl. Compliment her; she will preen. Touch her arm; she will tremble. Speak to her of serious matters as if you thought she had a brain bigger than the dropping of a pigeon; she will be dazzled and perhaps convinced of your viewpoint."

257

Lis shook his head in frank wonderment. "I'll do what I can. But I'm afraid I'm better with a slide rule than table conversation."

The prince got to his feet. "I will leave you now with Chris. She will answer any questions you may have." He glanced at his watch. "Even now I am late for a meeting with Lucian and Dorothea and some others, and I am sure they have already sent her looking for me, like a mastiff on the trail of a dying criminal."

Lis walked with him to the door. "I appreciate the information. And we'll make this work out all right."

Prince David turned, his expression different. "Do not allow the political scheming and manipulation to blind you to Monravia, my friend. It is a very beautiful and great country. Please understand that. Our petty quarrels cannot undermine the greatness of the country."

Lis was touched by his intense sincerity. "I understand."

With a wave, the prince stepped out into the corridor, magically transforming himself with a boyish gait and a bright, vacuous smile.

Lis closed the door and went back to Chris Ingels. "He's playing a deep game, your prince."

"He has to."

"You think the plotting and counterplotting is truly serious?"

"It is why I am here," she told him bluntly. "I believe Lucian Derquet and his kind will overstep themselves one day. I am dedicated, as long as I work here, to being on the scene the day they go too far."

"I wonder if they know you're watching for their misstep."

"I am just one of many," the amazing young woman said grimly. "They cannot watch us all . . . as we watch them. One day they will make a mistake, and we will have them, and this intrigue will have ended."

Lis continued to smile at the girl, but he felt a small chill inside. Excalibur, he saw, was only one of perhaps many symbols in a large power game. That made the outcome of the mission completely unpredictable.

14

From the opening session of actual business talks on Excalibur, Ken Lis knew that his gut feeling of difficulty had been, if anything, understated.

Nothing seemed to go well.

Although Lucian Derquet couched every question in the friendliest possible terms, it was clear that he had done his homework and was eager to point out every area where Excalibur might possibly be seen as inferior to another aircraft. He knew, for example, about higher maintenance costs involved in checking and maintaining the slot-wing fixtures. And he had sharp questions as to why Monravia should select a plane with Excalibur's range and payload in the face of other planes such as the LC-1011.

Forewarned, Lis tried to answer every objection calmly. The first round of meetings, however, never got to substantive issues, as Derquet continued to question, and clearly some members of the Queen's advisory cabinet were impressed by his negative points.

The second and last day's early talks seemed to go no better. Lis had begun to conclude privately, with a profound depression, that Derquet had a deal brewing with some other firm and was bound to torpedo thoughts of buying Excalibur.

Very late the second afternoon, the talks were concluded. A state dinner was scheduled for the evening. Turning down an offer of tennis or golf, Lis was headed for his room and a telephone call to California when he was intercepted by Derquet himself.

"Mr. Lis," Derquet said quietly, "a few words with you, I beg."

"In my room?" Lis asked.

"Splendid."

They went to the large, handsome guest room on the west side of the palace main building. The last rays of sunset poured through massive windows. Complimentary liquor was arranged on a cabinet, and Lis poured brandies for both himself and Derquet before sitting to face the minister near the fireplace.

"Mr. Lis," Derquet told him soberly, "you must realize that I care only for the future of Monravia. I am impressed with your aircraft. What I fear is the fact of being first in Europe with it, especially in view of the crash."

"We've tried to show that the crash was not Excalibur's fault," Lis said.

"Yes." Derquet frowned. "And as I have thought about it, I see that this may be true, Mr. Lis. Now, at the conclusion of our talks, I am almost convinced to swing my support to purchase of the Excalibur. But I must be honest with you, sir. There is a question of politics. I have spoken out rather strongly against this purchase. If I were to change my position now, for no obvious reason, it could make me appear weak and vacillatory to many of my associates."

"Are you saying you're locked into a position you no longer like?"

"I am saying, sir, that perhaps I have been wrong. And now we must find some method whereby I can change my position without appearing a fool or a weakling."

Lis told himself to be careful. It sounded good, but he suspected a hook in this bait. "Do you have something in mind?"

"It is possible, sir." Derquet got to his feet and walked to the windows, looking out for what seemed a long time in silence. "Are you aware, sir, that Air France will soon update portions of its domestic Common Market fleet?"

"Yes," Lis said, surprised. "As a matter of fact, we've filed papers to compete for that purchase. But I understand that any orders are at least a year away."

Derquet turned to look at him, and it was impossible to read this man's expression, although it seemed to be hiding something. It was *too* sincere for sincerity.

He said, "France's purchase may not be that far in the future, Mr. Lis."

"I wasn't aware of that."

Derquet began to pace nervously. "Allow me to make my theory clear. I have many friends in high places within the French Government. I have learned, in doing research about our own proposed purchase, that Air France may be expected to move much sooner than anyone had believed, in a matter of weeks, or months at the most."

"I'm surprised," Lis said. "With recent Concorde developments, I thought they might be two years from new expenditure."

Derquet held up a finger as if he were about to lecture a class. "Suppose, Mr. Lis, France were to order a rather large number of airplanes from your company. If this order were announced soon, consider what this would do for my situation. One. Monravia would no longer be the lonely pioneer. Two. France's order would be obvious public motive for me to change my position of antagonism to our own entry into the field with your airplane. Three. The existence of such a large European order might even allow you to make some small reduction in per-unit cost to us, further giving me obvious reason for changing my position without loss of face. In other words"—Derquet turned and pointed at Lis—"an Excalibur order by France would allow an immediate order by Monravia, without damage to me."

"There's only one thing wrong with that," Lis said slowly, digesting it. "Our competitive position is not good with France. Lockheed has already put its foot in the door with the military version of—"

"But you forget, Mr. Lis, what I told you! I have many good and powerful friends in the French Government."

Lis stared at the minister. "Meaning?"

"Mr. Lis, because this matter is sensitive, I must pledge you to total secrecy. Is that agreed?"

"Of course."

"Excellent. Now, what I am saying is this. It may be in my interest, and that of my country, for you to sell us the Excalibur. But it will be much easier for all of us if we have another country's purchase—say, France's purchase—as precedent. I wish this to happen. It may be that between us, you and me, we can *make* it happen."

"From what you've told me, you can be sure we'll redouble our sales efforts in Paris at once. Beyond that—"

"Mr. Lis, there are many ways things are accomplished in politics." Derquet watched him carefully.

"I'm sure of that," Lis said.

"There are ways, my friend Mr. Lis, to assure the order of your airplane by France. I feel this. I am confident of it. You see, the government of our neighbor to the north, as beloved a neighbor as she is, that government is not as strong and free of influence as our own. I believe that the application of the correct pressures could bring a quick settlement there—a decision to order your airplane. I know the right people, and for the good of Monravia, I am willing to take extraordinary measures to see this done." Derquet paused and sighed. "But now, sir, we are at what you Americans would call the nitty-gritty."

"Money?"

"Yes, sir." Derquet sighed again. "Certain favors must be given. I myself would not be involved, you understand. But it would be necessary, to make this take place swiftly and smoothly, that certain gratuities be exchanged . . . certain entertainments lavished upon officials—I leave details to your imagination, sir, as I am sure you know the things of which I speak."

"If I understand you correctly," Lis said, "my company would provide you with a certain sum of money. That sum would be used to buy action in France—"

"Public relations, sir," Derquet said quickly. "Call it a fund for public relations if you will."

"We would hand you a certain public-relations fund," Lis corrected himself. "This money would then be passed on to certain people in France, and as a result, France might buy Excaliburs for its fleet."

"Air France, sir, might buy as many as forty planes. And this would allow Monravia to enter its own order with no loss of prestige by anyone."

Lis went to his suitcase and got out a cigarette, making a big thing of lighting it. He hoped Derquet would believe he was considering immediate acceptance. "How much money are we talking about?" he asked.

"I believe, sir, one million would be adequate."

"Dollars?"

"Oh, yes. Dollars."

Lis almost smiled. Poor Lydia, with her little bag of fifty thousand dollars. "How would this be paid?"

"It would be necessary that it be delivered to me."

"In cash?"

Derquet appeared startled. "Yes, of course."

"You realize that I am not empowered to make a decision such as this on my own."

"Of course." Derquet smiled, apparently feeling he was past the worst of it now. "But when you take this idea to your Mrs. Baines, please stress the urgency. You understand."

Lis made his face completely neutral. "I appreciate your position, Mr. Derquet. I will relay this information to Mrs. Baines, and I feel sure we will be back in touch very shortly."

"Excellent! You understand, Mr. Lis, that there is nothing in this for me. It is only for love of my country that I would ever become involved, even indirectly, in such a course."

"Oh, yes, certainly," Lis said.

"It is the French companies. They simply do business this way."

"Right. Of course. That's all understood."

Derquet extended his hand. "This will be our secret for now, Mr. Lis. I hope it will lead to an arrangement which will help both of us, and most of all my beloved Monravia!"

After showing the minister out, Lis went to the window and looked out at the evening for a long time. He had a great deal to assimilate.

It was much bigger than he had anticipated, and much dirtier. If Lucian Derquet could influence a decision of this magnitude by a company in a country like France, he had very powerful allies. But Derquet would not easily promise what he did not really think he could deliver. . . . It had been done like this, Lis thought suddenly, when Derquet changed his position on a rail line linking Monravia to other countries in the Common Market, and there the minister had obviously not only delivered, but affected the commerce of several other countries.

It was a nasty game. There was no way of guessing how much of the million dollars, if delivered, would be Derquet's. Certainly he would get some of it as the central architect of the scheme. And there would probably be rake-offs all along the line, on deliveries, on scheduling favoritism, on custom outfitting of the planes as they were delivered. And—amazingly—Derquet would get a piece of all of this while only—to all outward appearances—working hard for his own country.

Lis knew that one of his options was to notify Prince David at once. But there was absolutely no proof. The prince might believe him, but they would still be helpless. This was not the time for Lis or anyone else to try to blow a whistle.

No, Derquet was more clever than that. To involve Derquet, Hempstead Aviation had to involve itself—with a payoff. And then no one would want to see another party caught.

Lis wondered what Lydia Baines's reaction was going to be. He knew what Jason would have said. But it was now a different ball game . . . a more dangerous and complicated one.

15

A day later, Ken Lis and Janis Malone sat side by side in the first-class cabin of the Excalibur, inbound for the East Coast of the United States.

"Glad to get home?" Lis asked, breaking a long silence.

Janis, her thoughts snatched back from thousands of miles, nodded. "I'm tired."

"We all are." Lis tapped the London newspaper on his lap. "But I think we've got our work cut out for us."

An article on an inside page, which he had found and pointed out to Janis earlier, was datelined Washington. It said Senator Clifford Sweet's committee in the U. S. Senate was expected to report favorably on a new weapons system appropriation within the next few days. The system was Hempstead's Eagle.

"We'll be going into production immediately?" Janis asked.

"Very quickly," Lis replied, his lips compressing.

"It won't hurt Excalibur."

"Not directly . . . not very badly, anyway. I think we can find and train new line personnel, and God knows the company can use all that extra income. But you know how some of us feel about depending on defense work."

"The morality?"

"Leaving the morality aside, we build that big production capability. Then we go full-bore for a few years. Then the contract is over. People are out of work. Our equipment and buildings are languishing. We get in a corner. We have to look for another one-shot contract to keep everything going a while longer. There's no continuity in defense work of this nature. Bigger companies, like Boeing and Lockheed, can absorb the ups and downs. We can't. We're trading some fat years immediately for a series of crises in the future."

"Wouldn't Mrs. Baines say that Eagle will open the door for more contracts?"

Lis smiled thinly. "Precisely. They've said that a lot of places—and some of the biggest who said it have had to have government loans to bail them out in the long run, after the proposition was proven untrue."

"But obviously," Janis said, "your view isn't prevailing at Hempstead." She almost added, *any more.*

"Right again," Lis said. "Aerospace will probably be the biggest division within a year. Even if Excalibur does all we dreamed for it—which I still believe it will—Harvey will have the glamour division now." He glanced down at his newspaper and frowned. "And probably the presidency."

"It's none of my business, but what will you do if that happens?"

"There are a lot of roads to cross before we have to face that one. Some of the private talks with Monravia were very interesting. I have some unusual aspects to report to Lydia. Depending on how all that goes, I could be around a long while yet."

Janis did not reply at once. The implication was so clear that it astonished her. In any event, Ken Lis was now facing the possibility of leaving the company. The question, by implication, seemed not to be *if*, but *when*. It was an eventuality that Janis had known might exist; but she had never before confronted it.

She did not know what Hempstead Aviation would be with Ken Lis and his kind gone and those like Harvey Coughlin in control. But she had a suspicion. There would be a great many new regulations, continual blizzards of memoranda, and a tremendous bureaucratic aura of efficiency. There might even be massive company profits. But there would be none of the sense of really owing anything to a company, like the feeling she had always had at Hempstead.

It was such an unhappy prospect that she had to find a way to avoid thinking about it. "Maybe," she said, "we'll be lucky. Congress could vote down the whole thing."

Lis grinned at her. "Right. And then if Monravia will buy, and we get a clean bill from the NTSB, we're home free."

"A lot of people at Hempstead like you," Janis said. "I think there are a lot of people who look at you as the main reason they're even there."

"That's nice to know, Janis. But we're too large a company for any personality cults. The idea is ridiculous anyway. If things go well, Hempstead will go right on. And if things go not so well . . . for some of us . . . Hempstead will keep right on going for a long time yet anyway."

"You're not really thinking of—leaving—any time soon, are you?"

Lis shook his head. "I told you: there are a lot of roads to cross before that one. It may be silly, but I still owe a lot to Hempstead. And I feel a responsibility for Excalibur. I intend to see it through. I'm not going to go off in a pout because of Eagle or anything else. As long as I can make a contribution, I'm committed."

Janis peered out the window. Far below, through broken cloud, she could see the East Coast just coming into view. "We're almost home," she said.

"Looking forward to seeing Hank?"

"I don't know," she admitted, and then was ashamed of herself. "Yes. I guess so."

"He's a good man, Janis. He's got some dumb ideas, but he's basically a good man."

Janis stared at her employer. "You *know*, then?"

"I've guessed."

The intercom loudspeaker overhead crackled, and the pilot's voice came over: "*Mr. Lis? Can you come to the flight deck, sir?*"

Frowning, Lis unbuckled. "Wonder what this is about."

"Maybe we're lost," Janis suggested with a smile.

"I can fix that. I'll tell them to fly straight west." Lis got out of the chair and went forward.

Left alone in her row, Janis looked back at some of the others. Most, including Barton MacIvor, were asleep. She turned to the front again.

She did not think the Monravian visit had gone well. Like Lis, she was hardly overjoyed with the news about Eagle. Anything that was likely to increase Harvey Coughlin's power in the company was bad, from her viewpoint. She knew he was a hero, but she could not bring herself to like the man. She felt insecure enough, without worrying about the future of Hempstead. There was the hearing coming up, and all the PR problems that was sure to cause. And there was Hank.

She yearned for a more stable relationship with Hank Selvy. But could it ever be if he simply would not understand that there was a life available to her beside the traditional status of barefoot and pregnant?

She brooded, wondering what she was going to do.

Then Ken Lis came back, and one look at his face told her that they had something new—and worse—to worry about.

Lis sat down. There was no color in his face.

"Another Excalibur has just crashed," he said.

16

At Pittsburgh, an Excalibur carrying eighty-seven passengers and a crew of six had been inbound for landing in marginal weather: light rain and patchy fog. Approximately one thousand feet from the runway threshold, the plane's engines roared to full power just as it pitched steeply left, entering a nose-down configuration. There was some sign of partial recovery, but the big jet impacted at a nose-down attitude of about 20 degrees, bursting like a can of tuna.

Miraculously there was no fire, and the first emergency crews on the scene managed to pull a dozen persons from the wreckage still alive. Three of these died on the way to the hospital, but the remaining nine still clung to life.

One of the survivors was the captain of the flight, a seventeen-year veteran named Scott Persons. He was terribly injured, and doctors held out little hope for him; he was unconscious and probably would not ever come out of it.

This was generally the extent of Jace Mattingly's information as he faced his superior, George Pierce, in Pierce's littered office.

"Well, it's bad," Pierce told him through the cigarette smoke. "It's very bad. We're already getting calls from Congress and the public. Naturally the press is really on our ass. This one looks just like the other one. We're going to have some hysteria if you don't find out something, and fast."

"We'll be meeting our guys already on the scene in less than two hours," Mattingly told Pierce. "We'll have tapes this time."

"We'd better have tapes," Pierce said. "We're going to have to make some kind of a statement within the next eighteen hours.

Those reporters are not stupid. They're already asking us how come the Excalibur is still licensed to fly passengers when we've had two almost identical crashes involving apparent stall on approach to landing. The *Post* was already preparing a depth piece on the simple wing—how new and revolutionary it is, et cetera. They'll hurry that up now. We're in trouble on this one and we have to *move*."

Mattingly knew the kind of pressures that were mounting without having them explained in any great detail. Leaving the office and hurrying to the airport, he found the "Go Team" waiting for him, and their plane left immediately for Pittsburgh. On the way, he mentally reviewed.

A single crash, although a cause almost always could be assigned, might sometimes be a true fluke. Two crashes, within weeks of one another and involving the same airplane—a new airplane—in almost identical situations, meant that a fluke was no longer possible. If two Excaliburs had crashed on approach to landing, there was an obvious pattern. If he could not immediately find some evidence of cause at Pittsburgh that clearly could not have also been the cause at New York, then Excalibur had to be ordered grounded for commercial traffic until things could be untangled: the flaw located and corrected to everyone's satisfaction.

More Excaliburs could not be allowed to fly and risk another crash.

Only Jace Mattingly knew how hard people had already worked on the first tragedy, and without results. That probe was already very, very costly. It had cost more than $50,000 just to salvage the wreckage at Kennedy. And Mattingly knew some of the other expenses by heart: $4,000 for photography, $3,800 for telephone tolls, $17,000 in per diem expenses, $5,300 for guards and security, $4,200 for travel, $19,000 in lab costs, $7,000 in preliminary computer time, salaries over $65,000 at minimum. And instead of being nearer a solution, they had only worse pressure and a new tragedy as goad.

The team landed at Pittsburgh in the very late afternoon. Mattingly had a headache. First editions of the morning papers were already on the news racks at the airport lobby. There were the inevitable grisly pictures of mangled wreckage and a glaring set of headlines:

SECOND EXCALIBUR CRASHES

84 Die as TW Jet
Crashes on Approach
Here; 9 Survive

Circumstances Look Same
As in Kennedy Disaster

Mattingly split his team: to the tower, to approach control, to emergency, to a pair of reported witnesses whom police had detained. Using an airport truck, he and two of his aides went directly to the crash site.

By now it was starting to get dark, and the scene was dismally familiar: portable floodlights, emergency trucks, ambulances, technicians, scattered wreckage. The stench of jet fuel hung like a pall in the wet, foggy air.

Two technicians were already inside the tail assembly, working to remove the recording devices. The word was that they were intact.

Mattingly located the airport traffic-safety man, a man named Clayton whom he had met earlier under happier circumstances. "Tell me how you have it happening."

Clayton squinted out toward the east, beyond the runway threshold, and pointed. "She was right down the middle and the pilot had visual contact with the ground. No turbulence, no wingtip vortices, nothing like that. A very little bit of rime ice reported, but nothing serious at all. The tower man says it looked like a stall break to him: the left wing fell sharply and the nose pitched over."

Mattingly nodded wearily. It was the same story. He looked out over the tangled wreckage, seeing how the wings had been sheared off at impact and the fuselage ripped open as if by a can opener. "Anything else?"

"Yes," Clayton said. "The tower said it definitely looked like a partial recovery was made in the split-second prior to impact."

"*Exactly* what did he say?" Mattingly demanded.

"He said the left wing dipped and it nosed over. But then, as he heard the engine roar, the left wing started back up again toward horizontal. He said the nose might have come up just a shade too— but it was too late."

"Hell! If that's true, then whatever happened was reversible! I mean it wasn't something that broke, or malfunctioned permanently. It was something the pilot or copilot caught, and started to fix." Mattingly slowly drew in his breath. "And to correct for whatever it was, they had to know what it was. *That pilot had to know exactly what had gone wrong!*"

"That's how it sounds to me," Clayton agreed.

"Don't you see what this means, man?" Mattingly asked. "It means that guy in the hospital had the answer!"

Clayton's eyes widened, then dimmed. "Maybe so. But he'll never help you, Jace. My God, he was broken terribly. It's a miracle he's stayed alive this long—"

"I'm going to the hospital," Mattingly said. "Can that truck take me back to the terminal?"

"Yes, but you're wasting your time! He's unconscious—dying."

"I'm going," Mattingly repeated, and ran for the truck.

The pilot *knew*. This was the single fact that Mattingly kept reverting to as he rushed to the airport and managed to convince a policeman to rush him toward the hospital in his patrol car. The pilot had been there and had reacted to *something*—something definite and identifiable and correctable. Given perhaps another few hundred feet of altitude—another few seconds—he might even now be sitting in a briefing room, giving them the solution to the whole mystery.

Scott Persons had not had that much time. But he was alive.

When he reached the hospital, Mattingly was confronted by a senior nurse on the eighth floor.

"Is he on this floor?" Mattingly demanded.

"Yes, sir, but he certainly cannot have visitors."

"I'm not a visitor." Mattingly showed his credentials.

The nurse did not blink. "It's just the same, Mr. Mattingly. The patient is very, very badly injured and you cannot see him."

"Who's the doctor in charge?"

"I am not required to give out that information, and I fail to see—"

"Listen, goddammit, I'm not some grieving relative you can bully. In about two seconds I'm going to start kicking doors in."

The nurse took one more look at his face and turned to pick up a telephone. She said a few words into it and turned back to Mattingly. "Wait one moment, please."

Mattingly lit a cigarette and paced. In about two minutes a very young doctor in a white floor coat came striding down the long corridor. His face was pink with anger.

"What's this all about?" he asked the nurse.

"This man—" she began.

Mattingly held out his wallet with the card in it. "Doctor, that pilot may have information that can solve two very bad crashes. I want to know if there's any reasonable chance I can talk with him."

The doctor smiled as if Mattingly's stupidity was amusing. "The man is unconscious. Unless you know how to talk to a man in that condition—"

"It strikes me," Mattingly cut in, "that somebody gave everybody on this floor some wise-ass pills. Do I get a straight answer or do we go to the administrator?"

"The man is not going to wake up for you, Mr. Mattingly. He has a broken pelvis, five broken ribs, smashed bones in his face, and a fractured left arm. We think his spleen has been crushed. There is evidence of intercranial pressure, and we have him on a pacemaker. We may have to take him to surgery at a moment's notice, although we would prefer to wait until he stabilizes a bit. Now, what the hell makes you think you or anyone else can make a man in that condition *talk?*"

"Could he talk if he came to? I mean, is his face so torn up he couldn't talk?"

"He could talk if he regained consciousness, Mr. Mattingly, but believe me: he is *not* going to come to."

"Let me sit in the room with him. Sometimes a man in a coma will come around for just a few seconds, won't he? I mean, he might mutter something. Believe me, doctor, this is important. Even a *word* from him might be crucial."

"Any word he spoke—assuming he spoke one—would only report to us how badly he's hurting. Unfortunately, we can't give him as much medication as we might like because of all the complicating factors."

"He's a professional," Mattingly argued. "Whatever is left of his mind right now is still at that moment of trouble in the airplane. If

273

he were to rouse, the first thing he would do would be tell us what
went wrong."

"I find that a bit far-fetched, Mr. Mattingly."

"Doctor, what in the goddam hell is wrong with me just *sitting*
there in his room?"

"You would be wasting your time!"

"It's my fucking time, isn't it?"

"All right. Come with me."

Mattingly put his cigarette in a can and followed him down the
long corridor to another nursing station. Behind the oval desk, four
nurses worked near a bank of TV-like monitor screens. One was dark
and silent. Each of the others portrayed periodically peaking green
lines, and below them numbers continually changed in digital
readout windows. Although he did not know a lot about hospitals,
Mattingly realized that each of the devices was attached electrically
to a patient in a nearby room. The nurses were monitoring the life
death struggles of a dozen patients at this station. Any major change
anywhere would set off alarm devices.

"This is Mr. Mattingly," the doctor told the head nurse here. "He
will be in that pilot's room. If he causes any disturbance, you're to
contact security at once and have him escorted out. I'm telling the
nurse in the room the same thing. Understood?"

The nurse gave Mattingly a glance of increased respect. "Yes, Doc
tor."

The doctor took Mattingly on down the hall and then into a
room.

It was cold and dim. A nurse sat in a straight chair beside a bed
On the bed lay Scott Persons, or what was left of him. Covered by a
light sheet, he lay very still, face up into a light. His head was
swathed in bandages. Tubes extended from both hands to bottles
suspended on gleaming racks. Wires ran out from under the coverlet
to a machine on the wall not unlike those out at the desk. This ma
chine blipped softly, regularly.

"Sit there," the doctor ordered curtly, pointing to a chair against
the bare far wall. Then he went over and bent over the nurse to have
a brief conversation with her, very low. Mattingly assumed he was re
peating all his threats.

After the doctor left, the nurse returned her attention to a maga
zine in her lap. The room, except for the regular blipping of the

monitor, was still, with a distant rush of air conditioning. Mattingly began to wonder why hospital chairs had to be so uncomfortable. Possibly someone specially designed them that way. He waited.

Seven o'clock came, then eight. The doctor came back once, only cracking the door to look in for a moment. As more time passed, the nurse occasionally flipped pages of her magazine, the stiff paper making sounds that seemed loud in the silence. Mattingly watched clear fluid trickle down one of the tubes to Persons' left hand and bubbles drift upward in the feeding bottle. He noticed that more tubes snaked out from under the covers, running to things under the bed: a plastic bag in a bucket, holding perhaps a cup or two of golden urine. They were pumping it in and draining it out, he thought, and it was probably good procedure. He wondered if they knew why they did it, or if it was just something the books said was a nice idea.

On the wall monitor, the pilot's heartbeat raised regular peaks of green on gray, with the line even along the bottom of the screen between beats. Another screen portrayed less jagged lines, which appeared almost as regular as the heartbeat.

Keep beating, Mattingly thought, almost in awe. *Keep beating, heart. Keep moving, blood. Keep dripping, bottle. Keep waving, you little squiggly lines that tell us his brain is still functioning.*

Even now, in this cold and silent room, Scott Persons' body was trying to begin mending itself. Ruptured cells were trying to get organized again, make repairs, replicate themselves. Blood was coagulating. In its own mysterious way, the body was fighting back against the shocking things that had been done to it. The body did not stand still; it was working beneath this quiet façade. A fantastic, hidden battle was being fought.

Every minute he lived must increase his chances, Mattingly told himself. Every second. Scott Persons could not know it, because his body had shut his consciousness out of this fight. With its own wisdom, it had seen how terrible the pain was and how awful the damage, so it had simply shut off all communication with the part of the brain that was Scott Persons, putting him to sleep while the automatic systems tried to make their initial repairs. You can sleep, intellect, and hide from this. This fight is beyond you. This is the kind of struggle that was taking place in the primitive slime of the earth when the first few cells were organizing to form the first life. You are

275

much too sophisticated for this kind of fight, intellect. You must sleep. This fight is ours.

Mattingly rubbed his eyes. The time was past nine o'clock. He had to have a cigarette. He left the room on tiptoes and went down the hall and located a rest room. He urinated and washed his face and hands and smoked three cigarettes, one right after the other. They made him dizzy. When he got back to the room, a different nurse was there.

She gave him a slight smile. "A friend of yours?"

"Yes," Mattingly lied. It was so much simpler that way.

At ten, the nurse changed one of the fluid bottles. At ten-thirty, the doctor came back. He peered under the covers, probed at some bandages and tubing, glared at Mattingly, and left again. Scott Persons continued to sleep, his face the color of ashes. But the chest rose and fell, rose and fell, and the instruments on the wall blipped normally.

Mattingly decided he could wait at least until morning. He knew how small the chance was, but it was a chance of some kind. It might save days of tape analysis. And there had to be some turning point. Scott Persons could not stay like this indefinitely. He had to start rallying . . . or go under. Mattingly had to be here in either case. He knew his crew was doing its job. His place was here, with this long-shot hunch.

Shifting his aching buttocks around on the unyielding chair, he yearned for another cigarette, and thought for a while about Nell Emerson.

Midnight.

It was a fool's errand, Mattingly thought. And then his eyelids began to itch and grow heavy.

He dozed sitting up.

It was a quick movement by the nurse—her feet scuffling on the floor—that shocked him awake. He saw that she was out of her chair, leaning over the bed and simultaneously reaching for a call button. The red light over the door had gone on.

Mattingly jumped to his feet, moving forward. The monitors were going crazy—jagged lines and beepers going off—and the tubes to the bottles were shaking, making everything jangle.

Scott Persons was awake. He was staring, wide-eyed, trying grotesquely to sit up.

"Be still!" the nurse hissed, pressing his shoulders down.

Persons rolled his eyes to Mattingly. His chest heaved.

He said, *"The brakes caught."*

"What?" Mattingly rasped. *"What?"*

"Get out of the *way*, damn you!" the nurse ordered angrily. She jabbed the call button again.

Persons made a convulsive movement that shook the entire bed. He coughed. The monitor on the wall began to wail. Persons was perfectly still. Mattingly stared at the monitor, stunned. The heartbeat line was now completely flat.

The door burst open and a nurse ran in, followed by two more hauling a wheeled cart with equipment on it. The first nurse hurled the sheet off the bed and pulled two long, thick, black electrical wires out of the cart. Mattingly backed up, getting out of the way. A doctor ran in, almost knocking him down.

"Out of here," the doctor snapped without even looking at him.

Mattingly retreated into the hall. Another nurse was running. He got out of her way and then leaned against the wall, shaking, He lighted his cigarette directly under the NO SMOKING sign.

"He's dead."

"Persons is dead?" George Pierce said over the telephone. "Shit."

Mattingly stood in the lobby telephone booth, watching patrons and staff trickle into and out of the nearby hospital cafeteria. Everything looked very normal and he was still shaking. "I was here at the hospital when he died. I was in the room."

"Shit," Pierce repeated.

"The brakes caught," Mattingly said.

"What? What did you say?"

"Just before he died, he woke up for a second. He looked right at me. He said, 'The brakes caught.' That's all he said."

There was a silence on the line, then Pierce said, "That doesn't make any sense, does it, Jace? What did he mean, 'The brakes caught'?"

"I don't know," Mattingly admitted. "But he must have meant something about the speed spoilers or something about the dimple wing. I think he must have meant something went haywire with the spoilers. That cut speed so drastically that there was a stall."

"The recording gear will verify it if it's true," Pierce said.

"There won't be anything much to show. Whatever it was, he had corrected it before impact. That's why I came here and waited. I thought there was a chance he might wake up and talk."

"It paid off, Jace."

"I wish he had said more. 'The brakes caught.' That's so damned little!"

"It's enough for right now. Maybe the tapes will tell us the rest. In the meantime, it gives us a start, and the director needed something to tell the press."

Mattingly was surprised. "He's making a statement already?"

"He already did. And he'll have to make another one in the morning, I'm sure. This thing is really hitting the fan here."

Mattingly looked through the glass door of the booth and watched people in the cafeteria. It seemed very strange to see people acting so normally. *One over easy, please, and, oh, I just can't decide between hash-browns and toast. . . .*

It was not easy, seeing someone die.

"I'll call you in the morning," he told Pierce. "I wish I had had a tape recorder when Persons said what he did. But I guess we'll just have to like as much as we got."

"It's something, Jace, and we needed it. It gives the director something to base his decision on, anyway."

Mattingly tightened. He had guessed this would happen. "They're going to postpone the public hearings on the Kennedy crash, right? We'll wait until we have some preliminary data on this one, right. Well, I can't say I'm sorry."

"I wouldn't be sorry either," Pierce said, "if that was all we had to do."

"What else?" Mattingly asked.

"The director says he has no choice now. We're postponing the Kennedy hearings. But in the meantime we're grounding the son-of-a-bitch."

17

I t was early afternoon the following day, California time, when the commercial jetliner carrying Ken Lis and Janis Malone skimmed high over the Rockies and began descent toward San Francisco.

It had been a worry-filled night and morning.

Television news in New York the previous night had played the latest Excalibur crash big, and the morning news, and the *Times*, had the grounding of the Excalibur fleet, as ordered by the National Transportation Safety Board, as a fresh angle for renewed display.

General Collins, director of the NTSB, had stressed in his announcement that the grounding was on his own initiative and was "precautionary." He made it clear that the board had not yet issued a finding in the earlier, New York crash and certainly had had no time to collect even the most preliminary findings at Pittsburgh. All the stories, however, pointed out similarities between the crashes, leading the unstated conclusion that something was drastically wrong with the airplane and it showed its fangs on approach to landing.

Collins had expressed hope that flight-data recorders from the Pittsburgh crash might soon provide some concrete evidence.

He and the NTSB were promptly praised by some spokesmen in government, notably J. L. Hallock, of Maine, who reinforced his reputation as a critic of commercial aviation by saying, "This is the DC-10 case all over again. The Board should have acted much sooner. Our entire system of overseeing the airlines in this nation must be drastically overhauled if we are to protect our citizens from this kind of negligence and tragedy."

Hallock had said the NTSB should be taken out of politics and a nonpartisan expert appointed to clean the mess up. Pressed by reporters, he suggested a retired engineer for the job. The *Times* pointed out that the engineer was also from the state of Maine.

Some others in the government, notably Vice-President Nathan Colby, had criticized the Excalibur grounding as "rash, premature, and overzealous." Colby, once an executive of a large airline, did not elaborate.

The *Times* had done an accompanying analysis tying together the crash and its unfortunate aspects for Hempstead Aviation with the fact that the company had had good news about another project, its Eagle, only hours before the Pittsburgh debacle. With the Eagle matter due to clear committee and reach the Senate floor within a week or ten days, the newspaper said, Hempstead Aviation had experienced an amazing and coincidental streak of good news mixed with bad in a very brief interval.

The *Times* had editorialized against Eagle.

Because no one had had word of Lis's arrival in New York, he had been spared interviews and stayed very close to his hotel room through the evening. A call to San Jose put him through promptly to Lydia Baines.

She had no more information than he did. The plant was being besieged by reporters and Janis Malone's staff was in a tizzy. Lydia had not wanted to discuss the crash on the telephone, nor did she want to talk about the Eagle news. She already had Lis's cable saying the Monravian visit had had mixed results, and she snapped that Lis should get back as early the next day as possible, at which time they could try to sort things out. She told Lis she expected to return to San Francisco; she ordered him to wire his arrival time after he had booked a flight and to plan to come from the airport directly to her apartment on Russian Hill.

Lis had put up a good front for Janis Malone, who was obviously shaken by the news, but he himself was far more upset than he allowed her to know. In recent days his confidence had been rebuilt by new tests of the plane and constant thought about them, and he had been speaking honestly in Monravia when he spoke of having complete faith in Excalibur once more. But Pittsburgh had changed all that.

No one would order on the assumption that the flaw could be found and corrected. As of this moment, Excalibur was dead. Only location of the fault—which must surely exist, after all—and correction of it could get Excalibur back into the competitive scene.

Now, with Eagle moving forward so swiftly, Lis wondered if he had that much time. No debacle ever befell a company without someone being made the alleged culprit and fall guy. He was the obvious choice in the case of Excalibur, and he did not doubt for a moment that Lydia Baines would sacrifice him if it became necessary to restore luster to the Hempstead reputation. . . .

Now, however, Lis could not dwell on yesterday's confusion.

The plane landed at San Francisco. He arranged for a rental car for Janis Malone, bade her good-by, and hopped into a taxi for the city. He rode in on the curving freeway without much appreciation, for once, of the way San Francisco seemed to gleam under a brilliant, clear sky.

When he reached Lydia Baines's building, he was whisked immediately to the top floor, where Lydia was waiting for him. Pacing back and forth the length of the living room, the cuffs of her silver jumpsuit swishing angrily, she was in a foul mood.

"You shouldn't have gone to Monravia personally," she told him almost at once. "You should have been here. We *needed* you here yesterday!"

"We weren't counting on another crash."

"God damn it, when I need one of my executives, I want him where I can touch him! With Excalibur already under investigation, it was bad judgment for you to leave the country!"

Lis sat in his chair silently, not reminding her that she had thought the mission a good idea only a few days ago. She was not in a mood for reminders of that sort.

"There was no factual basis for grounding, either," she said. "I've already lodged a written protest in Washington, and our lawyers ought to be calling on Collins right about this minute. Those bumbling fools are going to regret this."

"I don't like it any more than you do," Lis said. "Obviously. But under the circumstances, what else could he do?"

"Are you defending the bastard?"

"I merely asked what else he could do."

"No one has proved anything against our plane. Until they do, they have no right to hit us with this kind of blockbuster!"

"As recently as yesterday," Lis said, "I was saying that the New York crash meant nothing. I was satisfied with Excalibur. But, Lydia, the Pittsburgh crash is just too similar. There *is* something wrong. There isn't any other conclusion to be drawn. The NTSB had to do what it did to prevent the chance of still another crash."

"Collins will pay for it," Lydia said. "I'll have his job."

Lis wondered if she had power that extended that far. "He did it to save lives."

"To hell with that! You talk like one of them! Don't you see what this does to our *income?*"

Lis did not answer.

"Besides," Lydia said, resuming pacing, "what the hell does that mean anyway, about the brakes? It's nonsense. The words of a dying man who didn't remember his own name, much less what caused the accident."

"I don't know what you're talking about," Lis said quickly, with a jolt of interest.

Her face twisted, betraying that she must not have intended to give this away. "The pilot at Pittsburgh didn't die instantly. That probe expediter, Mattingly, spoke with him."

"The pilot? What did he say?"

"He was dying, Ken. Delirious. Just as he died, he said a few words which Mattingly *thought* were, 'The brakes caught.'"

"The brakes?" Lis repeated. "What does *that* mean?"

"Nothing. That's precisely the point. But when I called Collins after giving me his bleeding-heart solo about passenger lives, he had the gall to try to bolster his stand by pulling *this* bit of magic out of his hat. He said he didn't understand what the pilot's words mean either. But he said it obviously indicated that something definite and specific did go wrong—which, he said, made it all the clearer that Excalibur cannot be allowed in commercial service again until it's found out."

"'The brakes caught,'" Lis said, probing it. "I don't understand."

"That's because there's no meaning there! It's nonsense! There nothing wrong with Excalibur, and our lawsuit will demonstrate that to the American public!"

"It might be a good PR gambit, Lydia," Lis said. "But it can't change the facts. We're in deep trouble now."

"I know that," she said, stopping to glare down at him. "It's your division. What do you intend to do about it?"

So it was now in his lap. The lamb was being shorn for sacrifice. "First, we announce the testing we've already done since the first crash, and the dearth of results. Then we state continued confidence in the airplane. Then we announce new and more strenuous testing which will center around the spoilers and flap systems."

"That would give away what the pilot said, and the NTSB isn't releasing that. Why should we?"

"All right," Lis amended. "We simply announce new testing, then, based on new information."

"And then what do we do?"

"We test. And we hope those flight-data recorders give us the answer."

"It's the dimple wing," Lydia said. "I knew it was mad to believe anything Barton MacIvor said. I *told* Jason."

"Pappy," Lis countered quietly, "is a genius. It isn't that wing."

"Keep saying that as long as you can. It's the wing. I know it. Once the facts bear me out, *then* where are we on Excalibur?"

It was an eventuality that he had already been forced to consider, and he could reply with more calm than he felt: "Then Excalibur is done for."

"We couldn't refit it with a conventional wing?"

"Excalibur began with the wing. We built on the wing. It's not even a good conventional jet with a standard-lift wing. It would take total re-engineering—heavier engines, for one thing. It would be simpler to design an entirely new airplane."

Lydia stared out the wall of glass at the bay, where sailboats dotted the blue. She did not see them or anything else. "Jesus," she said almost reverently.

"It isn't the wing," Lis repeated.

With a visible effort, she became outwardly calm. Going to a table, she removed a cigarette from a gold box and offered one to Lis. He accepted it. They smoked in silence.

"I expect daily reports," she told him. "And if anything significant happens, I expect to be notified immediately."

Lis nodded.

"*Immediately*," she repeated. "You understand?"

"I understand."

She exhaled a long plume of smoke. "All right." She sat down for the first time in the interview. "Tell me about Monravia."

Lis did so, detailing Derquet's thinly disguised demand for a bribe. Lydia Baines leaned forward tensely as he got to this portion of the oral report, trying to give it to her word for word.

"Why should a man like Derquet risk his high position in the government for a payoff?" she asked when he had concluded.

"I've thought about that. Derquet must know that Prince David won't tolerate his power games once Queen Sophia has formally handed control of Monravia to the prince."

"You think Prince David intends to dump Derquet when he becomes King?"

"Yes, I feel confident of that. And Derquet must see it too."

Lydia Baines nodded. "So he intends to get his now, while the getting is good."

"That's my guess."

"How much does Derquet want from us?"

"A million dollars."

Lydia blinked, but otherwise did not betray her shock. She was still a consummate actress, Lis thought. It was a thing to remember.

"In cash," he added. "Delivered personally to him in Monravia." He watched her closely then, keenly interested in what she would say to this.

She frowned, tapping a long, crimson fingernail against one of her front teeth. She dropped her hand in a gesture of impatience. "We might be able to get it. We might arrange it." Her lips compressed. "But until we know what they're going to say in Washington about the airplane, it's moot."

"I'm sure Monravia will be postponing any definite action until they hear some word on the investigation too," Lis said. He was only slightly surprised that she would consider the dangerous, illegal path outlined by Derquet. The ease with which she seemed able to accept the amount of the pay was more surprising. It emphasized her own desperation. He added, "I intend to keep Monravia fully informed."

"Yes," she said, preoccupied perhaps with thoughts of raising the cash in ways that could not be traced. "And France. We have to redouble our efforts in France, grounding or no."

Lis nodded.

"The only thing that's going right these days is Eagle," she said.

"May I ask if you still expect congressional approval in this session?"

She appeared surprised by the question. "Of course I do. It will reach the floor next week. I'm sending Harvey Coughlin back to Washington earlier to contact just as many senators and representatives as he can—wine and dine them, have some parties, try to make some additional friends. All our indicators look excellent, but we'll take no chances when we're *this* close."

Lis got to his feet after extinguishing his cigarette in the ashtray. "I'd better head for San Jose."

"There's a memo on your desk down there about the second phase of transition to Eagle production. Please give it your earliest attention and call me about it."

He simply would not argue today about this. "May I use your telephone? I tried to call my wife several times last night, but she must have been out to a late meeting or something. There wasn't time this morning. This should be a good time to catch her at home."

Lydia Baines pointed to a Princess phone on a nearby end table. "Use that one if you like."

Lis dialed direct, using his personal credit card. When the call went through, he listened to the instrument in his home ring a number of times without response. She was out again, he thought, and was about to hang up, worried that she had gone back to the old, hectic pace, when the telephone at the other end finally was picked up.

"Hello?" someone said.

It was a woman's voice and it sounded much like Amy. But it was not. Lis surprised himself with his recognition of it.

"Jill?" he said.

"Yes. Who is this?" It was Amy's sister. But what was she doing in California? And why did her tone suggest such tension?

"This is Ken," he said. "What's—"

"Ken! My God, we even tried calling you in Monravia, but you had gone, and then we had no idea how to find you in New

York, and your assistant at the company, Miss Hemingway, didn't know—"

His insides began to chill and shrink. "Jill," he said, "what's happened?"

"Amy tried to kill herself."

18

There were two cars in the driveway of Ken Lis's home when he arrived. One was a dusty Nova bearing Arizona plates; that would be Jill's, the one she had driven through the night after hearing of her sister's suicide attempt. The second car, a blue Pinto, looked like a rental vehicle and would belong momentarily to Ted, Amy's brother, who had flown in from Dallas.

Lis parked behind them and hurried inside, using the kitchen entry.

Jill and Ted were both at the kitchen table, having TV dinners. Younger than Amy, Jill bore a striking resemblance, though she was thinner and her hair was done in the more contemporary, loose style. Ted, the older brother, was thickening around the middle now and had aged greatly since Lis had last seen him. His hair was almost gone, and crow's feet tracked his eyes.

Both of them rose as Lis entered. He went to the table and Jill quickly embraced him. "Oh, Ken—! We're glad you're back!"

Lis shook hands with Ted. "She's in bed?"

"Yes," Jill said. "She's sleeping right now. If you want to go up—"

Lis sat at the vacant chair. "Go ahead and eat. I want to stay here right now and hear exactly what happened."

"Do you want some coffee?" Jill asked. She was obviously still strained from the recent ordeal.

"Just eat," Lis told her gently. "And maybe you can repeat for me exactly what happened. I was so stunned on the telephone, I probably didn't get it all right."

Ted dug into his little tin tray of watery lasagna, but Jill showed

287

no interest in the food. She reached for a crumpled package of Camels and lighted one, exhaling nervously. "All right. The night before last, a little after midnight, I got a call from a doctor Aroundson—Arrand—"

"Arronson," Lis broke in. "Our GP."

"I don't know why I can't remember his name. It's some kind of defensive block, I guess—I've seen him three times since I got here—"

"Jill, just go ahead. Please."

She nodded and frowned at the cigarette between her fingers. "All right. Some of Amy's friends had found her in her car in the parking lot beside the country club about an hour earlier. It was late, and it was a miracle they found her. The car was parked down by the tennis courts, which were all dark and deserted at that hour. I guess she thought it was a place no one *would* find her . . . until it was too late. But the people who found her were going down with the tennis pro because one of them had lost a valuable watch, and she thought she might have left it in a locker—"

"All right," Lis said impatiently. "Go on."

His wife, Jill said, had been unconscious inside the locked car. After repeated attempts to awaken her by tapping on the windows had failed, the women and the young tennis pro had become alarmed enough to break a window on the other side and examine her. Her pulse was so weak it could scarcely be detected, her breathing ragged and shallow. On the floor of the car were a spilled, partially consumed paper cup of 7-Up and an empty package that bore a prescription for a dozen sleeping pills.

A prominent doctor lived less than a mile from the country club, in a huge new home backing up to the fifteenth fairway. Someone had enough presence of mind to remember this and shove the unconscious Amy onto the other half of the front seat and drive her to the doctor's house in her own car. The doctor happened to be an orthopedic surgeon, but he certainly remembered emergency treatment for an overdose and initiated it while one of the women contacted the hospital and Amy's own doctor.

Treatment had been in the emergency room, and although Amy began to show quick recovery at once, the hospital kept her overnight. Dr. Arronson, unable to contact Lis at home and hesitating to provide anyone at Hempstead Aviation with details of the situation, rifled Amy's purse and found Jill listed as next of kin, after Lis, on an insurance information card. He called Jill immediately.

Jill, although shocked, had taken hold quickly. She told Arronson that Lis was out of the country. She promised to drive all night and be at the hospital by morning. She called her brother in Dallas. The next morning, on her arrival in San Jose, she found Amy weak but conscious. Over the doctor's protests, she acceded to Amy's wishes and drove her home.

"I wanted to get her *out* of there," Jill explained. "It hasn't been in the papers. But the hospital has to call the police in cases like this, and there was a report. I had to . . . talk to the police. But the doctor thinks it won't be used by any of the news people. He says now I did the right thing. By taking her home so quickly, I made it look less serious than it was, and that's probably part of the reason no one picked it up for the paper or anything."

"How is she now?" Lis asked. "Was the doctor afraid she might have a relapse? Is that why he wanted to keep her at the hospital?"

"No," Jill said. "He was afraid she might try to do it again."

"Christ," Lis said.

"Ken," Ted broke in with quiet urgency, "what the hell are you going to *do*? Jill and I can't stay around very long. She has her kids, and my job is really pressing me right now—"

"I have to decide that after I talk to her," Lis said. "Tell me how she is now. Tell me how she's acting."

Jill stubbed the cigarette in an ashtray. Dr. Around—"

"Arronson."

"—Arronson said she couldn't have taken the pills very long before they found her. He spent a long time with her this morning. He took blood and urine. He called right after I talked with you in San Francisco and said it looks like she's going to be fine. There's no kidney damage . . . no brain damage."

"Thank God for that."

"But she's so depressed. She frightens me. I think she *might* do it again."

Ted leaned forward. "She's been in a mess for years, Ken. We both know that. Hell, you can't fool a brother and sister that easily. But we never expected *this*. We wonder what the hell you're going to do."

Lis looked at their earnest, caring faces. He wished he had some

fine and intelligent suggestion for them, something to cheer them up
with hope for his brilliant new scheme.

"I don't know what I'll do," he admitted. "I have to see her first."

He had to wait more than an hour for that.

When Jill came out of the darkened front bedroom and said Amy
was now awake again and knew he was there, he entered with anxiety and dread of how she would look—how she would respond to
him.

But he had reckoned without some of Amy Lis's pride.

Just as he entered, the overhead lights flashed on, startling him.
He saw his wife just turning back in the big bed from having flicked
the switch built into the headboard. She was pale and looked as
though she had been very, very sick, but as she recognized him she
also snatched up a hairbrush from the table and began pulling it
through her hair.

"You didn't give me enough time!" she said.

Lis went to the bed, sat on its edge, and kissed her on the cheek.
"Are you all right?"

"I think I feel very well for a woman who just botched her first suicide attempt."

"Amy, what the hell went wrong? Why did you do it?"

As quickly as it had appeared, her bravado vanished and tears
sprang to her eyes. "I don't know. *Everything*."

"When I left, I thought things were better."

She angrily pulled a Kleenex from a box at the bedside and
dabbed at her eyes. "It was. I thought it was better. I didn't want
you to go. Then I had some drinks . . . and some pills . . . and
some more drinks, and then I just got sick of it all. I went out there
and took the sleeping capsules and just *sat* there—a half-hour, forty-
five minutes, not sleepy or anything. Then I went to sleep, but I
knew it when they came up to the car and started tapping on the
glass. I pretended I was unconscious. I don't know why. I was groggy
but not that far under. It just seemed so *stupid*, not even to be able
to kill myself properly!"

"Amy, what have I been doing to make you this unhappy? What
do you want me to do?"

She shook her head, refusing to look at him. "I don't know."

Lis was in tumult. He had not known until this moment how

much emotion for this woman remained buried within him. Whatever troubles they had had—however close to parting they might have come—their emotional investment in one another was too deep and too intense simply to write off. He groped for her hands. "Amy, I won't leave you any more."

"You have your work—"

"Maybe that's the trouble. I've put my work first, when I should have put you first."

"If I had said that, you would have had a fit."

"Amy, I don't know what's the matter with me. Some of your troubles have been of my making. I know that. I've neglected you. I don't pretend we can fix things overnight, but I'd like to try."

"Maybe we could both try."

"Yes. . . . My God, when I think how close you came to killing yourself! That's—I really want to help you, Amy. We *have* to get ourselves together so nothing like this ever happens again."

She drew her hands away from his, but her expression was one of quiet amazement. She gave him a faltering smile. "Let's not talk any more right now . . . okay? I need some rest. And you look kind of . . . rotten yourself, darling."

"Okay," he said quickly, afraid to press her right now. "Maybe we can talk when you get feeling better."

"I *intend* to get better," she said. "The hospital has a regulation on all suicide attempts. You have to see a psychiatrist before they'll discharge you. I saw him there yesterday. I have another appointment with him tomorrow. I'm going to try. I *am*." She shuddered. "I didn't like the feeling of . . . dying."

Lis clasped her hands tightly within his, catching them for just an instant. "We'll whip it, then. I swear to God, I'll do anything to help you."

There was a sound at the bedroom doorway. It was Ted.

"Ken, there's a man at the back door, says he wants to talk to you about some yard work."

"Hell," Lis said sharply, "I don't have time for that kind of stuff now."

"Go," Amy said, mustering a smile. "Heavens knows the yard needs some effort!"

He hesitated, then obeyed her, hurrying downstairs and through the kitchen to the back door.

The youth standing there was lanky, with brownish-blond hair and a little drooping mustache. He had wild blue eyes and an engaging smile. He wore Levi's and a threadbare work shirt.

"Mr. Lis?" he said. "Hi, there. My name is Harold Smith, and I'd like to be your yardman."

19

I n the few seconds that his quarry stared out at him through the screen door, Harold was terribly careful to maintain his wide, friendly grin and look as brainless as possible. This was made more difficult by the hot, flashing excitement that had overwhelmed him when Ken Lis appeared there, within his very reach.

Lis looked like his newsmagazine photographs, although he was slightly shorter and more slender than Harold had imagined. He seemed . . . *diminished* in real life, less mythic, somehow. But that was all right. Harold was not really disappointed. A smaller man might be easier to kill.

"What makes you think we might need some yard help?" Lis asked him now, suspicion in his narrowed eyes.

Harold chuckled and looked around. "I sure don't like to knock anyone's yard, sir, but I do several yards in the neighborhood, and I've noticed yours. It sure looks like it needs some work to *me!*"

Lis slowly smiled. "Well, I can't argue with that observation. Actually, though," he said, frowning, "this isn't a very good time for us to discuss it. We have sickness in the house."

"I won't take more than a minute, sir," Harold said. "I certainly understand about illness, I certainly do. That's why I'm doing outside work all summer myself, sir. You see, a year ago I had tuberculosis. —Oh, I'm fine now; I mean, no more germs or infection. But outdoor work will help me build myself up again. And I enjoy it. So you can be sure I understand about the need to be real quiet around a house like this."

"You say you work other places around the neighborhood?" The man was still suspicious.

"Yes, sir. The Quinns, the Laceys, the Steiggers—they're all regular customers. Then I've worked several other places, odd jobs."

"I'm not interested in trying to make the place look like *House Beautiful*. We could use better help on mowing and trimming—"

"That's fine, sir," Harold said eagerly. "And I think I could make sure your sprinklers turn off and on properly, by the timer, and you need quite a bit of pruning, if you don't mind my saying so."

A scant smile touched Lis's face. "That's putting it mildly."

"I'll take care of all of that, and after you see the quality of my work, we can talk about what my wages will be in the future. Does that meet with your approval, sir?"

"I want to reiterate that we can't have a lot of noise—"

"I use all electric equipment, sir, even the mower."

"And I don't even want you to have a try at it unless you really are interested in doing top work."

"That's the only kind worth doing, sir," Harold said, grinning enthusiastically.

Lis held his right hand out through the screen opening. "Ken Lis. And if you can do your demonstration work before the weekend, I'll make an immediate decision on the future."

"I'll do it tomorrow, sir!" Harold promised.

"All right, fine. Let's try it."

"Thank you, Mr. Lis! Thank you!"

Backing and bowing and scraping off the patio, Harold chuckled and grinned all the way to the side-fence gate and beyond. Then, jamming his baseball cap back on his head, he went immediately down the street toward the battered Datsun pickup parked in the next block.

It would be all right now. It was going to be just fine. He could take his time—weeks if need be, or within days; he could be ready for instant action if the perfect opportunity presented itself. The trick was to be flexible: willing to wait patiently, ready to strike on a moment's notice.

20

On the day following his return from Monravia, Ken Lis did not go to the office until nearly 10 A.M. Fatigue tugged at him, but his primary reason for being so late was that he stayed home until he had assured himself that Amy was in reasonably good spirits. Her brother and sister would stay another two days, then would have to go to their own homes. Before they left, Lis intended to have a practical nurse on duty at least for a few more days.

When he reached the office, he was painfully conscious of pressures relating to Excalibur closing around him. Clippings about the Pittsburgh crash had been stacked neatly in the center of his desk. There was a typed transcript of a telephone report, from the Transwestern manager at the site, which added little to the news accounts. Kelley Hemingway had been in contact with Jace Mattingly, of the NTSB, and preliminary conclusions from him dovetailed with those already formed in Lis's mind: the Pittsburgh crash had been a ghastly carbon copy of the one at Kennedy.

In a brief talk with Janis Malone, Lis made suggestions for handling inquiries from the press about the grounding of Excalibur. There was no way to put a very bright face on this disaster. Until they found what had caused the crashes—and now it appeared that pilot error could not possibly be involved twice in such similar circumstances—it was exceedingly unlikely that there would be any more Excalibur orders, or even interest from anyone in talking about later possibilities.

Shortly after eleven o'clock, Lydia Baines called direct, on the inside line from her office. Lis agreed to report to her at once.

She was alone in her office when he arrived. Standing behind her large desk, she appeared crisp and lovely in a jade suit, with a minimum of jewelry. Her face was grim. "Please close the door, Ken." She touched an intercom button and told the secretary in the next room, "No interruptions."

Lis sat down facing her. Her expression bespoke more bad news.

"Tell me about your wife," she said.

Lis did so, expressing hope and telling her about his plans for a practical nurse. He was slightly surprised that Lydia Baines would even mention the matter; her incredibly single-minded way of doing things ordinarily precluded any such personal considerations. He wondered if he had misjudged her a bit.

When he had finished, however, and she spoke again, he saw that no misjudgment had been involved: she had asked because it related to business.

She told him, "I'm sure it would be a very bad time for you to turn right back around and return to Monravia."

"It would," Lis agreed. "As a matter of fact, there's no way I can leave Amy right now, Lydia."

"Even if the entire future of Excalibur is at stake?"

"I could leave for a few hours. I could go to Pittsburgh or Washington, if that's what you have in mind. I can't go back to Europe. Amy needs me right now."

"I wonder, Ken, if you would put personal considerations over business if it were Jason asking you."

Lis almost lost his temper. "As you've reminded me on several occasions, Jason is dead. So the question is moot."

Her lips hardened into a thin line. "As a result of the things you told me about Lucian Derquet, I have done some quick checking into certain related factors. The fact of the matter is that I want someone who is absolutely trustworthy to return to Monravia or a neighboring country—quietly—to meet Derquet at once."

"You're going ahead with the payoff, then?"

"It's a public-relations fee, Ken. The money will be used—"

"Spare me, Lydia. We both know *exactly* what it is."

Her eyes shot angry sparks. "Something has to be done, and fast, to try to counteract some of this publicity about Pittsburgh. We *must* keep moving on attempts to enter the European market.

There's no telling how long this crisis may last now. We can't stand still."

"We may need every cent we can rake up before this is over," Lis said. "Hempstead is going to face a deepening financial crisis. Can we really afford a million dollars, handed over illegally, to a foreign functionary who might not even deliver on his promises? And what do we do if we get caught?"

"We don't get caught," Lydia replied sharply. "That's why I wanted someone in whom I can put complete trust—you—to take the cash."

"Sorry. If the Amy situation weren't in this, you might have me on the horns of a real dilemma. But I'm spared the decision. There's no way I'll leave her again so soon."

"Thank you, Ken, for showing me a little of where your loyalties really lie."

"If you can't understand what I'm saying, Lydia, then go ahead and interpret it that way."

She reached a crimson-tipped hand for her intercom. Lis, assuming he had been dismissed, rose.

"Stay," she snapped. Into the intercom she said, "Please see if Mr. Coughlin can join us at once."

Lis said, "I'm needed here now anyway, Lydia. The first word from Pittsburgh is that the black box came through this one in good condition. We'll have data now. Whatever went wrong will be the subject of some intensive engineering study. I have to be on the ground to supervise it and handle the press."

"You have aides who could handle that."

"I intend to handle it myself."

"I understand that. Despite my wishes."

"Lydia, this payoff is risky as hell!"

"I've decided, Ken. I'll hear no argument."

She was, Lis realized, much angrier than he had first thought. It showed the level of her desperation, and he could dimly understand this. She had always been bright and ambitious. Jason Baines's death had given her her big chance to prove what she could do as head of a corporation. But nothing had been going right for her. She knew how desperate a payment to a man like Lucian Derquet really was, but she was reduced to such measures. If he had been good enough of heart, Lis saw, he might have felt sorry for her. All he could actu-

297

ally think was that Hempstead was heading for even worse trouble . . . and he had perhaps just kicked away his chance for the presidency. He felt slightly sick at his stomach; he had not truly known how much he wanted it.

There was, he thought, time to turn around. The temptation flashed before him. Amy would be all right for two days, surely. And was a payoff really so bad? Didn't everyone do it?

He felt the words of recanting on his tongue. The force of the impulse stunned him. He struggled with it.

"What is it?" Lydia asked sharply.

"What?"

"You just shook your head so violently, I thought you were going to pass out."

He took a deep, ragged breath. "Nothing. I'm okay."

Moments later, Harvey Coughlin tapped on the door and entered the office. It was Lis's first chance to observe his fellow executive at close range since his return. Coughlin appeared ruddier, in shining good health, and there was a springier bounce in his step as he entered, brimming with confidence.

"Good morning!" Coughlin said in a voice that reeked reassurance.

"Harvey," Lydia said after he had seated himself, "I want to be sure I understand the situation in Washington. You told me earlier that Eagle will definitely be docketed for next week?"

Harvey Coughlin nodded vigorously. "I'm told the docket is already in the print shop and will be released Friday morning. Eagle will be discussed again next Tuesday, and I believe I can assure you, Lydia, that we will have the votes to get it out and onto the floor this time!"

"That's wonderful news, Harvey, and you know how pleased I am."

"Thank you. When one has a product as fine as Eagle, the selling job is reward enough in itself."

"There is another matter of pressing concern," Lydia said. "It involves Excalibur overseas. For several reasons, Ken can't handle it. It will require the utmost discretion. A trip to Europe is involved—a flight over, a single meeting, in secrecy, and a return. Will you handle this matter for me?"

Harvey Coughlin's face was a study in uncertainty. "Of course I will do whatever you ask, Lydia. I had planned to be in Washington the day after tomorrow . . . a number of matters to attend to prior to the weekend—"

"This is urgent, Harvey."

"Then, of course I accept the assignment."

Lydia Baines turned to Lis, a smile on her lips. "It appears our problems have just been solved, Ken. I can handle the details with Harvey. You may be excused."

Not trusting himself to speak, Lis left the office without a word, quietly closing the door behind him. Of all the thoughts and emotions churning through him as he walked back to his own office, the uppermost was entirely selfish, and devastating: he had just closed the door on his future at Hempstead Aviation.

21

I n a frigidly air-conditioned laboratory in Washington, Jace Mattingly bent over a worktable, scowling at a special computer printout. It skimmed data taken from flight recorders, observer reports, and conclusions drawn by experts who had checked instruments and controls that had come through the Pittsburgh crash reasonably intact. Random and in some ways superficial, it nevertheless presented Mattingly a general view of what had been happening to the Excalibur just before its flight had ended in disaster.

SPECIAL XMOS   MATTINGLY

Excalibur FT 3875901-B (TW 23)

Acft. del. to TW	4 March
Modifications (seats, carpet)	7–10 March
Radio install	11–13 March
Flt. test	14 March
Check OK	YES
In service	24 March
Maint	13 April, fuel booster inop
	22 April, ROUTINE
	3 May, primary navcom inop
	intercom inop

20 May ROUTINE
   Replace nose-gear
      housing
   pilot-seat track inop
   track inop

OTHER MINOR REPAIR

5 March, clog sink
6 March, galley wiring
8 March, torn carpet
   cracked mirror
   galley sink inop
   pilot-seat track inop
5 April, bent fuel-filler cap
   seat back broken
   clogged toilet drain
   4 courtesy lights inop
11 May, 2 seat belts inop
None other

Crew reports (special
probs)   NONE
Tach. flt. time, date incident   1350 hours

Incident flt. data:
Loading—Normal cargo
      load   YES
   Normal pasgr.
      load   YES
   CG range   INSIDE ENVELOPE
   Fuel   61 per cent
   management   nominal—balanced
   other   NONE NOTED

Controls and instruments—
   Fuel boosters   ON

Aux. pumps	STANDBY, GREEN
Main elec.	ON
Standby	GREEN
Servosystem pressures	NORMAL
Seat-belt, no smoking signs	ON
De-ice	ON FULL
Wipers	ON
Aux. systems	STANDBY
Primary navcoms	ON
Backup navcoms	IDLE
Transponders	ON
Ground-proximity warning	MANUAL OVERRIDE OFF
A/C	40 per cent
Autopilot	OFF, LOCKED
Gear	DOWN, 3 GREEN
Flaps	15 DEGREES
Slat controls	FULL OUT
Power	35 per cent
Stall warning	ON
Radar	ON
Intercom	STANDBY
Brakes	OFF
Start systems	OFF
Fire-warning system	ON, GREEN
Pumpers	ARMED
Panel 1	GREEN
Panel 2	GREEN
Panel 3	GREEN

Approach	ILS
Discrepancies noted	NONE
Approach speed	140 stated
TAS time of incident	123 est.
AGL altitude time of incident	200 ft.

Incident description—THIS AIRCRAFT WAS MAKING A NORMAL APPROACH TO POINT OF INCIDENT. AIRCRAFT THEN PITCHED FORWARD IN 1.5 SECONDS 30 DEGREES DOWN AND STARBOARD WING BELOW NORMAL ROLL ATTITUDE 5–8 DEGREES EST. STALL-WARNING DEVICES SOUNDED. CREW APPLIED FULL POWER. SINK RATE APPROACHING 1000 FPM NOTED 1 SECOND. ENGINES DEV. FULL TAKEOFF POWER TIME OF IMPACT, NOSE DOWN 19 DEGREES AT IMPACT.

There was more, much more. Mattingly had only to scan the remainder of highly technical support data. Rolling the computer printouts up like a calendar, he headed for the office of his superior.

"What have you got?" Pierce asked as Mattingly walked in.

"It wasn't pilot error," Mattingly said.

Pierce noted the printouts in his hand. "Not this time, you mean?"

"Not this time, and almost certainly not the other time."

"You think you know what happened, and why?"

"I know what happened, anyway," Mattingly told him. "It stalled."

"Impossible. The first thing we got was a normal approach speed."

"It stalled," Mattingly insisted. "There's just no question about it. That plane was coming in at a true airspeed of a hundred and twenty-three miles per hour—incredibly slow for any other plane, but a nice, sanitary margin of safety for an Excalibur, with that slat wing. Then, with no warning, it stalled instantaneously. The nose pitched over and a wing dipped. The crew tried to recover, but there wasn't enough altitude."

Pierce stared at him with sagging eyes. "I find that very hard to believe."

"It's right *here*, goddam it!"

"Okay, Jace, okay. If it's there, it's there. But, my God, man! That wing can't stall at that speed. The FAA certification—"

"There's something about that wing, or the airplane, that we didn't see tested," Mattingly said. "It *should* have flown smoothly at that speed, but it *didn't*. And I'd be willing to bet that the same thing happened in the Kennedy crash: a low-speed, low-altitude stall, much too low to give the crew time to initiate a successful recovery."

Pierce lighted a cigarette. "Hempstead Aviation tested that plane for two years. The FAA tested it until the pilots' rear ends were falling off."

"It's got a flaw," Mattingly insisted. "Something small. Something subtle. Something you can't predict. But it's there. The data all indicate that, this time."

Exhaling a thick cloud of smoke, Pierce nodded glum agreement. "Well, we'll just have to keep combing the facts. We can make the postponement on Kennedy last until the first of the year if we have to. And the plane is already grounded . . . the damage is already done. It sounds like a tough one yet, Jace, pinning down what caused a stall to happen when all logic says it couldn't. You've got your work cut out for you."

"I think I've got an idea for a possible short cut," Mattingly said.

"You know there aren't any short cuts in this business."

"I know, I know. But call it an idea to make faster progress, then."

"What?"

"I want to go to California."

Pierce stared at him. "It can't be for a suntan."

Mattingly grinned. "Listen, you racist bastard. I want to lay it on the table for Ken Lis at Hempstead. I want some more stall tests run. This ties in with what the pilot told me about the brakes catching. Maybe, if the spoilers are partially extended, it somehow changes the flight characteristic of the slat wing in a very narrow parameter—"

"You're needed here."

"Simms can oversee the work here."

"Why Hempstead? Why not Transwestern?"

"I know Lis better than I know those guys. I can work with him. He can be trusted to keep his mouth shut. He wants to find this problem worse than we do. He'll co-operate. They've already done a lot of tests, and we can go over his earlier results and eliminate a hundred possibilities that we might have to sift through from scratch if we went to TW or the FAA."

Sighing, Pierce leaned back in his chair. "You know, Jace, by the time you retire from this job, you'll have destroyed every regulation, every standard operating procedure, we ever had. I'm not aware that we've ever done anything like this before—"

"Have you ever had a special trouble shooter assigned exactly the way you have me assigned already?"

"No, but I can't help worrying. You may be going too far."

"Didn't you tell me to cut corners to try to solve this thing?"

"Yes. Of course I did."

"And," Mattingly added, smiling to show it was in good will, "have you ever had anybody quite as willing to let his ass hang out on a gamble as I obviously am right here and now?"

Pierce studied his face with sober concentration. "You *do* recognize that it is your ass."

"Oh, yassuh, boss, ah sho do!"

Pierce threw up his hands. "Go, you maniac!"

Mattingly headed for the door, jerked it open.

"One thing!" Pierce called after him.

Mattingly turned in the doorway. "What's that?"

"Write down the office phone number someplace. Call us every once in a while, just to reassure us you're still earning your money."

"Would a postcard do?" Mattingly asked, and was gone.

Within a few hours after Jace Mattingly left his superior's office, Harvey Coughlin was in Washington. The stopover was not entirely necessary; arrangements had already been made for delivery of the money through a Swiss bank. But on the pretext of making a few telephone calls about Eagle, Harvey managed an overnight layover.

"Europe!" Dena Forbes said, kneeling naked in the bed, hairbrush in hand. "And you waited until *now* to tell me?"

"Yes," Harvey said, returning from the dresser with a glass of chilled wine in each hand. "First things first, Dena."

She made a face at him as she took her glass and moved over a little for him. "You were afraid I would beg to go."

"No, I know better than. that. The truth of the matter is, I'm going to miss you. I hate to mention being gone that long."

"How long is it?"

"Well, only a couple of days, actually. But it will be lonely."

"Your wife isn't going?"

"No. I wish *you* could."

"It would be lovely. But we both know how impossible it is, for several reasons."

Harvey rubbed the edge of his cold-beaded glass along her nude thigh. "I know . . . but I can't help dreaming."

"Stop that, darling. You know how kinky I am, and I want to *talk* now, not get all turned on again so soon."

He took the glass away. Suddenly, as happened often, he was overwhelmed by the splendor of her body, her youth, her nearness. "God, Dena! I don't know how I ever stay away from you!"

"You don't have to," she replied calmly. "When you have time, I'll always try to have time too. I like you just as much as you like me, you know."

"Do you?"

"Of course, Harvey."

He stared at her. "Why?" he blurted.

"We're not going to analyze it," she said. "We agreed on that, remember?"

"All right—yes, I remember," he said. "It's just that—there haven't been that many women for me, Dena, and sometimes when I'm with you, I'm so happy that I get this awful fear I'll lose you."

"Now, why should you fear that? We have fun. We like each other. And we're awfully good together—God, how good we are together!"

"But it isn't just the sex, Dena. It might have started out that way. But the way I can talk to you—that's something precious to me too."

"You don't tell your wife everything?"

"Hardly!"

"All right, you know what I mean!"

"She doesn't know a fourth the things you know about me, Dena —about the things I really like, or even the things I've really been doing to promote Eagle."

Dena put a finger on his lips. "No more talk about that. I told you the last time, I just don't want to know any more about your business transactions!"

"But I *want* to tell you! There's nothing I want hidden from you."

"And maybe," Dena said slyly, teasing him, "you hope I'll get just a little more turned on, hearing about your power maneuvers?"

"Would I resort to trickery to turn you on?"

"Would you?"

Harvey grabbed her and bowled her over backward across the bed, spilling both glasses of wine. "Of course I would!"

They wrestled gently for a minute or two, and then he pinned her wrists and got across her torso at an angle, pinning her hips, too, and kissed her. Laughing, she gave in.

"I'll miss you, too," she said fondly.

"I've got to go, though. This is important."

She watched him, her eyes darkening with worry.

"There's nothing to be concerned about," he told her.

"You're sure?"

"Of course. And this is a feather in my cap. It doesn't even have to do with Eagle. It's an Excalibur sales negotiation."

"Fantastic! Monravia, then?"

For an instant, Harvey felt a stab of suspicion. Was she too quick to make the guess? Was he being pumped? He elected to test. "Not necessarily," he said.

"Oh," she said. "Okay." She rolled off the bed and walked to the dresser, opulent hips swaying. She poured more wine and came back.

"Don't you want to know the details?" Harvey asked.

"Details of what?" she asked blankly, handing him his glass.

"Details of my trip to Europe!"

"You'll be back by the weekend, so maybe we can still go to that concert. That's all I have to know."

"This is a very important and delicate trip I'm about to undertake!"

"I'm sure it is, darling." She sipped her wine.

"And you could care less?" He was stung.

"Of course I'm interested," she said. "But if you want to tell me, you'll tell me, and if you don't want to tell me, you won't. I can live either way, darling. But I am *not* going to pry. Not now and not ever."

Harvey thought about it a moment. "I want to tell you about it," he said then. "I have to tell *someone*."

She smiled and kissed him. "Whatever."

Once the Monravian trip was over, Harvey thought—once Eagle

had been approved and he had the presidency—he would marry this amazing girl. A quiet divorce and an even quieter marriage, after a suitable waiting period. Then his every dream would have been fulfilled.

He knew Dena held nothing back from him. She had already told him things about herself that opened her totally to him, made her completely vulnerable. She had not asked anything in return, but he wanted this closeness and sharing. He got a strange and frightening pleasure in opening himself and making himself vulnerable to her. He had never done so with any other human being.

"Now, about Europe," he said.

Dena stifled a little yawn with her fingertips.

"You're not even interested!" Harvey said, aggrieved.

"I'm sorry, darling." She sat up straighter. "Go on."

Harvey began telling her all about it . . . and if he exaggerated the personal danger a bit and made it appear more cloak-and-dagger than ever it could possibly be, no one could really blame him, could he? For he *had* her now; she was hanging on every word. And he embroidered a little, to please her.

22

T he sky is intensely blue seven miles straight up. Most cloud
layers are far below, and while it is not high enough yet to betray the darker fringes of space, the altitude is sufficient to give the
distance a violet tinge. The sunlight is very brilliant too, with a thin
yet harsh quality that makes the shadow of a structural member on
the wing or body of an airplane stand out like the slash of a piece
of charcoal.

With an experienced copilot beside him, a crash flight engineer at
his back, and fourteen technicians in the second cabin with their instruments, Hank Selvy felt, as always during the crucial moments of
a test, very much alone.

The test Excalibur was throttled drastically far back. With flaps,
gear, and slat-wing surfaces fully deployed, it waddled through the
thin, treacherous air on the brink of a complete stall. Dripping
sweat, Selvy hung onto the control yoke and played pressures with
his feet on the rudder pedals, with all the sensitivity of a concert pi-
anist. A lesser pilot would have let the plane stall long before now.
Even Selvy wondered how he was keeping it straight and level, and
in the air.

Feeding in the slightest additional bit of back pressure on the
yoke, he bled off perhaps a dozen engine RPMs, such a slight
amount of extra power that the gauges scarcely registered the
change.

"Just about ready," he told the crew.

"IAS is right on the red line," his copilot, Bert Beggs,
said.

"Okay, fine," Selvy said very softly, as if even the vibration of his vocal cords might disturb this great beast's delicate balance. "Are we all ready, then?"

"Go."

Selvy touched the yoke and pedals, putting Excalibur into a gentle turn to the left.

Ordinarily this would have been the simplest maneuver. A big jet has amazingly light aileron response, thanks to servomechanisms, and Selvy's effortless touch of the yoke would have resulted in a 5-degree bank under normal circumstances.

A plane is turned in flight, however, not because the nose changes direction or the tail is blown around, as most people think, but because of a lifting-vector tradeoff. Flying straight and level, the wing's vector of lift is straight up. Tilt that same wing, and the vector is no longer straight up but either left or right, depending on which way the tilt was made. Thus it is that an airplane turns: the wing is tilted, the lift vector goes one direction or the other, and the plane lifts itself into that new direction, left or right.

It stands to reason, however, that a wing with part of its lift vector off to one side will no longer have as much straight-up lift. This is where the tradeoff comes in. Ordinarily a plane has so much lift that it can afford to give some up momentarily in order to make a turn.

Close to the stalling speed, however, the wing has no lift to waste. If tilted very much so that the lift vector is no longer straight up, it simply doesn't have enough reserve—and stops flying.

In turning the controls at such a low speed, Hank Selvy knew all this. He was deliberately initiating a stall by tilting the wing and thus dumping off lift. Called an accelerated maneuver stall, it is one of the more dangerous stalls.

The moment Selvy touched the yoke, lights flashed overhead on the ceiling panel and the yoke began to shake violently. A horn went off and more lights exploded alive, and Excalibur plunged sickeningly off level and into a downward-plunging spiral. Because it was being asked to do more lifting than the left, it was the right wing which first dipped sharply, making the plane swoop from left to right.

The instant the stall began, both Selvy and Beggs leaped on it to bring it under control. Their hands flew. Gravitational forces built up in a split-second, throwing them hard against their chairs and trying to render them helpless. The sky pinwheeled past the windows.

They got the control yokes forward, then back again in normal position, and with full power on, Excalibur began to recover.

"Okay, anything broken?" Selvy asked sharply.

"Looks okay here," the engineer called.

"Let's start easing the slats off," Selvy ordered.

As they did so, he mopped sweat from his face, tasting it in the corners of his mouth. You might know all the odds and all the procedures, but you did not hurl a big airplane like this into such gyrations without severe strain on your nerves. Every time you did it, you were risking your life. It was that simple.

Again, however, Excalibur had been maddeningly docile.

PART THREE

1

A pall of dense humidity and pollution hung thick over Washington, D.C., and with it—for insiders, capable of making such an observation—an equally palpable ambience of something wrong—something big about to happen.

As recently as the 1950s, Washington had retained a small-town atmosphere despite its thriving downtown, sprawling suburbs, and impressive buildings and monuments centered around the famous Mall. That atmosphere had changed subtly but steadily during the sixties and seventies, so that little of it remained now. Here now, clearly, was a dense and troubled major city, with its traffic snarls, crime, and air of indifferent cruelty. But here, too, was power. And while the administrative machinery of that power had grown enormously over the decades, its central control area remained relatively small. Congress, one major facet of this control, had changed very little through the years; its procedures were essentially the same, its general size, even some of its membership. And the new congressmen who made the trek to this center of government every two or six years soon lost some of their initial idealism and individualistic drive: The system was large enough, and had endured long enough, to swallow up any firebrand. One adapted and became like the others. So Congress remained as it had been for many decades, in its atmosphere, its gossip, its secrets, and its incredibly sensitive ability to detect rumors or even shadows of change or trouble.

Now, in the first week of August, this acute political organism sensed that something unusual was in the wind.

It was extremely difficult for any member to ascertain precisely what this something might be. The political "window" for important actions was soon to close, and a whirlwind of activity had sent dozens of bills to the White House for signature. An attempt to override the President's veto of an additional $6 billion in programs for Health, Education, and Welfare had failed, but this failure had been expected. There was considerable speculation over who might be named to the vacant space on the Supreme Court, but—again—this kind of "crisis" was normal here. No one really believed that the general feeling of tension and uncertainty had anything to do with the quite nasty marital crackup being undergone by the Secretary of State. That sort of thing went on all the time, and seldom reached the newspapers.

This was something else again, a miniature version of the kind of feeling that had prevailed during some aspects of the Watergate investigation or one of the several episodes that had followed, engulfing members of Congress in personal scandal and allegations of malfeasance. The organism detected some threat to its own equanimity.

The outward signs were very slight. Certain senators known for their good attendance at roll calls were seen to miss a few. Senator D. L. Boudoin made an unscheduled trip home for a weekend. Two representatives known as personal enemies were seen having lunch together. Some expected opposition to an environmental-impact bill failed to materialize. A few reporters, ordinarily among the last to sense such events, began asking their sources what the hell was brewing beneath the surface, and these questions elicited no information, because the sources probably did not honestly know; but the asking of the questions in itself contributed to further growth of the general feeling of malaise and worry.

For Senator Matthew Johns, the sense of impending trouble began to have individual significance when the Eagle matter was not formally reported out for consideration on the Senate floor, as scheduled.

At first Johns assumed this was an oversight, and thought little about it. Such administrative snags were almost the rule. But in checking on the matter, he found that it was not listed anywhere in the pipeline for floor consideration, and the clerks he asked about it seemed to have no idea why.

Funds for Eagle had been in the original Pentagon budget as submitted by the White House. They had been stricken by mutual agreement after certain pressure groups and the so-called "peace lobby" in the House had threatened a major confrontation over the entire budget if that item was left in. Eagle had been allowed to remain as a line item, but without funds, for two years now. It was not ordinarily a complex matter to fund a system that already existed on paper, if the necessary preliminary politicking had been done and enough support lined up.

Johns believed he had the support, and when the irritating snag came fully to his attention, he called a few colleagues to see if they would nudge the right people to get things moving again. That was when his surprises became more threatening.

"Matt, I would like to help," Senator Barker told him on the telephone, "but I'm just up to my ears. Can't possibly do a thing."

"You still support Eagle, however," Johns said.

Barker sounded like a man hedging his bets. "Well, I certainly have an open mind, Matt. I'm certainly not *against* it . . . *per se*."

In the cafeteria a little later, Johns made it a point to touch base with two other colleagues on whom he had counted for active support.

"Matt, I heard that wouldn't come up after all," one of them said frowning.

"Where did you hear that?" Johns demanded softly.

"I don't know." The man was lying. "Can't seem to remember. . . . One of those rumors, you know. A man can't keep track of everything he hears. . . ."

"When it comes up, are you going to support it?"

"Well, Matt . . . I wouldn't want to limit my options. . . ."

And the other senator had been even more evasive.

The matter had begun to worry Johns now, but he was a very busy man and he knew he might be getting alarmed over nothing. For two days, he was engrossed in other matters. Then, at a cocktail party where he happened to run into several of his friends from the House, he raised the Eagle question to them as casually and indirectly as possible.

They all had heard "rumors" that it was a dead issue for this session.

The following morning, Johns made two more telephone calls, using the pretext of other matters. In each case he asked what his

317

associate had heard about scheduling the Eagle funding debate. One said he had heard nothing, and acted so mystified that Johns believed he was being truthful, and the second was more blunt: "Matt, it's not coming out."

"Where did you hear that?" Johns asked.

"I heard that D.L. doesn't want it to come out, and Cliff Sweet is going to go along with him and routinely lose the whole damned matter until it's too late for action this year."

Johns was stunned. "D.L. supports this appropriation!"

"Does he?" his associate asked quietly.

In a simpler universe, Johns would next have picked up the telephone and called Boudoin directly. But this might have been misinterpreted as a pressure tactic or interference in the operation of the Sweet Committee through an intermediary. Johns explained his mystification to his top administrative assistant, and that assistant wandered off to meet his counterpart in the larger, Boudoin office over coffee, by accident.

The aide was gone more than two hours. When he came back, he looked a shade tense. Closeted in Johns's office, he reported precisely what he had been told, off the record and largely on the basis of hearsay.

Johns made it a point to give his assistant a relaxed smile after asking a few questions and assuring himself that there was nothing more to be learned from this source. "Well, obviously it's a tempest in a teapot, Ralph! I'm relieved. Thought we might really have some trouble!"

His aide studied him closely, concerned. "Steinell is onto something about Eagle. But as long as there's no basis for what they've heard—"

"There isn't," Johns assured him, spreading his hands wide. "How could there be? Damn! It's irritating, but it's nothing to worry about, And I thank you for clearing it up for me, old man!"

The assistant went back to the large, "bull pen" front office. Johns allowed his forced smile to die. He tried to examine his scanty information from every angle, checking what he had heard against verifiable data. It was too early to tell just how much trouble they were really in, but it was not too early to make sure that everyone knew the extent of the danger.

Johns punched up his private line, the one with no outlets in the

318

other office. He used his personal credit card for the billing, and hit the buttons with suppressed anger and worry.

The transcontinental circuits were open and the call went through at once. The telephone at the other end rang four times, and then it was answered. Johns recognized the voice.

"Hello, Lydia?" he said.

2

K en Lis did not expect Barton MacIvor to like the idea.
MacIvor didn't.

Lis found the old man in a corner of his jam-packed cubicle, surrounded by engineering drawings and debris. The air was dense
with tobacco smoke, and MacIvor's fingers flew over the keys of a
desk-top computer, making green digits flash on the display window.

"Won't take long, Pappy," Lis said from the doorway.

"Come on in!" MacIvor half turned in his chair. "What would
you be doin' doon here in the slum areas?"

There was no use delaying it. "I've had a telephone talk with Jace
Mattingly, the NTSB man. The data on the Pittsburgh crash indicates the wing stalled."

MacIvor stiffened. "Bool."

"The Flight Recorder showed a stall."

"Impossible."

"Mattingly said he wanted to come out here. He has some ideas
for some further tests. He'll be here the day after tomorrow."

"Wal, enjoy yerself." MacIvor turned grumpily back to the computer.

"Pappy—"

"Lemme finish these figgers, an' then I'll make us a spot of tea."

Lis patiently waited. MacIvor hit computer buttons and glared at
the panel as it flickered and blinked some more, very rapidly, then
displayed a long sequence of numbers to about five decimal places.

"Ah-ha!" MacIvor said in triumph, and penciled a notation on the
back of an old bank deposit slip. He glared at Lis. "What would you

think of a range of eleven hundred miles with a thirty-minute reserve, a cruise of two-sixty knots, a ceiling of sixteen thousand, an' a landing speed of one-one-oh?"

"Goddammit," Lis said, "you're not supposed to be down here working on old Songbird drawings, Pappy!"

MacIvor picked up some pencil sketches, incredibly intricate and beautifully drawn, and whacked them with the back of one hand. "We can use the dimple wing with a manual control! It's as simple as the flap lever on the Cherokee." He jerked his right arm forward and back as if moving a Cherokee flap handle. "Whap! Slats open, dimple wing. Whap! Slats closed, normal wing. We could even build a solid dimple wing, put in a Lycoming one-fifty engine an' a fixed gear, 'n' sell her as a trainer!"

Lis looked at the drawings and felt a pang of pleasure mixed with regret. Barton MacIvor had taken their earlier designs for Songbird and drastically modified them. The earlier plans had shown a sleek and lovely mid-wing airplane with a very large engine and front-flapped wings for extra lifting surface at low speeds, capable of seating four in relative comfort. These drawings, though preliminary and done in pencil, had both MacIvor's exquisite drawing ability and a profoundly new concept built right into them.

Songbird was now a sleek, longer, low-wing aircraft with a three-bladed prop. Its tall rudder and wide stabilizer promised excellent control characteristics. And clearly sketched in was a dimple wing.

They had first uncovered MacIvor's long thought about the dimple wing in late-night discussions of Songbird. At the time, it had been ruled out, because the machinery to move the slats would make the plane too large, heavy, and costly for the private aviation market. They had gone on to the priority project, Excalibur. But now. . . .

"Would it work?" Lis asked.

"I'm tellin' you! Do you think I'm daft?"

Lis studied the lovely detail drawing, in one corner, showing how a simple set of mechanical extenders would move the wing slats. The plane would not only work, he thought. It would be a marvel to fly. If it could be produced for a sales price under twenty-five thousand dollars, it could stand the private aviation industry on its ear.

He became aware of MacIvor's keen scrutiny. With an effort, he beat down his flush of enthusiasm and put the plans carefully on the edge of the littered desk. "Interesting."

"*Interesting!*" MacIvor grunted. "Is that all you got to be sayin'?"

"Pappy, I came down here to talk about the new Excalibur tests. We want to start day after tomorrow, high altitude, hanging all the spoilers out to try to induce a stall—"

"Yer wastin' yer time," MacIvor said. "I checked an' rechecked all the figures, and it won't stall."

Lis felt a pulse of anger. "It *did* stall—twice."

"It wasn't the wing."

"What was it, then?"

"I don't know, but it wasn't the wing. She won't stall. Numbers don't lie. I asked the computer."

"Pappy, the plane is grounded. Maybe the tests can tell us what went wrong."

"Pilot error! Pilot error! Can't be anything else!"

"Look, I came down here to ask your advice about speed and throttle settings."

MacIvor grumbled over to his cabinet, where the decrepit kettle had been steaming. He poured something black and nasty out of a cup into the wreckage in a cardboard carton, dumped some tea leaves into the soggy bottom of the cup, and poured steaming water over it. His lips moving silently, shaggy eyebrows twitching, he found a spoon and stirred vigorously, then began blowing into the cup. The actions seemed to calm him.

"Aw right, lad," he said finally. "I'll git you your settings before quittin' time. But you're wastin' your time."

"Give me an alternative suggestion."

"I did! Pilot error!"

"Give me another."

MacIvor's good eye rolled. "Sun spots."

"Oh, shit," Lis said.

"Sun spots is as good a theory as sayin' the wing stalled!"

Lis stood. "Okay, Pappy. Thanks. Send the figures up by messenger, all right?"

"I'll tell you," MacIvor growled. "When all's said an' done, they're gonna find the crashes were caused by something real stupid. *Real* stupid. But if they don't find a cause soon, they won't have to be blamin' you for pushing the project, and me for designing that wing. That big whoor will be blaming us long afore they even think of it."

"Lydia is behind Excalibur all the way."

MacIvor snorted. "I had a friend once, name of Coffin Johnson. Ended up in prison, he did. He was always getting behind things too. Then one day a couple of nuns an' the sheriff seen him gettin' behind a sheep."

Lis grinned. "We aren't sheep."

"*I* ain't, fer shooer! Before she can break it off in me, I'm gonna be long gone from here!"

"That again?"

"Ah, lad," MacIvor sighed with genuine regret, "she's fixing to have your balls, and you don't even know it!"

Lis shook his head and started out.

"Tell me how is yer missus," MacIvor called after him.

It gave Lis an idea. MacIvor had always had a way with Amy, and she had always liked him—his wild hyperbole and unpredictability. Lis turned back. "She's better, Pappy."

"You think I could proper call her 'n' say how-dy-do?"

"I've got a better idea. Her brother and sister have been with us, but they leave tomorrow. I plan to ask Amy to have dinner out tomorrow night, over at The Grotto. Why don't you join us?"

"I'd be puttin' ye oot."

"Bullshit. How about meeting us there about seven-thirty?"

"You sure?"

"Amy can use some cheering up. And you and I might even find time to argue some more about Songbird."

"Wal, I dunno aboot arguing, but I'd like seein' her again, and I guess we could put up with your company if you promise to keep real quiet."

"Tomorrow night. Seven-thirty. The Grotto."

"Aw right." Then MacIvor fixed him with his good eye. "But don't think this will change my mind aboot more tests, lad! That boy from Washington can come, and we can fly the plane forever, but it'll all be baloney, an' nothing is going to change my mind on that!"

"Pappy," Lis said, "changing your mind on anything was the farthest thing from my mind.

The impulse to ask the old man to dinner sprang from more than a vague hope of convincing him. Lis was more upset by the data from the second Excalibur crash than he liked to admit, and at times like this he had always gone to Jason Baines or MacIvor for advice. He needed whatever support he could get from the old man, but was too proud to say it outright.

As it turned out, the dinner the following night had little to do with Excalibur. But MacIvor was in rare form and the evening was a success.

The old man appeared in a linty-looking suit with coat-hanger marks in the shoulders of the coat. A waiter seated them in a corner of the large, cavern-like room, not far from a crackling fireplace made possible by frigid air conditioning. Illumination at the table was by candlelight, and it was flattering to Amy. She looked lovely, the havoc softened by the dimness, and her liking for the old man surfaced immediately as MacIvor began tugging uncomfortably at this collar.

"Stop that," she scolded him gently. "You look very nice."

MacIvor obeyed grouchily. "Tell me how yer feelin'."

"Better."

"You're lookin' purtier'n I ever seen you. You'll break half the hearts in the country tonight!"

Amy turned to Lis. "Remind me to have him visit us at least once a week to repeat some of these compliments."

A cocktail waitress approached them. Lis was aware of a tightening in his gut as she asked if they would have drinks before ordering.

MacIvor cast a look with his good eye that showed tension of his own. "Would ye be havin' beer?"

"Yes, sir. Budweiser, Schlitz—"

"Say no more. I'll have the Bud. I like their horses."

The girl turned to Amy. "For you, ma'am?"

"Yes." Amy smiled and Lis's insides sank. Then she added, "I think I'll have a Coke."

"One Coke . . . and for you, sir?"

"Nothing," Lis said, meeting his wife's smile.

"Now," Amy said to MacIvor after the waitress had gone away. "I'd like to hear what *you* think of the Excalibur grounding, and Lydia Baines, and everything else. Ken doesn't like to talk shop at home, and I never know what's going on."

"Wal," MacIvor said cautiously, "there isn't much to say."

"Nonsense. First. Excalibur. Is there something badly wrong with

the airplane or isn't there? I assume there isn't, or you two perfec-
tionists would never have had anything to do with it."

"That's true," MacIvor replied, leaning his elbows on the edge of
the table. "And there ain't. But how do you convince the Washington fellers of that? It takes more'n character references, you know."

"You have your own tests ongoing, don't you?"

"Shooer."

"Well? Tell me about them!"

Lis became the silent partner at the table, listening in quiet
amazement as Amy expertly, and with genuine interest, drew Mac-
Ivor out. After a while they were interrupted to order their meals,
and by delivery of their drinks. As they sipped, the conversation
drifted to Lydia Baines and changes in the company since her take-
over.

MacIvor did not handle her as Lis did. The old man held back
nothing, voicing his animosity and fears for the future. Lis was afraid
he was going too far and would only worry Amy, but she seemed
tranquil. Was there a lesson here? Lis wondered. In trying awkwardly to shield her from his own worries, was he really denigrating
her and contributing to her low self-esteem?

It was not a pleasant thought. If it was accurate, then the only
way to begin repairing the situation was to begin at once—tonight—
with a new candor. Caution whispered that she was not ready. He
told himself he had to try.

By the time the meals came, the subject had switched to Mac-
Ivor's own future. While they ate, he returned to his morose thoughts
about that, making no attempt to hide them.

"If I want to work on Songbird," he told Amy, "I must be getting
on with it. I don't have forever, you know."

"You talk like a decrepit old man," she teased him. "And half the
women in here are trying to flirt with you by long distance."

"Ay, they know they can flirt with me, because my hearin' 'n' sight
are so bad any more I can't be receivin' any of their messages!"

"Pappy," she said, "*have* you ever thought of getting married
again?"

"At my age? You're daft!"

"You have lots of years ahead of you!"

"It's fine fer you to say that. You're in your prime. I might be
kickin' off anytime. An' I got things I wanna do before my time is

oop. Songbird, for example. I might be an old fool, but I'd shooer like to see her fly!"

Amy turned to Lis. "Is there a chance Hempstead will develop it? I know how long the two of you have talked about it."

"I don't know," Lis said. "Once we get Excalibur sales rolling, the investigation all behind us—"

"Lydia," MacIvor snorted, "will never go for it, and you know it!"

"Is that true?" Amy asked.

"I don't know," Lis said.

"She'll never let us try it!" MacIvor said. "That's why one of these fine days I'll be movin' on."

"Oh, Pappy. You wouldn't do that. You and Ken have been together so long now."

The old man scowled from under his shelf of eyebrows. "You sound like your hubby now, playin' on my emotions. I'm s'posed to be a scientist. I ain't s'posed to be ruled by emotions."

"We're all ruled by our emotions," she said. "The only difference is that some of us spend half our lives pretending we don't *have* emotions, and that's when we get in trouble."

Lis had never heard her say anything remotely resembling this before. Was it her discovery, or was she quoting the new doctor? In either case it might be a hopeful sign.

They finished their meals. The conversation turned to happier topics. MacIvor told them some stories about his childhood, and of the first gliders he made—and crashed in—during his teens. One of the crashes had been on—and through—the roof of a village church. He had emerged with only a broken arm, but his father had threatened him with considerably worse if he ever "toyed with them contraptions" again. After that, MacIvor had journeyed all the way in to the next valley for his earliest flying experiments.

When they left the restaurant, about nine-thirty, there was no question that the evening had been a buoying experience for all of them. MacIvor gallantly kissed Amy's hand and secured from her a promise to visit his apartment soon to diagnose a mysterious illness going through all his house plants. Amy, in turn, had made the old man say he would not leave Hempstead Aviation—or get married to any young girl—without first letting her know about it. Standing with them in the parking lot for a moment while the cars were brought around, Lis reflected that they were the two persons remaining in the world who meant the most to him. And he might be on the verge of losing them both.

In the car on the way home, Amy told him, "That was fun."

"I'm glad you had a good time, because I did."

"Ken, why had it been so long since we went out with Pappy, or anyone else, like that?"

"I don't know. But we won't wait so long again."

"It was my drinking," she said. "And those damned pills. And all my meetings. When could we have gone out when I was going twenty hours a day to prove to myself that I was important?"

He glanced at her, again surprised by the insight it seemed to stem from. "Let's not start assigning any blame. Let's just continue from tonight."

"I'd like that. I think I'll be all right."

"You know, tonight Pappy told you some things about the company and our troubles that I never would have said."

"I know that. But I don't understand why."

"I didn't want to be dumping my troubles on you. I don't want to come home and start telling you how miserable I am. That's not a very supportive thing for a husband to do. I thought if I kept things to myself—"

"But when you keep everything to yourself, isn't that a sort of lying?"

He thought about it, driving. "I guess maybe it is."

"I always thought you had stopped telling me things because you figured I didn't care. So I tried *not* to care."

"I know you didn't like Jason, Amy. But he was a very special man. I'll never forget him. I think it might be a long, long time before I stop grieving over what happened. But how could I have told you something like that even a week ago? How can I say it to you now? It makes me sound like a crybaby, and I don't want to upset you—"

"We have to try to stop that sort of behavior," she told him firmly. "We have to be out front with things."

They drove in silence. Lis thought about Harvey Coughlin's trip to Europe. He had intended to tell her about that sometime tonight, and be open in saying what a difficult position it left him in with Lydia Baines. But things had gone so well that he decided to carry it inside himself, and alone, a little while longer.

327

After a while she said quietly, "I hope Pappy gets feeling better about Lydia, and the new tests."

"He will."

"Will he?"

"I hope so, Amy. I've got to work like hell to make him feel better."

"Maybe we can go out with him more—see him more."

"Yes."

"Because I really enjoyed tonight, darling. I think I feel better than I have in a long, long time."

"I hope so," he said, and then added, "Amy, your getting better means more than anything else."

"I got through today."

"Yes."

"And we've made a fine start."

He reached for her hand on the seat between them.

"There's one thing you do have to understand, though," she said.

"That being?"

"I have to say this, Ken. I think I can get better. And I *think* I can learn to stand on my own feet while being your wife. But I *will* get better this time. If it begins to seem that the only way I can control the drinking—be self-realized—is by going my own way—"

"Let's not consider the possibility!"

"We must," she said somberly. "There are all the years . . . the ways we habitually relate to each other, and the problems. We're doing just fine. I think we *will* do fine. But I'm just saying that I intend to make it this time, and be a whole person. It's possible I might have to . . . think seriously about changing almost everything in my life in order to get myself reorganized."

He glanced at her for as long as the task of driving allowed. He was newly shaken. She could never have said a thing like this before. The suicide attempt had worked profounder changes in her than he had realized. He saw that she might have to jettison him in order to be able to stand alone . . . and the thought shocked and frightened him.

It occurred to him to play the old power games with her. He caught himself.

All he said was, "We'll hope it doesn't come to that, babe."

"It probably won't."

How calmly they spoke of changing their entire lives!

The remainder of the drive home was in silence. When they reached the house it was quite dark, but the new yard boy they had hired was just loading his mower into the back of his old truck. Skinny and blond, he grinned and waved at them from across the yard as they drove into the garage.

3

I t might be easy to do the job instantly, Harold thought, watching Ken and Amy Lis drive into their garage. Follow them by going around the house to the back door; use the plastic credit card on the cheap lock; go through the kitchen and confront them either in the living room, or upstairs if they went directly up the stairs.

Jesus, it was a tempting proposition! He was getting sick of waiting, wanting to be absolutely sure! He wanted it *over* with!

But rushing was the best way to get caught, he told himself quickly. And his flesh shriveled at the thought of being caught and put in prison, behind walls, in a little room, with more rooms on top of you and on all sides of you and underneath you, a teeming, squirming warren, and you *in* it somewhere, unable to *move*.

The thought gave him screaming claustrophobia and drove him to get into his truck fast and drive away before he caught another glimpse of the Lises and felt more temptation to attack before the time was ripe and his plans were fully ready.

It would not be long now, Harold told himself, trying to calm down. He needed just a little more information on the interior of their house, and more observation of their habits and those of the neighbors most likely to observe. Then he would be ready. Then he would see Ken Lis's blood spill.

Driving unsteadily, Harold reached his temporary home. It was one of four small cubbyhole apartments over a dry cleaner's and a drugstore. The corner building had been a showplace once, probably in the thirties. It had pink walls, a false stucco finish, a crenelated edge over the hidden roof. Below, the little neon sign read SAY-

LORS in the cleaners, and a bluish sign extended from the corner entrance of the drugstore. *Rexall*, it said. The windows of the apartments overhead were dark cavities of heat.

Pulling down the gravel alley past the Dempster Dumpster, Harold parked the pickup in his slot behind the fallen-in garage. Something scurried away from the trash cans as he got out and slammed the door hard to lock it. He went around the side of the garage to the metal fire escape and climbed up, intent on thoughts of his revenge. The voice consequently startled him badly.

"What?" he said, looking around sharply.

"Sorry, man," the voice said softly from nearby. "Didn't mean to shake you up. I just said you worked late."

Harold located the man, about his own age although he was heavier, running to fat. He was Harold's neighbor, and right now he was sitting on the fire escape just above Harold's position on the stairs, bare feet dangling. Harold took a breath and climbed on up.

"No use coming home," he said. "Too hot to do much."

"You can say that again, man," the fat neighbor said. "You can say *that* again! I think it must be a hundred and forty in my pad!"

"Hot everywhere," Harold said unlocking his door.

"You don't have any cold beer, do you?" the fat man asked.

"No," Harold said, and remembered his neighbor's name. "I don't drink beer, Joseph."

"Well," Joseph said, "I've got some orange soda. It's not very good, but it's real cold. Would you like to have one?"

Harold hesitated. He had to appear normal, not reclusive. "Yes, that would be very nice, Joseph."

His neighbor got up. "I'll bring it right over." He shambled toward his own door, bare feet splaying, almost-female breasts swaying under the sweaty gray material of his tee shirt.

Harold went inside. The apartment was so hot it took his breath away, made him shudder. He turned a table lamp on, revealing the green velveteen couch, brown plastic armchair, pale blond end table, wicker plant stand with two dead ferns in it, and girlie magazines and weight-lifter publications scattered over the thin, mat-like rug. He felt a burst of sheer hatred—hatred of the crummy apartment, hatred of the crummy furniture, hatred of the heat, hatred of his own slowness to act on Ken Lis, hatred of everything and everyone, including Joseph. The fat bastard was always fawning around, flop-

331

ping his teats, shaking his long, dirty hair, sticking his ugly bare feet out into the middle of the room, wanting to borrow weight-lifter magazines, asking if Harold wanted to go to a porno movie, seeking to share ice cream or a Coke. Harold knew it was necessary to be friendly; he could not afford to arouse suspicion of any kind by being overly remote or mysterious. But he hated the fat son of a bitch, detested these frequent conversations and visits.

Before he could change clothes or even think about a shower, the door rattled and Joseph lumbered in, carrying two sweaty bottles of orange soda. He handed one over and flopped onto the couch. Sipping, he grinned. "Good for what ails you, man."

"I need a shower and early rest," Harold said. The orange drink tasted like piss, and he yearned to tell Joseph so. "That's all that will help me: some rest and some cooler weather."

"It was ninety-four today," Joseph said.

"I knew it was hot."

"You look tired," Joseph said, calf-like eyes watching closely. "You should stay in during the heat of midday."

"That's when I make my money, in the heat of the day."

"You know, the moment you moved in here, I knew we would be friends. I wish my health were better, that I were stronger. I'd like to do the kind of work you do. I could get off some of this weight."

"If you want to lose weight," Harold snarled, "try not eating so much."

"I know I should. When I see the way the exercise has given you such a wonderful shape, I know I should do something about my own condition."

"You'll be all right," Harold said. "Listen, you have to excuse me now. I need that shower."

"Go ahead," Joseph said. "I'll just finish my drink."

Gritting his teeth, Harold started for the doorway to the bedroom-bathroom area. "Just lock the door on your way out."

Closing the bedroom door, he stripped out of the sweaty clothes. Bits of grass clippings clung to his torso, arms, and legs. He hoped the shower would cool him off. He went into the bathroom, startling two or three large brown roaches with the overhead light, and went immediately to the shower stall.

The water was lukewarm and would not get cooler, but it felt good. Harold lathered carefully and shampooed his hair and rinsed well and got out of the stall with reluctance. But he did feel cooler, and the air that swirled into the bathroom from the darkened bedroom, when he opened the door, was almost refreshing. He walked into the dark with the towel over his shoulder.

"I hope you don't mind," a furry voice said out of the darkness. "I hope you understand, man."

Revulsion beginning in his gut, Harold turned. He could just make out the figure on the bed—*his* bed. It was a very large figure, white, shapeless. He could see the pile of clothing on the chair nearby.

"I know it's not very subtle," Joseph said thickly, unmoving. "I've run out of subtle hints."

Harold stared at him through the darkness, seeing him better, feeling the nausea tug at his throat.

"I think we understand each other," Joseph said, "don't we?"

Harold felt the short circuits let loose in his brain, each with a little elastic snap of pure pain. He walked to his dresser and opened the top drawer. Then he turned and went toward the pale, blubbery figure on the bed.

"I'll be nice," Joseph cooed. "You'll be nice too, won't you, lover? I can always spot a kindred spirit. I knew you the moment I first saw you."

Harold leaned across the bed and seized Joseph's greasy long hair with his left hand, pulling his head up and back.

"What are you—" Joseph's voice became a bubbly outrush of air as the blade of the big knife began slicing under his left ear, slashed through cartilage and carotid artery, destroyed the voice box and windpipe, and came out under the other ear in a great, steamy splash of hot blood. Joseph's fat, bare legs kicked spasmodically and the bed rocked as though it would go through the floor, but he did not get fully to a sitting position before he pitched sideways, twitched violently several times, and was still.

Harold sat very still, shaking from head to foot, listening to something drip. He realized that it was Joseph's blood, and ran to get towels to sop it up before it leaked throught the floor to the store below. *What a mess*, he thought, *what a mess*. It would take half the night to get everything even halfway cleaned up, and he would have to practically rupture himself to haul this fat slob down the stairs in the dead of night and get him into the truck under the grass for hauling to the dump. Christ, it was just a mess all around, and he would be exhausted tomorrow.

Then it dawned on Harold that there was one fringe benefit: He had not thought about how hot it was for almost two minutes. And it was, after all, good practice for Ken Lis, was it not?

Harold stood in the dark holding a blood-soaked towel, and began laughing.

4

When Harvey Coughlin returned from Monravia a day later, his first act was to seek out Lydia Baines. When he learned that she was at her San Francisco apartment, he called there.

"It went fine, Lydia," he told her at once. "Naturally, details should be told in person. But the, ah, transaction went without a hitch, and in perfect discretion."

"We have a problem, Harvey. I must see you at once."

Harvey tightened. "About my trip? I assure you—"

"It's another matter. Come to San Francisco at once."

"Now? —I mean, I just walked into the office—"

"*Now!*" Lydia said, and slammed the receiver in his ear.

Harvey was shaken by her angry tone but reassured himself that he was in such good graces now that nothing serious could be wrong. He told his secretary he was going to San Francisco, and departed at once.

Thanks to snarled traffic, he did not reach the apartment tower on Russian Hill until noon. Night fog had broken a brief heat wave, and although the sun shone brilliantly over the city, fog remained over the bay. The city itself was crisp, cool, and dazzling, but the view out toward Marin County was extremely hazy, and he could only barely make out the green flats and dun-colored hills around Berkeley.

The view would be better, Harvey thought, from Lydia's wall of glass.

When he was ushered into the large, cool living room on the top floor, however, he had no time to inspect the view. The oriental girl bowed out immediately, closing the door behind her. And Lydia Baines, who had been standing at the windows and smoking a cigarette, turned on him with naked anger in her eyes.

"I expected you an hour ago."

"There was traffic all tied up, Lydia. They're working on the highway."

She strode around the end of the long couch, the legs of her flared white jumpsuit swishing with every angry movement. She stabbed her cigarette into a large crystal tray. "Sit down."

Harvey obeyed. He was beginning to get upset. *She's just a woman*, he tried to remind himself.

Lydia put hands on hips and glared down at him. "You recognize that Eagle has been delayed again."

"It's irritating," he said. "But I'm sure it's merely routine—"

"I doubt it. That's what I intend to find out. I have some questions. I want straight answers. Don't try to lie to me or hide anything. I'll find out and have your balls."

"Of course I would never lie or dissemble to you, Lydia! My life is an open book. My loyalty is all to you and Hempstead Aviation."

"When did you first meet General Mallory?"

The question was out of left field, and it took him a few seconds to adjust. "Black Jack Mallory?"

"What other General Mallory *is* there?"

"Well, let me see. . . ." Sweat began to form on his brow. "I think I first met him last year, when we made that slight attempt to see what the future of Eagle might be. But Jason called off any effort at that time—"

"That was a courtesy call at the Pentagon?"

"Well, you might call it that. We had a soft drink in a cafeteria somewhere, and talked for about ten minutes."

"When did you see him the next time?"

"Well, we talked on the telephone before my first trip East this summer—"

"And then you saw him at the party given by Matt Johns."

"Let me think . . . yes, he was there. We said hello—hardly more."

"Then?"

"The next time . . . let me see . . . it was at the hearings. We talked over cups of coffee in the corridor, as I recall."

336

Lydia tapped her foot. "I want to know about *major* meetings."

"A major meeting—with a general? I think there's a pun there. Ha, ha." Her look could have killed. He cleared his throat, feeling his panic grow. *What was going on here?* "I had one session of perhaps thirty minutes with him and two other staff officers on one of the later trips, and he attended the Thursday-night party I gave at the hotel during my last visit—"

"Do you believe you caused Mallory's support for Eagle?"

Ordinarily he would have claimed so. But caution ruled now. "I would like to think I . . . contributed, Lydia. But the general has always been in favor of the system."

"I want a careful, complete answer to this. Did you at any time offer Mallory any sort of inducement?"

"Inducement?"

She gestured. "Money. Favors. Liquor. A girl. Anything."

"No! —It wasn't necessary, you see."

"Would it surprise you to hear that General Mallory has received a formal letter of reprimand concerning Eagle?"

Harvey sucked in his breath. "God! He did?"

"He did. And it came right from the top. It said his conduct in the whole matter, and his friendship with, quote, officials high in the manufacturing company, unquote, compromised his reputation. He was directed to make no more statements about Eagle, or take any further action in the matter in any way."

"How do you know this?" Harvey asked, stunned.

"I know."

"Poor Jack! This is terrible!"

"It isn't the end of his career. It's happened before. I remember a case—another missile case, as I recall—where a general got such a written reprimand and then was promoted in turn next time around. And the government ended up buying the missile, too. I'm more concerned with this as a symptom of the trouble, not for what it may or may not do to one damned fool's career."

"Does this mean other people are being asked questions too? Is someone trying to make trouble?"

"Tell me about your relationship with Senator Barker."

"Barker?" Harvey was really worried now. He racked his brain. "I saw him in his office once—no, twice—and I talked to one of his administrative assistants a couple of times . . . and let me see . . . he

was at one of the last parties, I think. I have my lists. I could check
that—"

"Did you give him any presents?"

"No! —Well, let me see. . . . I might have sent a bottle of bour-
bon around—I bought several cases and handed them out, strictly
as a friendly gesture—"

"Anything more?"

"No."

"Parkhurst," she said. "What about him?"

"Essentially the same. —Lydia, what *is* this? What's happening? I
think I have a right to know!"

"What did you do to get Clifford Sweet to change his position?"

"I—I didn't really do anything! I was just persuasive, I guess!"

"Don't lie. We sent Interspace, in his home state, a letter saying
we considered their cost estimates the best in their category. Isn't
that right?"

"Didn't I tell you about that at the time, Lydia?"

"You didn't. But that probably had an impact on Sweet, right?"

"Well, we *hoped* so—"

"*Was* Interspace the lowest and best bidder?"

"Yes!"

"Are you sure of that?"

"Yes! I swear it! You can check the files yourself if you don't believe me!"

"I intend to, Harvey. Now. What else might you have done to
influence Sweet?"

"Nothing else!"

"What about D. L. Boudoin? Isn't it true that you had Matt
Johns arrange a meeting with him at Matt's party? Didn't you talk
in the garden, alone? As a result of that meeting, didn't you subse-
quently make a contact with a man named Joe Wind, identified as
Boudoin's son-in-law?"

She had been talking to Johns. There was no telling how much
more she knew. The panic was fullblown now. He could not risk another half-truth. "Yes. I saw Joe Wind. Matt Johns suggested that I
needed to be nice to him—that's the way things get done in
Washington—"

"Did you make some investments with Wind?"

"Yes. Strictly *personal* investments! My own money, Lydia; I'm completely loyal to Hempstead, and if that was what it took—"

Lydia Baines took a pad and pencil from the end table, sat down, and poised the pad on her crossed knee. "How many investments?"

"Three. —No. Four."

"How much, and approximately when?"

Harvey rubbed his face, slick with sweat that dripped between his fingers. "Let me see. . . . The first time, right after I met Boudoin. Wind came around and we talked—"

"How much?"

"Ten thousand dollars."

She jotted the figure. "Next?"

"Not long after that, he said he had a new deal and he could let me in—" Harvey saw her rage and cut straight to the point: "Seven thousand."

"The next."

"A month ago. Two thousand."

"There was a fourth time?"

"Two weeks ago. Another two thousand."

"How were these investments made?"

"My personal check, mailed to his office."

Lydia ticked off the figures with the point of her pencil. "So you've made payoffs to Wind in the total of twenty-one thousand dollars."

"They weren't payoffs! They were personal investments!"

"Do you have stock certificates?"

"No."

"Do you have *anything?*"

"No, but he's a fairly legitimate broker, I'm sure—"

"Wind is being investigated by the Securities and Exchange Commission and the FBI. Every person I've mentioned, and some others we haven't identified yet, have been the subject of an ongoing investigation of some kind by the news media. Craighead and Little of the *Post* are asking questions. So is Jake Steinell. He apparently had an early start on it all. Virtually everyone we've been counting on for active support in Washington is scared shitless and gone underground. No one knows exactly how this happened, or even why, but it looks like Eagle is going right down the tubes unless something

339

can be done to make certain that no one can allege any wrongdoing by Hempstead—any influence peddling."

Harvey stared. He was numb with shock. He remembered his one brief meeting with Steinell. "My God, Senator Johns had Steinell at his party that time! I thought they were friends—"

"Steinell is syndicated in over two hundred daily newspapers, and he would print a story that might help circulation if it meant the Pope would be excommunicated as a result. A lot of this information he apparently is working on—and others are now working on—had to come from somewhere. Did you ever confide in him?"

"My God, no!"

Lydia got to her feet again and began pacing. "It's very bad, Harvey. Very, *very* bad. We not only stand to see Eagle go down, but if a lot of unfavorable publicity comes out to damage the company, God only knows what that will do to Excalibur sales, even if we ever succeed in getting the damned NTSB off our backs. This can be ruinous."

"I know what it must look like," Harvey said. "Influence peddling —corruption—but none of that is true—"

"You have to do two things," she cut in. "You have to get to Washington and contact this Joe Wind. You have to get out of that investments game he's been playing."

"I don't know if I can get my money back out that easily. I—"

"To hell with your money! Just contact him—tell him you want out—insist that you are terminating all connections at once, and demand a letter to that effect. Take your letter of demand to his office if you have to. If he won't co-operate, at least get your demand on file. That's first. You *must* get yourself entirely divorced from him, in writing, and fast."

Harvey thought of his savings vanishing, never to be reclaimed. It made him sick, but he couldn't even pause to worry about it now. Much more was at stake. "I'll handle it at once—leave tomorrow—"

"Leave today. Secondly, it's crucial that we try to find out who has been feeding the press, especially Steinell, some of this inside information. Surely you've met some people there by now whom you could discreetly question about this. Giving away nothing, you understand, but putting out feelers. Do you think of any people you know like that?"

Harvey cast around. "There's one . . . young girl."

"I know about her. She works for Matt Johns. He's checking her out now, most carefully."

"It couldn't be Dena! She—likes me. And she doesn't like Steinell at all."

Lydia Baines stopped pacing. "Talk to her if you're absolutely certain she's trustworthy. If there is any doubt, leave her out of it. Matt Johns is trying discreetly to gather more information, and you can call him at his office but not at home—repeat, not at his home—and after you identify yourself, he'll make arrangements to call you somewhere else from a pay phone. Together the two of you may be able to get to the bottom of this, find our source."

Harvey stared at her, his mind reeling. Calling from *pay phones*? Looking for *informers*? He remembered Watergate. Was it going to be like that? A horror of plot and counterplot and trusting no one? Did she really suspect phone taps?

"I'll . . . get right on it," he said. "I'll be . . . very careful."

"You'd better be," Lydia told him coldly.

He looked up at her, trying to read her meaning.

"You've been our man in Washington," she said. "As far as anyone can determine, you are the common denominator in several of these vague rumors and allegations. Someone—Steinell, the *Post*—someone has been backtracking many of your activities, and it's obvious that someone thinks he smells illegal influence peddling. Matt doesn't think they can have much to go on, or they would have already broken some half-assed story. But we have to eliminate what smoke they think they see. You have to get out of any connection with Wind—and repudiate him, and you have to do that fast. And if you can get any hint of where all this is originating, you have to help Matt do that, too."

"I'll do everything I can."

"I've liked you, Harvey," Lydia said. "I have had high hopes for you . . . and for Eagle. But if you've made some stupid mistake . . . or if there is no other way to save the reputation of Hempstead Aviation . . . you must understand my alternatives. No one is bigger than the company. If I must, to save what I can, I'll sacrifice you in a second."

"Yes," Harvey choked. "Yes, of course, I understand—I'll do my best."

"You'd better get moving, then." She turned her back on him and walked to the windows.

Somehow he found his own way out and down the plush express elevator, and to his car. It was only after he was behind the wheel that he took a shuddering breath and began to shake uncontrollably with a deep, nameless, all-engulfing terror.

·

5

Low scud veiled the early-morning sun the next day as test pilot Hank Selvy and a crew of a dozen technicians watched several mechanics make final adjustments to a special wind-velocity and angle-of-attack indicator boom-mounted on the nose of the test Excalibur. As soon as the final fittings were secure, the crew would be taking the plane up for the latest in the continuing series of high-altitude stall test procedures.

Exactly on schedule, Ken Lis and Jace Mattingly walked out of the MA Building and to the waiting aircraft. Lis made introductions to the ground crew and to Hank Selvy.

"Hope we're not going to wreck our bird," Selvy said.

"I'm with you on that," Mattingly replied, his face sober.

Selvy pointed to a boom rigged on the front of the lab plane. "We've got the extra wind-flow gear in place, I was noticing."

"It looks good," Lis said. "You've studied the proposed flight plan for today?"

"Yes. Full load, dummy weights. Approach to landing stalls with everything hanging out. Maneuver stalls with and without the gear extended."

"You don't look happy about it," Lis said.

"We've done this test series before."

"You didn't read the fine print. We're going much deeper into the stall this time, unless you can make her stall prematurely."

"Excalibur won't stall prematurely."

Lis was watching Jace Mattingly and saw his face stiffen. Mattingly said carefully, "The Pittsburgh Excalibur stalled prematurely."

"That's what the instruments say," Selvy replied.

"You don't believe the instruments?"

"Excalibur doesn't stall that way," Selvy said.

Lis intervened. "Let's start flying and stop talking, gentlemen."

Selvy turned and walked toward the airplane.

Mattingly smiled thinly. "A lot of people have an almost mystic faith in this piece of equipment."

"Hank Selvy has wrung Excalibur out a thousand times. You can't blame him."

"No, but the black box doesn't lie."

There was no solution to that puzzle. Lis could only nod and walk with the grim NTSB investigator toward the waiting airplane.

A few minutes later they were inside the passenger cabin, which was sweltering with no air conditioning yet on. A dozen technicians swarmed over the computers attached to every vital component and member of the plane. Much of the gadgetry was already in operation, monitoring. Lis walked Mattingly through, briefly explaining, and then they went up to the flight deck.

Hank Selvy and the test copilot, named Trusdale, were already in their seats, panels of lights glowing amber and green overhead. The flight engineer was on his hands and knees in the narrow aisle behind them, banging with a wrench on the underside of Selvy's seat while Selvy rocked forward and backward in it rather violently.

"What's the problem?" Lis asked.

"Same old thing," Selvy grunted, perspiring. "We build a perfect airplane, but we can't install a seat that doesn't get hung up on its forward-backward track every once in a while."

The engineer whanged away. "Try it now."

Selvy lurched forward in the seat and it slid up. "Okay. Nothing is perfect," he told Mattingly. "Even Excalibur."

Lis and Mattingly strapped themselves down on a special bench seat installed behind the engineer's position in the narrow aisle.

Within minutes, preflight checks had been done and Selvy flicked a final switch and keyed his intercom mike. "We're firing them up, gentlemen."

The engines turned and Excalibur throbbed to life. Cool air began whispering from ceiling vents. The doors were up and locked, radios set, the final portions of the second check list read off. Selvy unlocked the brakes and spread his ample hand over the ganged center throttles, nudging them slightly forward. Excalibur began to move, trundling away from the MA Building.

The flight plan called for initial climb to FL 39—thirty-nine thousand feet above sea level—and a cruise east to put the testing over the desert of Nevada. Once they were airborne, Lis took Mattingly to the back for a few minutes, where they briefly watched the engineering technicians monitor the maze of instruments plugged into miles of extra cable that intersected every vital conduit in the airplane's central nervous system. Satisfied that all was well, they then returned to the flight deck.

They were now over the test area. Lis and Mattingly buckled in again.

"Okay," Selvy said on intercom, glancing at his clipboard of notes. "Ready for number one?"

"We're ready back here," the voice of an engineer came from the rear.

"Okay, sequence one."

The autopilot was disengaged, and Selvy flew the airplane. He turned the yoke gently, and both pilots scanned the sky high and low as the Excalibur described a massive, high-altitude clearing turn. Broken cumulus cloud shone silver far below, and here and there in holes. Lis could see the rumpled brown patterns of mountains and canyon country. He felt himself being caught up in the moment and it felt good.

Rolling Excalibur back precisely out of a full circle, the compasses swinging back to their original heading, Selvy began issuing orders from the clipboard strapped to his knee. Power was reduced and additional nose-up trim inserted to maintain altitude at the cost of decaying airspeed. Flaps were extended first to 2, then 5, then 7 degrees. Airspeed continued to bleed off and more back pressure was added to the yoke; then the pressure was trimmed out. The plane moved sluggishly through the thin air, its nose very high to give the wings additional bite in compensation for the low speed.

At a precisely calibrated point, the airplane's wings would no longer improve their ability to fly at reduced speed by increasing their angle of attack. Beyond a point, wind would burble fully over the top surface and even the dimple wing would stall. It was the wing's stall tendencies they were being forced to re-explore in increasingly exotic ways, because it had been some kind of stall that had brought death at New York and Pittsburgh. Until the wing could be made to pull its killing trick under controlled conditions, there was no way to pinpoint the exact parameters of trouble . . . and start figuring out how to fix things.

Nudging below 160 knots, Selvy gently moved a handle on the central control pedestal, beginning deployment of Excalibur's wing slats. A yellow light flickered in the overhead panel.

"Slats open six," the engineer called.

"Six," Selvy repeated.

"Ten."

"Rog. Ten." Selvy's hand, working by feel as he scanned instruments and horizon referents, continued to tease forward the red, star-shaped knob on the end of a small handle behind the ganged throttles on the center pedestal. The slat-control knob, like none other in any aircraft, had been given its multiple-pointed head precisely to make sure that no pilot could ever grasp it in the mistaken belief that it was any other control.

"Fifteen," the engineer said. "Full fifteen."

"Full fifteen."

"Okay, a little more back pressure."

The airspeed indicator continued to spiral downward: 150 . . . 145 . . . 140. . . . And both pilots were helping hold pressure on the control yoke to maintain a rock-solid altitude and heading. Excalibur was not being given enough engine power to maintain this altitude at any speed above its minimum. The addition of any more drag would push it over the brink into a near stall.

They were purposely pushing through the limits.

As the airspeed indicator hit 130, a whining beeper started and red lights flashed in a triangular pattern overhead.

"Okay," Trusdale said calmly, "automatic gear-extension warning."

"Okay. Go ahead and put them down."

Below a speed ordinarily reached only in the final stages of landing, automatic mechanisms sensed the conditions and warned the pilots with the beeper while starting the gear down for landing without being told. When Trusdale flicked the gear-down switch, the beeper fell silent. The massive gears, already going down, dropped on into place and locked with a thump that was both audible and felt throughout the length of the aircraft.

"Gear down, three green lights."

"Okay, watch the airspeed now. Give me the flaps."

The landing-gear assemblies and open wells from which they had descended were adding tremendous drag components, making Excalibur harder to hold to its low-power altitude. Airspeed was down to 123 and dropping. As Trusdale's hand moved and new switches were thrown, servomechanisms whined distantly and the plane's nose nudged higher, as if shoved up by a massive hand. Flaps were extending, increasing the effective surface of the wings again, but once more with the effect of making the plane seem to waddle through the sky, nose pointing sickeningly high.

"Okay," Selvy called on the intercom, his voice higher with controlled tension. "Be ready, everybody. We're right on it." He closed the switch and glanced back over his shoulder at Lis. "All the way through?"

"Yes," Lis told him.

Selvy riveted his attention on his flying.

Excalibur was now at the speed where it ordinarily landed in the cushion of ground effect. The wings simply could not fly more than a few more seconds. They were gouging great, invisible troughs through the atmosphere, leaving a wake of boiling commotion. Lift was almost all gone. Excalibur had begun to tremble in warning. Blinker lights started going off like a Christmas tree. The airspeed continued to bleed. Both pilots hung onto the yokes, forcing the ship to hang on its nose and struggle to maintain its attitude.

"Just keep the ball in," Selvy said tautly. "If that ball gets out—"

"It's in."

"Keep on it. If it breaks, we don't know which way it will roll."

A horn began blaring in the low ceiling. Simultaneously, a large red light flashed on the panel and both control yokes began to buffet —a little at first, then much more roughly, shaking both pilots like rag dolls.

"What keeps the mother *flying?*" Trusdale asked.

"Spoilers," Selvy ordered.

Large flaps on the upper surfaces of the tortured wings were raised abruptly. Lift was destroyed. Excalibur lurched. The wing stopped flying. A panoply of lights exploded all over the panels and ceiling of the flight deck. The control yokes broke abruptly backward, fully into the pilots' chests.

Majestically, the long, needle nose of the airplane began to pitch forward—across open sky and then through the horizon. It was falling into a rock-heavy dive.

Selvy's hands flew. The yoke back pressure was released and full recovery power slammed home. Spoilers were already off and Trusdale had the gear coming up. Air whistled around the windows. The windscreen was filled with the earth, far below, and the altimeters were spinning madly in descent.

Both pilots eased back slowly on the yoke. The plane shuddered like a wet dog and began to pull out . . . began to fly again.

"Jesus," Jace Mattingly said beside Lis. His face dripping sweat.

Lis smiled grimly. Excalibur had just lost almost six thousand feet of precious altitude in seconds. His ears were popping and his stomach had been lost somewhere up above. But for Lis this was expected.

What was significant, and perhaps what had caused Mattingly's exclamation, was the fact that nothing untoward had happened. The stall break had been docile and predictable, and *below* the book stall speed.

The great airplane had been docile as a kitten.

Which meant that still another test had just failed.

6

As the test Excalibur glided in over the city on its way to a landing, some fifty minutes later, Harold Zelmer observed it with mixed feelings of hatred and elation.

It was unlikely that he would ever again view any large jetliner without the feeling of hate. His elation stemmed from the more specific knowledge that his day of final retribution was near at hand.

Harold paused and mopped a bandana across his face, saw the Excalibur dip out of his view below the distant horizon and house-tops, then turned back to the power mower he had been operating in a yard less than a block from the home of Ken and Amy Lis.

He had known his luck was running well, and that he was nearly ready to complete his vengeance, when the Lises departed from their house together for their dinner engagement with Barton MacIvor a few nights before. This presented Harold with his first chance to explore their house, which was to be the scene of his vengeance, and he had taken full advantage of the opportunity.

The door leading into the kitchen from the rear of the house had presented no problems. Using a thin plastic card as he had seen one used in a movie, Harold opened the simple lock and stepped boldly inside. He conducted a quick search, memorizing the room layout and looking into closets and cabinets.

In a small nightstand in one bedroom, Harold found a Smith & Wesson .38 revolver. All five chambers of the cylinder were loaded with the kind of hollow-nose bullets Harold had himself used in his attack in New York. The gun looked new, and had no odor of powder

349

at its muzzle. Evidently his prey kept it there for possible use against intruders, and perhaps had never even fired it.

Harold put the gun back in the drawer exactly as he had found it, smiling as he closed the drawer. Now that he knew where it was, it was no hazard to him. All he had to do was strike before Lis could make any move in its direction.

If he was lucky, Harold thought, Amy Lis would never even know what was happening, and he would not have to hurt her in any way.

He would enter the house late, through the kitchen door. Once upstairs, he could glide down the hall to the bedroom and enter without sound. Other homes were too close—and Mrs. Lis too near —for him to use the gun this time. That was why he had purchased the heavy hunting knife. He would use the knife this time. It had the advantage of being soundless, and it amused him to think he would have his revenge with a hunting instrument.

One strike would do it, with any luck, Harold knew. He had bought a cheap book on the human anatomy at a shopping-center bookstore and had pored over the full-color chart of an adult male until he even knew many of the Latin names for various organs. He would cut the throat if he had a choice. If it was more difficult than that, he would order Lis to turn with his back facing him, and then plunge the blade up past the spine and into the heart from the rear. His third option was a front strike, directly in the center, under the breastbone, to sever the aorta.

If he made no sound, Harold thought, he could risk leaving as he had entered. But if there was any commotion he could quickly open one of the bedroom windows, hop out onto the porch, run across it, and drop to the driveway. There were plenty of shrubs to mask his route from any neighboring house, and he knew that it was only thirty strides from the spot he would drop to the fence in the back yard. From there, his route would be through the vacant lot, between houses on the next street, and to the rental car he would have parked there. His own automobile would be about three miles away, and he knew how he would ditch the rental car and get to his own too.

Going back downstairs, Harold looked through the study, the dining room, the den, and the living room. He carefully opened closets so nothing would be overlooked. There was no gun cabinet. As long as he kept Lis from that one revolver in the nightstand, he had no problem. And he was pleased that it was a nice, uncluttered house: nothing to trip over in the dark on the way upstairs.

So all was in readiness.

Continuing to work in the neighbor's yard, Harold mentally reviewed everything. He knew he was ready. The crash of a second Excalibur had confirmed in his mind the justice of what he had done in New York and what he would do here within the next few days. It was required.

It would feel good to have Mother fully avenged. Then he could drive to Florida, where he would begin his new life under a new name. He intended to find a job in a nightclub and resume his work as a guitarist. Within a few weeks or months he would be discovered as a great talent and would start on the road to becoming a star. Then, as soon as he was rich, he would buy a big house in the Bahamas or someplace like that, and retire from music, and write books with all his philosophy in them. Some people would hate him for his genius, but he would have many followers.

It was all planned.

7

Harvey Coughlin, meanwhile, was reaching a state verging on hysteria.

His twenty-four hours in Washington had been the stuff of nightmare: calls not returned, secretaries saying people were out when obviously they were not, even Senator Matthew Johns refusing to take his calls. Harvey had not even been able to locate Dena Forbes. He had the insane feeling that he was a Rip van Winkle. Everything was different and he was at a loss to understand it.

There was simply not any way he could continue such helpless thrashing. Pacing his hotel room, he decided on a desperate gamble. One person, he thought, would talk to him: a person perhaps at the center of all the rumor. It was dangerous, but his desperation left him no choice.

He was so nervous that he had to ask the hotel operator to help him locate a number for Jake Steinell.

"Cloakroom Intercom," a woman answered the telephone briskly when the call was put through.

"Is Mister Steinell there?"

"I'm sorry, he's out of the office now. May I ask who is calling please?"

Harvey hesitated. He could still turn back. . . . But no, he could *not* turn back. Whatever was going on was serious. He had to take some action, and this was all he could think of. "Yes," he told the woman, trying to make his voice sound stronger. "This is Harvey Coughlin. Hempstead Aviation. I want to speak with Mister Steinell." He gave the hotel number, and his room.

52

"Sir," the woman said with a different tone, "I'm sure Mr. Steinell will call you back shortly."

"Thank you," Harvey said, and hung up.

The change in the secretary's voice had added to his sense of alarm. *She had recognized his name.* It could only mean Steinell *was* near the heart of the rumors and fear . . . was working on something, and Harvey himself was somehow involved.

He was beside himself. He paced the floor again, waiting. It might be hours before Steinell replied, but Harvey felt he did not dare do anything but wait.

The trip had been a fiasco from the start.

His first action, after checking in at the hotel, had been to call the number he had listed in his book for Joe Wind. There was no answer on the first attempt, but this was during the lunch hour. When he called back, he got an answering service.

Two hours later, Wind had called back. "Harvey! How are you, good buddy? What's going on?"

"Joe, I've had some bad financial news lately . . . a personal problem. I needed to contact you—"

"Say, Harv! I'm genuinely sorry to hear that! Ordinarily, I think we would have seen some immediate return on our original investments; you remember, the ones from my first trip to Europe. Unfortunately, the fiscal situation over there is a little depressed. It might be a few weeks yet. But buck up, friend. Right now, as I read the indicators, we're looking at a return of about 82 to 83 per cent, which ain't bad for a two-month transaction, eh?"

Harvey believed it for a few seconds. But the pressure on him forced continuing on the planned line. "That sounds awfully good, Joe. But, ah, unfortunately, my own situation is pressing."

"What are you saying, Harvey?"

"I am . . . forced . . . to withdraw all my investments immediately."

"Say, I'm not sure I heard you right, Harv. Withdraw? You can't just withdraw, man! I mean, your money is *out* there, *working!*"

"I need whatever money I can get back at once, Joe. I'm sorry about this, but as I said, it's a genuine emergency."

Wind's voice became flat and hostile. "I'm sorry too, buddy. Right now there's no way we can return any part of your personal fund without destroying the investment integrity of a dozen other accounts. I just value all my other clients too much for that."

"You mean you won't return anything?"

"I will when the investment returns come in, Harvey. Not before. It's manifestly impossible. Sorry."

Harvey felt a pulse of turgid anger. "I am writing a letter as of this date, severing all connection with you and your firm, and demanding return of my funds."

"Yeah? Well, it's your funeral, Harvey. Just remember. You don't have any contract, and no signed investment certificates. My firm operates on good will, and strictly confidentially, as I once explained. Legally, you don't have a leg to stand on. If you want your money back—and at a handsome profit, I might add—then you'll be patient a little while—leave well enough alone."

"I am writing the demand letter, Joe. Our relationship is severed as of this time. I—"

Wind hung up on him.

It shook Harvey even though he had tried to steel himself for a bad scene. It was possible, he thought, that this was a serious mistake. If Joe Wind was absolutely on the up-and-up, he was now offended. This would be relayed to D. L. Boudoin. Whatever tenuous support Boudoin might have been providing lately would be eliminated. And Harvey stood to lose all his own personal funds. He could not really afford that, and was deeply worried and chagrined about it.

It had been necessary, however. Lydia Baines had been explicit. Harvey already had the demand letter typed up—had brought it with him from California—and now sealed and mailed it, special delivery. . . .

But the Wind problem had been only the first, and one of the more predictable ones. Failure to be able to make contact with others who had earlier been friendly was even worse. He had become a pariah. Even his call to General Black Jack Mallory, at his home that first evening, had been more than discouraging.

"I'm not talking to you," Mallory snapped the moment Harvey identified himself. "I'm sorry."

"I heard about your difficulty," Harvey said. "I want to say I regret it. If in any way I may have contributed—"

"That's water over the dam. From now on, we don't communicate. That's the way it has to be. Understood?"

"If you could just tell me whether you have any idea how this all got started—"

"Sorry. Good-by." And again a line went dead in Harvey's ear.

All through the lonely evening, Harvey had periodically dialed the number for Dena Forbes's apartment. The instrument rang and rang, leaving him dreadful visions of her with another man.

Now he continued to pace, awaiting Steinell's call back. . . .

It finally came, shortly before five.

"You called me?" Steinell's bray was unpleasant.

"I think we need to talk," Harvey said.

"I couldn't agree with you more," the reporter said. "When I heard you were back in town, I wrote myself a note to get in touch with you at the first opportunity. I think I have something you ought to see."

"What is it?"

"Not on the phone, Mr. Coughlin. Where could we meet?"

"Here. In the bar off the lobby."

"All right. In thirty minutes?"

"That will be fine." Harvey's patience tattered. "But see here! I've become aware of the existence of some sort of rumors—allegations—and they may concern me. If that's true, I'm calling to demand an accounting!"

"Mr. Coughlin," Steinell said with a frigid calm, "we both want to talk about the same thing. In the hotel bar. In thirty minutes."

There was nothing more to say. Harvey murmured assent and hung up.

He was not able to sit still for the allotted thirty minutes. Within ten, he was already in the bar, where he ordered a bloody mary, which he did not touch. His instinct had been correct. He was going to get to the heart of something here, he thought. He had the feeling of a man being drawn inexorably into the center of a web where a monster waited. . . .

His bloody mary was a mess of melted ice by the time Jake Steinell arrived, a full thirty minutes late. The reporter looked tired and as sloppy and ragged as ever. He sat down across the booth table

355

from Harvey without greeting, and without offering to shake hands. He had a manila folder, which he placed on the edge of the table.

"Hello, Mr. Coughlin. Long time no see."

Harvey leaned forward, keeping his voice low to avoid being over-heard by the handsome young couple at the next table. He could not keep his words from sounding shaky with a combination of anger and fear. "My company is very, very upset about delays encountered in Congress on the Eagle matter. I've come here to try to find out what's going on. I hear reports that you're conducting some kind of half-baked investigation—spreading some sort of rumors. I demand to know about it."

Steinell raised his eyebrows. "Well, that's getting right to the point."

"Is it true?"

"Is what true?"

"Is it true that you've been spreading malicious rumors of some kind?"

"No, sir. I've been asking questions."

"About Eagle?"

"Among other things."

"Don't play games with me! I have my rights! You're invading my privacy! If you've damaged my good name, you'll face the biggest lawsuit you ever heard about!"

Steinell's weary eyes seemed to sag in their sockets as he contem-plated Harvey's face with a cynicism as old as the ages. "Mr. Coughlin, you have every opportunity to comment on anything I may print. As a matter of fact, that's why I'm pleased you called, and saved me the trouble of making the initial contact."

"Since I've done nothing wrong in any way, I don't know what you're talking about!"

Steinell's nicotine-stained fingers went to the large envelope and opened it. He withdrew a sheaf of papers on which there was dense, sloppy typing. "I think you should read this. Then we can continue the conversation."

Harvey took the papers. He glanced at them, then began to read with a mounting sense of horror. The sheets obviously represented a column for distribution to Steinell's subscriber newspapers.

356

DELAY ON EAGLE
VEILS STRANGE BEDFELLOWS

COPYRIGHT J. STEINELL ENTERPRISE

BY JAKE STEINELL

WASHINGTON, D.C.—That "mysterious delay" in moving the case of the Eagle missile on to the floor of the Senate for further action is the result of panic in the halls of Congress over possible disclosure of influence peddling and purported illegal inducements to certain friends of friends, our research shows.

At the center of the strange-bedfellow situation are two markedly different men, each with an ax to grind.

One is HARVEY COUGHLIN, middle-aged vice-president of California-based Hempstead Aviation Co., and chief of the Hempstead division which hopes to market the Eagle to the Pentagon at a cost to the taxpayer of a cool $1 million each. (Several hundred are contemplated.)

The other, a chum of Coughlin's, is JOE WIND, operator of an investments plan currently under super-secret probe by the Securities and Exchange Commission and, insiders whisper, the FBI. Preliminary evidence, according to one source, links Wind's outfit with telephone-solicitation land sales in Florida. The FBI is interested because the land is useless swamp and both interstate telephones and the federal mails have allegedly been used in the swindle.

What makes the case more interesting, in light of the Eagle delay, if that WIND is the son-in-law of SEN. D. L. BOUDOIN, formerly a candidate for the presidency and vice-presidency, and a powerful figure within the majority party.

It is a well-known fact that SEN. CLIFFORD SWEET, once opposed to letting Eagle out of his committee, changed his tune only weeks ago. This change of heart, it is reliably reported, came in part because BOUDOIN convinced him that the full congress should be allowed to consider the matter.

357

BOUDOIN got interested in Eagle some two days after COUGHLIN made the first of several personal investments in the WIND operation.

COUGHLIN has been much in evidence around the Hill this summer. He met a number of influential people, including BOUDOIN, at a party given by SEN. MATTHEW JOHNS.

JOHNS, it is said, not only holds stock in two of the Florida land companies being serviced by WIND; he also holds some stock in Allied Aviation, a Colorado-based alloy-treating company whose primary customer is none other than COUGHLIN's Hempstead Aviation. JOHNS and Hempstead Board Chairman LYDIA BAINES have been a social item on several occasions in the San Francisco area over the past two years.

An early casualty in the political fallout is GEN. BLACK JACK MALLORY, Pentagon supporter of Eagle and a friend of COUGHLIN. MALLORY has been handed an official reprimand for "taking too active an interest in a political matter," i.e., for pushing Eagle too hard on the Hill.

COUGHLIN has openly boasted that he has influenced a number of other congressmen to support his firm's pet project. (It is especially a pet right now, with the same company's Excalibur commercial jet grounded by the NTSB for alleged unsafe control systems.)

It remains to be seen whether more flak catches more personages. Right now, they're running for cover in all directions, and Eagle looks dead, dead, dead.

At least for this session . . . until the public forgets.

—30—

Harvey put the sheets of paper down with trembling hands. "You can't print that!"

"It's for Sunday release. We mail it day after tomorrow."

"Lies! All lies and filthy innuendo!"

Steinell's eyes seemed to sag further. "You want to give me any comment for the record?"

"How could I? It's all a lie—character assassination—!"

The reporter placed the sheets of paper carefully back into the envelope. "Mr. Coughlin, let's put it all out in the open. Very frankly, you're small game. I'm much more interested in Boudoin, Wind, Johns, and any others who might be implicated. You and Mallory are in it, yes. But I'm not vitally concerned about either of you. I'll give you the same offer I gave him. Make a clean breast of the whole thing. I'll be just as gentle on you, in exchange for useful information, as I possibly can."

"Leave my name entirely out of it?"

"Sorry. There's no way I can possibly do that."

"Then, what are you offering me? Nothing! . . . And I haven't done a thing that's illegal or even unethical! I'm an innocent man who is guilty of nothing more than trying to sell his company's product."

"When your product happens to a be a million-dollar missile, Mr. Coughlin, and selling it will hang your company from the public teat for three to five years, then it's no longer a simple business transaction. The taxpayers have a right to know."

"What makes you think I've done anything wrong? My connections with Joe Wind are personal—a personal investment! That's all! If he's illegal in any way, I certainly knew nothing of it!"

"The last part of that may be true, Mr. Coughlin. But you went in with Wind to curry favor with Boudoin. That's as clear as that window pane over yonder. And I have many more facts which I intend to publish just as soon as I collect some substantiating testimony: other congressmen you influenced in one way or another."

"But I never—!"

"Mr. Coughlin," Steinell interrupted wearily, "I *know* some of the other people you influenced. I have names. It's just a question of tracking everything down. Now, listen to reason. My primary interest is in official corruption on the Hill and over in Virginia at the Pentagon. You're small potatoes. Co-operate. It will go much easier on you."

"I have nothing more to say," Harvey said thickly. "It's all a lie. I'll sue."

Steinell sighed and picked up his envelope. "Very well. You will have until tomorrow night if you happen to change your mind or want to offer any additional information by way of mitigation. After that, this item goes in the mail—and I expect to make it the first in a series."

"You bastard. You *enjoy* hurting innocent people!"

The reporter stood. "No, sir. I don't even enjoy hurting guilty ones. You know how to reach me if you change your mind."

Harvey reached for his bloody mary.

"Incidentally," Steinell said turning back, "I've mailed a copy of this column to your boss, Lydia Baines. Perhaps if you don't want to make any comment or try to work out a deal, she will."

The bloody mary sloshed violently in Harvey's hands, spilling redly over his fingers and onto the table top.

8

D espite two sleeping pills, Harvey Coughlin had a largely sleepless night. As first dawn crept across the windows of his lonely hotel room, he felt his sense of desperate isolation becoming intolerable. He clung to his plan to start calling Dena Forbes early. He no longer cared that she had spent the night somewhere else . . . probably with someone else. He had to have someone. He needed her now.

Fuzzy-minded and trembling, he dialed her apartment number once more. He waited. There was an odd clicking sound on the line and then a rapid series of rings, and then a louder click.

"*I'm sorry*," a man's tinny, recorded voice said in his ear. "*The number you have reached is not in service. Please make sure you are dialing the correct number.*"

Hissing with frustration, Harvey broke the connection and tried again, punching the buttons with great care and checking each one against his book.

Again there were the strange noises. "*I'm sorry. The number you—*"

He hung up again and pulled the directory out of the end table, ripping pages in his frustrated haste. Not on this page . . . not on this page . . . oh, Jesus. . . . Yes. Assistance in dialing.

He punched the three buttons furiously. An operator answered. He gave her the number and said he was having trouble. She dialed the number for him and the same maddening recording came on the line.

"I'm sorry, sir," the girl told him. "That line has evidently been disconnected."

"It can't be disconnected! I just called it yesterday!"

"Sir, a disconnect can be made at practically any time. Will you hold? Let me check the records."

Harvey held, the receiver slippery in his sweaty hand. He already had a numbing headache. Why did everything go wrong for him? My God, had Dena changed apartments or something—had she perhaps been home last night, while he vainly called a wrong number about to be taken out of service? They might have been together last night . . . she might have already suggested some way she could help him around Jake Steinell—

"Sir, I've checked the records, and that number has been disconnected at request of the subscriber."

"Give me the new number."

"I'm sorry, there is no new listing."

"God damn it, there has to be a new listing! Look. The name is Dena Forbes. She must be moving or something. Check it out and—"

"I've already checked, sir. It's a straight disconnect order."

"I tell you, that's impossible!"

"Would you like to have the number to which Miss Forbes's final billing is to be mailed?"

"I don't understand. You said she doesn't have a new number."

"Sir, I have a listing for a business number account that will receive the final billing on the residential disconnect."

Dena would be furious when she heard how much trouble he had had, Harvey thought.

"Give me that number," he ordered.

The girl complied and he curtly hung up on her, having scribbled the number in his notebook. He punched it into the telephone immediately. The number seemed familiar, which was very odd, but he didn't take time to think about it.

The telephone rang a long time, but no one answered.

Harvey showered, shaved, and dressed, then tried once more. Again, no answer. He did not understand it, and everything happening made him more mystified. He felt his time was running out. Jake Steinell's copy of his column, "Cloakroom Intercom," would reach Lydia Baines in California today. Senator Matthew Johns might already have seen a copy and notified her by telephone. Harvey had to do something, and fast. He had tried to tell himself to sleep on the problem and then some avenue would be clear when he was rested. But he had not rested, and things only looked worse.

The more he thought about it the more he believed that Dena was his only hope. She did not like Jake Steinell, he remembered, and she had once helped against him, making the meeting with Boudoin possible at Johns's party. If she knew anything that might damage Steinell—anything even possibly embarrassing—then perhaps Harvey would be able to use it for some leverage.

He tried the number given by the operator once more, again with no results. He went down to the hotel coffee shop and ordered breakfast, but the food was like dry cardboard in his mouth and he could not even get all the rancid-tasting coffee down. In twenty minutes he was back in his room, trying the number again.

It was now almost 7:30 A.M.

The telephone rang four times, and then it was answered.

It was a woman's voice and he had heard it once before. But it was not Dena Forbes.

"Cloakroom Intercom," she said.

Ice flooding his veins, Harvey hung up as if the instrument were a deadly viper. He stared at the telephone. For just an instant, he thought he had read the wrong number out of his book. He consulted it even as the realization was beginning to dawn on him.

No. He had called the number given by the operator. The number he had written down for Jake Steinell's office was not even on the same page.

He found that page and compared the numbers. They were identical.

The notebook dropped from Harvey's lifeless fingers. He now made all the connections: the mystery of how Steinell had gotten some of the allegations . . . the memory of boasting to Dena, in bed, of political manipulations and conquests he had not even really made but only conjured up to impress her . . . how Dena's eyes had shone, and how she had pressed for all the details.

Now, of course, in this shattering moment, it was all too clear.

"Oh, Jesus," Harvey said, burying his face in his hands. "Oh, Jesus; oh, Jesus."

He might have broken then, but he did not. For almost an hour he sat virtually motionless, seeing what a fool he had been and how he had been betrayed. For much of this time his reaction was of sheer pain and shock. He had been tricked and used—everything she had told him had been a vicious lie. She did not care for him at all.

This last realization, for a while, hurt more than anything.

But he could not wallow in self-pity. The more his mind began to take hold and remember some of the outrageous, boastful lies he had told Dena Forbes the more he saw how devastating this alleged information could be if Jake Steinell had the temerity to use it without substantiation. My God! He had made Dena believe that he influenced people he had not even met! If much of that came out, he would look like a mastermind of unethical and illegal influence! No wonder Steinell believed he was onto a major scandal!

It could not be allowed to continue. As bitterly hard as it was to accept Dena's betrayal of him, he at least now understood the source of the allegations.

And he thought he could fight them.

After taking a tranquilizer and an ounce of scotch to steady himself, he called the "Cloakroom Intercom" number.

"I'm sorry, Mr. Coughlin," the girl told him. "Mr. Steinell is unavailable until this evening. But he left a message that he would return your call early this evening, if you happened to call."

So Steinell was so sure that he would come crawling, Harvey thought with a burst of rage. But he did not show this in his tone of voice. "Please tell Mr. Steinell that I want to see him as early tonight as possible. Also, please tell him that I now know his source of information."

"Yes, sir," the girl replied, with that distracted sound of someone writing a note.

"Have you got that? —That I want to see him as soon as possible?"

"Yes."

"And that I know his source of information?"

"Yes."

"Make sure he gets the information as soon as he calls in."

"I will, Mr. Coughlin." The girl sounded respectful. She probably had no way of knowing whether he was friend or foe.

"And if he wants to get in touch with me before tonight," Harvey added, "on the basis of this new information, I'll stay close to my hotel room, or leave a forwarding number."

"Oh, I doubt that he'll be able to call earlier, sir. He isn't even in the city right now."

Harvey hung up. He wondered how he was going to endure the time between now and nightfall. But at least he had one more thing to do that could help his situation, and he intended to do that just as soon as it was late enough in California for Lydia Baines to be awake.

He calculated that to be ten o'clock Washington time.

Promptly at ten, he dialed Lydia's San Francisco apartment direct. The maid said she did not know if Mrs. Baines could be disturbed. Harvey snapped his name and ordered her to go find out.

A moment later, Lydia's voice came on the line. "Good morning, Harvey. You're calling very early."

"I have important information," Harvey told her, fighting to keep his voice strong-sounding and confident. "First, Jake Steinell is the one behind all the investigation. He has half this town scared out of their wits."

"He's a powerful man, Harvey."

"Yes, and I happen to have done some detective work, and I know he even has the draft of a column written that makes unfounded allegations about several persons, including, I'm afraid, myself."

There was a silence on the line.

"By applying some pressure," Harvey went on, "I've forced him to mail a copy of the proposed column to you. You should receive it sometime today. I wanted you to see just what kind of swill this man has been circulating. But listen, Lydia. I have also learned the source of his information. It's a rotten source, and later today or tonight I intend to reveal to him that I know this."

"What will that accomplish?" Lydia Baines asked.

She did not sound worried, and that gave Harvey heart. "I believe his entire so-called investigation has been a sham—a trick to make people panic and blurt out some real information. Believe me, Lydia, Steinell has nothing of real consequence. The only hard fact he has is my investments with Joe Wind. But I've already severed all connection with Wind, so Steinell really doesn't even have that.

"Tonight, when I see him," Harvey went on, "I intend to let him know that I've uncovered his source, and his tricky plan. It's time to get tough. I intend to make it clear to him that unless he ceases and desists at once, I will reveal his underhanded methods to the owners of the news syndicate, and if he pushes me, to other newspapermen as well. I believe they could make quite a big story of how this man has been trying to persecute innocent people on the basis of blackmail from a source that has fed him nothing but demonstrable lies!"

"I see," Lydia said. "It sounds like you've been very busy. You feel sure you have the situation in hand?"

"It's tricky," Harvey said. "But I believe I have him, Lydia. I believe I can face him down, because I know his source and I know the truth!"

"I want you to proceed," Lydia said after a brief pause, when she seemed to be digesting the information. "It's too early to be relieved, I think, but I want you to know I admire the way you have dug into this."

"It's a pleasure to fight scum like Jake Steinell."

"Will you report tonight?"

"If I possibly can, yes."

"Good. Thank you, Harvey. Good-by."

He hung up the phone with a feeling almost bordering on genuine confidence. What he had said was half true, anyway. He would simply tell Jake Steinell the truth—that he had bragged to Dena to impress her. He would have to explain how little he really had done. This would be terribly humiliating. But he could do it. He had to do it. And he knew Steinell would see that it was the truth and there was really very little story here.

The prospect of debasing himself to Steinell was a terrible one. But at least it would save the situation, Harvey thought. At least it was now salvageable.

Across the breadth of America, however, Lydia Baines saw the matter quite differently. Sitting in her living room with Senator Matthew Johns, she lighted a cigarette and inhaled angrily. "He's bluffing. He seems to have a genius for it."

Johns watched her warily. He had taken a severe tongue-lashing from her only minutes earlier, when he had revealed his own miscalculations. "Did he mention Dena Forbes as the source for Steinell?"

"Not by name, but apparently he's tumbled. Jesus, Matt, that was incredibly stupid of you!"

"I checked her out, I tell you! I believe Steinell got to her after she was hired by my office manager. There's no way you can prevent things like that from happening."

"But you should have seen what she was up to!"

"Granted. But I didn't, and now the damage is done."

"Yes," Lydia said. "And there's nothing to do but try to cut our losses."

"How?"

"I'm going to call Bert Jerno and dictate a letter to his secretary at once. Harvey has had it."

"You're firing him?"

"The letter will mention suspension during internal investigation. It can be dated a week ago, to establish for the record that we were looking into his activities well before anything surfaced from Steinell."

Johns nodded approval. "That way, it will look like someone at Hempstead leaked the information to him and that he's reacting to Hempstead, rather than vice versa."

"Correct. It won't save us from bad publicity, but it will put us in a slightly better light."

"It won't save Eagle, either," Johns said.

"What will happen?" Lydia asked. "It won't be lost *forever*."

"Congress has never gone through military appropriations quite so piecemeal," Johns frowned. "I suppose virtually anything could happen, but I think it's pretty safe to guess what will, as far as Eagle goes, after all this has hit the fan."

"Tell me."

"All right. Eagle exists as a defense project without funding. The House Committee on Military Spending is not going to report out any more individual military spending projects unless requested to do so by the Senate. Eagle—the question of feasibility and therefore of spending—is in effect locked up in Cliff Sweet's Senate committee, just as it has been."

"I know all this," Lydia said impatiently.

"I realize you do, Lydia, but I'm trying to make it all clear as to my conclusions."

"Go ahead."

"If the Sweet Committee had voted Eagle out of committee, the Senate would then have voted on addition of a line item to the budget for funding. That vote, as a rider probably to the water-con-

367

servation or energy-expenditure bill, would have gone to the House. The House would then have called up its own committee report on Eagle, and we would have gotten a definitive vote."

"But none of that will happen now."

"That's right, I'm afraid. Sweet will just let the question lie there in the committee papers. As far as the whole Senate is concerned, then, it simply will not exist. We already know the item won't be considered by the House without prodding."

"So," Lydia said bitterly, "no consideration by the Sweet Committee means no reporting of Eagle to the Senate, which means no Senate vote on an appropriation."

"Which means no House action, either," Johns nodded, "and the matter is dead until next year."

"Damn it!"

"I don't like to think what all this will do to Coughlin," Johns said after a thoughtful pause. "His public image has been the center of his life."

"So what? He made the mistakes, didn't he?"

"This action of yours will just kill him, Lydia."

"Better Harvey," Lydia snapped, "than my company."

9

When Harold Zelmer walked out of his apartment, onto the fire escape/front porch, the police were there.

Two of them; apparently, because there was only one black-and-white car parked in the alley below. One of them, a flabby uniformed sergeant, stood at the far end of the metal porch as if guarding the doorway to Joseph's rooms. The doorway was open, so Harold assumed the other one was inside.

He was not surprised, nor was he frightened.

He walked down the porch toward the stairs. "Morning, officer!"

"Good morning," the sergeant said. He looked Harold up and down, taking in the faded blue work shirt, Levi's, heavy shoes, sweat-stained baseball cap. It was the kind of uniform that tended to reassure police of the wearer's hard-working honesty, and the sergeant seemed to relax a bit. "Nice morning."

"Going to be hot." Harold grinned. He looked out over the rooftops, power lines, billboards. There was a yellowish cast to the distance. "I'm afraid the smog is still with us too."

The sergeant consulted a page of a notebook covered with engraved leather. "You're Harold Smith?"

"That's right. Anything I can do for you?"

"Are you acquainted with your neighbor, Joseph Kleppnitz?"

"Well, we've met, and we had a soda at the drugstore once. But I haven't seen him for a day or two, come to think about it. I hope nothing is wrong!"

The sergeant ponderously played it close to the vest. "We've just been trying to determine his whereabouts recently."

"Well, you might try the used-book store down the street. I remember he said he worked down there."

Of course the sergeant would have already checked there, but offering the information made a nice show of open helpfulness. He appeared quite at ease now. "You known the subject long?"

"Actually, I hardly know him at all. I've lived here only a short time."

"What kind of work do you do?"

"Yard and garden work."

The sergeant scribbled a note in his book. "Employed by?"

"Self-employed."

"Uh-huh. Where did you live before you moved here?"

"Just before here I was in the Army. Before that I lived in LA."

There was a slight sound inside Joseph's apartment, and a second officer appeared in the doorway. He was younger, just beginning to put on the lard that marked his older partner. Dusting his hands, he came out and let the screen door bang. "Nothing," he said.

"This is Harold Smith," the sergeant said. "He lives next door."

"Hello, Mr. Smith," the younger officer said, going by the book. "Have you seen your neighbor Mr. Kleppnitz lately?"

"I've questioned him," the sergeant said quietly.

"Oh," the younger officer said.

"Is Joseph in trouble?" Harold asked, showing concern. "I had only talked with him a couple of times—we were strangers, really—but he certainly didn't seem like a lawbreaking kind of person."

The younger officer began looking at him with eyes that were definitely disturbing. Harold was now being sized up by an intelligence. "Tell me, sir. You and Mr. Kleppnitz didn't have any problems, did you?"

"No, certainly not! —Listen, what's going on here? What kind of trouble is Joseph in?"

"You live next door, here?"

"Yes, that's right."

"We're making a routine check. Would you have any objection to our looking around your place?"

Harold grimaced. "Well, ordinarily I wouldn't. But I wish you wouldn't . . . right now."

"We can get a warrant," the younger officer said quickly.

Harold shuffled from one foot to the other. "It's just that—this is embarrassing. There's a—well, I've got a girl in there, see, and she wouldn't like it, being seen—"

Both officers visibly relaxed. So they *had* known Joseph's predilections.

"That won't be necessary." The sergeant smiled. "We might come back some other time, if you don't mind."

Harold grinned. "Just give me a minute's notice, okay? I mean, Suzie's mother would be *really* angry if—"

"Sure," the sergeant chuckled. "We understand. Come on, Jack. Let's go see the landlord again."

"Joseph was sort of a . . . weirdo," Harold added. "I know people like that sometimes get roughed up. I hope this isn't something like that."

The sergeant paused, but they both trusted Harold now. Having a girl hidden in his room made him one of them. "Mr. Kleppnitz is dead," the sergeant told him.

"Oh, no! That's terrible! How did it happen?"

"Somebody cut his throat from ear to ear and dumped him over the fence into the city dump in a black plastic bag."

"Oh, my God! That's terrible! That's horrible! And you're here to look for clues? You mean, you don't have the person who did it?"

"We have some good leads," the sergeant said mysteriously, looking out over the rooftops. "He was a queer, Mr. Smith. Did you know that?"

"I thought he might be. That was one of the reasons I tried to shun him."

"Well, that was smart on your part. Queers like him, they cruise the streets and bars, looking for pickups, you see. Our guess is that he found one who was just a little kinkier than he was ready for."

"Still, it's an awful thing," Harold said solemnly, "the taking of a human life."

"Yeah," the sergeant said. "Well, Jack, let's get on downstairs. Thanks, Mr. Smith."

"If you want to look at my apartment, I'll get Suzie out in just a few—"

"That won't be necessary." The sergeant yawned. "Come on, Jack."

They went below. Harold went back to his apartment to carry out that much of a pretense that he had a girl there. He waited by the window, out of sight.

If the police suspected him, his cover was tissue thin. His phony ID material, purchased in San Francisco's Tenderloin, would not stand up to any careful scrutiny. All the police really had to do was *wait*, and notice that he did not—could not—produce a girl. Then a search would find the stains on the bed. There was no way he was going to be able to get rid of those.

But Harold did not think the police were going to do any of these things. He was a workingman, clean-cut, heterosexual, and sort of dumb and ignorant, just the kind police liked. His cover was fine and his destiny to avenge Mother would not be thwarted by accident.

So he waited, calm.

Within five minutes the officers appeared below, walked to their cruiser, and drove away. They were probably not terribly excited about the killing of one faceless homosexual, anyway.

Harold waited another ten minutes to make sure they were gone, then went down to his truck and drove off for work, whistling.

10

There was a rap on Harvey Coughlin's hotel-room door. Nerves jangling, Harvey walked to the door and unlocked it.

Jake Steinell came in. The reporter wore a plaid sport coat, bright green slacks, pointed loafers, and a perky beige suede cap. He had a Uher tape recorder slung over his shoulder.

"I see I'm first," he said, glancing around the room.

"First?" Harvey echoed. "Nothing was said about anyone else being here for our meeting!"

Steinell put the suitcase-sized Uher on the floor and unrolled an extension cord. "No problem, Mr. Coughlin. I assume you have no objection to taping our conversation?"

"I certainly do. Now, see here. I know now where you got all your so-called information, and the sad truth for *you*, Mr. Steinell, is that you actually don't have a thing!"

"Let me get this plugged in and running before we go on, Harvey, okay?"

"I just told you—" He was interrupted by someone else at the door.

Steinell walked over and opened it. Dena Forbes walked into the room. She wore a summer dress and heels, and was barelegged. She looked so young and lovely that Harvey's breath caught in his throat even as his outrage bloomed.

"You here?" he said. "I'm surprised you would show your face!"

"Dena is working closely with me on this," Steinell said. "I thought she ought to be here as a reality check on anything you may have to tell me."

373

"A reality check? Is that what you call it when you bring in a Judas to reverify previous lies?"

"Harvey," Dena Forbes said softly, with something like regret. "I wish it hadn't turned out this way—"

"Bitch! Whore! Get out! Get out!"

Steinell took a deep breath. "Okay, Dena, let's go." He unplugged the extension cord and started re-rolling it.

This would not do. However he felt, Harvey had to prove to them that the "information" they had was bogus, with no basis in reality. It was the only way he could save himself and short-circuit the entire investigation.

"No," he said weakly. "Wait."

Steinell, bent over the recorder on the floor, looked up. "Are you going to be nice?"

"Yes, I'll . . . behave myself."

Steinell plugged the machine back in and turned it on. As he adjusted the controls, Harvey went to the bed and sat on its edge, weak and sick with tension and the effort of suppressing his emotions. Phrases and arguments tumbled like dominoes through his brain, in rehearsal. His apprehension was extreme. Having Dena Forbes here made everything infinitely more painful, tangling him up in his mortification and regrets.

Dena sat in a chair near the bed, crossed her legs, and met his eyes with an expression approaching genuine regret. "I just want you to know, Harvey—I did like you. Honestly. That part wasn't fake."

"But you tricked me. You betrayed me!"

Dena grimaced. "I'm sorry. That's my job; the way it turned out this time, anyway, wasn't planned. It just happened. But getting this information and everything—I know you must feel awfully bitter. I don't blame you. That's why I'm sorry it turned out the way it did. Using the information and everything—it isn't against you as a person. It's just my job. There's nothing personal."

Harvey could not believe his ears. "Nothing personal? It wasn't *personal* when we fucked? It wasn't *personal* when you pretended to come, and told me those lies about how good it was with me?"

Steinell extended a microphone on a coiled cord. "Look. Let's cut out all the hearts and flowers. I don't want that kind of crap on the tape."

"I'm very sorry you don't want it on your precious tape!" Harvey said. "But what I hear her saying is so insane, there's no way I can sit silent and accept it! My God, Dena, you tricked me as cruelly as a woman can trick a man! You—you built me up. You made me think I was special to you. You had me where I was dreaming about you every minute of the day. I thought—I even thought I was in love with you. And all your talk about how I was a better man than I realized, and how I ought to have more confidence—and the way you made love with me—and *everything* was a lie. And then you say it wasn't *personal?* Somebody is crazy here, and I don't think it's me!"

Steinell had finished adjusting the recorder and placing the microphone. A loud click announced that he had turned it on. The reels began turning very slowly.

"Harvey Coughlin interview," Steinell said for the machine. "All right, Harvey, you understand this interview is being recorded?"

"Yes," Harvey said, fighting for self-control.

"All right, sir. You know that we are developing information for a series of columns on influence peddling and possibly other illegal activity surrounding the Eagle appropriation matter. You have agreed to meet with me to discuss that. Do you have any opening statement to make?"

"Yes," Harvey said. "You could have been saved no much trouble —it would have been so much simpler for a lot of us—if you hadn't accepted the things I told Dena Forbes."

"Why shouldn't I accept them? You had no idea she worked for me. Those statements you made to her were free and voluntary."

"And lies," Harvey said.

"Of course you would say that now."

"No, what I'm saying now is the truth. It makes me squirm to have to admit it now . . . under the circumstances. But most of the things I told Dena were simply made up—pipe dreams I fed her because I wanted to appear important to her, and because she seemed to enjoy such stories so much." Harvey glanced bitterly at the beautiful young girl. "She talked about power as an aphrodisiac, so I tried to tell her stories of power to . . . excite her."

"True stories," Steinell interjected.

"False, almost every one of them. . . . Made up on the spot to excite her . . . and make me appear more important in her eyes."

The two of them watched him intently, Steinell's expression one of frowning disbelief, Dena's bordering on quiet dismay.

"This costs me a great deal of pride to admit this," Harvey told them. "You probably have no idea. But it gives me some pleasure, too, to see how much I really did fool the both of you with my pitiful little tales of things I had done—things I really couldn't have done if I had wanted to, because I wouldn't have known how!"

Steinell took out a pack of cigarettes and lighted one. He said nothing.

"So you see," Harvey added, "you really don't have a thing. You can threaten all you want, and there's no more information you'll ever uncover, because the things you're trying to track down have no basis in fact. You came here believing you would get a lot of juicy new items, and what I'm giving you is the end of your entire house of cards!"

Steinell exchanged looks with Dena Forbes, and puffed his cigarette in silence.

Finally Harvey could stand it no longer. "Well?"

"Well, what?" Steinell asked calmly.

"What do you think of *that?*"

"Are you finished?"

"Just one more thing. I may not sue you. I haven't decided yet. But I *may* not sue you, assuming you destroy all copies of that scurrilous column you showed me yesterday, and apologize, and never bother me again!"

Steinell's expression slowly changed. It became a grin.

"What?" Harvey asked, alarmed.

"Harvey, you really amaze me. You're cleverer than I thought. It's a very nice gambit, it really is. The neatest part is that I'm sure it has a grain of truth in it . . . an aging businessman, a beautiful, eager young girl . . . of course he would boast and even elaborate on some things. I assumed some exaggeration in your claims from the start. But it won't cut it, Harvey. You're in this thing up to your ass, and nothing will change that."

"Print anything," Harvey said, "and you'll be hit with the biggest lawsuit—"

"The line forms on the right."

"But, my God, man! I've just told you! You have nothing! No facts—"

"The Joe Wind connection is a fact."

"That was personal. I have now withdrawn—"

"The connection was *there*. It's verified. Wind is being interviewed by agents right now, and he's chirping like a canary, trying to make a deal so they won't prosecute on the land frauds in Florida that were another aspect of his operations."

"I had nothing to do with that," Harvey said weakly. "I had no idea—"

"Of course you didn't. We recognize that. You were a dupe. —And don't say you never got anything back from your investment money. Of course you didn't! No one did. You and a hundred other people paid Joe Wind large amounts of money to curry favor with his father-in-law, D. L. Boudoin. He's one of the big fish in this net, Harvey, and he's netted just as firmly as you are."

"You can't *prove* illicit influence."

"The Black Jack Mallory connection is there too," Steinell told him. "Mallory has already been reprimanded. That's verified; I have a Xerox of the letter that went into his file."

"Then, you're a thief as well as a character assassin."

Steinell shrugged. "Then there's the matter of the con you worked on Interspace Industries. I'm still pursuing that. Do you want to tell us about that? Make a clean breast of it?"

"You're power crazy—insane! You don't have a thing! Is that the way you usually develop so-called information? Threaten witnesses and frighten them into saying anything you want, just to have you give them a little mercy?"

"Let's talk about Senator Jacobs," Steinell suggested. "You had a number of meetings with him. He's in trouble at home over some large amounts of money that seem to have turned up in his accounts. What did you have to do with that?"

"Nothing!" Harvey said quite truthfully.

"You told Dena that you, quote, turned Jacobs around, unquote. How did you do that?"

"I was just—that was just one of the things I *told* Dena, to impress her! There was no truth to it at all!"

"So you lied." Steinell's eyes were like lead.

"Yes!"

"You lied then . . . or you lied just now?"

"I lied then! This is the truth, every word of it! —Oh, you bastard, you're twisting everything I try to explain to you—"

"There's only one way to help yourself now, Harvey: Start at the beginning. Make a clean breast of everything. Do that, and I'll be just as light on you as I can. You'll be involved, yes. There's no way around that. But I'll try to be merciful, and use your information as a route to other sources who can be named whenever possible."

"I'll never do that," Harvey said hoarsely. "My future is at stake. My company can be maligned. I can lose my position. I'm not a young man. This can ruin me—wipe me out—and almost all my savings are gone to that damned Joe Wind. You can't destroy me this way! Where is your—your decency? Your compassion?"

Steinell walked to an ashtray and jabbed his cigarette into it. "I'm giving you one last chance. Start from the beginning. Were you acting specifically on orders from Lydia Baines? What's the connection between Boudoin and Matthew Johns?"

"I won't tell you a thing because there's nothing to tell, and if you pursue this matter, you'll be very, very sorry!"

The reporter sighed and turned off the tape recorder. He pulled the extension cord from the wall outlet and began rolling it up. "I'm sorry you choose to follow this line, Mr. Coughlin. It will wind up making things tougher for you."

Harvey stared at him, and at the beautiful, silent Dena Forbes. He had thought he could show them the truth, even bully them after they saw their error. But it had all gone wrong. They were going ahead. He was filled with a sickening sense of impending disaster. His mind raced down blind corridors, seeking any way out.

An idea came. "You said Boudoin was a big fish. Would Johns be a big fish, too?"

"Not as big, but a keeper."

"What if I could document for you how it was *Johns* who was working to influence everyone on Eagle?" Harvey asked eagerly. "You remember his party, the one where we first met. Suppose I could tell you about certain other meetings he had to promote Eagle—certain people he called, and even wrote letters to? Wouldn't that be good information?"

"It would be very nice, Harvey, yes."

"You could show that it was *he* who really did everything," Harvey said. "I could provide a lot of this information." Now his mind was really racing. "And what about this? You know my company's Excalibur jet is grounded right now. What about some juicy information on that? What if I could tell you how a vice-president of our company pushed the Excalibur project ahead after development and test difficulties? I'm not saying it's an unsafe plane, mind you, but a detailed story, with actual documents, showing when and where and how we hit all sorts of snags in developing and testing Excalibur—it would show how one man pushed it through, and now he has finally been caught, and the mistakes caught up with him, and the plane grounded. How does that strike you for another story?"

Steinell put his hands on his hips and looked down at Harvey with unmasked distaste. "I was almost feeling sorry for you for a while there, man. But you'd sell your mother, wouldn't you." Steinell hefted the tape recorder. "Come on, Dena."

"Wait!" Harvey said. "There's more! That other vice-president— Ken Lis—went to Europe recently and handed a million-dollar bribe to a foreign official! I know this is true! The Monravian's name is Lucian Derquet. The cash went through a Swiss bank—"

"Harvey," Steinell said, staring at him with eyes like those of a corpse, "that won't wash either."

"But it's true! It's all true! Lis and Johns are the big fish you really want! I can give you details—"

"Harvey, it's too late for you to try to turn state's evidence. It's like Watergate. Once the ball starts coming unraveled, it's just too late for anyone to escape. Don't you understand it *yet*, man? You've *had* it!"

11

For a very long time after the hotel-room door closed behind Jake Steinell and Dena Forbes, Harvey stood rooted by shock. He saw that he had made a serious blunder in trying to blame the Monravian payoff on Ken Lis. He remembered only now, too late, that he had told Dena too much about it for that story to be believed.

So in his desperation he had destroyed the last vestiges of his credibility. Jake Steinell was going to go ahead. What could be done? There had to be a way out. There was always some way out!

He had another ounce of scotch and an additional tranquilizer, but they seemed to have no effect whatsoever. He was trembling and making little moaning sounds to himself as he paced back and forth, trying to find some avenue of escape. Everything was ruined . . . everything. How could he delude Lydia Baines about this? What could he do to keep the things known by Jake Steinell a secret? Did he know *anyone* with sufficient power to silence a man like Steinell?

Time passed . . . perhaps an hour. *What could he do?*

In a little while the telephone rang, startling him. He snatched it up. Steinell, he thought, had changed his mind—!

"Hello? Harvey Coughlin speaking!"

"Harvey? This is Bert Jerno in California."

The connection was not the best, but Harvey recognized the voice of his fellow company officer. Desperate pride made him alter his voice to his accustomed sound of bluff confidence. "Bert! How are you, old man? Say, aren't you burning the midnight oil out there tonight? It must be well past quitting time!"

380

Jerno's tone was hollow. "Harvey, I'm afraid I have some serious news."

Harvey's insides tightened painfully. "Bad news? What could that be?"

"At the direction of Mrs. Baines, Harvey, a letter has just been mailed to you there at your hotel, special delivery. Mrs. Baines wanted me to call you, however, and tell you about its contents tonight."

"Letter? What letter? Say, Bert"—and Harvey tried a laugh that came out a ghastly cackle—"what is this, anyway?"

"Let me read the letter," Jerno said.

Harvey closed his eyes and sank to the edge of the bed.

Jerno's voice droned, "It's addressed to you, Harvey, as chief of Aerospace, Hempstead Aviation, and it's signed by Mrs. Baines. The text is as follows.

" 'Dear Mr. Coughlin,

'It is with personal regret that I inform you that I am ordering your immediate suspension as vice-president, Aerospace, for this company.

'This administrative action does not constitute dismissal at this time. Regular pay and benefits remain in force until further notice. However, you are suspended from all duties with the company as of this date and until other notification. You may not speak for the company in any matter.

'It is my hope that the investigation now being conducted here may be completed within one calendar month. During that period you are not to enter the premises of Hempstead Aviation Company or contact any of the firm's employees or officers.

'For your information, this investigation is of allegations of serious wrongdoing on your part, including, but not limited to, attempting illegally to influence members of Congress and the defense establishment; mishandling of specification bids for the Eagle missile, and conducting personal business with persons now under investigation by the United States Justice Department.

'You will be notified by certified mail when the company hearing will take place. You will be expected to appear at the appointed time, with your legal counsel.

'Sincerely, Lydia Baines, chairman.' "

"She can't *do* this!" Harvey said.

"Harvey, I'm sorry. You'll receive the letter by tomorrow after-noon, I imagine. This is a really nasty thing, and I wish I could help in some way."

"Nasty! Is that all you can say about it? A man gives his life to a company, and then he's treated like this on the basis of half-cocked, unfounded rumors? And you say it's *nasty*? I have a contract with Hempstead Aviation! I have rights—legal rights and—and human rights! I demand to know the basis of this action!"

There was a pause, and Jerno's voice sounded different again, as if he were bracing himself. "I'm sorry, Harvey. Our instructions are that no information at all will be given out to anyone."

"Even to me? I'm the accused here! Yes! The accused! And with-out due process of any kind! Bert, she can't get away with this! I'll see my attorney! I'll—take legal action if I must!"

"Harvey, your pay and allowances continue. There's no legal re-course. If the investigation fails to prove anything, then I assume—"

"*If* it fails to prove anything! How could it prove anything when I'm being crucified with not a shred of proof of anything at all?"

"Just calm down a little, man."

"I am calm! Jesus Christ almighty, I'm completely calm! I have *perfect* control of myself! But what am I supposed to do? Here I am in Washington, doing my very best for Eagle—"

"Harvey, the letter ought to make it clear that you no longer rep-resent us on Eagle or anything else. Why don't you just hop the next plane back home? Let this thing work itself out. You mentioned a lawyer. My personal advice, as a friend, is that you should see a law-yer, at once. In the meantime, if you have personal items in your office that you want, I'll be glad to meet you at the gate and escort you there long enough for you to claim them—"

"You act like—like I won't even be allowed on the grounds!"

"Those are Lydia's orders. But no one wants to . . . inconvenience you."

"*Inconvenience* me! *Inconvenience* me? She can't do this to me! It's wrong! It's vicious! She's—she's setting me up as a villain in this whole case, and if there's bad publicity or anything, she can say it was all me—I was the culprit! She's sacrificing me, Bert, she's a vicious—cruel—horrible person, and it's not right . . . it's not right—" To his horror, Harvey began sobbing.

"Take it easy," Bert Jerno's quiet, unhappy voice said in his ear.

"If there's nothing wrong, Harvey, it will all work out. Sometimes we have to get through some bad things—"

"You don't understand. You don't understand *anything!* She's ruining me—destroying me—and I haven't done anything wrong!"

There was a long silence at the other end of the line while Harvey sobbed.

Finally Jerno spoke again, his own pain clear in his tone. "Harvey, I just don't know what to say."

"Well," Harvey said, frightened rage coming up from the depths to try to save him, "I'll tell you what you can tell Lydia for me, and I think you'd better tell her at once, do you hear me? At once! You tell her that if she tries to make *me* the goat in this matter, there's a certain situation in Monravia that *everyone* is going to be hearing about!"

"Monravia?"

"That's right, Monravia! You tell Lydia for me that Harvey Coughlin isn't taking the rap for everything by himself! You tell her that she'd better back off, instantly, or people are going to be hearing *the rest of it*—all that juicy information about Lucian Derquet!"

"My God," Jerno said. "We're not involved in *that*, are we?"

"In what?" Harvey asked. "You mean you *know* Derquet?"

"I remember he was in the party that visited us to look at Excalibur. That's why I picked up his name immediately tonight on the evening news. You mean, you didn't see that?"

"See what? What are you talking about?"

"CBS had a long report on it. Evidently Derquet was arrested today in Monravia after agents took pictures of him handing a large sum of money to a man representing some faction in the French Cabinet. The way CBS told it, some people in Monravia evidently have been watching him for months. He handed this package of money over today, presumably to buy some kind of industrial or trade favor from someone in the French Government. But the Monravians caught him at it, and the Frenchman is in trouble too."

"If he—paid someone off," Harvey said slowly, having trouble with his breathing, "then he must have been using Monravian money!"

"No, that's the strangest part. Apparently the Monravians are charging Derquet with influence peddling in both directions: taking money from outside in payment for his favors, then using parts of the same money to help buy more favors elsewhere, too. I tell you what, it's going to be some sort of mess before they get through with it. Harvey? Are you still there? Harvey?"

12

At midnight, Harvey Coughlin left his hotel room and began walking aimlessly.

He could not sleep. He could not stand still, remain in the hated room another moment. He had nowhere to go, but he had to do something. Every frantic telephone call had been refused. Even a try to re-establish contact with Jake Steinell had failed. Then Harvey had finally taken two sleeping pills and sat facing a television set where people were pretty and filled with laughter, and the pills had had absolutely no effect. When he could endure it no longer, he thought a walk might wear off some of the tension.

He walked without concern for direction, heading away from the large public buildings and monuments which seemed to mock him in their floodlit grandeur. The warm evening had become a still and humid night, and as he walked, the neighborhood deteriorated and he moved now under streetlights that were not so bright, past storefronts not so lavish. He passed an all-night convenience store, catching the warm odors of roasting chicken inside a glass-walled rotisserie near the window, and a novelty shop that smelled sweetly of candy-coated popcorn.

No one would help him now, he thought, dazed in his bitterness. He was quite alone. And there were some who would even enjoy his tragedy. There were always some who would delight in the downfall of a nobler man.

In the morning he would get on an airplane and return to California, and to his wife. He would have to tell her a little of it, enough so that she would imagine she understood what was happening. This would require clever lying, but he was good at that. She would never know any of the truth.

And then, he tried to convince himself, there was a chance the company would never be able to prove anything against him, and after Jake Steinell's lies were branded openly for what they were, Lydia would have to take him back. He might yet win vindication.

But it was a feeble hope, one he recognized as such. The tumble had begun, and once great men began to slide, their movement only accelerated; it was seldom arrested. The planting of a doubt was enough. They had done in a President that way, one Harvey had revered and still profoundly respected as a person ensnared and cruelly mistreated by his political enemies.

Harvey came to a dimly lighted bar. He thought a drink might help. He went inside, into smoke and small red lights over a long mahogany bar, a juke box in the back, and a few couples rubbing together in a travesty of dancing. Everyone was black. Instantly he felt not only alien but in danger. Ordinarily he would have turned and walked back out on the spot. But now a stab of fury with himself—for his own eternal timidity—forced him to stand his ground and even walk on the rest of the way to the end of the bar.

A big black bartender came over, grinning and showing a gold tooth. Harvey did not know what to order, so he asked for a scotch on the rocks. The black men nearest him at the bar subtly put space between them, so that by the time his drink was served, there was a place about four feet wide that gaped on his right, his left side being against the back wall. He felt angry and reckless, and did not care. He tossed the scotch back and, shuddering, signaled for another.

The couples were still dancing, holding one another and scarcely moving, in loose time with the soul music blaring from the smoky back of the hall. Harvey felt hostile eyes on him but ignored them, setting his teeth and staring at the rows of bottles along the back glass. They extended all the way to the cash register. He had never seen so many bottles.

His sense of danger persisted, but he allowed it and would not yield. *You may never be in this city again, and this is your only adventure away from Dena.* He would not run from it. He was sick of his fear, which seemed to radiate infinitely in all directions.

As the first drink began hitting him, he realized that he had not eaten all day. He wondered if he could find his way back to the hotel. Perhaps he should leave at once, because if he got any drunker, he might really be in trouble.

At that point, he almost laughed aloud. It would be terrible, he thought, if he were to get into *trouble*.

So he did not move, but nursed the second drink. No one would frighten him away. He was a citizen and he had every right to be here. And if something should happen to him . . . ah, Christ, with the feeling of self-loathing now sour in his throat, would it really matter? Would it matter at all?

A little later, he became conscious of someone standing near him on his right. He turned and stared into the eyes of a very tall black woman. She was much taller than he, slender, with large breasts half exposed by the sagging silk of her dress. She had a towering Afro and she was young, and she was smiling at him with a look he instantly understood.

"Hi," she said. Her voice was honey-milk.

"Hello," Harvey said thickly.

She moved marginally nearer, her thigh bumping lightly against his. Out of the deep, fleshly cleavage of her breasts came a perfume that was like nothing he had ever experienced before, rich with her blackness, her femaleness. It gave him a jolt that penetrated deep.

She asked softly, "You like to be my honey man?"

"What?"

"You like to be my honey man? You like to have some fun with me?"

"You don't—know who I am."

She laughed almost soundlessly. "Don't matter, baby. I know you ain't no cop. You a senator?"

The question gave Harvey his turn to be struck by a sense of the wildly incongruous. "No. I'm far from that."

She placed long, black fingers on his forearm. He looked down at her hand and wrist, encased in multiple bracelets and large rings. There was something brazen and primitive about the jewelry that again touched something within him.

She said, "Don't matter who you are, honey man. You want to be *my* man?"

"You don't understand," Harvey told her, realizing how drunk he was now. "I don't have any money, I don't live around here—"

"We can go to my place. I got a nice little place just around the corner. Would you like to see my place?"

Harvey stared at her. He did not quite remember how he had gotten there. He was more aware now of the black menace in the crowded, smoky room. He wanted to run. But he wanted to stay, too. He thought of Dena Forbes. She was the only pitiful adventure he had ever had in his miserable life, and what difference did anything make now?

He took a breath. "How much?"

Her thigh pressed insistently. "Fifty. You won't be sorry, honey man. Anything you want. Fifty."

Was that how much Jake Steinell had paid Dena Forbes? Harvey wanted to cry. He was getting very confused, the drinks had come too fast. "No."

The girl did not blink. "Okay. I'll suck your dick for twenty-five."

Was that how it worked? Had Dena been earning less from Steinell when she did for Harvey what no woman had ever done before, making him *know* she loved him?

"Come on, baby. What you say? Twenty-five? I do it real nice."

"I'm lost," Harvey told her, suddenly seeing in her the only person who had cared anything about him all day . . . perhaps forever.

The girl misunderstood. "That's okay, honey man. Now, listen. We can't walk outta here together. Some of these dudes is real mean. I'll leave, you dig? Then you wait a minute or two, you walk out. You turn right. *Right.* Get it? And I'll meet you up the block and we'll go to my place for a nice little quickie. Now, does that sound nice?"

Harvey tried to focus on her face, this woman who had seen him as a person, had even talked to him. But his vision was blurred. He thought he might be crying.

She squeezed his arm briefly, with great strength, and moved to the door. Harvey heard the door open and close.

So she was gone. *Right.* He tried to think about it rationally, but rational thought made very little sense. If he went after her now, there would be at least a few moments of a touching. No matter what ever happened, he would remember this. Why should he be careful? Why should he worry about anything at all? Had anyone else spoken to him this day? Did he have any farther to slide? Did he want to go back to the hotel room, and pace?

To hell with it, to hell with everything. What did he have to lose?

Driven by a feeling that he must degrade himself to prove his strength—to rid himself of something—he carefully nursed down the last of his drink. How much time had elapsed? Enough. He put both hands on the edge of the bar and slipped off the stool to his feet. He felt unsteady. He turned and with great dignity walked to the front door.

It was hotter and more humid outside, and the air smelled sweetly of decaying garbage. He saw blackened apartment windows, deserted stores. He turned to his right and started up the block, which was very dark. After all, what did it matter? He would have this. And then he would sleep. Tomorrow he would go home. After that—

"Honey?"

He turned. The voice had called softly from the doorway to an apartment building. He could just make out her figure standing in the door, which was ajar. The corridor into the building behind her was like pitch. He hesitated, some elemental warning system trying to operate.

"It's okay, baby," she whispered. "Come on. It's real safe."

He walked to the darkened doorway. Her teeth gleamed as she backed inside. He followed, and found her cool hand. She clasped his fingers and led him deeper into the darkness. The hallway smelled faintly of dust and decay.

"Hey," the girl whispered, moving against him, her pelvis insistent against him. "You my man, huh?" Her breath was hot on his face and then her lips pressed against his, her tongue darting, and her arms went around his arms, squeezing—*pinning his arms to his sides*.

That was when he knew, but it was too late. He tried to pull away, but there was movement behind him—a scuffling—and something smashed with paralyzing force low into his back, into his kidneys. He cried out and went to his knees as the girl danced nimbly back out of the way and something hit his skull a glancing blow. The floor was gritty with filth. A flashlight sprayed blindingly into his eyes. Something—a foot—exploded in his mid section, hurling him over backward and against the wall. Then something hard and metallic crashed into the middle of his face. Hands grabbed him—rifled his pockets—took his billfold—

"Motherfucker! He ain't got hardly nothing on him!"

Another blow slammed to the side of Harvey's head, making a

brilliant yellow flash, and then bombed out to blackness in his consciousness. Feet scuffled. A door slammed.

Harvey lay still. He did not think he lost all consciousness. The pain assaulted him. He listened and heard nothing, and then he began to know he was going to suffocate. Despite the pain, he sat up. The agony tore through him and he threw up, the sour whiskey splashing hot down the front of his shirt and onto his hands and thighs. Gagging, fighting for air, he rolled to his hands and knees and retched again. The pain was unbelievable.

Finally the paroxysm slowed. His breathing was like that of a wild animal, trapped, and he listened with horror. It had all been a trick. A fool—he had been a fool again. He was a fool in everything.

As his dazed eyes adjusted, he made out a rectangle of faint light ahead. He realized that it was the doorway to the street, left ajar. Everything was silent. He wondered if he had lost consciousness, after all. Was he alone? Had they gone? Why was there no help? How many people cowered behind doorways, perhaps only a few feet from him, having heard the beating but too terrified to look out?

He crawled to the doorway and used the edge of the door as a crutch to climb to his feet. The pain as he stood erect almost dropped him again.

Once outside, on the sidewalk, he looked in both directions, seeing a totally deserted panorama. Again he had the feeling that eyes were watching but from safe hiding. The fear struck him again then, too, very hard. He had to get out of this neighborhood. He had to get back to the hotel. It was a miracle he was alive.

Limping, he started south.

After a few blocks, he saw a car approaching down the street, and recognized the outline of the flasher unit on the top. His first thought was to rush into the police car's path—this, after all, was help. But just as quickly he realized how he looked, and what had happened. The police would be sardonic. "*After a little of that black stuff, pal? Well, some of you never learn. Let's go downtown and talk about it for the report.*" And then the inevitable headline; *Streetwalker Lures Business Figure into Mugging, Robbery.*

He dodged like a fugitive into a storefront doorway until the police car had cruised on.

He hurried now, moving into the brighter and better section of the city, and ahead saw the marquee lights of his own hotel. He frantically checked his pockets. They had taken everything, even his key.

The pain was more intense now. In the better light he saw the figure he made: blood-spattered, stained by his own sour vomit, his coat and shirt badly torn. Tears came to his eyes, but they were not from the pain but from mortification. Now he was reduced to *this*.

With every ounce of his will power, he limped into the hotel lobby with his head up. It was deserted except for a lone clerk behind the desk. The elderly man was reading a magazine. He did not look up until Harvey cleared his throat.

"I seem to have misplaced my key. Coughlin. Room 728."

"What happened, sir? Are you—all right?"

"A little accident. Not as—bad as it may look. My key, please."

The clerk got the extra key from the box and slid it across the counter. "If you would like the house doctor to look in on you, Mister Coughlin—"

"I'm fine," Harvey snapped, and turned away to walk as stiffly and soberly as he could to the elevator, waiting, vacant.

The doors slid blessedly closed and the car carried him upward. He limped down the silent hall to his own room, got it unlocked, went inside, locked and bolted everything.

In the bathroom, he stared at himself. He beheld a ragged, filthy tramp, clothing ruined, clotted with blood and vomit. His left eye was already closing, blood leaked from his nose and mouth. Testing his teeth gingerly with his tongue, he could see some of them wiggle. He would lose some of them. He had paid five thousand dollars to have them all capped, and now he would lose some of them.

Stripping out of the stained clothing, he stood shivering at the bowl as he washed himself. A large, purple bruise had begun to show itself low on his side, and when he probed it with gentle fingertips, the pain made him cry out. He wondered about the offer of the hotel doctor, but rejected this. He would have had to explain.

Explain . . . *explain*. All his life had been spent explaining. And in being afraid. Now, in the morning, he would have to call Junetta for money, and he would have *this*, too, to explain to her. Explain this . . . explain his suspension . . . explain the hateful story when it appeared in Jake Steinell's column, and when people began to whisper.

He had to sleep. He yearned for oblivion now more passionately than he had ever wished for anything in his life. He looked around, still shaking, and found the sleeping pills. Tapping the bottle lightly, he rolled two more out into the palm of his hand.

Then he hesitated, because two would not do any good. And tonight would be like last night. Like all the nights.

Was there no end to the explaining?

And he could not stand it.

In a spasmodic movement, he dumped all the pills out of the bottle into his hand. A few rolled to the floor. He threw all the rest into his mouth and held them cool against his tongue and the roof of his mouth and sloshed water into the drinking glass and gulped it down, carrying all the pills down with the water.

He stared at himself in the bright mirror again, and realized what he had just done.

It was all right, he told himself. It absolutely did not matter. This was the one freedom they could not take away from him. They could never get at him again, once he had done this. And they would be sorry.

He left the bathroom and walked into the bedroom and turned off the lights. The room was overly warm and he felt nauseated. The pain pulsed on the horizon of his consciousness as he lay back across the bed, naked. He saw that there was still light in the room. The bathroom light. He had forgotten that. In a minute he would get up and turn it off.

Still sleep did not come. He stared at the ceiling, thinking about what a fool he had just been and conjuring up a little fantasy in which he had that black whore and her aides in *his* control, and what he would do to them, and especially to her. He got half an erection imagining it. Then, however, the figure in the fantasy became Dena Forbes, here, in bed with him, and the sound of her voice gasping. He began crying then.

After a while, he decided not to bother getting up to turn off the bathroom light. He was starting to feel nice and warm and sleepy, and not so tense. Why had he been so . . . upset? It would work out. There was nothing really that serious, was there? Of course not. He was fine. . . . He could not even quite remember, now, what all the worry had been about, and he was going to get a good night's sleep at last.

Harvey slept. The sleep became very deep, and then deeper still, and then, very quickly, it became an abyss of sleep, and his chest rose and feel evenly, softly, at peace, and then after a while his body was entirely still.

13

An unseasonal rain came down steadily from a low, gray sky the following morning, and members of the board of Hempstead Aviation Co. filed into the room for emergency session. The Sales Department had been using the regular board room to lay out and discuss proposed campaigns, so the emergency meeting was to be in Lydia Baines's office. Chairs had been drawn into a semicircle facing her huge desk. The draperies at the back had been opened, providing a long vista out over wet tarmac, the roofs of smaller buildings with water streaming off their walls, and the dreary, dwarfed grass surrounding the black ribbon of the test-field runway. The hills beyond could not be seen, and the bright fluorescents in the office ceiling accentuated the drabness of the weather.

With a sense of genuine impending doom, Kelley Hemingway entered the office at Ken Lis's side. He was pale, carrying a clipboard scrawled full of various notations. Both of them had been swamped since early in the day, helping Janis Malone try to respond to questions from the press concerning Harvey Coughlin's death, in Washington. There had been time for no talk except of how to answer some of the questions for the best interests of the company, with so many aspects of the death still unanswered by authorities in Washington. Kelley had not really been able to probe Lis's personal reaction, although it was clear the event had deeply shocked him.

The meeting obviously had been called in response to the news, and Kelley was anxious to learn what Lydia Baines knew, and what it was going to mean to all of them.

They were all there, the rest of them: Lydia herself, wearing a dark business suit that made her appear waxen, with the cold beauty of a classic statue, behind her desk, slim hands folded before her; rotund Bert Jerno, rumpled and sickly in color, nervously fingering the folder of correspondence on his lap, which he stared at fixedly; youthful Dean Busch, shooting Kelley a glance that clearly asked her if she knew what was going to come out in the meeting; Seymour Trepps, chief of Ocean Research, sitting very straight and smoking an unaccustomed cigarette; and Richard Cazzell, the elderly chief of Finance, who seemed to have been aged by this latest development, so that the fine lines of his face and throat were deeper, wearier today.

As Lis and Kelley took chairs alongside the others, Lydia Baines leaned forward, her face glacial in its control. "Kelley, will you swing the door closed, please?"

As Kelley complied, Lydia punched her intercom to order no interruptions. Seymour Trepps awkwardly stubbed out his cigarette in a tray on his knee, showering sparks on the carpet and nervously rubbing the sole of his shoe over them in embarrassment. Lydia seemed not to see this. Her eyes swiveled around the group, from face to face. There was a very great anger there, and frustration. But no sign of panic.

"Until a coroner's jury can meet," she began, "there will be no formal finding in Harvey Coughlin's death. As most of you know, the first news reports have already been on radio and TV, and they quote police as saying the death was an apparent suicide."

"That's absurd!" Richard Cazzell said. "Everything was going well for Harvey, and there was no motive of any kind! I hope we can issue some statement to counteract this calumny!"

"We'll issue no such statement," Lydia said.

"But surely Harvey—"

"Police say it appears he died from a combination of alcohol and tranquilizers, and possibly from sleeping pills as well. Further, there was evidence that he had been assaulted earlier in the evening."

"Assaulted!"

"There's no way to tell at this point whether it took place in the hotel or somewhere else. Police are starting to question all the night employees to try to find that out. I mention it only because it's a part of the factual picture." Lydia Baines paused, frowning, then

395

went on. "In actuality, the assault, or whatever it was, probably had nothing much to do with Harvey's taking his own life."

"You believe he *did* do that?" Cazzell asked incredulously.

"You said, Richard, that everything was going well for Harvey and he had no motive for taking his own life. As long as it's possible, our official position will be the same. But the fact is that things were *not* going well for Harvey. Not at all. And I personally believe it probably was suicide."

Cazzell leaned back, shock registering on his deeply lined face. "I see there are some things here I didn't know about!"

"Recently, I learned that Harvey's transactions in Washington were being investigated by segments of the media. I looked into this. The early evidence suggests that he did reprehensible things to try to build support for the Eagle system, completely without my knowledge or authorization."

It was Dean Busch's turn to blurt a comment. "I don't understand what sort of things you're suggesting."

"Influence peddling. Payoffs to a relative of a high-ranking senator. Gifts to both members of Congress and key officials at the Pentagon. Rigging of certain bids on Eagle to favor companies in the home districts of wavering senators or representatives."

"And the press was onto him?" Busch said.

Lydia opened a thin folder on her desk. "I have here copies of a column that was scheduled to run in some two hundred newspapers this coming Sunday. Now that Harvey is dead, I'm sure a different sort of piece will be published. It shows the tip of the iceberg." She handed the stapled pages out over the rim of the desk. "This is confidential, of course, and no copy will leave this room."

Kelley Hemingway stared at the Xeroxed pages, instantly recognizing the Jake Steinell by-line. She read swiftly, then looked up to see most of the others still reading in stunned silence. She said, "But none of this is substantiated!"

"We've already done some investigating," Lydia Baines told her. "There is considerably more to the case than what you see here presented by innuendo. There's little possible doubt. Harvey had made a long string of very stupid blunders."

"How long," Dean Busch asked, "have we known about this? What were we doing about it?"

"Yesterday, on my direct orders, Bert, here, wrote a letter for my signature addressed to Harvey in Washington. I suspended him from his job, with pay and allowances, pending a full internal investigation."

Now it was Ken Lis who spoke. "And was Harvey notified of the letter prior to last night?"

"Bert telephoned him, I understand."

Every head turned to Bert Jerno, who seemed to shrink in his chair, his face a picture of anguish and remorse. "I was . . . instructed to call Harvey, and I did so. I . . . read him the letter. . . . But I didn't think he would do anything like this! My God, I didn't ever imagine he might kill himself!"

There was another brief, shocked silence. Then Richard Cazzell said hoarsely, "So it's true—Harvey did take his own life—because he was in disgrace!"

"He was stupid," Lydia said.

Cazzell's lean face lengthened with amazement. "But he was our . . . associate . . . our friend!"

"Harvey Coughlin," Lydia said, "may have done any number of stupid, illicit things in trying to exert undue influence on behalf of Eagle. It's obvious that parts of the story have already leaked; that's why Eagle did not come up for final discussion in committee this week. My sources in Washington indicate that no one will touch Eagle this year—and perhaps not ever—because they're all terrified that a favorable word could be interpreted as evidence of taking favors from Harvey . . . or from someone else in this company. I'm not here to talk about Harvey Coughlin. He's dead. There is a small chance that we acted swiftly enough with the suspension letter to avoid some of the worst publicity and/or prosecution. But our job now is to try to save this company. I'm telling all of you as much as I know at this point, because, frankly, I believe much worse publicity and difficulty is ahead of us."

"This is terrible," Cazzell said, rocking nervously in his chair. "Nothing like this has ever happened to us before."

"This is the way it's going to be," Lydia said coldly. "No officer or employee of this company will make any comment whatsoever about Harvey Coughlin, Eagle, or anything else relating to those or allied subjects. If any statements are made, they will be made by me personally. Second. Despite the cost factors involved, we will maintain the Eagle change-over operation for the present; if we were to start disbanding it at once, word would leak and our case would be further damaged."

"Then," Busch broke in, "*you* think Eagle is dead now too?"

Lydia's eyes were diamonds. "I'm being realistic."

No one dared speak. Kelley Hemingway wondered how the man beside her was really reacting to this. Harvey Coughlin had not been a friend, but she knew that Ken Lis's loyalty to Hempstead Aviation ran incredibly deep. What was he feeling? Relief? Anguish at seeing how serious the trouble for the firm had now become? A trace of personal uncertainty for his own future? But Lis's face was rigidly controlled; she could not read his stony expression.

"Third," Lydia said into the silence, "each division chief will begin at once preparing a confidential report for my eyes only. This report will be in two parts: the first will project income and cost figures based on known—not hoped-for—developments; the second part will detail procedures, including personnel figures, for cutbacks that may be made within a ninety-day period if company income slacks due to failure to land the Eagle contract and possible continued grounding of Excalibur."

"Are you speaking," Cazzell asked quietly, "of a routine reduction in force through attrition, or—"

"I'm speaking of slashing everything to the bone, Richard, to avoid a calamity."

Again no one spoke, as the import sank in.

Lydia Baines spoke again, addressing herself to Cazzell, and in a tone that was suddenly gentle, as if she knew how much this hurt the old man. "You know better than anyone here, Richard, how slender our margins have been. The outlook cannot be described as anything but bleak. We'll have no Eagle contract this year. We can't predict what's going to happen with Excalibur, and income from that division at the moment is zero. We are not facing a belt-tightening. It's far more serious than that, and in the confines of this office we have to face it, and face it now, if we're going to come through."

She paused, then looked around the room. "We can expect . . . more bad publicity. Steinell and his kind are jackals. They'll swarm on this corpse. God knows what else they might uncover."

Into the silence, Seymour Trepps spoke like a man emerging from a coma: "I thought everything was going so well!"

The hint of a bitter smile turned Lydia Baines's lip. "We'll get through it."

"What happens with Aerospace?" Ken Lis asked quietly. "Who takes over?"

Lydia opened the folder again and took out a single sheet of paper. "I ask the board to ratify the following changes: Dean Busch from chief, Consumer Products, to chief, Aerospace; Kelley Hemingway from administrative chief, Airplane, to chief, Consumer Products. Ken, you may appoint a new administrative aide of your own choice. These changes to take effect immediately."

There was a faint but definite galvanizing effect in the room. Even as she felt the shock of this unexpected promotion, Kelley saw how well conceived and clever it was. They were going forward, it said; they were not beaten; old annoyances were being buried with the appointment of both her and Dean Busch; and new people in new jobs would give at least an appearance of new directions—the hope of new leadership.

Lydia looked at Busch. "Will you accept this appointment if the board offers it, Dean?"

Busch stared, wide-eyed. "Yes."

The eyes turned. "Kelley?"

Kelley knew she had been maneuvered. But it was too good to turn down. They *could* save the company, she thought. She said simply, "Yes."

"Will the board ratify these appointments?"

The vote was instant, with a grim unanimity.

"Ken, do you have immediate thoughts about a new administrative chief for your division?"

Lis spoke without hesitation. "I recommend Janis Malone."

"Janis," Lydia said, "is going to be badly needed in PR."

"She has the ability for this bigger job. For the time being she can wear two hats if necessary. She deserves it."

Lydia frowned, then nodded assent. "Done, then. Several of us will be wearing more than one hat, as you put it. You and Dean and I will work intimately on handling matters pertaining to the Coughlin-Eagle matter. At the same time, it becomes increasingly clear that our whole future may depend on finding the flaw in Excalibur and getting it into the air again. May I ask if there have been any new developments on that line?"

"We flew two missions yesterday," Lis said. "We had two more scheduled today."

"Fly them. You still have the NTSB man here, don't you?"

"Yes. He's down in Engineering now, with Barton MacIvor."

The pencil Lydia Baines held in her hand was clutched so tightly that her knuckles were white. "Standing as we do now, we must have Excalibur. There is simply no option. And we can't wait weeks or months for whatever Washington may finally conclude in its investigation. So fly the missions today. Use as many aircraft as you might possibly need. If we can't ourselves find what's wrong with Excalibur now, and find it quickly—"

She did not have to finish the statement.

When the meeting broke up, Ken Lis stayed behind.

Lydia Baines looked up and saw him. "A question, Ken?"

"Several."

"Close the door."

He did so.

"Now," she said.

"You didn't bring up Derquet's arrest in Monravia."

Her mouth hardened. "No. I did not."

"What if Derquet is telling them everything? It might all come out: the payment we made, Harvey's involvement."

"I'm gambling that Lucian will keep his silence."

"I've looked into it a little bit. You know, when I was over there I met a young woman who was part of a loyalist faction devoted to supporting the prince and getting rid of trouble makers for him, like Derquet. It was her group that caught him. They had key people inside the secret police, and Derquet has made few moves in recent weeks that were not monitored. There's a good chance his meeting with Harvey in Switzerland was watched."

"I'm gambling, as I said, otherwise."

"Do you believe Harvey heard of Derquet's arrest?"

"Oh, yes. Bert Jerno mentioned it to him on the telephone that night."

"That must have been a factor in his suicide . . . if it was suicide."

"Oh, it was suicide, I think. Weaklings always take some cheap way out like that."

Lis stared at her with amazement. "Lydia. You ordered him to carry that cash to Derquet."

"What if I did? *He* was the one who did it!"

"You were ready to sacrifice him in a minute," Lis said. "He must have seen that you were going to suspend him, then fire him if you had to, and let him be the one who had done all the wrongdoing."

"Precisely. Grow up! This is serious business and we're all big boys and girls now. Harvey knew the risks he was taking. He happened to lose. My concern is the company now."

"I remember a time when people counted too, around here."

"Spare me your insufferable sermons. Our job is to salvage what we can from this mess. Your job, very specifically, is to find what's wrong with Excalibur."

"And if I fail, I'm the next fall guy?"

"Why talk nonsense?"

"Is it nonsense?"

"You'll find the problem. I have complete confidence in you."

"But if I don't?"

"It's up to you to make sure we never have to face that eventuality."

Lis turned and walked out of her office.

Heading back for his own floor, he was in turmoil. He could not pretend deep grief over the fate of Harvey Coughlin. They had never gotten along, and he had known Coughlin was willing to sacrifice him in an instant to win the top position in Lydia's reorganized company.

The way Coughlin had been used, however, was profoundly upsetting. It demonstrated better than any words how Lydia Baines would run the company in the months and years ahead. Personal loyalty meant nothing now. No one could have been more dedicated, in his own warped way, than Coughlin. He had been rewarded by being made the fall guy.

For the first time, nearing his own office, Lis thus faced the consequences of Jason Baines's death and the shift of power. Hempstead Aviation was no longer the kind of place he wanted to work. It would never be so again, even if it weathered this crisis and came out whole.

He could not remain.

But there was Excalibur. It was clear now that the airplane carried within its miles of wiring and hundreds of subassemblies some tiny, elusive, fatal flaw. The aircraft had been Jason Baines's dream, and his own. He had to continue until that flaw was uncovered, and corrected.

Then, he told himself, walking into his office, he would face the consequences of the insight he had just experienced about the future.

Kelley Hemingway was at her desk. Hiding his true feelings, Lis winked at her like a conspirator as he passed. She immediately left her desk and followed him into his own office.

"No stealing secrets from the Airplane Division," he told her.

"I'm in a state of shock," she said.

He studied her. She was very pale, her eyes enormous. She had never appeared more beautiful, and something in him stirred once more. "You deserve it, Kelley."

"I'll miss you," she said with a crooked smile.

"Right." He grinned at her. "You're going to be all the way up there on the next floor."

"You know what I mean!"

"Yes. I know what you mean."

"Have you been to see Janis?"

"No, I'm going down in a few minutes to tell her."

"She'll be floored."

"It's getting to be a big club."

Kelley moved nearer the desk, which separated them. "Are there things about this situation involving Harvey's death that I don't know?"

"Nothing special," he lied. Then, meeting her eyes, he could not leave it at that. "I've got divided loyalties, Kelley: to you and to the company. If there's further trouble, it certainly won't involve you directly. Your job is to get Consumer moving faster, try to start finding new projects. Any other information has to come from Lydia."

"You're even more upset by all this than I thought."

"Yes, I'm a little upset."

"Would you rather I didn't take the job as chief of Consumer Products?"

"Hell, no! You deserve it, Kelley. Dean Busch has been stagnating, battering his head against walls. He'll be a tonic for Aerospace, and I'm betting you'll work wonders in his old division. It needs the kind of new thinking you can provide."

"But if you need me here," she said, "I'll stay."

"No. I want you to take this opportunity."

"It's funny," she said with a half smile that had no real humor in it. "We've spent the last months tiptoeing around one another, one just as aware as the other . . . I think . . . of the attraction. Now, all at once, that seems to be gone too, and we're two executives circling warily."

"I don't feel that way," he told her, surprised yet relieved that in this way it had finally come into the open. "You're always going to be very special to me, Kelley."

Her eyes were even larger. "And you to me."

"I just wonder," he said, the words dragging from him, "what might have happened if I had made that pass."

"I thought you were going to, that night we left late together right after the New York crash."

"Yes. I almost did that night."

"I'm glad, in retrospect, that you didn't."

"Meaning that at the time you felt differently?"

"I don't know how I would have responded, Ken. I feel a very strong attraction to you. I have for a very long time. But there's nothing at all seriously wrong with my marriage. I'm committed to it. I love the guy."

"Then, it's better I didn't have the nerve."

"It wasn't nerve."

"Wasn't it?"

"No. I think you still love Amy a lot more than you sometimes realize."

"You're right, and I know it now. I didn't then."

She smiled at him. "So we're both glad it turned out as it did, right?"

"Amy is talking about leaving me."

"Oh, no."

"She's mentioned it several times. It's damned hard for me to understand. We're getting along better than we have in years. She's seeing that doctor and he's helping. She hasn't had a drink or a pill for what begins to seem like a reassuringly long time. And then, right in the middle of a conversation, she'll mention that she has to keep her options open—that she might have to leave me for a while . . . or for longer. And I can't understand it. She's tried to explain, but I can't comprehend her reasoning."

"She loves you."

"I think she does. But she still maintains she might have to leave me to go off on her own . . . be her own person. I want her to do what she feels is best. But the thought of her leaving me now—well, it's almost more than I can stand."

"I've got an idea that it's part of the process she has to go through," Kelley said. "You've got to let her find her own way."

"I am if it kills me. But I can't understand it!"

"I don't know Amy all that well, Ken, but the times I've been around her, I've had a very strong feeling that her life has always been almost totally bound up in yours."

"She's had all her clubs, all her—"

"Those have been attempts to establish her own self, her own importance. But they didn't work very well, did they? If they had, would she have been drinking, taking those pills?" Kelley gestured impatiently. "Look, I'm just guessing. But sometimes one woman understands another at levels below logic. I think Amy loves you. But I think she's very mixed up, trying desperately hard right now to try to realize *herself* as a person. Maybe . . . she's been submerged by you, your personality, your strengths, so long that the only way she'll *ever* find her own way is to be away from you for a while."

"That's the kind of things she says, and it doesn't make sense!"

"It will," Kelley told him quietly. "You're trying—both of you. It's going to work out. Give her all the freedom she can take. *Trust* her! Trust your love! It's going to work out."

Lis had to smile. "You know, this strikes me as just a little weird. After fiendishly lusting after your body for months, I finally find the subject out in the open. Then, instead of falling madly into each other's arms, we talk about my problems with Amy."

"We're very weird people," Kelley said. "That's why we get along so well."

He looked at her, and a sense of relief flooded through him. He was liberated from wanting her by the very fact that it was acknowledged. He wondered why his other problems could not be solved so easily.

As she did often, Kelley seemed to read his mind. She gave him her brightest smile. "You'd better go tell Janis. I intend to move out of here by nightfall and start trying to figure out ways Consumer Products can steal some of Airplane's thunder."

"I'll fight you tooth and nail."

"Good. I wouldn't have it any other way."

15

For Janis Malone, Ken Lis's visit with the news that she could be his new administrative aide—second in command of the Airplane Division—was a distinct shock.

"I'm not qualified!" she gasped.

"You can grow into the job, Janis," Lis told her. "You have the capability and everyone is enthusiastic about your having the chance."

"But I'm not—*ready!*"

"You'll never feel any readier. . . . Okay, I know what you're going to say. You haven't had college training in management, you're too young, you've just learned your PR job really well, and so on, and so on. If you really don't want the job, then fine. There are others we can consider—"

"No!"

"No, you don't want it?" Lis asked. "Or no—"

"No, I want it! I mean—no, don't give it to someone else! My gosh, if you're crazy enough to let me try it, then I'm crazy enough to *take* it!"

"You'll do fine," Lis said. "You know some of the things Kelley handles: you manage the office force, you trouble shoot, and frankly you do PR for me and the rest of the division. It's not as if I were asking you to take over Engineering."

"You make it sound so easy."

"Oh no, it's not easy. There will probably be some older hands who resent you, and you've got a tremendous amount to learn about production control systems. But your job in PR has taken you into all areas of the company, and you know more than you probably think you do. You know how to find the right expert to get something done, and as my first assistant, that's one of the things I'll be asking you to do often."

"The whole prospect scares me out of my wits," Janis admitted.

"But there is something else you have to consider. You have a pretty good idea of how troubled this company is right now, don't you?"

"Eagle . . . Excalibur . . . the Harvey Coughlin thing," Janis said. "Yes. I think I have a pretty horrible inkling."

"You might want to consider that before you give me a final yes or no. And let me add that I'm sure you'll have Kelley nearby, to ask questions of. And coming in during a time of turmoil is not always the worst way. No one is going to accuse you of rocking the boat. It's already rocking like crazy."

Janis stared at Lis, trying to read his face. It occurred to her that this promotion would move her out of the employee class and into the ranks of the executives. It was more than she had ever dreamed about.

"Why *me*?" she asked.

"I've told you. You have a broader understanding of the division than almost anyone around. You can grow into the job. You've earned the shot at it. So what do you say? Would you like to think it over until tomorrow?"

"Yes," Janis decided. "At least that will give me time to get used to the idea a little."

Lis nodded. "Come by the office in the morning."

The remainder of the working day, after that little bombshell, was a blur. At first, Janis cycled back again and again to the gut feeling that she simply did not *know* enough. But, as the first surprise passed, she found herself analyzing the situation in broader terms. The very aspect of her present job that at first seemed to disqualify her now began to look like her best asset, just as Ken Lis had indicated.

She could think of more-mature people, experts with more longevity, in practically every office. But as she thought about it, she realized that they *were* specialists. Often she had been surprised, talking with someone in Engineering or Production, to learn how little he or she really understood about how the various parts of the company fitted together in a single, cohesive effort. She saw that Lis was right, that this was her strong point: a broad overview and a grasp of how sections interlinked.

Her own office, she recognized without conceit, had grown from a one-girl operation to a full-fledged section with four full-time and six part-time employees, all under her lone supervision. The PR office was a far cry from Division, but at least part of her duties would be managing another office. It was not as if she were being thrust into some alien world.

By suppertime, she had just about decided to take a flier at it. She would have Kelley to ask questions of, and after reviewing the other staff members in the administrative office itself, she thought she could handle them. As for the other myriad duties she would have to perform—well, she would just have to learn them!

Hank Selvy was due at her apartment about eight, and she knew he might present a problem. Nervously she awaited his arrival, using the time to plan her approach with him. She thought she knew just how she would introduce the topic so that he would not see it as further involvement on her part that might detract from their relationship.

But she had forgotten that Selvy would have been in the air all afternoon with Lis and that they might already have talked.

Selvy arrived at eight-ten, and when she opened the door she knew he already had at least part of the news. He hugged her briefly and went past her into the apartment. There he dropped onto the couch, one lanky leg extended to the coffee table.

"Sorry I'm a little late," he said wearily.

"How did the flights go?"

"Normal. Absolutely no progress."

"You look tired, honey. Would you like some tea?"

"What I would like, chicken, is to know what you've decided about this fancy new title Ken Lis wants to stick on you."

"Oh, Hank. I wanted to tell you in my own way."

"Well, it got mentioned while we were flying back this evening."

"Damn."

Selvy was grim but strangely calm. "So what are you going to do about it?"

Janis restrained the reply that almost came out. Instead she asked quietly, "What do you think I should do, Hank?"

He frowned. "Well, for a person who wants a career, it's a fantastic opportunity."

"Even with Hempstead in trouble?"

"Listen, we'll find the glitch in that airplane. And, I don't like the lady much, but Lydia Baines is going to get it back together if she has to steamroller the damned *world*."

"Then, you think I should take it? I'm not qualified."

Selvy surprised her. "Ah, hell, dumpling. You're qualified. You just don't really recognize how damned smart you are, how much you've got on the ball."

"Then, you think I should take it?"

"Do you want a career?"

"Hank, I just don't know how I can turn down the chance, even though it scares me half to death."

"Then, there's your answer."

"Is that *your* answer?"

Selvy's chest heaved and he reached for a cigarette. "You know, I'm not the brightest guy in the world."

"Hank—"

"No, let me finish. I'm not the brightest guy in the world. I'm a pretty good pilot, you've got to give me that. But you get me away from airplanes and charts, and I don't have a whole lot going for me. I know that."

"Hank, everyone respects you—"

"And," Selvy went on as if she had not spoken, "I've got this problem. I've been thinking about it, and I know it's *my* problem. After Ken told me about his offer to you today, I thought about it some more."

Selvy paused and inhaled smoke deeply. "Rationally, I know it shouldn't make a damn if you were barefoot and pregnant or head of PR here or president of the damned company, as long as you said you loved me. But the more I tell myself that, the more upset I get. Janis, I want all of you, not the leftovers from Hempstead Aviation or some other job. In the daytime, I tell myself that's stupid. Then I lie awake at night, thinking about you at work giving the best of yourself to the job instead of to me, and I get so upset I can't sleep for hours."

"Hank—" Janis began.

"No, let me finish, okay? Please."

"I can be a better wife by developing my potential—"

"I *know* that! But tell it to my gut at three o'clock in the morning."

"Maybe it just takes more getting used to!"

"We used to have great times, *all* the time," Selvy said staring into space. "Remember the time we got roped into taking that kindergarten class to the park and I fell in the wading pool?"

Janis giggled. "Or the bowling?"

Selvy grinned, but then the grin faded instantly. "We haven't had much fun like that in recent months. Half the time we've been together, we've either been fighting about your job, or trying not to, which is just as bad. I've acted like a dumb shit. I just . . . can't . . . accept the idea of sharing you. Not with another guy, not with a job, not with *anything*."

She thought she saw what was coming now, and it did not really surprise her. She had never confronted it before, but it had been there, a probability, all the time, and a part of her had known. "What are you saying, Hank?"

"I don't like being a dumb shit," he said. "I don't like being the heavy. I know I ought to change, but there's something about me—I just can't. Not really. I could pretend, but that would be all I was doing and you'd see right through it."

"What are you saying, Hank?" she repeated quietly.

His eyes were bright with suppressed anger and pain. "I think you'd be crazy not to take the job."

"And you'll—try to accept it? If we both try—"

"No, chicken," he said softly, with infinite regret.

"What?"

"You're the best, Janis. You deserve a guy who has it all together in the upper belfry, a guy who can let you have the freedom someone like you has to have, and deserves. And me—well, maybe someplace there's a dumb old, old-fashioned country girl, all ready and willing to be barefoot in the kitchen when I get home and wear chintzy, dumb aprons and bake apple pie—"

"Hank, *what are you saying to me?*"

He stood, his eyes definitely bright now, and perhaps wet. "I'm tired of fighting. I don't want to do it and I can't stop. I'm just too hung up. I've read that feminist stuff you gave me to read, so I know probably I'm really worried about my own balls or something, but that doesn't matter. None of it matters logically. I am what I am, and you're what you are, and I just won't hold you back or try to change you any more than you can change me. And we won't . . . fight any more."

"Hank—?"

He came to her, heartbreakingly good-looking and earnest, and took her hands. He pulled her close and kissed her very lightly on the tip of the nose. "Let's have lunch sometime, okay?"

She had wondered how things like this ended. She had never expected it to be like this. She was in tumult but could not speak as emotions warred within her.

Selvy released her and walked, stony-faced, to the door. He opened it and did not look back. The door closed behind him.

Janis stood where he had left her. The impulse came to run after him. She knew instantly that she could not do this. He had not devised this as a test. It went deeper and farther than that, and she saw that he was right.

It had been a long time since they had had the old kind of fun together such as he had mentioned. This moment had been coming for a long time.

That did not make it any easier. She knew she would always remember him in this moment, and love him, a little, for having seen the truth before she could face it.

Tomorrow there was going to be the start of a new job, and a continuation of the old one. Both were going to seem very lonely.

Janis went into the bedroom. Distantly she heard Selvy's car start and drive away. It would be fine, she told herself. Then she started to cry.

16

In the week following Harvey Coughlin's death, Hempstead Aviation was repeatedly in the news on both sides of the Atlantic.

In Monravia, formal charges were filed against the disgraced Lucian Derquet. Although the name of his alleged American connection was not released, speculation was widespread that he had been dealing with Hempstead, and the suggestions of linkage were bolstered by reports telling about the trade visit to Monravia that had been led by Ken Lis only shortly before the arrest. There was no direct suggestion that Lis was involved in reported payoffs, and a number of theories were introduced to tie the Derquet case to Coughlin, whose visit to Europe had also been uncovered.

Much to Lydia Baines's relief, it appeared that Derquet was not helping Monravia in its investigation. News stories said he was accused of taking "about $200,000 from an American firm," which tended to explain why the diplomat could afford to play it close to his vest: evidently only about a fifth of the money paid to him through Coughlin had been located, and he seemed willing to risk a longer jail term for non-cooperation if the trade-out was access, at some later time, to the remaining $800,000.

A cool letter from Prince David Peltier to Lydia's office verified Derquet's fall from grace and said that Prince David himself would handle all future negotiations for a commercial jet to be added to his country's fleet. Further evidence that Derquet was maintaining silence came in the prince's statement that Hempstead had not been eliminated from consideration by possible wrongdoing involving a few.

When Monravia announced that Derquet's trial might be months in the future, press interest in his case seemed to decline, although Janis Malone had a few further questions from reporters on the subject.

"The Coughlin story," as it was first known, quickly broadened. In a series of three columns, Jake Steinell suggested widespread misdeeds in negotiations for defense contracts generally, and then turned his big guns on the Joe Wind – D. L. Boudoin connection, outlining a number of allegedly shady land deals perpetrated by Wind in Florida and Louisiana. Wind threatened a lawsuit.

An item appearing only in a few Colorado newspapers said Senator Matthew Johns had reorganized his administrative staff in Washington. A woman named Dena Forbes and a lawyer named Collins were dropped. When the New York *Times* ran a piece linking Johns to corporate interests doing business with Hempstead Aviation and detailing social events that Johns had hosted for key persons including Harvey Coughlin, Johns issued a statement saying he would not dignify gutter journalism by making a statement.

It was now deep into August and Congress adjourned, but not before D. L. Boudoin announced formation of an interim investigating committee to look into reports of "possible misconduct" in handling defense matters. In one of its last acts before adjournment, Congress approved the work of the committee as stated in its plans, including fourteen investigators, an administrative staff of nine, and a budget of $285,569.27 for the first six months of operation.

"This is tax money well spent," Boudoin told the press.

On August 26, the Atlanta *Constitution* reported that an electronics firm in the home state of Senator Clifford Sweet stood to lose more than $2 million as a direct result of collapse of support for the Eagle missile system. The newspaper said Interspace Industries had spent that amount acquiring a smaller, sister firm in order to have production capability for an Eagle subsystem. It was reported, without attribution, that Interspace had in its files a letter from Hempstead Aviation stating that it would be the builder of the subsystem once congressional approval was given to Eagle.

The next day, ABC-TV screened an interview with Sweet from Nashville, where he was making a speech on ethics in government. He categorically denied being influenced by "chamber-of-commerce factors in the conduct of this nation's defense business."

On the same date, General Black Jack Mallory announced his early retirement from the military in order to accept a position on the board of a major western coal company at a salary in excess of two hundred thousand dollars per year. The wire services moved a photo of Mallory being welcomed by members of the company's board, including a black vice-president named Joseph Johns, the senator's brother.

At Hempstead Aviation, confidential reports were prepared for a possible major cutback in all divisions. Harvey Coughlin's funeral was attended by all company officers, and his grieving widow was briefed on the broad range of benefits to be paid her from the company's insurance and retirement plans. At Lydia Baines's order, all files in Aerospace were started through a careful audit for signs of possible irregularities.

As an outsider, Jace Mattingly was aware of the pressures and crosscurrents but did not attempt to analyze them beyond recognizing that Hempstead desperately needed to find the flaw in Excalibur to try to get sales moving again. He attended two conferences between Ken Lis and representatives of Transwestern Airlines, which had been conducting certain aircraft and flight tests of its own. The TW test program was not as sophisticated as Hempstead's, and Mattingly was not surprised to learn that they, too, had run into blank walls so far.

In a number of lengthy calls to Washington, Mattingly kept up with probe developments there. An early indication of a wing-root failure on the Pittsburgh crash plane was ruled out on subsequent investigation. Files were being built on every witness, but, as in the New York case, new facts were hard to uncover. Although no official statement had been contemplated to date, official thinking now tended to the theory that the Excalibur slat wing, being a radical departure from traditional aerodynamic theory, simply had a margin of unpredictability that testing could not uncover routinely. This thought—violently opposed by Ken Lis and especially by Barton MacIvor—could give the agency a kind of official "out": the slat wing could be ruled basically untrustworthy, and further Excalibur crashes positively eliminated from possibility by the simple expedient of ordering that no Excalibur would ever fly with a slat wing again.

If he had believed this line of thought, Mattingly could have lived with the realization that permanent grounding of Excalibur might well wipe out Hempstead Aviation. He had seen government toy with the public safety as it kowtowed to private industry, notoriously in the instance of spray-can propellants and the long delays in banning them, and he would have accepted Hempstead's ruin if he had believed this was the only way to assure safety for the airline passenger. But as in the case of earlier attempts to pin the New York crash on pilot error, the idea of the wing being essentially faulty simply did not quite ring true. He continued doggedly working with Lis and MacIvor and the other engineers, trying to rig new tests.

The help was more welcome to Ken Lis than Mattingly perhaps realized. As each day passed, with more flights and negative results, Lis's sense of desperation was increasing. The latest financial reports from Richard Cazzell, passed out in utmost secrecy, were abysmal. Hempstead was now plunging deeper into the red with each passing day. News that TWA was ordering fifty of the new Boeing mid-range commercial jetliner did not help. Lis had been counting on TWA for new Excalibur orders.

There was still hope, he assured himself privately. United needed more planes and seemed intent on holding off a decision until early next year. Monravia was still in the picture, and France. So were Continental, American, Delta, and Eastern. Most of these were still flying some 707s. Once the queen of jet travel, the 707 was now a very old airplane; soon it would be seen only on foreign carriers or the small domestic ones, and it had to be replaced with something.

Lis made it a point to try to help Dean Busch in the sprawling confusion of Aerospace, Kelley Hemingway in Consumer Products, and of course Janis Malone as his own new administrative assistant. All seemed to be taking hold fast.

There was little communication with Lydia Baines. She had made four trips to the East Coast on unstated business.

At home, Lis maintained a constant close contact with Amy. The experience was a baffling mixture of hope and worry. His wife was blooming, staying dry and away from pills, and paradoxically embarking on a strict diet and exercise program of the kind she had not been able to maintain for years. She kept saying she was taking it a day at a time.

At the same time, however, the specter of Amy leaving—at least for a little while—remained constant. Lis understood only that somehow she felt she might have to do this, to prove to him—or more, to herself—that she could function successfully with no one as a crutch.

On Friday night, over a week now since the Coughlin death, Lis and his wife went out for dinner. As they drove home rather late, the topic came up again.

She was sitting close beside him, her hand lightly on his thigh. She squeezed. "It's been a terrible year for you, Ken."

"We'll make it," he told her with more confidence than he felt.

"I don't like to think I'm adding to your problems."

"You're not! Listen, if I were better with words, I could tell you how proud I am of you—how great it is that you're coming back the way you are."

"Would it bother you a very great deal," she asked abruptly, "if I were to desert you for a little while?"

He forced himself to sound very calm. "Go off somewhere, you mean?"

"I've about decided I just have to do that, you know."

He swallowed his feelings. "Where will you go?"

"Not far. Seattle, I think. I've never even seen Seattle, you know. I thought I could get an apartment . . . and possibly a job."

"It sounds . . . almost permanent."

"No. I don't think so. I don't think I'll—I don't even think I would stay away very long at a time. I mean, I would like to come back . . . sometimes . . . on weekends. Or you could come to see me there."

"If you'll let me, you know I will."

He said this with more force than he had intended, because she chuckled and then moved her hand teasingly. "Two old fogeys like us, shuttling back and forth all the time whenever we get horny?"

He risked taking his eyes from the street long enough to kiss her ear. "I don't feel very old tonight." But it was bravado; inside he felt nothing but frightened despair.

"I want to prove some things to myself," she said. "I suppose I've never . . . really had a life independent of you. If I go away for a little while, I can test myself . . . have time to think, and be alone, and see how I do."

"Are you ready this soon to be away from your doctor?"

417

"I don't know. I think I am. How will I ever know unless I try?"

They were nearing their home now, and he felt the pressure of things to say, the right words to give her. He wanted above all things to be supportive. He could not really understand. Why did she have to talk about going now, when they were doing better in every way than they had in years?

He knew he could not demand that she make him understand, because it might be impossible, and his very questioning might shatter the strength of her fragile, building resolve. And so he was placed in the position of accepting the unacceptable.

"I wish you could stay," he said slowly. "But if this is what you have to do, then this is what you have to do. I just hope it's not . . . too long."

"It's not that I want to be away from you, Ken. It's that I have to get closer to myself."

He turned the car onto their street and saw their house ahead. He felt a streak of inexplicable sadness. Would he look back on this night as the time it all finally ended?

He said, "When do you plan to make this move?"

"I don't know yet. Soon, I think."

"I'll help you, Amy, however you want. I'll try to help you find a place, and make arrangements, or I'll stay out of it."

"Seattle isn't so far. I think I can handle everything. And we'll talk on the telephone . . . and make our little horny trips back and forth."

"If that's what you have to do," he said again. It was all he could think to say.

"Let me think about it over the weekend," she said.

"Okay." He tried to recapture a happier mood. "And in the morning we go bike riding, but not to Seattle!"

"Just to Tiburon."

"Ouch."

With a press of the car transmitter, the automatic garage door opened and he drove in. They went into the kitchen and he locked up behind them. Amy went to the refrigerator for iced tea.

"That's funny," he told her. "This back door was open, and I could have sworn I locked it when we left."

"We need to replace the locks with dead bolts," she said, pouring a glass of the brown liquid.

"I'll put that on my do list."

Standing at the sink, she drank the tea in a long, steady motion, put the glass on the drainer, and walked to him. Her smile was tremulous. "You're not mad at me?"

"I love you."

She slipped back out of his arms. "I think I might just go slip into something indecent."

"Your room or mine?" Lis asked, following her to the stairs in the dark.

She didn't reply except for a soft chuckle. Although his clothes remained in the back bedroom, and he showered and shaved there, the bed had not been slept in for some time. They were together again in this way, too, and he still awoke each morning with a momentary sense of disorientation and wonderment as he discovered the feminine curtains and furniture, and her body warm beside him in the bed.

"I'm stuffed," Amy panted at the top of the stairs. "I shouldn't have had the medium-sized steak."

"Let me go change and I'll try to think of some suitable exercise for you."

She turned, toward the front bedroom. The light went on as she entered and turned the switch. He went the other direction, going to the back of the house and into his own room, which he was beginning to think of as a den.

Not bothering to turn on the main overhead light, he walked across the dark room to the bathroom door and flicked that light on as he stepped inside. Leaving the door ajar, he relieved himself, washed his hands, caught his reflection in the bright rectangle of the mirror, and stared for a moment. There were some new lines. He was starting to get old. He was also quite tired.

Something had to break on Excalibur, he thought. And he did not know how brave and calm and wonderful he was going to be able to act if Amy went ahead with this thing . . . and her stay away from him became prolonged.

He pushed the bathroom door open, and this cast a long shaft of light into the bedroom, across the unused bed. He felt stirrings of desire, and a gladness. But at the same time he was wondering which bed he would sleep in, alone, once she had gone.

Taking off his jacket, he tossed it across the end of the bed. He began unknotting his tie, deep in thought.

It was at this point that something—a tiny sound or perhaps some atavistic instinct—warned him. An incredible chill shuddered through his body. There was someone behind him in the room.

17

As Ken Lis turned, his primitive warning system shrieking in his bloodstream, he knew he would see someone or some-*thing*. His pulse was already crashing sickly in his ears.

Standing in front of the partly opened closet doors was Harold, the yard boy. Lis saw in a flash that he had been hidden in the closet; the clothes were all pulled aside, some fallen onto the closet floor. Harold appeared almost normal—jeans and a tee shirt and cheap canvas shoes—but his face shone with a deathly pallor, glinting under its film of sweat, and in his eyes was a look like none Lis had ever seen before anywhere.

The raw physical fact of his presence, uninvited, moved Lis back an involuntary step nearer the front wall of the room.

"What the hell do you want?" he demanded hoarsely.

Harold had his right arm behind his back. He came a gliding step closer, his right arm remaining hidden. "You weren't supposed to turn. It would have been easier. But nothing can help you."

"What the hell are you talking about? Get out of here, Harold!"

Harold's right arm moved, bringing what he held into view. Light glittered off the long, thick blade of the hunting knife.

"Put that damned thing down!" Lis said.

"You are evil," Harold said. He moved another step nearer, poised on the balls of his feet, the knife extended toward Lis.

"Harold, wait a minute! What's going *on* here?" Lis moved away from the knife, seeing that the youth was now close enough that he might strike with a single long bound. There was a revolver in the nightstand, but that was across the room diagonally. Harold had managed to cut him off from it. The only other avenue was the window. Could he dive through the glass before—

"You can't get away," Harold told him, with another careful step nearer. "Accept your fate. You have done evil and you must pay. An eye for an eye, a tooth for a tooth. Kneel!"

His flesh crawling as he comprehended the insanity facing him, Lis braced his legs. He had to move in and try to get the knife. There was no other way. The wild look in the boy's eyes said he expected this, even wanted it. He was moving the point of the huge knife in a little circle as Lis had once seen someone do in a combat training film.

A voice—Amy's—came from beyond the far doorway into the hall. "Ken?"

"Amy!" Lis called sharply. "Stay out! Get out of the house, fast!"

The door swung open and Amy stepped into the room. She was wearing a white, floor-length gown, perfectly transparent, and her hair had been brushed, new makeup applied, her face shining with a smile of anticipation.

She faltered on the doorsill, seeing Harold. One hand went to her throat in a convulsive gesture of shock. "I—thought I heard—"

Harold swung partway toward her, the knife describing a broad arc. "Stand back! Don't move! Don't come any closer!"

Amy's eyes began to swivel from him and the ugly knife back toward Lis. In the same split-second, Lis saw every aspect of the tactical situation. Harold was almost exactly halfway between them, his attention momentarily divided. His eyes had gone even wilder with alarm. He was going to strike any instant. Amy was frozen, defenseless and unmoving, and as the latest entry into the scene might be the object of the first instinctive surge of attack.

Beyond this, Lis saw that Harold's eyes had gone toward Amy in this fraction of time—were not watching him.

And the path to the nightstand, and the gun, would never be clearer.

Lis moved.

Harold screamed something incomprehensible and lunged after him.

Lis was already at the little table by the bed, had the drawer jerked open, plunged his hand inside for the revolver—fumbling for it. Harold closed the gap and started around the end of the bed, the knife raised. Amy screamed and rushed forward, hurling herself at the youth and knocking him sideways, momentarily off balance. The two of them tangled and fell to the floor. Harold was still screaming obscenities and thrashing around, and then Amy cried out and seemed to be hurled back away from him on the floor. Harold scrambled to hands and knees, bringing the knife up, but it was different now. It threw heavy red gobs of something . . . Amy's blood.

Lis slammed the cylinder of the .38 closed and swung it upward. He had had grave moral doubts about ever buying this gun. It had never been fired. With a spasmodic motion he pulled the trigger and it fired now. The bullet hit Harold somewhere in the front of his body, hurling him backward. The bloody knife clattered against the wall. Lis squeezed the trigger again, and then again, the deafening explosions unleashing something terrible within him. The bullets smashed Harold twice more, rolling him over onto his side. He twitched and lay still.

Shocked almost senseless by the noise and violence and stench of cordite suddenly filling the room, Lis turned in what seemed a hideous slow-motion action to look at where his wife had fallen. She lay flat on her back, one arm thrown outward, her eyes staring at him. She tried to say something. It came out a moan.

Lis threw himself to his knees beside her. She was conscious and in pain but could not seem to speak. There was blood everywhere—such a lot of blood—clotting the filmy material of the pretty gown, puddling on the floor. More blood was pumping out of her abdomen with an awful force.

"Oh, God," Lis said. "Oh, Christ." He hauled the bedspread off the bed and tried to wad some of it up and press it against the wound. It became drenched and hot instantly, and still the blood came. He was sobbing words that didn't make any sense.

The telephone.

He ran to the bedside extension, picked up the receiver, and punched the O. He waited. He was half out of his mind. The telephone buzzed, signaling a ring. It buzzed again. *Oh, Jesus Christ, come on—*

"Operator. May I help you?" The woman sounded bored.

"Get me the police! Get an ambulance! Emergency!"

"Sir, those numbers are listed in your—"

"God damn you! My wife has been stabbed and she's dying and I just killed a man! I'm at 30118 Poplar. Have you got that?"

"Yes sir," the woman said. She didn't sound bored now. "That's 30118 Poplar?"

"Yes! An ambulance! A doctor! The police! Hurry!" He dropped the telephone and ran back to Amy's side. He pressed more bedding against the wound. This seemed to help. He was crying.

She opened her eyes and tried to smile. ". . . not the welcome . . . I expected . . . darling."

"Just be still," Lis begged her. "There's help on the way. You'll be all right."

"I helped you," she whispered.

"My God, yes! You saved my life! Now be quiet, honey, *please*— don't try to talk—save your strength."

She obeyed. Her eyes closed. In the far distance came the sound of sirens.

18

The trip in the ambulance was the stuff of nightmare; Lis hunched helplessly in a corner, the windows bathed in flashing red light, two paramedics bent over the stretcher bearing Amy, one working on her while the other talked in rapid-fire question and answer to the emergency room ahead. Two police cars had arrived simultaneously with the ambulance, and two more had arrived as the ambulance departed. An unmarked car, a portable red flasher stuck to its top by magnetic clamps, could be seen through the back windows of the ambulance on the way to the hospital, and when the crew whisked Amy immediately into a treatment room, Lis was approached by a thickset man who identified himself as a local police detective named Mahoney.

"Can you tell us what happened there at the house, Mr. Lis?"

In his anxiety, Lis wanted to lash out. But he managed to control himself and tell briefly what happened.

"The dead man," Mahoney said. "He was part-time gardening around the neighborhood, you say?"

"He's dead?" Lis said. "I killed him?"

Mahoney appeared concerned and perplexed. "It was self-defense, wasn't it?"

"Is that supposed to make you feel better about killing a man?"

Sympathetic, the detective asked more questions: how Amy had been hurt, how long Lis had owned the gun, whether it was registered. But most of the questions were about Harold Smith, and Lis could not answer them.

"Unless memory fails me," Mahoney said thoughtfully, "there was a case something like this in the state of New York earlier in the summer. I remember the mail on it because the guy was a prominent businessman and the local authorities were looking for a yard boy who had disappeared. Funny, history repeating itself."

A doctor came from the emergency room to tell Lis that they were taking Amy to surgery.

"What is it?" Lis demanded. "How bad is it?"

"We can't tell a lot more until we get into surgery. But right now it looks quite hopeful, sir. It appears to be a slash wound that didn't penetrate any of the vital organs."

"Thank God! How long before you're *sure?*"

The doctor looked dubious. "Possibly an hour, sir. Now there are some consent forms we have to have you fill out. . . ."

Less than an hour later, she was in the recovery room. A doctor—a different one—smiled as he approached Lis in the waiting room and confirmed earlier guesswork. "She's a lucky lady. An inch deeper and we would have had very serious problems."

"But she's going to be all right?"

"It certainly looks that way, Mr. Lis. She should be out of recovery in another hour, and perhaps you can speak briefly to her. She's going to be in here a few days, and then she'll be mighty sore in the abdominal region for a while. But we don't anticipate any difficulty."

It was past midnight when he was finally allowed into her room. Woozy from the anesthetic and injections, she smiled and kissed him with slightly bluish, cold lips. Then she slept. Lis stayed firmly in the chair beside the bed, watching with fatigue-sticky eyes.

In the morning she was conscious but in some pain. She ate a special breakfast and a doctor came by, then her own physician a little later. The police were back—a different detective—with more questions. Lis telephoned Amy's sister and brother and reassured them.

The injury to Amy Lis and the killing of the intruder dominated local news coverage that Saturday morning, and by 9 A.M. Lis, still at the hospital, had to contend with three reporters. Shortly afterward, Barton MacIvor and Kelley Hemingway arrived together, followed only minutes later by Janis Malone, and then by both Dean Busch and Bert Jerno. Busch had talked with Lydia Baines in San Francisco, and she asked Lis to call her there at his earliest opportunity. It was mid-morning before he had a chance to do so.

"Amy is definitely all right?" Lydia asked at once.

"I've just been with her, and Pappy is with her now. Yes, Lydia, she's fine. They say she was awfully lucky."

"Ken, you sound exhausted."

"I've found that hospital chairs don't make very good beds."

"Anything Amy needs—special nursing care, whatever—please don't hesitate to order them and have all the billing done to the company."

"Thanks, Lydia. I think we're out of the woods."

"You sound like you need to go somewhere and sleep."

"I intend to do that very shortly."

"I'm sure MacIvor can oversee any Excalibur testing scheduled for the early part of the week."

This idea surprised him. "If Amy is doing as well as I think, there doesn't seem to be any reason why I can't be on the job Monday."

"If that works out, fine. But please don't sacrifice caring for her."

"I won't, Lydia," Lis said. "You can be sure of it."

At noon he was staggering. He paid Amy another visit and headed home.

The police had been thorough in locking up, and the cleaning lady, contacted from the hospital, had done a reasonably good job of cleaning things up in the front bedroom. Two ghastly dark stains persisted in the carpet despite obvious attempts to scrub them out. Lis took one look, then closed the door and went to the front bedroom, where he fell across Amy's bed and slept until almost six.

When he reached the hospital again, he found several familiar faces in the waiting room. One was the first detective, Mahoney, who said it was possible that the youth slain by Lis was the same who had killed a man in New York.

"Funny thing," Mahoney said. "His name was Trenor, and he had something to do with airplanes too."

It clicked in Lis's memory. "Nolan Trenor?"

"Yes, sounds right." Mahoney cocked his head. "You know him?"

"He was an officer in Transwestern. That's the airline company. He and I worked together in negotiating their purchase of some airplanes from us about a year ago."

Mahoney snapped his fingers. "May be more here than I thought. I'll be back to you later."

Lis went in to see his wife. She was partially sitting up, the head of the bed having been cranked up part way, and her color was almost normal.

"You look better," she told him, surprising him.

"I was going to say the same thing." He kissed her.

"My middle hurts."

"God, Amy, it was a close thing!"

"I was scared out of my wits."

"*You* were scared! When I saw the blood—!"

"But you stopped him."

"Yes," Lis agreed somberly. "I stopped him."

"My poor dear. It had to be awful for you."

"It's behind us, Amy. I'm going to keep it there."

She brightened. "They say I might get out of this place by the middle of the week. I'm all for that. The last time I was in here, I vowed never again."

"This will be the last time."

"Yes!"

They watched one another, holding hands.

"Ken," she said after a while, "I don't want you to let this interfere with your work. I know how badly you need to do these new tests."

"Assuming you're still feeling fine," he said, "I thought I would try to operate normally once Monday rolls around. I'll come by here on the way to work, and be back at lunchtime and in the evening. But we do need to run those tests."

"That's fine. And you can skip that morning visit if you want to. You know I'm always grouchy in the morning."

He grinned at her, loving her. "Not as grouchy as I'll be in the evenings if we don't find something pretty soon!"

He could not know that he would have the answer in less than forty-eight hours.

19

A thin layer of cloud obscured the sun Monday morning when Ken Lis walked out of the Hempstead Aviation MA Building and onto the tarmac ramp. The test Excalibur was already surrounded by electronics vehicles, fuel trucks, fire-protection units, and swarms of workers and technicians. Lis spied Hank Selvy, Barton MacIvor, and Jace Mattingly in earnest conversation under the sleek nose of the aircraft, and walked over to join them.

"Just going through the drill for today," Selvy said looking up from his clipboard.

"Fine," Lis said. "Go ahead."

"Nothing real unusual. We're a little heavier-loaded this time and we've got the CG just as far back as it can go and still be in the safety envelope. Everything is at thirty thousand or whatever alternate assigned by Denver Center. Test one, approach to landing stall, full stall break with asymmetric power reduction, port side lagging. Test two, approach to landing stall, full stall break with asymmetric power reduction, starboard side lagging. Test three, approach to landing stall, full break, kick left rudder. Test four, approach to landing stall, full break, kick right rudder. Test five—"

"No changes from the protocol, then?" Lis interrupted.

"No."

"Let's get going."

There was no social talk as they climbed aboard. All that had taken place in the coffee shop an hour earlier. There was nothing left now but the tests, and the tension they shared. Each of those maneuvers had been tried before, in largely the same circumstances, without making the test airplane show any bad manners whatsoever. But they could not relent on the testing now, of all times. And it had been—obviously—at a time when no one expected it that Excalibur had failed twice before.

About half the test instrumentation had been removed from the back for the latest tests, but the bare aluminum floor, studded with rivets, was awash in thick black electrical cables running in all directions. A half dozen engineers were at work in front of a computer console installed more or less permanently on one cabin-area wall, and two others were coaxing readings from circular scopes and instruments with glowing green digital readouts.

"Better strap in," Lis called to them. "We're going to kick the tire and light the fire today."

Up on the flight deck, some sick radios had been replaced, with the result that the usual odors of plastic and oil and sweat were overlaid by the sharp smell of resin-core solder. Both pilot and first-officer seats had been removed to facilitate tearing out some of the panels, and different chairs had been installed on completion in response to Selvy's continuing complaints about balky slide mechanisms on his back. The old seats had been dark red; the new ones, beige, appeared otherwise identical. The engineer's seat remained the old color, and a couple of jury-rigged stools, covered with black padding, had been bolted into the narrow aisle behind the control pedestal. The result was a cabin that looked like a plumber's nightmare.

Selvy seemed not to notice. Climbing over the console, he dropped into his pilot's chair and reached down for the slide-up handle even as Lis was clambering up beside him. Selvy depressed the seat control and rocked the chair forward. Nothing. It did not move. He rocked harder. Again, nothing.

"God damn it," he muttered, and began shoving forward and back so violently that the entire airplane could be felt to tremble.

"You know," Lis said, "you must have a genius for breaking these seats."

"The track is no damned good," Selvy fumed.

Lis reached down and touched his control. His seat slid forward and upward with soft, silent precision. "No problem on this side."

"Pappy," Selvy said, punctuating every few words with another spasm of effort to get his chair out of the far-back position, "why can't a man . . . of your talent . . . dream up a seat . . . that *works?*" As he finished the question, the seat broke loose and slid up about a third of the way, then seemed to jam again. At this point it simply would not move in any direction.

Selvy tested his reach with arms and legs. He was back farther than normal, and bitched about it. Lis said they could postpone until a new seat could be installed. Selvy said he would hack it, and prepared to light the engines. Twelve minutes later, they were taxiing off the ramp and toward the field's only paved runway.

It was crowded on the flight deck. Selvy and Lis were in the front seats, of course, and an alternate test-plane engineer named Trent was in the seat that faced the side and his wall of instrumentation. Mattingly and MacIvor were belted to the stools in the aisle, hanging on for dear life even at slow taxi. They reached the end of the runway and turned onto it, taxiing into position to hold as the make-shift tower—an engineer atop the MA building with binoculars and a walkie-talkie—suggested. Selvy and Lis continued with their checklist.

"Rear baggage-door light," Trent sang out.

"What?" Selvy said, leaning back.

Trent pointed to a red lamp aglow on the overhead panel. "Rear baggage-door light."

Selvy bared his teeth in irritation. "Cycle the switch."

Trent reached up and flicked a silver toggle back and forth repeatedly. The red light remained obstinately aglow.

"Well, shit," Selvy said after a moment's thought. He touched the throttles, advancing the port engine, and Excalibur began to turn back off the runway.

"Crew, get ready to check our back baggage door," Lis said into the radiomicrophone. "We're got a red light."

They taxied back, and the crewmen climbed up and opened and reslammed and latched the large metal door near the tail. The yellow light, when the detector circuit was again activated, blinked once and went out. The red light stayed dark. Selvy taxied Excalibur again.

This time the remainder of the checklist went flawlessly. Muttering to himself, Selvy shoved his chart folder, about three inches thick, in between his back and the recalcitrant-chair back while Ken Lis made conversation with San Francisco for routing out of the area. Wishing for a smoke, Jace Mattingly clung to his aisle perch beside Barton MacIvor and tried to overhear details of Lis's conversation. He failed.

Lis, however, supplied it after more talk back and forth including Selvy. "We've got a choice of a long straight-out to the west and climb back to come inland again at over twenty-eight thousand, or we can hook it around sharply to the south and save probably fifteen minutes. We're going to have to really stomp on it to get altitude quickly enough on the southbound leg. If anybody tends to get airsick, we'll take the longer route. Speak now, or forever hold it down." He was talking into the microphone that connected him to the engineers in the back, as well as to those on the deck.

"I'd say let's get it on," Mattingly said.

Lis was listening on his headphones. He keyed his mike again. "Nothing heard from the back. Anything heard from up front? Okay. We'll make up the time we lost with the door, then." He changed microphones to notify San Francisco of the election, and already the impatient Hank Selvy was adding power to all three engines.

Barton MacIvor nudged Mattingly and leaned close. "You don't git a takeoff like the one you'll be seein' now on a commercial flight."

"I'm ready." Mattingly smiled.

"Aye, good. An' you'll be seeing some of what Excalibur can do."

It was routine for all the rest of them, but Mattingly felt a stronger pulse of anticipation rising with the thunderous roar of the distant jet engines. Maybe this flight would change their luck, he thought. Maybe this would be the time when finally that elusive glitch showed itself. And whether it did or not, at least he was here, on the scene, taking as active a part as possible in this phase of the search. He expected a long and tiring day, but he was up for it.

With a few terse words, Hank Selvy released the brakes and let Excalibur begin to roll. The pavement in front of the down-canted nose seemed close enough to touch, and it moved very slowly for a few seconds. Then it began to move faster, and the grass off the edges of the asphalt started to become a blur. Over the roar, Ken Lis was calling out speeds and distances. Hank Selvy sat square to the control yoke, shoulders braced, his head straight ahead with intense concentration. Excalibur skimmed and bumped over humps in the pavement now, and half the runway had been used up. The old pilot's cliché went rapidly through Mattingly's mind: *"There are two things that will never help: the sky above you and the runway behind you."*

As the thought passed, Ken Lis said something sharply. Both pilots pulled back firmly, steadily, on their control yokes. The nose of Excalibur rose majestically as the great aircraft rotated, lifting its nose wheel, changing drastically the angle at which the wing was attacking the air. By all the laws of aerodynamics, increasing the angle of attack would make the wing fly. . . .

And fly it did. Excalibur seemed to *leap* off the ground. With a speed and sharpness that almost unnerved Mattingly, the plane was airborne and, hanging on her nose, clawing for altitude. He glanced outside and saw the field and then the hills dropping away like those views taken from the tail of a rocket in flight, and then he got a glimpse of the altimeters on Lis's side of the panel; one was going around too fast to read, and the other's digital readout was constantly changing as numbers increased.

Hank Selvy laid Excalibur on her side. Suddenly, out the one window there was nothing but cloud, and out the other was a view straight down to the pinwheeling earth. Mattingly's cheeks and jowls sagged painfully under the force of the Gs. He wondered if he was going to be sick after all, and even as he wondered, the tightness of the turn *increased*, making him hurt more. *These people are crazy. This* was the performance of an airplane grounded for alleged lack of safety?

As quickly as it had begun, the sharp bank ended. Excalibur rolled back level again, in terms of its lateral axis, nose still high. Mattingly saw that Selvy had on full power, his hand holding the ganged throttles full forward, while Lis had gotten the gear up and the flaps retracted. The slat-wing control, however, remained also fully forward, giving the wing maximum lift for this full-performance climb-out dictated by the radar control center.

Mattingly managed to get another glimpse out the window. The earth was far below now, and they had climbed over the Rockies. He saw Ken Lis flick a switch, and was startled when the voice came from the ceiling loudspeaker: *"Hempstead test one, we show you at twenty-four thousand, and your traffic at zero niner zero degrees is American Flight 40, inbound San Francisco, at fourteen thousand."*

Lis said something in reply that no one else could hear.

Then: "*Hempstead test, this is American 40. You guys look like you're in some kind of hurry today.*"

Lis grinned and said something monosyllabic. He was looking off to the right side and down, and Mattingly caught a brief flash of sunlight on aluminum that must have been American Flight 40.

Looking uncomfortable, Selvy twisted up in his seat a bit, said something to Lis, and allowed the yoke to move forward slightly. The plane began to ease out of its steep climb. At the same time, Selvy began slipping the ganged throttles back inch by inch, and as the engine sounds changed and the world began to be right side up again, Mattingly saw that they had left the gauze layer of cloud far below. They were in clear blue air and nearing a level flight configuration. Selvy pulled the throttles farther back.

Suddenly everything went wrong.

The first warning was an explosion of flickering, flashing lights, like fireworks all over the overhead panels. Before anyone could react in any way, the control yokes began buffeting violently forward and back. Selvy yelled something. A loud horn klaxoned. There was a thumping sound of some kind, and then the long, needle nose of Excalibur pitched majestically forward, and the whole sky went up past the window, and Jace Mattingly's stomach came up in his throat as earth wheeled past the front windscreen.

The klaxon was still blaring and lights flashing. At the engineer's position, Trent's hands flew to switches but seemingly to no avail. Mattingly saw Selvy and Lis both hook forearms over forward-position control yokes and start drawing back. Selvy had full power restored. Slowly Excalibur began to recover. The earth righted itself again. Mattingly felt a new downward tug at his jaws as the plane came out of rapid descent, putting several Gs on itself and everything inside.

"Okay," Lis said sharply, "airspeed is one eighty."

"Straight and level," Selvy said.

"Stall system on, armed, normal," Trent called.

"Go see how they came through it in the back," Lis ordered, and Trent unbuckled from his chair and climbed past Mattingly and MacIvor to go to the back cabin.

"What made 'er stall?" MacIvor asked, bewildered.

"I don't know," Lis said, scanning instruments. "She seems okay now—"

The overhead loudspeaker squawked: *"Hey, Hempstead test, where did you go?"*

Lis picked up his mike. "We're okay, American. We just lost some altitude."

"Looked like you flat fell out of the sky!"

"We're okay; thanks for your concern."

Selvy pointed to the now-quiescent altimeters. "You know how much altitude we lost in about five seconds? Almost three thousand feet."

"I still don't know what happened," Mattingly admitted huskily.

"Nobody knows what happened! Jesus, we were coming out of our climb perfectly normally, and all of a sudden we got a full stall!"

"But why?" Lis demanded, turning to stare at MacIvor.

The old man slowly shook his head. "I don't know, lad."

Selvy clicked the autopilot on and sat back in his chair, dazedly rubbing his right elbow and forearm. "We were well above normal slat-wing stall speed."

"We got the lights, the horn, and the warning buffet virtually simultaneously," Lis said.

"Don't I know it!"

"So she stalled very suddenly—very fast."

"I still can't believe it," Selvy said. "After all the times of trying to make it stall, there it is, just like that—like a rattler from under a rock."

"When we least expected it," Lis said grimly.

"Just like those landing accidents." Selvy continued to rub his arm. He held it up and examined it, frowning. "I banged myself," he said, displaying a red welt near the elbow.

Jace Mattingly looked at him, looked at the welt, and had a tingling flash of insight. "For the love of God!"

Lis, Selvy, and MacIvor all stared at him.

"You can turn this thing around," Mattingly told them. "We don't need any more tests today." He smacked his forehead with his palm. "God! That it could be this simple—so damned, unbelievably, impossibly *simple!*"

"You think you know what happened just now?" Lis asked sharply.

"Yes," Mattingly said. "Get us back to the field and on the ground and I'll show you. I *know*, I know!"

435

here was a brief colloquy about returning immediately to the
Hempstead field, and Lis ruled that they should terminate the
flight at once whether Jace Mattingly really had the solution to the
long-standing puzzle or not.

"For Christ sake, Jace," he said as Selvy banked the plane, "if you
know the answer, after all these weeks of agony—!"

"Let us get it back on the ground," Mattingly pleaded, "and I'll
show you. If I don't demonstrate for you, you won't believe it!"

"Yer not grandstandin'?" Barton MacIvor growled.

"No, sir, I'm definitely not!"

They flew back quickly enough, descending through heat haze and
light smog in a straight-in approach over the city. Hank Selvy flew
the Excalibur with exaggerated caution now, keeping her far over the
normal stall speed. Mattingly watched him carefully, intent on warning him if he got near another dangerous situation, but Selvy did not
do so. The landing and taxi were uneventful.

After shutting down the engines near the MA Building, Lis went
to the back of the plane briefly to confer with the technicians, and
then, through the exit door, with someone on the ground. Trent was
given some debriefing chores, and left the flight deck. When Lis
came back, it was the four of them in the rapidly heating cabin: Lis,
Selvy, MacIvor, Mattingly.

"Okay," Lis said. "Let's have it."

"I'd like to change places with you, Hank," Mattingly said.

Selvy shrugged and climbed awkwardly out of the stuck seat and
over the center console. Once he was in the aisle, Mattingly climbed

the other direction to take his pilot's seat. It was so far back that he couldn't reach the rudder pedals.

He grabbed the yoke and shook it. *"Thruum! Thruum!"* he said.

"He's gone daft," MacIvor said.

"Sorry," Mattingly said. "I'm just so damned stunned and delighted—"

"Let us in on it," Lis said in a tone that said he was losing patience.

Mattingly took a deep breath and complied. Holding the yoke with his left hand, he turned to his right and touched the star-shaped knob of the slat-control lever behind the ganged throttles. "Okay. Let's say we're on approach. The flaps are down, gear is down, throttles are well back, and this little dude, the slat control, is full forward. Right?"

"Sure," Hank Selvy said, staring hard as if still worried that Mattingly might have flipped.

"Okay," Mattingly said. He moved his hand to the throttles. "Now. Let's say we're on approach and we're just a little high near the fence. What do we do?"

"Probably nothing," Selvy grunted. "You've usually got a thousand-foot landing envelope down the runway. You just sit there and let her settle in."

"But you *might* slightly reduce power, right?"

"Well, yes," Selvy said.

"Okay," Mattingly said. He started drawing his right hand back with the throttles. "This much?"

"Yeah," Selvy said.

Mattingly raised his arm and looked at them triumphantly.

"What?" Ken Lis said, baffled.

None of them saw it.

"The slat-control lever!" Mattingly said. "*Look* at the mother!"

Selvy, Lis, and MacIvor leaned forward to look.

"Wasn't that lever full forward?" Selvy asked sharply.

"Yes," Lis said. "And it's *moved.*"

Mattingly shoved the slat-control lever fully forward, readjusted the throttles, and again went through the procedure for retarding power. "Watch my arm, back near my elbow."

As he drew the throttles slightly backward, his forearm pressed

437

down against the slat-control lever, moving it back an equal amount. This time, everyone saw it.

"For *God's* sake!" Selvy said.

"You took 20 per cent of the slats off!" Lis said.

Showers of sparks fell over MacIvor's chest as the pipe almost fell from his mouth.

Mattingly banged his palms on the control yoke in jubilation. "You get it? You get it? Hank gave it away when he rubbed his arm. He bonged the slat knob with it, moving it back as he began retarding power, but when the lever moved there was instant stall and he was so shook up by that, he didn't realize what had happened."

Lis put a hand to his forehead. "*Of course* the plane will stall at a low speed if the slats are partially closed! And if the same thing happened at New York—and Pittsburgh—but hold on! Didn't you get the center pedestal out intact at Pittsburgh? Wasn't the slat lever in normal, full-open position?"

"Yes. But witnesses had already told us that the plane there started a partial recovery. Hank, isn't checking the slat handle part of your standard stall recovery in this plane?"

"Sure it is," Selvy replied. "Slats full open, release back pressure, full throttle, gear up, flaps up."

"They had time to slam the lever back to the right position, then," Mattingly concluded. "So there was nothing for us to find in the wreckage."

"But they didn't have time," Lis said, "to get flying again, because they were simply too low."

"Only, there's a wee problem, lads," Barton MacIvor said.

They all turned to look at him.

"We ordinarily use only 70 per cent slats fer a landing," the old man said. "Yer arm didna move the handle far enough to git it outside that range."

"Well, sure," Mattingly said after a few seconds of total silence. "But let's think about it. Both crashes came in marginal weather, at busy airports. Let's imagine the crew on approach, maybe a little late, on an ILS. Maybe, groping for the ground, they use a little more slat, to allow for a slower approach on short final. That's not restricted in the manual, is it?"

MacIvor scowled. It was Lis who answered. "I remember the wording in that section exactly. We say *normal* slat position is 70 per cent, but full slats are available. We give throttle and speed settings for full slats."

"So," Mattingly said, "I'm betting both crews were on full slats and flying just as slow as they felt they dared. Then, they were a little high, and the weather is crappy, and a go-around will mean another twenty minutes minimum, so the pilot eases off a little power."

"And he has no margin to work with, and he gets a stall the instant his arm nudges the slat lever," Lis said. "Good Lord!"

"It fits the facts," Mattingly said. "We couldn't find anything wrong with the aircraft because there wasn't anything wrong with it. It was an accident of hitting this lever in unusual circumstances."

"But wait a minute," Selvy said. "I've flown this dude a million times. How come I never hit the lever before?"

"Maybe," Mattingly said, "you never flew with the seat so far back.

"The seat!" Selvy said. "The goddam, miserable, maladjusted seat! Sure! With it back the way this one is stuck, you're not only back nearer the lever; the seat is *lower* on the track, so the chances of your elbow hitting it are enhanced that way, too!"

"I think maybe that's what happened," Mattingly said. "I can't be absolutely certain, but I think the maintenance report on the Pittsburgh Excalibur showed some work had been done on the flight-deck seats at least once."

"God only knows how many times they whanged on it themselves to get it going," Selvy said.

"So," Lis said, "maybe in both cases the pilot's seat was not quite ideally situated. I don't mean it was stuck all the way back—no one would be idiot enough to fly a real mission with it jammed all the way to the rear—"

"But it could have been messed up a little," Selvy said.

"Which gives you a damned strange combination of coincidences," Mattingly added. "A seat messed up on its track, an approach in bad weather, a slightly *high* approach, necessitating throttle retardation—"

"And the guy's arm happens to bonk the slat lever," Selvy said.

"His arm, or his sleeve."

"The sleeve could do it," Selvy agreed. "That knob has those sharp little star-shaped projections on it; it could catch easily."

"We thought we were adding a safety factor when we put that unusual shape on the slat knob," Lis said. "No other control feels anything like it. We wanted to make sure no pilot ever grabbed for it by touch and pulled on it thinking he had hold of something else."

"But what you actually did," Mattingly said, "was to—"

"Make it easier for it to hang up on a coat sleeve," Lis finished.

"No wonder we couldn't find it," Selvy said. "It was a goddam fluke!"

"It might never have happened again," Lis agreed.

"Aye," MacIvor rumbled. "Or it might have happened ten times in a row. Odds are a little funny, lad. The chances of this happening must be on the order of one in ten million. Only, it happened twice and it might've happened again any time."

The men stood or sat very still. It was stifling hot in the cockpit and they were all bathed in sweat.

"A stupid little design flaw," Lis said. "A jagged shape on a handle."

"And a crummy seat-tracking system," Selvy added.

"Which will be fixed damned fast."

"Lads," MacIvor said, "let's git out of here and have some tea."

They climbed out. On the ground, the warm breeze felt cool after the intense heat of the flight deck.

Walking to the main building with the others, Mattingly actually felt weak in the knees. The aftermath of the excitement would probably stay in his memory as long as he lived. He could not wait to call Pierce. It was going to become a very famous story around the agency, no doubt about it.

"Well, we could have looked forever," Lis said as they entered the air conditioning. "You did it, Jace."

"I wonder if we could possibly have considered cockpit arrangement sooner if I hadn't been thrown off the lead by what Scott Persons told me in the hospital," Mattingly said.

"The Pittsburgh pilot?" Lis frowned. "Yes. Why would he say the brakes caught? He must have been delirious."

"When I think of all the time and effort spent checking spoilers and flaps—"

"Maybe," Hank Selvy said, "that wasn't what he said."

"No, Hank, I heard him."

Selvy held up his right forearm. "Right along here, on the TW uniforms, members of the flight crew have strips of heavy gold braid.

Three for the captain, two for the copilot, one for the engineer. Pretty thick stuff. It could have caught the handle. Maybe it was even frayed, or coming loose."

Mattingly tumbled. "Then, Persons wasn't saying the *brakes* caught—"

"He was saying *the braid* caught."

"And the other tapes, from Kennedy," Mattingly said. "I remember that one shout—I've played it a hundred times—it sounded like, '*The antel cough.*'"

"The handle caught," Selvy translated instantly.

"We had it all right there in front of us. We just couldn't see it."

"Every plane," MacIvor said, "is a brand new ball game."

"But we're cleared now," Lis said triumphantly.

"You know the board," Mattingly cautioned. "It only deals in verifiable facts, not supposition. But when we've shown how this control lever hangs up, and add the other circumstantial evidence, they can't reasonably keep Excalibur on the ground once some modification is made on the seat and/or the slat-control lever."

Lis held the door to the main building. "That's good enough for me, gentlemen."

Once inside, they started for MacIvor's office and some "tay." But Mattingly begged off for a minute to make a telephone call.

Actually, he made two.

The first, to Pierce, took almost ten minutes.

The second, to Nell, was more brief.

"We found it," Mattingly told her when she came on the line.

"Oh, Jace."

"It wasn't pilot error, Nell. No one will ever be able to say that again. It was a design flaw on a control."

"Jace, that's wonderful. Thank you. Thank you. And you're calling me from California to let me know at once?"

"Yes. We just got back on the ground. Are you happy, Nell?"

"Yes!"

He hesitated, but then he had to say it. "When I get back to Washington, Nell—I would like to see you again."

She did not reply at once. He knew her thought: there was no longer an excuse for them to meet. And so finally it was in the open between them, and he held his breath.

When the silence lingered, he had to say something more. "I want to be your friend, Nell. I won't rush you. But I want to see you and be with you and see the kids."

There was another, slighter pause, and then she said, "I think that would be very nice, Jace. Because I want to see you again too."

21

The atmosphere in the board room at Hempstead Aviation was far different from any recent meeting, when key personnel gathered on order of Lydia Baines three days later. Those attending were Ken Lis, as chief of the suddenly viable Airplane Division; Kelley Hemingway, as head of Consumer Products; Aerospace Chief Dean Busch; Seymour Trepps, Bert Jerno, Richard Cazzell.

Lydia, looking cool and lovely, walked in briskly on the stroke of the appointed hour of ten. Placing a few thin folders on the table before her chair, she remained standing.

"Ken, good morning," she said, giving him a particularly bright smile. "Good morning, everyone. This is spur-of-the-moment, but I have just quite a lot of good news that I wanted to share with all of you without delay. And we have some decisions to make."

She picked a copy of *The Wall Street Journal* out of one of her folders and held it up. Lis, like everyone else in the room, knew the contents of the top-right story almost by heart. The story, leaked by persons unknown within hours of the Excalibur discovery, reflected with remarkable accuracy what was wrong with the controls and how simple it would be to make modifications.

"This story," Lydia said, "continues to pay incredible dividends for us. I've just been informed informally—a letter is to follow—that Excalibur's grounding order is being lifted as of midnight tonight, the only proviso being that suitable safety changes have to be incorporated to prevent the kind of mistake we found in our testing here."

There was a general murmur of pleasure and approval. Several pairs of eyes turned to Lis with congratulation.

"Really great news," Dean Busch exclaimed. "Tremendous! Now all I want to know is, how long will it take us to make the necessary modifications?"

Lis replied, "We already have a new slat-control-lever handle drawn. Pappy has people fabricating a special seat track that ought to end sticking problems once and for all. As soon as we get the seat-track devices built—probably later today—we'll start testing them. But we ought to have prototypes of both fixes in Washington before the end of the week."

"And in the meantime," Lydia said, "we can begin delivery of planes again immediately. As you remember, we have two aircraft for Transwestern that have been ready for weeks. A call a little while ago from TW headquarters said they'll fly two test crews in within hours, and they'll fly the Excaliburs to Oklahoma City to start refitting."

"TW plans to start flying Excalibur again as soon as cleared?" Kelley Hemingway asked gladly.

"Not only that," Lis told her. "That new order that's seemed a mirage on the horizon now looks firmer than it ever has. Off the record, the NTSB call should have cinched it. We should have a new TW order for eighteen more Excaliburs before Friday."

"That's grand news, Ken!" Lydia said. "And I believe you told me that Sales is very excited about indicators from Delta and United."

"Delta, United, TWA, and Eastern," Lis corrected her. "They're all receptive again. I personally believe we have an order for thirty-six from United sewed up right now."

"Three dozen?" Bert Jerno said. "That will keep us busy awhile!"

"It's only beginning again," Lydia said smiling. "We have a long way to go yet, but quick leaking of that information to the press was one of the smartest things we ever did."

"We were the source?" Bert Jerno asked. "I heard we disclaimed any knowledge of *how* it got—"

"Of course we disclaimed it, Bert," Lydia said. "The NTSB is not at all happy to have details of their probe in the newspapers before their own reports are written or new dates selected for public hearings. But we needed the relief at once, and it was handled very discreetly . . . through the office of a friend of mine in Washington.

It will never be traced back to us. And as a result, we not only have the good effects of the news at once, as you've just heard; in addition it's my understanding that the board is now under pressure to set the hearings on both the New York and Pittsburgh crashes for the middle of next month."

"Of course," Lis pointed out guardedly, "we won't be entirely vindicated in the hearings."

"No," Lydia said frowning, "that's true. Both crashes appear to have been caused by accidental snagging of a control. Fixing the control is simple enough. The orders are already flowing again, so we have a future. However, as to lawsuits—" She looked toward Bert Jerno. "What's the situation there?"

Jerno puffed out his cheeks. "The latest tally in the Legal Department shows three hundred and eighty-some lawsuits already filed, of which almost half are against Hempstead Aviation."

"People suing for wrongful-death damages in both crashes," Lydia said. "I think, unfortunately, that the total cases will go even higher."

"They can't win these cases," Jerno said. "They can't prove negligence on our part."

"Who can predict what a damage-suit jury might do these days?" Lydia countered.

"Well," Jerno said reluctantly, "that's true. . . ."

"We have to face the reality of more lawsuits, and some catastrophic decisions in a few of them," Lydia said. "And that's the other side of the coin."

"You mean," Richard Cazzell said speaking for the first time, "the other reason you asked us to meet today?"

Lydia's eyes hardened. "We now know what caused the crashes. Excalibur is in the process of being cleared. Orders are starting again. But it's no time for undue celebration. These lawsuits will continue for years, if not decades, and the dollars drain will be severe. We *must* economize in every way possible."

For a long minute no one responded, and Lis sensed the renewed tension in the room. None of them even yet knew this woman well. What was she driving at?

She did not make them wait to find out. "I have some preliminary ideas," she said, tension clipping her words. "I think, Dean, we will have to consider some major personnel cutbacks in Aerospace, at least until a new major project is on the boards. Consumer Products, Kelley, is simply going to have to start pulling its weight or face a phase-out." She turned toward Seymour Trepps. "Ocean Research *must* come up with a new government contract or it will fast become a luxury we can't afford."

Again no one spoke. In a handful of words this remarkable woman had raised the prospect of doom for every division of the company with the exception of Airplane. *And she would do it.*

It was Bert Jerno who spoke. "You make it appear we face . . . drastic measures, Lydia."

"I don't know if anyone realizes just how drastic, Bert," Lydia replied. "No one is likely to be unaffected. You and Richard, for example, must be ready to combine your divisions into one, and take on certain other duties that heretofore have been handled in the branches at Laredo and Nashville."

"You're not thinking of closing the branches!"

"Most definitely. We can do all billing and sales out of San Jose. The public-information and PR functions will be *better* handled here."

"This is not just a belt-tightening operation," Jerno said. He was pale and slick with sweat now. "This is a—a real cutback."

"That's what I've been trying to say," Lydia replied.

Again silence fell. Lis knew that this was not a quick decision on Lydia's part, nor was it motivated entirely by the threat of more lawsuits perhaps extending over a period of years. No, this was a major and sustained upheaval in the structure of the entire company, and it had probably been in Lydia's mind since the day she took office.

"You look glum, Ken," Lydia said.

"Shouldn't I?"

"It's no time to give in to despair. It may be difficult, but the way you have Airplane flying again, we'll come out of this in fine shape. We all just have to continue thinking reorganization and economy. I didn't want us to forget that in the glow of our present upturn in fortunes."

"You have some immediate instructions?" Lis asked.

"Yes," Lydia said coolly. "For each of you." She opened a folder and studied its contents—a single sheet of paper—for a moment.

"Kelley," she said then. "It's unfortunate that you and Dean have to take the brunt of some actions after you've been in new jobs such a short period, but we can't afford any more delays. I want you to prepare a program for the elimination of your separate administrative staff and laying off of fifty shop employees."

"At once?" Kelley said, her voice hoarse.

"We won't do anything at all just yet." Lydia smiled. "This is preparedness. If Consumer Products should experience a definite upturn in the weeks ahead, perhaps none of this will have to be done."

Kelley looked down at her folded hands. "I see."

Lydia turned. "Dean?"

For Dean Busch the news was slightly worse: plan a 60 per cent cutback of all personnel; prepare a list of executives who could be cut to make a 30 per cent cost cutback in the front offices.

For Seymour Trepps the planning was to be most devastating of all.

"Seymour," Lydia told him, "unless we have new government work, the division is simply an appendix, an organ without visible function. We can't afford that. You do see my point, don't you?"

"Our ships," Trepps said thickly. "The port facilities—the research bell, and the labs—"

"Begin quietly," Lydia told him, "to find what we might be able to salvage by selling all of it on short notice. —Come on, Seymour! Back up, now! You won't be out of work yourself, and possibly some new contract will come along to make this all unnecessary!"

A pall of gloom began to deepen over the room. It was a far cry from the mood only minutes earlier. Lis watched Lydia prepare Bert Jerno and Richard Cazzell for gaping cuts in their divisions too, and had to feel an instant's dismal admiration; she was very, very good at this. She was going to have her own way, and now would be able to turn misfortune—the crash lawsuits—into a weapon on her side in the internal company struggle.

"Don't look so glum, Ken!" she said now, smiling again. "Your division is hardly going to be touched! As a matter of fact, as a corollary of all the slashing we have to be ready for, I want you to prepare quite a different kind of planning proposal."

Lis watched her, sure there was a knife somewhere. "What is it?"

"Songbird," she said.

He stared, not understanding.

"If we can expand anywhere," she said, "it will be in Airplane. I've thought a lot about that small plane you and Barton MacIvor keep dreaming about. Well, I think you've shown the management ability, and possibly we'll have the chance. So let's have from you a complete proposal, all right?"

For just an instant—for a part of a second—something inside Lis wanted to get up and start running.

Which was when he suddenly understood.

Every one of them had been given a new carrot on a new stick. For all the others, the threat was sufficient motivation: *unless you drive yourself and your people harder—hard enough to win a new contract or project—you may be eliminated*, Lydia had told all of them.

And to Lis she had said, *I can't threaten you, because you've done so well. But I can still drive you harder. I can still control you by making you run. For you, the carrot will be Songbird. Drive yourself; support me; this, too, you may have.*

She even, as he saw this, added something more. "We all have much to do. I think we should adjourn and be about it. I'll be available for individual consultations, and urge you to come see me. If I'm away when you need a decision, by all means see Ken." She smiled at him. "I intend to hold to my intention of operating without a formally named president until after the first of the year. But the way things have been going, I don't imagine anyone is going to have difficulty guessing the ultimate choice."

So there was the last of it—the ultimate reward, dangling in front of him.

Within minutes, the meeting broke up.

"Ken," Lydia said, "can you come with me to my office, please?"

He followed her to the crisp, contemporary room. It seemed very cold in there. He stifled an impulse to shiver as she closed the door to afford them privacy.

"Well?" she said. "How do you think they reacted?"

"I'm not even sure how I reacted," he told her.

"Nonsense! You're getting everything, and you know it."

"You shouldn't drive people the way you like to do, Lydia."

She stared. "Are you telling me how to operate my business?"

"No. I'm not. And I see I never could."

"Buck up, Ken." She smiled again. "You'll get used to my way of doing things."

"But it isn't fair to Dean, or to Kelley," he said. His mind was already made up in this moment, but he had to say it. "They've just gotten their jobs. You could push them too far."

"I'll push them until they succeed for me."

"Or until they break?"

"All right, then, yes. Until they break, if they're that kind of people."

Lis took a deep breath. "I want to thank you for everything, Lydia."

"What do you mean by *that*?" she demanded.

He did not answer. He walked out of her office and went downstairs, saying nothing to anyone. He got the folders of old Songbird drawings and specifications out of his personal safe, and dumped a few pictures and personal possessions into his attaché case. It occurred to him to write a formal letter, or let Pappy or Kelley or some of the others know, but tomorrow would be soon enough for that. Right now he wanted to get home.

It was hot in his car, and the sunlight on pavement was blinding as he pulled away from the MA Building for perhaps the last time, heading for the distant gates.

As he reached the gate and slowed, a great roar began to gather in the distance. For a second he did not know what it was, but then a little thrill ran through him as he did. He turned, and could look almost directly down the runway, and up out of the heat fumes and distortion of the afternoon sunlight came a screaming, prehistoric monster, all gleaming scales, drooping snout, lizard wings extended. It leaped from the earth and thundered over his head, tucking in its feet, tilting its nose toward the heavens, twisting its narrow silver wings as it fought toward the sun. It breathed a little wisp of gray smoke, and its voice faded, and then it was gone—swallowed up by the sky, its home.